H. E. Goldschmidt

**German Poetry**

with the English versions of the best translators

H. E. Goldschmidt

**German Poetry**
*with the English versions of the best translators*

ISBN/EAN: 9783337882518

Printed in Europe, USA, Canada, Australia, Japan

Cover: Foto ©Andreas Hilbeck / pixelio.de

More available books at **www.hansebooks.com**

# GERMAN POETRY

WITH

## THE ENGLISH VERSIONS

OF

## THE BEST TRANSLATORS.

~~~~~~~~

EDITED

BY

## H. E. GOLDSCHMIDT,

MASTER OF THE MODERN SCHOOL, LORETTO, MUSSELBURGH.

———————

## WILLIAMS AND NORGATE,

14, HENRIETTA STREET, COVENT GARDEN, LONDON;
AND 20, SOUTH FREDERICK STREET, EDINBURGH.

1869.

# Meiner lieben Mutter

gewidmet.

# PREFACE.

Nec levis, ingenuas pectus coluisse per artes,
Cura sit, et linguas edidicisse duas.

In these days of Internationalism, when the inhabitants of Great-Britain and Germany are constantly brought into contact with each other, a general knowledge at least of the literary treasures of both countries is looked for from every educated man; an attempt, therefore, like the present, to render a fair knowledge of German Poetry of easy acquisition, may be expected to meet with some share of public favour and support. The literature of my native land abounds in gems of lyric and dramatic Poetry of the highest beauty. Of these a large number are already well-known to the British public through translations, which have appeared, from time to time, in Books, in Periodicals, and in daily papers; my aim has been to gather the best of these together, and thus to present to the Reader, in one Collection, a number of the fairest gems in their choicest settings.

In many cases I have experienced, with regard to the translations, quite an e m b a r r a s  d u  c h o i x, and, accordingly, the task of selection among different versions of the same poem has not always been an easy one. I can hardly expect, of course, that a l l my readers will be pleased with the selection made; but let me humbly suggest that—as, according to M a c a u l a y, Frederick the Great, with a truly royal superiority to grammar, used to say — "de gustibus non est d i s p u t a n d u s." Moreover, opinions differ widely as to what constitutes a good translation. Some are especially anxious for the preservation of the metre and rhythm of the original, not recognising that the genius of one language invariably requires a different thought - mould from that of another. Others, again, allowing a certain latitude, on the part of the translator, with regard to the f o r m, insist upon a strict (and literal) adherence to the m a t t e r, even though, what is beautiful and appropriate in one language, may appear strange, perhaps absurd, in another.* For my part, I care more for the preservation of the spirit, the a r o m a of the original, than for any mere reproduction of either form or matter. To translate thus, is, I readily grant, no easy thing: it is indeed, no less than the former

---

\* "Nec verbum verbo curabis reddere, fidus Interpres."

Ho r a c e, Ars Poetica, 133.

ones, a high standard by which to judge of a translation; but that it is a point of perfection attainable in many instances — the translations contained in the present volume afford ample proof.

The collection is one of specimens and no more. I do not pretend to have finished the harvest, nor even to have brought home all that is good; the field is too large, the growth too luxuriant, my time too limited for the attempt. I am but as a dweller among the busy haunts of men, who, in his scanty leisure-hours, strolls among waving corn-fields and through green lanes — and who, to gladden for a time his dull home in the city, brings back with him, not a bouquet from the flower-garden, but a rough nosegay — say, some rich and mellow ears of corn, some wild-flowers gathered by the wayside, and, in memory of those who have passed away, a forget-me-not or two. I shall be glad if other eyes than mine will rest awhile on what I have gathered, and I trust that my readers will feel something of the exquisite enjoyment which the work of collecting has afforded to me!

Many fine versions of German poems have been, most reluctantly, omitted — for various reasons, of which the limits of space, and a desire not to encroach unduly upon any publication in particular, were the most cogent. The truly national Volkslied, and such songs as have been, from time immemorial, most popular among the German student-world, are almost entirely left out; mainly, because ample justice has already been done to them by such works as H. W. Dulcken's "Book of German Songs." For similar reasons, I quote but a few select specimens of the Devotional Poetry of Germany.

It only remains for me to express my sincere thanks to all, who have either allowed me to reprint translations, which have already been published, or who have contributed new ones to the Collection. And first: place aux dames! — I quote by special permission, from Lady John Manners "Gems of German Poetry" [Blackwood and Sons]; from "Hymns from the Land of Luther" [Kennedy, Edinburgh] and "Thoughtful Hours" [Nelson and Sons] by H. L. L. My Readers and myself are indebted to the owner of these initials for the happy translation of Sigmund Kunth's beautiful hymn on everlasting rest; the translation was written specially for this Collection. Ferdinand Freiligrath's daughter, Mrs. E. Kroeker, kindly sent various translations, and Miss Marion Hutchison contributes a version of one of Heine's sweetest poems. Lastly, Miss Winkworth is represented by two translations; permission to quote them having been purchased from the owners of the copyright.

I have to express also the deepest gratitude for the kindness of Thomas Carlyle, Dean Alford, Lord Lytton, Professor Longfellow, Rev. W. W. Skeat, Mr. Theodore Martin, Professor Blackie, Mr. Bowring, Dr. Baskerville, Dr. James Steele, Mr. A. D. Coleridge, Mr. Garnett, Mr. Peter Gardner etc. in allowing me to make use of their translations; and I have to thank Mr. Lumley, who owns the copyright of "German Ballads etc." for granting me permission to quote from that interesting work. — A list of the Books from which I quote is appended to these lines, and every contribution, which appears for the first time in print, is marked with an asterisk in the Table of Contents. The Reader may notice some alterations in such translations as are already known to him; they are all made, either at the request or with the sanction, of the individual translators. In most instances the different contributors have kindly corrected their own proofs.

My thanks are also due to the Rev. Dr. Merivale for his permission to reprint some of his father's translations, notably the very fine version of *Schiller's* "Commencement of the nineteenth century," which the reverend gentleman himself has reproduced, most happily, in that delightful volume, the: "Arundines Cami." — Through the Earl of Ellesmere's courtesy I am enabled to reprint some of the late Earl's spirited translations; and Mrs. Anster very kindly permitted me to avail myself of the late Dr. Anster's translations — his "Faust," and his versions contained in "Xeniola," the "Dublin University Magazine" etc. The mention of Dr. Anster's revered name brings to my memory his gifted, but unfortunate countryman—whom his gentle hand vainly tried to rescue from utter shame and ruin: James Clarence Mangan. Alas, poor Yorick!

In conclusion I beg to thank all who have, in any way, helped and advised me in the selection and arrangement of the contents of the Collection. Especially my thanks are due to the Rev. W. W. Skeat, M. A., late fellow of Christ's College, Cambridge, and to Alexander E. Shand, Esq., M. A., of Edinburgh; to the elegant taste and sound scholarship of both I am indebted for many valuable suggestions.

And now, what more have I to say? Only to crave the kindly criticism of an indulgent public. That there are many shortcomings in the execution of what has, in truth, been to me a labour of love, I do not doubt; but:

*Ut desint vires, tamen est laudanda voluntas.*

Loretto House,
Musselburgh, NB. April 1869.

**H. E. Goldschmidt.**

# CONTENTS.

~~~~~~~

_____

\* not previously printed.
† see notes.

# TRANSLATIONS ARE QUOTED FROM THE FOLLOWING WORKS:

**Alford,** (Henry, Dean of Canterbury): *The Year of Praise.*

**Auster,** (Dr. John) Goethe's *Faust.* Part I and II. *Xeniola.*

**Aytoun,** (William Edmonston, and Th. Martin.) *Poems and Ballads of Goethe.*

**Ballads,** (German) *and Songs.* — [Lumley.]

**Blackie,** (John Stuart): Goethe's *Faust.*

**Bowring,** (Edgar Alfred): *Poems of Heinrich Heine.*

**Bryant,** (William Cullen): *Poems.*

**Carlyle,** (Thomas): *Life of Schiller.*

**Coleridge,** (Samuel Taylor): Schiller's *Wallenstein.*

**Coleridge,** (Arthur Duke): Goethe's *Egmont.*

**Ellesmere,** (Earl of): *Poems.*

**Garnett,** (Richard): *Poems from the German.*

**Gower,** (Lord Francis Leveson [Lord Ellesmere]) Goethe's *Faust.*

**Hymns,** *from the Land of Luther.*

**Körner:** *A Selection from the Poems and Dramatic Works of Theodor Körner.* By the Translator of the "Nibelungen-Treasure" (Madame Davesies de Pontès).

**Longfellow,** (Henry Wadsworth): *Poetical Works.*

**Lyra Germanica.**

**Lytton,** (Lord): *The Poems and Ballads of Schiller.*

**Mangan,** (James Clarence): *Poems.*

**Manners,** (Lady John): *Gems of German Poetry.*

**Martin,** (Theodore): Goethe's *Faust vide also* **Aytoun.**

**Merivale,** (C. Hermann): *Minor Poems of Schiller.*

**Richardson,** (G. F.): *The Life of Körner with Selections from his Poems, Tales and Dramas.*

**Shelley,** (Percy Bysshe): *Poetical Works.*

**Skeat,** (W. W.): *The Songs and Ballads of Uhland.*

**Taylor,** (William, of Norwich): *Historic Survey of German Literature, interspersed with various Translations.*

**Thoughtful Hours** by H. L. L.

# Gottfried Auguſt Bürger,

born 1748, died 1794.

„Hoch klingt das Lied vom braven Mann,
Wie Orgelton und Glockenklang!"

# Lenore.

Lenore fuhr um's Morgenroth
    Empor aus schweren Träumen:
Bist untreu, Wilhelm, oder todt?
    Wie lange willst du säumen?


Er war mit König Friedrichs Macht
    Gezogen in die Prager Schlacht,
Und hatte nicht geschrieben,
    Ob er gesund geblieben.


Nun jedes Heer mit Sing und Sang,
    Mit Paukenschlag und Kling und Klang,
Geschmückt mit grünen Reisern,
    Zog heim zu seinen Häusern.


Und überall, all überall,
    Auf Wegen und auf Stegen
Zog Alt und Jung dem Jubelschall
    Der Kommenden entgegen.

# ELLENORE.

At break of day from frightful dreams
    Upstarted Ellenore:
My William, art thou slayn, she sayde,
    Or dost thou love no more?

He went abroade with Richard's host
    The paynim foes to quell;
But he no word to her had writt
    An he were sick or well.

With blore of trump and thump of drum
    His fellow-soldyers come,
Their helms bedeckt with oaken boughs,
    They seeke their long'd-for home.

And evry road and evry lane
    Was full of old and young
To gaze at the rejoycing band
    To haile with gladsom toung.

„Gottlob!" rief Kind und Gattin laut;
  „Willkommen!" manche frohe Braut.
Ach! aber für Lenoren
  War Gruß und Kuß verloren.


Als nun das Heer vorüber war,
  Zerraufte sie ihr Rabenhaar
Und warf sich hin zur Erde
  Mit wüthiger Geberde.


Die Mutter lief wohl hin zu ihr:
  „Ach! daß sich Gott erbarme!
Du liebes Kind! was ist mit dir?"
  Und schloß sie in die Arme. —


„O Mutter! Mutter! hin ist hin!
  Nun fahre Welt und alles hin!
Bei Gott ist kein Erbarmen:
  O weh, o weh mir Armen!" —


„Hilf Gott! hilf! Sieh uns gnädig an!
  Kind, bet ein Vaterunser!
Was Gott thut, das ist wohlgethan;
  Gott, Gott erbarmt sich unser!" —


‚O Mutter! Mutter! eitler Wahn!
  Gott hat an mir nicht wohlgethan!
Was half, was half mein Beten?
  Nun ist's nicht mehr vonnöthen!' —

"Thank God!" their wives and children sayde,
    "Welcome!" the brides did saye;
But greet or kiss gave Ellenore
    To none upon that daye.

And when the soldyers all were bye,
    She tore her raven hair,
And cast herself upon the growne,
    In furious despair.

Her mother ran and lyfte her up,
    And clasped in her arm,
"My child, my child, what dost thou ail?
    God shield thy life from harm!"

'O mother, mother! William's gone,
    What's all beside to me?
There is no mercie, sure, above!
    All, all were spar'd but he!'

"Kneele down, thy paternoster saye
    'Twill calm thy troubled spright:
The Lord is wise, the Lord is good;
    What He hath done is right."

'O mother, mother! saye not so,
    Most cruel is my fate:
I prayde, and prayde, but watte avaylde
    'Tis now, alas! too late.'

„Hilf Gott! hilf! Wer den Vater kennt,
     Der weiß, er hilft den Kindern.
Das hochgelobte Sakrament
     Wird deinen Jammer lindern." —


,O Mutter! Mutter! was mich brennt,
     Das lindert mir kein Sakrament!
Kein Sakrament mag Leben
     Den Todten wiedergeben!'


„Hör', Kind! Wie, wenn der falsche Mann
     Im fernen Ungarlande
Sich seines Glaubens abgethan
     Zum neuen Ehebande?


Laß fahren, Kind, sein Herz dahin!
     Er hat es nimmermehr Gewinn!
Wenn Seel und Leib sich trennen,
     Wird ihn sein Meineid brennen!"


,O Mutter! Mutter! hin ist hin!
     Verloren ist verloren!
Der Tod, der Tod ist mein Gewinn!
     O wär' ich nie geboren!


Lisch aus, mein Licht! auf ewig aus!
     Stirb hin! stirb hin in Nacht und Graus,
Bei Gott ist kein Erbarmen!
     O weh, o weh mir Armen!' —

"Our Heavenly Father, if we praye,
　　Will help a suffring child:
Go take the holy sacrament,
　　So shal thy grief grow mild."


'O mother, what I feele within
　　No sacrament can staye,
No' sacrament can teche the dead,
　　To bear the sight of daye.'


"May-be, among the heathen folk
　　Thy William false doth prove,
And put away his faith and troth
　　And take another love."


"Then wherefor sorrowe for his loss?
　　Thy moans are all in vain:
But when his soul and body parte,
　　His falschode brings him pain."


'O mother, mother! gone is gone:
　　My hope is all forlorn,
The grave my only safeguard is —
　　O, had I ne'er been born!'


'Go out, go out, my lamp of life,
　　In grizely darkness die,
There is no mercie, sure, above!
　　For ever let me lie.'

„Hilf Gott! hilf! Geh nicht ins Gericht
　　Mit deinem armen Kinde!
Sie weiß nicht, was die Zunge spricht;
　　Behalt ihr nicht die Sünde!

Ach Kind! vergiß dein irdisch Leid,
　　Und denk an Gott und Seligkeit,
So wird doch deiner Seelen
　　Der Bräutigam nicht fehlen!" —

,O Mutter! was ist Seligkeit?
　　O Mutter! was ist Hölle?
Bei ihm, bei ihm ist Seligkeit!
　　Und ohne Wilhelm Hölle!

Lisch aus, mein Licht! auf ewig aus!
　　Stirb hin! stirb hin in Nacht und Graus!
Ohn' ihn mag ich auf Erden,
　　Mag dort nicht selig werden!' —

So wüthete Verzweifelung
　　Ihr in Gehirn und Adern.
Sie fuhr mit Gottes Vorsehung
　　Vermessen fort zu hadern;

Zerschlug den Busen und zerrang
　　Die Hand bis Sonnenuntergang,
Bis auf am Himmelsbogen
　　Die goldnen Sterne zogen.

"Almighty God! O do not judge
    My poor unhappy child;
She knows not what her lips pronounce,
    Her anguish makes her wild.

'My girl, forget thine earthly woe
    And think on God and bliss;
For so at least shal not thy soul
    Its heavenly bridegroom miss.'

"O mother, mother! what is bliss,
    And what the fiendis cell?
With him 'tis heaven anywhere,
    Without my William, hell."

'Go out, go out, my lamp of life,
    In endless darkness die:
Without him I must loathe the earth,
    Without him scorn the skie.'

And so despair did rave and rage
    Athwarte her boiling veins;
Against the Providence of God
    She hurlde her impious strains.

She bet her breast, and wrung her hands,
    And rollde her tearless eye,
From rise of morn, till the pale stars
    Again orespred the skye.

Und außen, horch! gieng's trap trap trap,
        Als wie von Rosses Hufen,
Und klirrend stieg ein Reiter ab·
        An des Geländers Stufen.


Und horch! und horch! den Pfortenring
        Ganz lose, leise kling ling ling!
Dann kamen durch die Pforte
        Vernehmlich diese Worte:


‚Holla! holla! Thu auf, mein Kind!
        Schläfst, Liebchen, oder wachst du?
Wie bist noch gegen mich gesinnt?
        Und weinest oder lachst du?' —


‚Ach, Wilhelm! du? — So spät bei Nacht? —
        Geweinet hab' ich und gewacht;
Ach! großes Leid erlitten!
        Wo kommst du her geritten?' —


‚Wir satteln nur um Mitternacht,
        Weit ritt ich her von Böhmen;
Ich habe spät mich aufgemacht
        Und will dich mit mir nehmen!' —


‚Ach, Wilhelm! 'rein, herein geschwind!
        Den Hagedorn durchsaust der Wind:
Herein, in meinen Armen,
        Herzliebster, zu erwarmen!' —

When harke! abroade she herde the tramp
　　Of nimble hoofed steed;
She herde a Knight with clank alighte,
　　And climbe the stair in speed.


And soon she herde a tinkling hand,
　　That twirled at the pin;
And thro her door that opend not,
　　These words were breathed in.


"What ho! what ho! thy door undo:
　　Art watching or asleepe?
My love, dost yet remember me,
　　And dost thou laugh or weepe?"


'Ah! William here so late at night?
　　Oh! I have wachte and wak'd:
Whense art thou come? For thy return
　　My heart has sorely ak'd.'


"At midnight only we may ride;
　　I come ore land and see:
I mounted late, but soone I go;
　　Aryse and come with mee."


'O William, enter first my bowre,
　　And give me one embrace:
The blasts athwart the hawthorn hiss:
　　Awayte a little space.'

‚Laß sausen durch den Hagedorn,
　　Laß sausen, Kind, laß sausen!
Der Rappe scharrt, es klirrt der Sporn,
　　Ich darf allhier nicht hausen!


Komm, schürze, spring und schwinge dich
　　Auf meinen Rappen hinter mich!
Muß heut' noch hundert Meilen
　　Mit dir ins Brautbett eilen.' —


‚Ach! wolltest hundert Meilen noch
　　Mich heut' ins Brautbett tragen?
Und horch! es brummt die Glocke noch,
　　Die elf schon angeschlagen.' —


‚Sieh hin, sieh her! der Mond scheint hell;
　　Wir und die Todten reiten schnell;
Ich bringe dich, zur Wette,
　　Noch heut' ins Hochzeitsbette.' —


‚Sag an! wo ist dein Kämmerlein?
　　Wo, wie dein Hochzeitsbettchen?' —
‚Weit, weit von hier! Still, kühl und klein!
　　Sechs Bretter und zwei Brettchen?' —


‚Hat's Raum für mich?' — ,Für dich und mich!
　　Komm, schürze, spring und schwinge dich!

"The blasts athwarte the hawthorn hiss.
    I may not harbour here;
My spurs are sett, my courser pawes,
    My hour of flight is nere."

"All as thou lyest upon thy couch,  ·
    Aryse and mount behinde;
To night we'le ride a thousand miles,
    The bridal bed to finde."

'How, ride to night a thousand miles?
    Thy love thou dost bemock:
Eleven is the stroke that still
    Rings on within the clock.'

"Looke up; the moon is bright, and we
    Outstride the earthly men:    .
I'le take thee to the bridal bed,
    And night shall end but then."

'And where is then thy house, and home,
    And bridal bed so meet?'
"'Tis narrow, silent, chilly, low,
    Six planks, one shrouding sheet."

'And is there any room for me
    Wherein that I may creepe?'   ·
"There's room enough for thee and me
    Wherein that we may sleepe.

Die Hochzeitsgäste hoffen;
    Die Kammer steht uns offen.' —


Schön Liebchen schürzte, sprang und schwang
    Sich auf das Roß behende;
Wohl um den trauten Reiter schlang
    Sie ihre Lilienhände.


Und hurre hurre, hop! hop! hop!
    Gieng's fort in sausendem Galopp,
Daß Roß und Reiter schnoben,
    Und Kies und Funken stoben.


Zur rechten und zur linken Hand
    Vorbei vor ihren Blicken,
Wie flogen Anger, Heid' und Land!
    Wie donnerten die Brücken!


„Graut Liebchen auch? Der Mond scheint hell!
    Hurrah! die Todten reiten schnell!
Graut Liebchen auch vor Todten?" —
    ‚Ach nein! doch laß die Todten!' —

"All as thou lyest upon thy couch,
　　Aryse, no longer stop;
The wedding-guests thy coming wayte
　　The chamber-door is ope."


All in her sacke as there she lay,
　　Upon his horse she sprung;
And with her lily hands so pale
　　About her William clung.


And hurry-skurry off they go,
　　Unheeding wet or dry;
And horse and rider snort and blow,
　　And sparkling pebbles fly.


How swift the flood, the mead, the wood,
　　Aright, aleft, are gone!
The bridges thunder as they pass
　　But earthly sowne is none.


Tramp, tramp, across the land they speede;
　　Splash, splash, across the see:
"Hurrah! the dead can ride apace,
　　Dost feare to ride with me?


"The moon is bright, and blue the night;
　　Dost quake the blast to stem?
Dost shudder, mayde, to seeke the dead?"
　　'No, no, but what of them?'

Was klang dort für Gesang und Klang?
　　　Was flatterten die Raben?
Horch Glockenklang! horch Todtensang:
　　　‚Laßt uns den Leib begraben.‘

Und näher zog ein Leichenzug,
　　　Der Sarg und Todtenbahre trug.
Das Lied war zu vergleichen
　　　Dem Unkenruf in Teichen.

‚Nach Mitternacht begrabt den Leib
　　　Mit Klang und Sang und Klage!
Jetzt führ’ ich heim mein junges Weib;
　　　Mit, mit zum Brautgelage! —

Komm, Küster, hier! Komm mit dem Chor
　　　Und gurgle mir das Brautlied vor!
Komm, Pfaff’, und sprich den Segen,
　　　Eh wir zu Bett uns legen!‘ —

Still Klang und Sang — die Bahre schwand —
　　　Gehorsam seinem Rufen,
Kam’s hurre! hurre! nachgerannt
　　　Hart hinter’s Rappen Hufen.

Und immer weiter, hop! hop! hop!
　　　Gieng’s fort in sausendem Galopp,
Daß Roß und Reiter schnoben,
　　　Und Kies und Funken stoben.

How glumly sounes yon dirgy song!
　　Night-ravens flappe the wing.
What knell doth slowly tolle ding dong?
　　The psalms of death who sing?

Forth creepes a swarthy funeral train,
　　A corse is on the biere;
Like croke of todes from lonely moores,
　　The chauntings meete the eere.

"Go, beare her corse when midnight's past
　　With song and tear and wail:
I 've gott my wife, I take her home,
　　My hour of wedlock hail!

"Leade forth, o clark, the chaunting quire,
　　To swell our spousal soug:
Come, priest, and reade the blessing soone:
　　For our dark bed we long."

The bier is gone, the dirges hush:
　　His bidding all obaye,
And headlong rush thro briar and bush
　　Beside his speedy waye.

Halloo! halloo! how swift they go,
　　Unheeding wet or dry;
And horse and rider snort and blow,
　　And sparkling pebbles fly.

Wie flogen rechts, wie flogen links
    Gebirge, Bäum' und Hecken!
Wie flogen links, und rechts und links,
    Die Dörfer, Städt' und Flecken!


‚Graut Liebchen auch? — Der Mond scheint hell!
    Hurrah! die Todten reiten schnell!
Graut Liebchen auch vor Todten?' —
    'Ach! laß sie ruhn, die Todten! —


Sieh da! sieh da! Am Hochgericht
    Tanzt um des Rades Spindel,
Halb sichtbarlich bei Mondenlicht,
    Ein lustiges Gesindel.


‚Sa! sa! Gesindel! hier! komm hier!
    Gesindel, komm und folge mir!
Tanz' uns den Hochzeitsreigen,
    Wenn wir zu Bette steigen!' —


Und das Gesindel, husch! husch! husch!
    Kam hinten nach geprasselt,
Wie Wirbelwind am Haselbusch
    Durch dürre Blätter rasselt.


Und weiter, weiter, hop! hop! hop!
    Ging's fort in sausendem Galopp,
Daß Roß und Reiter schnoben
    Und Kies und Funken stoben

How swift the hill, how swift the dale,
　　Aright, aleft are gone!
By hedge and tree, by thorp and town,
　　They gallop, gallop on.

Tramp, tramp, across the land they speede;
　　Splash, splash, across the see:
"Hurrah! the dead can ride apace;
　　Dost feare to ride with mee?

"Look up, look up, an airy crew
　　In roundel daunces reele,
The moon is bright and blue the night
　　Mayst dimly see them wheele.

"Come to, come to, ye ghostly crew,
　　Come to and follow me,
And daunce for us the wedding daunce
　　When we in bed shall be."

And brush, brush, brush, the ghostly crew
　　Came wheeling ore their heads
All rustling like the witherd leaves
　　That wide the whirlwind spreads.

Halloo! halloo! away they go,
　　Unheeding wet or dry;
And horse and rider snort and blow
　　And sparkling pebbles fly.

Wie flog, was rund der Mond beschien,
  Wie flog es in die Ferne!
Wie flogen oben überhin
  Der Himmel und die Sterne!


‚Graut Liebchen auch? — Der Mond scheint hell!
  Hurrah! die Todten reiten schnell!
Graut Liebchen auch vor Todten?‘ —
  ‚O weh! laß ruhn die Todten!‘ —


‚Rapp! Rapp! mich dünkt, der Hahn schon ruft;
  Bald wird der Sand verrinnen!
Rapp! Rapp! ich wittre Morgenluft;
  Rapp! tummle dich von hinnen!


Vollbracht, vollbracht ist unser Lauf!
  Das Hochzeitsbette thut sich auf!
Die Todten reiten schnelle!
  Wir sind, wir sind zur Stelle!‘ —


Rasch auf ein eisern Gitterthor
  Ging's mit verhängtem Zügel;
Mit schwanker Gert ein Schlag davor
  Zersprengte Schloß und Riegel.


Die Flügel flogen klirrend auf,
  Und über Gräber ging der Lauf;
Es blinkten Leichensteine
  Ringsum im Mondenscheine.

And all that in the moonshyne lay
    Behind them fled afar;
And backward scudded overhead
    The skie and every star.

Tramp, tramp, across the land they speede;
    Splash, splash, across the see:
"Hurrah! the dead can ride apace;
    Dost feare to ride with mee?

"I weene the cock prepares to crowe;
    The sand will soone be run:
I snuffe the early morning air;
    Downe! downe! our work is done.

"The dead, the dead can ride apace:
    Our wed-bed here is fit:
Our race is ridde, our journey ore,
    Our endless union knit."

And lo! an yron-grated gate
    Soon biggens to their view:
He crackde his whyppe; the locks, the bolts,
    Cling, clang! assunder flew.

They passe, and 'twas on graves they trodde,
    "'Tis hither we are bound:"
And many a tombstone ghastly white
    Lay in the moonshyne round.

Hasi! hasi! im Augenblick,
        Hu! hu! ein gräßlich Wunder!
Des Reiters Koller, Stück für Stück,
        Fiel ab wie mürber Zunder.


Zum Schädel ohne Zopf und Schopf,
        Zum nackten Schädel ward sein Kopf,
Sein Körper zum Gerippe
        Mit Stundenglas, und Hippe.


Hoch bäumte sich, wild schnob der Rapp
        Und sprühte Feuerfunken;
Und hui! war's unter ihr herab
        Verschwunden und versunken.

Geheul, Geheul aus hoher Luft,
        Gewinsel kam aus tiefer Gruft;
Lenorens Herz mit Beben
        Hang zwischen Tod und Leben.

Nun tanzten wohl beim Mondenglanz
        Rundum herum im Kreise,
Die Geister einen Kettentanz
        Und heulten diese Weise:

And when he from his steed alytte,
 His armure, black as cinder
Did moulder, moulder all away
 As were it made of tinder.

His head became a naked scull
 Nor hair nor eyne had he:
His body grew a skeleton
 Whilome so blithe of ble.

And at his dry and boney heel
 No spur was left to bee;
And in his witherd hand you might
 The scythe and hourglass see.

And lo! his steed did thin to smoke,
 And charnel fires outbreathe;
And pal'd and bleachde, then vanishde quite
 The maid from underneathe.

And hollow howlings hung in air,
 And shrekes from vaults arose:
Then knewe the mayd she might no more
 Her living eyes unclose.

But onward to the judgment seat,
 Thro' mist and moonlight dreare
The ghostly crew their flight persewe,
 And hollowe in her eare:

„Geduld! Geduld! wenn's Herz auch bricht?
    Mit Gott im Himmel hadre nicht!
Des Leibes bist du ledig;
    Gott sei der Seele gnädig!"

---

## Das Lied vom braven Mann.

---

Hoch klingt das Lied vom braven Mann,
Wie Orgelton und Glockenklang.
Wer hohes Muths sich rühmen kann,
Den lohnt nicht Gold, den lohnt Gesang.
Gottlob! daß ich singen und preisen kann,
Zu singen und preisen den braven Mann.

Der Thauwind kam vom Mittagsmeer,
Und schnob durch Welschland, trüb' und feucht,
Die Wolken flogen vor ihm her,
Wie wann der Wolf die Heerde scheucht.
Er fegte die Felder, zerbrach den Forst;
Auf Seen und Strömen das Grundeis borst.

Am Hochgebirge schmolz der Schnee;
Der Sturz von tausend Wassern scholl;
Das Wiesenthal begrub ein See;
Des Landes Heerstrom wuchs und schwoll;

"Be patient, tho thyne herte should breke
    Arrayne not Heaven's decree,
Thou nowe art of thy bodie reft,
    Thy soul forgiven bee.

## THE LAY OF THE BRAVE MAN.

Loud sounds afar the brave man's lay,
    Like bells' clear chime or organ's roll;
Sweet song, not gold, can best repay
    The man who shows a dauntless soul.
Thank God! who hath taught me to praise and sing,
For loud shall the brave hero's praises ring.

The warm wind came from the Southern sea,
    And Italy felt its humid breath;
The scattered clouds before it flee,
    Like flocks, when wolves bring fear and death.
It swept o'er the fields, the forest it brake,
And loosened the ice upon streamlet and lake.

Snow melted on the mountain-tops:
    A thousand plunging torrents fell:
Lakes buried field, and dale, and copse;
    Each river rose with sudden swell.

Hoch rollten die Wogen, entlang ihr Gleis,
Und rollten gewaltige Felsen Eis.


Auf Pfeilern und auf Bogen schwer,
Aus Quaderstein von unten auf,
Lag eine Brücke drüber her,
Und mitten stand ein Häuschen drauf.
Hier wohnte der Zöllner, mit Weib und Kind. —
„O Zöllner! o Zöllner! Entfleuch geschwind!"


Es dröhnt' und dröhnte dumpf heran,
Laut heulten Sturm und Wog' um's Haus,
Der Zöllner sprang zum Dach hinan,
Und blickt' in den Tumult hinaus —
„Barmherziger Himmel! erbarme dich!
Verloren! verloren! Wer rettet mich?"


Die Schollen rollten, Schuß auf Schuß,
Von beiden Ufern, hier und dort,
Von beiden Ufern riß der Fluß
Die Pfeiler sammt den Bogen fort.
Der bebende Zöllner, mit Weib und Kind,
Er heulte noch lauter, als Strom und Wind.


Die Schollen rollten, Stoß auf Stoß,
An beiden Enden, hier und dort,
Zerborsten und zertrümmert, schoß
Ein Pfeiler nach dem andern fort.
Bald nahte der Mitte der Umsturz sich —
„Barmherziger Himmel! erbarme dich!" —

Their channels the cataracts ploughed and tore,
And fragments of ice to the valley bore.

On piers and arches strongly planned,
 Well built of quarried stone and wood,
A lofty bridge the valley spanned,
 Whereon, midway, a cottage stood :
And here lived the tollman with child and wife :
"Oh, tollman ! oh, tollman ! flee fast for thy life !"

Loud roared, and howled, and beat, and rained
 The storm around that lonely home ;
At length the roof the tollman gained,
 And looked across the seething foam,
"Oh merciful heaven ! my trust is in thee !
I am lost, I am lost ! what refuge for me?"

The blocks of ice came rolling fast   .
 On either bank, both far and near :
On either side the stream rushed past,
 And swept away both arch and pier :
The timorous tollmann with wife and child,
Shrieked louder yet than the tempest wild.

The heaped up ice came rolling on,
 At either end both far and near :
Arch after arch away was gone,
 In fragments fell each ruined pier.
To the middle the turmoil had forced its way,
"Oh merciful heaven, now help ! we pray !"

Hoch auf dem fernen Ufer stand
Ein Schwarm von Gaffern, groß und klein;
Und jeder schrie und rang die Hand,
Doch mochte Niemand Retter sein.
Der bebende Zöllner, mit Weib und Kind,
Durchheulte nach Rettung den Strom und Wind.

Wann klingst du, Lied vom braven Mann,
Wie Orgelton und Glockenklang?
Wohlan! so nenn' ihn, nenn' ihn dann!
Wann nennst du ihn, mein schönster Sang?
Bald nahet der Mitte der Umsturz sich,
O braver Mann, braver Mann, zeige dich!

Rasch galoppirt' ein Graf hervor,
Auf hohem Roß, ein edler Graf;
Was hielt des Grafen Hand empor?
Ein Beutel war es, voll und straff. —
„Zweihundert Pistolen sind zugesagt
Dem, welcher die Rettung der Armen wagt!"

Wer ist der Brave? Ist's der Graf?
Sag' an, mein braver Sang, sag' an!
Der Graf, beim höchsten Gott, war brav!
Doch weiß ich einen bravern Mann. —
O braver Mann, braver Mann! zeige dich!
Schon naht das Verderben sich fürchterlich. —

Und immer höher schwoll die Fluth;
Und immer lauter schnob der Wind;

High on the farthest bank a crowd
    Of gazers, young and aged, stood;
Each wrung his hand, and wept aloud:
    But none would dare that dangerous flood:
The timorous tollman, with wife and child,
Shrieked loudly for help thro' the uproar wild.

When shall the brave man's lay be rung,
    Like organ's roll, or bells' pure chime?
When shall his noble name be sung,
    My sounding song? 'tis time! 'tis time!
To the midst hath the turmoil forced its way:
Brave hero! brave hero! now help, I pray!

Fast galloped up a noble knight,
    A horse he rode of stately build,
What hold his right hand forth to sight?
    A heavy purse with gold well-filled.
"Two hundred pistoles are here, I swear,
For him who to save them will nobly dare!

Will *he*·— this knight — those wretches save?
    Is *he* thy worthy theme, my song?
The knight, as Heav'n doth know, was brave,
    But one more brave shall come ere long.
Brave hero! brave hero! at length appear!
Their terrible ruin is drawing near.

And higher still the flood doth swell,
    And louder still the storm doth rave,

Und immer tiefer sank der Muth. —
O Retter! Retter! komm' geschwind!
Stets Pfeiler bei Pfeiler zerborst und brach,
Laut krachten und stürzten die Bogen nach.

„Halloh! Halloh! Frisch auf! gewagt!"
Hoch hielt der Graf den Preis empor.
Ein jeder hört's, doch Jeder zagt,
Aus Tausenden tritt Keiner vor.
Vergebens durchheulte, mit Weib und Kind,
Der Zöllner nach Rettung den Strom und Wind. —

Sieh', schlecht und recht ein Bauersmann
Am Wanderstabe schritt daher,
Mit grobem Kittel angethan,
An Wuchs und Antlitz hoch und hehr.
Er hörte den Grafen; vernahm sein Wort;
Und schaute das nahe Verderben dort.

Und kühn, in Gottes Namen, sprang
Er in den nächsten Fischerkahn;
Trotz Wirbel, Sturm und Wogendrang,
Kam der Erretter glücklich an:
Doch wehe! der Nachen war allzu klein,
Um Retter von allen zugleich zu sein.

Und dreimal zwang er seinen Kahn,
Trotz Wirbel, Sturm und Wogendrang;
Und dreimal kam er glücklich an,
Bis ihm die Rettung ganz gelang.

And more and more their courage fell. —
   O daring hero, haste to save!
Pier upon pier is burst in two,
Arch after arch is broken·through!

"Will no one dare? see here! see here!"
   The knight held out the tempting prize:
Each peasant hears, but shrinks with fear,
   Of thousands, none the risk defies.
In vain did the tollman, with wife and child,
Shriek loudly for help thro' the uproar wild.

But lo! a peasant, staff in hand,
   Comes striding up with hurried pace,
His·mean attire the gazers scanned,
   His stalwart frame, and noble face.
He hears the promise the knight had made,
And saw that their doom could scarce be stayed.

He trusted God's protecting power,
   And in the nearest skiff he leapt;
In spite of stream, and whirl, and shower,
   His way the daring hero kept;
Oh! horror! the boat is so frail and small,
It never can hold them and save them all!

In spite of whirl, and storm, and tide,
   Three times the dangerous course he braved;
Three times he safely reached the side,
   By God's good grace, till all were saved:

Kaum kamen die Letzten in sichern Port,
So rollte das letzte Getrümmer fort. —

Wer ist, wer ist der brave Mann?
Sag an, sag an, mein braver Sang!
Der Bauer wagt' ein Leben dran;
Doch that er's wohl um Goldesklang?
Denn spendete nimmer der Graf sein Gut,
So wagte der Bauer vielleicht kein Blut.

„Hier", rief der Graf, „mein wackrer Freund!
Hier ist dein Preis! Komm her, nimm hin!"
Sag an, war das nicht brav gemeint?
Bei Gott! der Graf trug hohen Sinn. —
Doch höher und himmlischer, wahrlich! schlug
Das Herz, das der Bauer im Kittel trug.

„Mein Leben ist für Gold nicht feil.
Arm bin ich zwar, doch eß' ich satt.
Dem Zöllner werd' en'r Gold zu Theil,
Der Hab' und Gut verloren hat!"
So rief er mit herzlichem Biederton
Und wandte den Rücken und ging davon. —

Hoch klingst du, Lied vom braven Mann,
Wie Orgelton und Glockenklang!
Wer solchen Muths sich rühmen kann,
Den lohnt kein Gold, den lohnt Gesang.
Gottlob! daß ich singen und preisen kann,
Unsterblich zu preisen den braven Mann.

And scarce for the last time he reached the shore,
Ere the last pier fell and was seen no more!

But wherefore call the peasant brave?
      Why make his praise thy theme, my song?
He risked his life those lives to save,
      But then — the hope of gain was strong!
And had it not been for the brave knight's gold,
The peasant might never have been so bold!

"Thy prize," exclaimed the knight, "is won:
      Come here, brave friend, receive thy due!"
Sure this was well and nobly done,
      By heaven! the knight was brave and true!
But the heart that beat 'neath the peasant's weeds
In kindness and worth the knight's exceeds.

"I risk not life for money's sake;
      I eat enough, tho' poorly clad:
Thy bounty let the tollman take,
      The flood has swallowed all he had."
In tones of compassion he said his say,
Then slowly he turned him, and went his way.

Now loudly rings the Brave Man's Lay,
      Like bells clear chime or organ's tone:
For song, not gold, can best repay
      The man who dauntless worth hath shewn.
Thank God, who hath taught me to praise and sing;
For aye shall the brave man's praises ring!

# Johann Wolfgang von Goethe,

born 1749, died 1832.

„Was glänzt, ist für den Augenblick geboren,
Das Rechte bleibt der Nachwelt unverloren."

# Zueignung zum Faust.

———

Ihr naht euch wieder, schwankende Gestalten!
Die früh sich einst dem trüben Blick gezeigt.
Versuch' ich wohl, euch diesmal fest zu halten?
Fühl' ich mein Herz noch jenem Wahn geneigt?
Ihr drängt euch zu! Nun gut, so mögt ihr walten,
Wie ihr aus Dunst und Nebel um mich steigt;
Mein Busen fühlt sich jugendlich erschüttert
Vom Zauberhauch, der euren Zug umwittert.

Ihr bringt mit euch die Bilder froher Tage,
Und manche liebe Schatten steigen auf;
Gleich einer alten, halbverklungnen Sage,
Kommt erste Lieb' und Freundschaft mit herauf;
Der Schmerz wird neu, es wiederholt die Klage
Des Lebens labyrinthisch irren Lauf,
Und nennt die Guten, die, um schöne Stunden
Vom Glück getäuscht, vor mir hinweggeschwunden.

Sie hören nicht die folgenden Gesänge.
Die Seelen, denen ich die ersten sang;

# DEDICATION. (FAUST.)

— Translated by Dr. Anster. —

———

Again, in deepening beauty, ye float near,
    Forms, dimly imaged in the days gone by —
Is that old fancy to the heart still dear?
    To that old spell will ye again reply?
Ye throng before my view, divinely clear,
    Like sunbeams conquering a cloudy sky!
Then have me at your will! My bosom burns,
Music is breathing — youth and joy returns!

Pictures you bring with you of happy years,
    Loved shades of other days are rising fast.
First-love with early Friendship reappears
    Like half-remembered legends of the past.
Wounds bleed anew; — the Plaint pursues with tears
    The wanderer through life's labyrinthine waste;
And names the Good, already past away,
Cheated, alas! of half life's little day.

But, ah! they cannot hear my closing song,
    Those hearts, for whom its earlier notes were tried;

Zerstoben ist das freundliche Gedränge,
Verklungen, ach! der erste Wiederklang.
Mein Lied ertönt der unbekannten Menge,
Ihr Beifall selbst macht meinem Herzen bang;
Und was sich sonst an meinem Lied erfreuet,
Wenn es noch lebt, irrt in der Welt zerstreuet.

Und mich ergreift ein längst entwöhntes Sehnen
Nach jenem stillen, ernsten Geisterreich;
Es schwebet nun in unbestimmten Tönen
Mein lispelnd Lied, der Aeolsharfe gleich;
Ein Schauer faßt mich, Thräne folgt den Thränen,
Das strenge Herz, es fühlt sich mild und weich;
Was ich besitze, seh' ich wie im weiten,
Und was verschwand, wird mir zu Wirklichkeiten.

## Aus: „Faust."

### Nacht.

In einem hochgewölbten, engen gothischen Zimmer Faust unruhig auf
seinem Sessel am Pulte.

### Faust.

Habe nun, ach! Philosophie,
Juristerei und Medicin,
Und, leider! auch Theologie
Durchaus studirt, mit heißem Bemühn.

Departed is, alas! the friendly throng,
    And dumb the echoes all, that first replied.
If some still live this stranger world among,
    Fortune hath scattered them at distance wide;
To men unknown my griefs I now impart,
Whose very praises leave me sick at heart.

Again it comes! a long unwonted feeling —
    A wish for that calm, solemn spirit-land;
My wavering song lisps faint, like murmurs stealing
    O'er Æol's harp by varying breezes fanned.
Tears follow tears, my weaknesses revealing,
    And silent shudders show a heart unmanned;
What is, in the far distance seems to be,
The Past, the Past alone is true to me.

## "FAUST." Act I. Scene I.

### Translated by Theodore Martin.

#### — Night. —

A vaulted Gothic chamber. — Faust seated at his desk.

#### FAUST.

All that philosophy can teach,
The lore of jurist and of leech,
I've master'd, ah! and sweated through
Theology's dead deserts, too,
Yet here, poor fool, for all my lore,

Da steh' ich nun, ich armer Thor!
Und bin so klug, als wie zuvor;
Heiße Magister, heiße Doctor gar,
Und ziehe schon an die zehen Jahr,
Herauf, herab und quer und krumm,
Meine Schüler an der Nase herum —
Und sehe, daß wir nichts wissen können!
Das will mir schier das Herz verbrennen.
Zwar bin ich gescheidter als alle die Laffen,
Doctoren, Magister, Schreiber und Pfaffen;
Mich plagen keine Scrupel noch Zweifel,
Fürchte mich weder vor Tod noch Teufel —
Dafür ist mir alle Freud' entrissen,
Bilde mir nicht ein, was Rechts zu wissen,
Bilde mir nicht ein, ich könnte was lehren,
Die Menschen zu bessern und zu bekehren.
Auch hab' ich weder Gut noch Geld,
Noch Ehr' und Herrlichkeit der Welt;
Es möchte kein Hund so länger leben!
Drum hab' ich mich der Magie ergeben,
Ob mir durch Geistes Kraft und Mund
Nicht manch Geheimniß würde kund,
Daß ich nicht mehr, mit saurem Schweiß,
Zu sagen brauche, was ich nicht weiß,
Daß ich erkenne, was die Welt
Im Innersten zusammenhält,
Schau' alle Wirkenskraft und Samen,
Und thu' nicht mehr in Worten kramen.

I stand no wiser than before.
They call me magister, save the mark!
Doctor, withal! and these ten years I
Have been leading my pupils a dance in dark,
Up hill, down dale, through wet and through dry —
And yet that nothing can ever be
By mortals known, too well I see!
This is burning the heart clean out of me.
More brains have I than all the tribe
Of doctor, magister, parson and scribe.
From doubts and scruples my soul is free;
Nor hell nor devil has terrors for me:
But just for this I am dispossess'd
Of all that gives pleasure to life and zest.
I can't even juggle myself to own,
There is any one thing to be truly known,
Or aught to be taught in science or arts,
To better mankind and to turn their hearts.
Besides, I have neither land nor pence,
Nor wordly honour nor influence,
A dog in my case would scorn to live!
So myself to magic I've vow'd to give,
And see if through spirit's might and tongue
The heart from some mysteries cannot be wrung;
If I cannot escape from the bitter woe
Of babbling of things that I do not know,
And get to the root of these secret powers,
Which hold together this world of ours,
The sources and centres of force explore,
And chaffer and dabble in words no more.

O sähst du, voller Mondenschein,
Zum letztenmal auf meine Pein,
Den ich so manche Mitternacht
An diesem Pult herangewacht:
Dann über Büchern und Papier,
Trübsel'ger Freund, erschienst du mir!
Ach! könnt' ich doch auf Bergeshöhn
In deinem lieben Lichte gehn,
Um Bergeshöhle mit Geistern schweben,
Auf Wiesen in deinem Dämmer weben,
Von allem Wissensqualm entladen,
In deinem Thau gesund mich baden!


## Aus: „Faust.“

Bauern unter der Linde.   Gesang und Tanz.

Der Schäfer putzte sich zum Tanz,
Mit bunter Jacke, Band und Kranz:
Schmuck war er angezogen.
Schon um die Linde war es voll,
Und alles tanzte schon wie toll.
Juchhe! Juchhe!
Juchheisa! Heisa! He!
So ging der Fiedelbogen.

Er drückte hastig sich heran,
Da stieß er an ein Mädchen an

Oh, broad bright moon, if this might be
The last of the nights of agony,
The countless midnights, these weary eyes,
Have from this desk here watch'd thee rise!
Then, sad-eyed friend, thy wistful looks
Shone in upon me o'er paper and books;
But oh! might I wander in thy dear light
O'er the trackless slopes of some mountain height,
Round mountain caverns with spirits sail,
Or float o'er the meads in thy hazes pale;
And freed from the fumes of a fruitless lore,
Bathe in thy dews and be whole once more!

### "FAUST." Act II. Scene III.
Translated by Peter Gardner.
Dance and Song.

The shepherd busk'd him for the dance,
In's tartan coat an' plaid to prance,
Sae braw, folk's een did row, man.
Lang syne below the trees was thrang,
There a' like mad they lap an' flang.
Hooch, hee! Hooch, hee!
Hooch, heeze, man! Heeze, man! hee!
Sae rung the fiddle-bow, man.

He pressed in, drivin' here an' there
An' stammered on a maiden fair,

Mit seinem Ellenbogen;
Die frische Dirne kehrt' sich um
Und sagte: „Nun, das sind' ich dumm!
Juchhe! Juchhe!
Juchheisa! Heisa! He!
Seyd nicht so ungezogen".

Doch hurtig in dem Kreise ging's,
Sie tanzten rechts, sie tanzten links,
Und alle Röcke flogen.
Sie wurden roth, sie wurden warm
Und ruhten athmend Arm in Arm.
Juchhe! Juchhe!
Juchheisa! Heisa! He!
Und Hüft' an Ellenbogen.

Und thu' mir doch nicht so vertraut!
Wie mancher hat nicht seine Braut
Belogen und betrogen!
Er schmeichelte sie doch bei Seit',
Und von der Linde scholl es weit:
Juchhe! Juchhe!
Juchheisa! Heisa! He!
Geschrei und Fiedelbogen.

His elbows garred her steer, man.
The sprichtly lassie swept her roun,
"Noo, gouk" quo' she, "ye're on my goun."
Hooch, hee! Hooch, hee!
Hooch, heeze, man! Heeze, man! hee!
"Oh! show some havins here, man."

Noo quicker gaed they thro' the reel,
To richt an' left a' set an' wheel,
Hoo swift the short-gouns' flicht, man!
Syne grew they red, an' grew they warm,
Syne rested, pechin', arm in arm.
Hooch, hee! Hooch, hee!
Hooch, heeze, man! Heeze, man! hee!
An' elbow-deep they sich'd man.

"An' dinna mak' sae free," she said,
"There's mony woo that never wed,
There's mony a broken vow, man."
But aye he fleeched — they stept aside,
Wide frae the trees there skreighed to chide
Hooch, hee! Hooch, hee!
Hooch, heeze, man! Heeze, man. hee!
Sae skreighed the fiddle-bow, man.

## Aus „Faust."

(Studirzimmer.)

Faust mit dem Pudel hereintretend.

Verlassen hab' ich Feld und Auen,
Die eine tiefe Nacht bedeckt,
Mit ahnungsvollem, heil'gem Grauen
In uns die beßre Seele weckt,
Entschlafen sind nun wilde Triebe,
Mit jedem ungestümen Thun;
Es reget sich die Menschenliebe,
Die Liebe Gottes regt sich nun.

Sey ruhig, Pudel! renne nicht hin und wieder!
An der Schwelle was schnoberst du hier?
Lege dich hinter den Ofen nieder,
Mein bestes Kissen geb' ich dir.
Wie du draußen auf dem bergigen Wege
Durch Rennen und Springen ergetzt uns hast,
So nimm nun auch von mir die Pflege,
Als ein willkommner stiller Gast.

Ach, wenn in unserer engen Zelle
Die Lampe freundlich wieder brennt,
Dann wird's in unserm Busen helle,
Im Herzen, das sich selber kennt.
Vernunft fängt wieder an zu sprechen,
Und Hoffnung wieder an zu blühn;
Man sehnt sich nach des Lebens Bächen,
Ach! nach des Lebens Quelle hin.

## "FAUST." Act II. Scene IV.

(Faust's study.)

FAUST entering with the Poodle.

Hush'd now the field and meadow lies,
Beneath the veil of deepest night,
And solemn thoughts within us rise,
Too holy for the garish light.
Calm now the blood that wildly ran,
Asleep the hand of lawless strife;
Now wakes to life the love of man,
The love of God now wakes to life.

Quiet thee, poodle! what frets thee so,
Running and suiffing to and fro?
Come, couch thee down upon the hearth,
Thou hast a comfortable berth.
And as without, on the mountain-way,
We joy'd to see thy gambols gay,
So here, my hospitable care,
A quiet guest, and welcome, share.

When, in our narrow cell confined,
The friendly lamp begins to burn,
Then clearer sees the thoughtful mind,
With searching looks that inward turn.
Bright Hope again within us gleams,
And Reason's voice again is strong;
We thirst for life's untroubled streams,
For the pure fount of life we long.

Knurre nicht, Pudel! Zu den heiligen Tönen,
Die jetzt meine ganze Seel' umfassen,
Will der thierische Laut nicht passen.
Wir sind gewohnt, daß die Menschen verhöhnen,
Was sie nicht verstehn,
Daß sie vor dem Guten und Schönen,
Das ihnen oft beschwerlich ist, murren;
Will es der Hund, wie sie, beknurren?


Aber ach! schon fühl' ich, bei dem besten Willen,
Befriedigung nicht mehr aus dem Busen quillen.
Aber warum muß der Strom so bald versiegen,
Und wir wieder im Durste liegen?

Davon hab' ich so viel Erfahrung.
Doch dieser Mangel läßt sich ersetzen;
Wir lernen das Überirdische schätzen,
Wir sehnen uns nach Offenbarung,
Die nirgends würd'ger und schöner brennt,
Als in dem neuen Testament.
Mich drängt's, den Grundtext aufzuschlagen,
Mit redlichem Gefühl einmal
Das heilige Original
In mein geliebtes Deutsch zu übertragen:

(Er schlägt ein Volum auf und schickt sich an.)

Quiet thee, poodle! it seems not well
To break, with thy snarling, the holy spell
Of my soul's music, that may not be
With bestial sounds in harmony.
We are well used that men despise
What to see they have no eyes,
And murmur in their peevish mood
Against the beautiful and good;
Belike the cur, as curs are they,
Thus growls and snarls his bliss away!

But, alas! already I feel it well.
No more may peace within this bosom dwell.
Why must the stream so soon dry up,
And I lie panting for the cup
That mocks my thirsty lips so often? why
Drink pleasure's shallow fount, when scarce yet
                                    tasted, dry?
Yet is this evil not without remeid;
We long for heavenly food to feed
Our heaven-born spirit, and our heart, now bent
On things divine, to revelation turns,
Which nowhere worthier or purer burns,
Than in the holy Testament.
I feel strange impulse in my soul
The sacred volume to unroll,
With pious purpose, once for all,
The holy Greek Original
Into my honest German to translate.

(*He opens the Bible, and begins to read.*)

GOLDSCHMIDT, German Poetry.            4

Geschrieben steht: „Im Anfang war das Wort!"
Hier stock' ich schon! Wer hilft mir weiter fort?
Ich kann das Wort so hoch unmöglich schätzen,
Ich muß es anders übersetzen,
Wenn ich vom Geiste recht erleuchtet bin.
Geschrieben steht: im Anfang war der Sinn:
Bedenke wohl die erste Zeile,
Daß deine Feder sich nicht übereile!
Ist es der Sinn, der alles wirkt und schafft?
Es sollte stehn: im Anfang war die Kraft.
Doch, auch indem ich dieses niederschreibe,
Schon warnt mich was, daß ich dabei nicht bleibe.
Mir hilft der Geist! Auf einmal seh' ich Rath.
Und schreib' getrost: im Anfang war die That!


Soll ich mit dir das Zimmer theilen,
Pudel, so laß das Heulen,
So laß das Bellen!
Solch einen störenden Gesellen
Mag ich nicht in der Nähe leiden.
Einer von uns beiden
Muß die Zelle meiden.
Ungern heb' ich das Gastrecht auf.
Die Thür' ist offen, hast freien Lauf.
Aber was muß ich sehen!

"In the beginning was the W o r d." Stops here
*In ipso limine* my course? In vain
I seek this mystic symbol to explain,
Unless some god my inward vision clear.
The naked word I dare not prize so high,
I must translate it differently,
If by the Spirit I am rightly taught.
"In the beginning of all things was T h o u g h t."
The first line let me ponder well,
Lest my pen outstrip my sense;
Is it thought wherein doth dwell
All-creative Omnipotence?
I change the phrase, and safelier write,
In the beginning there was M i g h t.
But even here methinks some warning voice
Makes me to waver in my choice —
At length, at length the Spirit helps my need!
I write, "In the beginning was the D e e d!"

Wilt thou share the room with me,
Poodle, thou must quiet be,
Thou must cease thy snarls and howls,
And keep for other place thy growls.
Such a noisy inmate may
Not my studious leisure cumber;
You or I, without delay,
Restless cur, must leave the chamber!
Not willingly from thee I take
The right of hospitality,
But if thou wilt my quiet break,

4 *

Kann das natürlich geschehen?
Ist es Schatten? ist's Wirklichkeit?
Wie wird mein Pudel lang und breit!
Er hebt sich mit Gewalt,
Das ist nicht eines Hundes Gestalt!
Welch ein Gespenst bracht' ich ins Haus!
Schon sieht er wie ein Nilpferd aus,
Mit feurigen Augen, schrecklichem Gebiß.
O! Du bist mir gewiß!
Für solche halbe Höllenbrut
Ist Salomonis Schlüssel gut.


Geister auf dem Gange.

Drinnen gefangen ist einer!
Bleibet haußen, folg' ihm keiner!
Wie im Eisen der Fuchs,
Zagt ein alter Höllenluchs.
Aber gebt Acht!
Schwebet hin, schwebet wieder,
Auf und nieder,
Und er hat sich losgemacht.

Seek other quarters — thou hast exit free.
But what must I see!
What vision strange
Beyond the powers
Of Nature's range!
Am I awake, or bound with a spell?
How wondrously the brute doth swell!
Long and broad
Uprises he,
In a form that no form
Of a dog may be!
What spectre brought I into my house?
He stands already, with glaring eyes,
And teeth in grinning ranks that rise,
Large as a hippopotamus!
O! I have thee now!
For such half-brood of hell as thou
The key of Solomon the wise
Is surest charm to exorcise.

*Spirits in the passage without.*

Brother spirits, have a care!
One within is prisoner;
Follow him none! — for he doth quail
Like a fox, trap-caught by the tail.
But let us watch!
Hover here, hover there,
Up and down amid the air;
For soon this sly old lynx of hell
Will tear him free, and all be well.

Könnt ihr ihm nützen,
Laßt ihn nicht sitzen!
Denn er that uns Allen
Schon viel zu Gefallen.


### Faust.

Erst zu begegnen dem Thiere,
Brauch' ich den Spruch der Viere:
    Salamander soll glühen,
    Undene sich winden,
    Sylphe verschwinden,
    Kobold sich mühen!


Wer sie nicht kennte,
Die Elemente,
Ihre Kraft
Und Eigenschaft,
Wäre kein Meister
Über die Geister.


    Verschwind' in Flammen,
    Salamander!
    Rauschend fließe zusammen,
    Undene!
    Leucht' in Meteoren-Schöne,
    Sylphe!
    Bring häusliche Hülfe,
    Incubus! Incubus!
    Tritt hervor und mache den Schluß!

Let us wait, a faithful crew,
Here to do him service true!
Who so oft hath served our pleasure
Pay him back with brimming measure!

FAUST.

First let the charm of the elements four
The nature of the brute explore.
  Let the Salamander glow,
  Undene twist her crested wave,
  Silphe into ether flow,
  And Kobold vex him, drudging slave!

Whoso knows not
The elements four,
Their quality,
And hidden power,
In the magic art
Hath he no part.

  Melting in flames glow
  Salamander!
  Rushing in waves flow
  Undene!
  Shine forth in meteor-beauty
  Silphe!
  Work thy domestic duty
  Incubus Incubus!
  Step forth and finish the spell.

Keines der Viere
Steckt in dem Thiere.
Es liegt ganz ruhig, und grinst mich an;
Ich hab' ihm noch nicht weh gethan.
Du sollst mich hören
Stärker beschwören:

Bist du, Geselle,
Ein Flüchtling der Hölle?
So sieh dies Zeichen,
Dem sie sich beugen,
Die schwarzen Schaaren!

Schon schwillt es auf mit borstigen Haaren.

Verworfnes Wesen!
Kannst du ihn lesen,
Den nie entsproßnen
Unausgesprochnen,
Durch alle Himmel gegoßnen,
Frevenlich durchstochnen?

Hinter den Ofen gebannt,
Schwillt es wie ein Elephant,

None of the four
In the brute doth dwell.
It lies unmoved, and grins at my spell;
Not yet I made it feel the pain.
With a stronger charm
Thou shalt hear me again.

    Art thou a fugitive
    Urchin of hell?
    So yield thee at length
    To this holiest spell!
    Bend thee this sacred
    Emblem before,
    Which the powers of darkness
    Trembling adore.

Already he swells up with bristling hair.

    Can'st thou read it,
    The holy sign,
    Reprobate spirit,
    The emblem divine?
    The unbegotten,
    Whom none can name,
    Whose word did the world's
    Infinity frame,
    Yet to death submitted
    Of sin and of shame?

Now behind the stove he lies,
And swells him up to an elephant's size,

Den ganzen Raum füllt es an,
Es will zum Nebel zerfließen.
Steige nicht zur Decke hinan!
Lege dich zu des Meisters Füßen!
Du siehst, daß ich nicht vergebens drohe.
Ich versenge dich mit heiliger Lohe!
Erwarte nicht
Das dreimal glühende Licht!
Erwarte nicht
Die stärkste von meinen Künsten!

(Mephistopheles tritt, indem der Nebel fällt, gekleidet wie ein
fahrender Scholasticus, hinter dem Ofen hervor.)


## Aus: „Faust.“


### Geister.

Schwindet, ihr dunkeln
Wölbungen droben!
Reizender schaue
Freundlich der blaue
Aether herein!
Wären die dunkeln
Wolken zerronnen!
Sternlein funkeln,

And seems as if he would fill the room,
And melt into a cloud away.
Down, proud- spirit, downward come!
And at thy master's feet thee lay!
In vain, in vain, thou seek'st to turn thee,
With an holy fire I burn thee!
Wait not, spirit, wait not till
My triple-flame I spread around thee!
Wait not till my magic skill
With its mightiest spell hath bound thee!

*(The clouds vanish, and Mephistopheles comes forward from behind the fire-place, drest like an itinerant schoolmaster.)*

## "FAUST." Act II. Scene V.

### Translated by Dr. John Anster.

*Spirits sing.*

Vanish, dark arches,
That over us bend,
Let the blue sky in beauty
Look in like a friend.
Oh, that the black clouds
Asunder were riven,
That the small stars were brightening
All through the wide heaven!

Mildere Sonnen
Scheinen darein.
Himmlischer Söhne
Geistige Schöne,
Schwankende Beugung
Schwebet vorüber,
Sehnende Neigung
Folget hinüber;
Und der Gewänder
Flatternde Bänder
Decken die Länder,
Decken die Laube,
Wo sich fürs Leben,
Tief in Gedanken,
Liebende geben.
Laube bei Laube!
Sprossende Ranken!
Lastende Traube
Stürzt ins Behälter
Drängender Kelter,
Stürzen in Bächen
Schäumende Weine,
Rieseln durch reine,
Edle Gesteine,
Lassen die Höhen
Hinter sich liegen,
Breiten zu Seen
Sich ums Genügen
Grünender Hügel
Und das Geflügel

And look at them smiling
   And sparkling in splendour,
Suns, but with glory
   More placid and tender;
Children of heaven,
   In spiritual beauty,
Descending, and bending
   With billowy motion,
   Downward are thronging,
Willing devotion
   Flowing to meet them.
Loving hearts longing,
   Sighing to greet them.
O'er field and o'er flower,
   In bank and in bower,
The folds of their bright robes
   In breezy air streaming,
Where loving ones living
   In love's thoughtful dreaming,
Their fond hearts are giving
   For ever away.
Bower on bower,
   Tendril and flower;
Clustering grapes,
   The vine's purple treasure,
Have fallen in the wine-vat,
   And bleed in its pressure —
Foaming and steaming, the new wine is streaming,
   Over agate and amethyst.
   Rolls from its fountain.

Schlürfet sich Wonne,
Flieget der Sonne,
Flieget den hellen
Inseln entgegen,
Die sich auf Wellen
Gaukelnd bewegen;
Wo wir in Chören
Jauchzende hören,
Ueber den Auen
Tanzende schauen,
Die sich im Freien
Alle zerstreuen.
Einige klimmen
Ueber die Höhen,
Andere schwimmen
Ueber die Seen,
Andere schweben;
Alle zum Leben,
Alle zur Ferne
Liebender Sterne,
Seliger Huld.

Leaving behind it
    Meadow and mountain,
And the hill-slopes smile greener, far down where
                        it breaks
Into billowy streamlets, or lingers in lakes.
And the winged throng, drinking deep of delight
From the rivers of joy, are pursuing their flight.
    Onward and onward,
    Wings steering sun-ward,
Where the bright islands, with magical motion,
Stir with the waves of the stirring ocean.
Where we hear 'em shout in chorus,
Or see 'em dance on lawns before us,
As over land or over waters
Chance the idle parties scatters.
Some upon the far hills gleaming,
Some along the bright lakes streaming,
Some their forms in air suspending,
Float in circles never-ending.
The one spirit of enjoyment
Aim, and impulse, and employment;
All would breathe in the far distance
Life, free life of full existence
With the gracious stars above them,
Smiling down to say they love them.

### Aus: „Faust.“

— — — — —

— — — — —

　　　　　Und Schlag auf Schlag!
Werd' ich zum Augenblicke sagen:
Verweile doch! du bist so schön! —
Dann magst du mich in Fesseln schlagen,
Dann will ich gern zu Grunde gehn!
Dann mag die Todtenglocke schallen,
Dann bist du deines Dienstes frei,
Die Uhr mag stehn, der Zeiger fallen,
Es sei die Zeit für mich vorbei!

— — — — —

— — — — —

### Aus: „Faust.“

#### Wald und Höhle.

##### Faust allein.

Erhabner Geist, du gabst mir, gabst mir alles,
Warum ich bat.　Du hast mir nicht umsonst
Dein Angesicht im Feuer zugewendet.
Gabst mir die herrliche Natur zum Königreich,
Kraft, sie zu fühlen, zu genießen.　Nicht

## "FAUST." Act II. Scene VI.

When to the moment I shall say,
Stay, thou art so lovely, stay!
Then with thy fetters bind me round,
Then perish I with cheerful glee!
Then may the knell of death resound,
Then from thy service art thou free!
The clock may stand,
And the falling hand
Mark the time no more for me!

## "FAUST." Act IV. Scene III.

*Wood and Cavern.*

FAUST. (alone)

Spirit Supreme! thou gav'st me — gav'st me all,
For which I asked thee. Not in vain hast thou
Turned toward me thy countenance in fire.
Thou gavest me wide Nature for my kingdom,
And power to feel her, to enjoy her. Not
Cold-wond'ring visit only gav'st thou me,

Kalt staunenden Besuch erlaubst du nur,
Vergönnest mir in ihre tiefe Brust,
Wie in den Busen eines Freunds, zu schauen.
Du führst die Reihe der Lebendigen
Vor mir vorbei, und lehrst mich meine Brüder
Im stillen Busch, in Luft und Wasser kennen.
Und wenn der Sturm im Walde braust und knarrt,
Die Riesenfichte stürzend Nachbaräste
Und Nachbarstämme quetschend niederstreift,
Und ihrem Fall dumpf hohl der Hügel donnert,
Dann führst du mich zur sichern Höhle, zeigst
Mich dann mir selbst, und meiner eignen Brust
Geheime tiefe Wunder öffnen sich.
Und steigt vor meinem Blick der reine Mond
Besänftigend herüber, schweben mir
Von Felsenwänden, aus dem feuchten Busch
Der Vorwelt silberne Gestalten auf,
Und lindern der Betrachtung strenge Lust.

O daß dem Menschen nichts Vollkommnes wird,
Empfind' ich nun.　Du gabst zu dieser Wonne,
Die mich den Göttern nah und näher bringt,
Mir den Gefährten, den ich schon nicht mehr
Entbehren kann, wenn er gleich, kalt und frech,
Mich vor mir selbst erniedrigt, und zu Nichts,
Mit einem Worthauch, deine Gaben wandelt.
Er facht in meiner Brust ein wildes Feuer
Nach jenem schönen Bild geschäftig an.
So tauml' ich von Begierde zu Genuß,
Und im Genuß verschmacht' ich nach Begierde.

But ev'n into her bosom's depth to look,
As it might be the bosom of a friend.
The row of living things thou mad'st to pass
Before mine eyes, my brethren mad'st me know
In silent bush, in water, and in air.
And when the storm loud blustereth, and raves
Through the dark forest, and the giant-pine,
Down-tumbling, tears with it the neighbour-branches
And neighbour-stems flat-strewn upon the ground,
And to their fall the hollow mountain thunders;
Then dost thou guide me to the cave where safe
I learn to know myself, and from my breast
Deep and mysterious wonders are unfolded.
Then mounteth the full moon into my view
With softening brightness; hovering before me
From rocky wall, from humid brake, arise
The silver shapes of times by-gone, and soothe
The painful pleasure of deep-brooding thought.

Alas! that man enjoys no perfect bliss,
I feel it now. Thou gav'st me with this joy,
Which brings me near and nearer to the Gods,
A fellow, whom I cannot do without;
Though, cold and heartless, he debases me
Before myself, and, with a single breath,
Blows all the bounties of thy love to nought.
Within my breast a raging fire he fans
For that fair image, busy to do ill.
Thus reel I from desire on to enjoyment,
And in enjoyment languish for desire.

5 *

## Aus: „Fauſt."

### Gretchens Stube.

Gretchen am Spinnrade allein.

Meine Ruh' ist hin,
Mein Herz ist schwer;
Ich finde sie nimmer
Und nimmermehr.

Wo ich ihn nicht hab',
Ist mir das Grab,
Die ganze Welt
Ist mir vergällt.

Mein armer Kopf
Ist mir verrückt,
Mein armer Sinn
Ist mir zerstückt.

Meine Ruh' ist hin,
Mein Herz ist schwer;
Ich finde sie nimmer
Und nimmermehr.

Nach ihm nur schau' ich
Zum Fenster hinaus,
Nach ihm nur geh' ich
Aus dem Haus.

"FAUST." Act IV. Scene IV.

Translated by Peter Gardner.

*Margaret's Room.*

(MARGARET alone, at a spinning-wheel.)

My peace is gane,
  My heart is sair,
I'll be mysel never —
  Ah! nevermair.

Where I na' hae him
  To me's the grave;
A' the warl's bitter,
  Sae sweet to the lave.

My puir head stounds,
  A madd'nin' pain
Is life in my soul,
  Is thocht on my brain.

My peace is gane,
  My heart is sair;
Rest find I nae way
  An' nevermair.

I look frae the window
  For him alane,
Savin' him, frae the house
  I gang for nane.

Sein hoher Gang,
Sein' edle Gestalt,
Seines Mundes Lächeln,
Seiner Augen Gewalt,

Und seiner Rede
Zauberfluß,
Sein Händedruck,
Und ach! sein Kuß!

Meine Ruh' ist hin,
Mein Herz ist schwer:
Ich finde sie nimmer
Und nimmermehr.

Mein Busen drängt
Sich nach ihm hin;
Ach, dürft' ich fassen
Und halten ihn!

Und küssen ihn,
So wie ich wollt',
An seinen Küssen
Vergehen sollt!

His braw, braw form,
  His step sae free,
His lauchin' mou',
  The micht o' his e'e.

His glamourin' words,
  Their flow o' bliss —
The grip o' his fingers,
  An' oh! his kiss.

My peace is gane,
  My heart is sair;
Rest find I nae way
  An' nevermair.

My bosom fills
  For him awa'.
Oh! micht I clasp him,
  Mine ain an' mine a'!

An' kiss, kiss, kiss him,
  I'm fain for sic bliss;
An' kissin, an' kissin',
  I'd dee on his kiss.

# Aus: „Faust."

### Zwinger.

(In der Mauerhöhle ein Andachtsbild der Mater dolorosa, Blumenkrüge davor).

### Gretchen

(steckt frische Blumen in die Krüge).

Ach neige,
Du Schmerzenreiche,
Dein Antlitz gnädig meiner Noth!

Das Schwert im Herzen,
Mit tausend Schmerzen
Blickst auf zu deines Sohnes Tod.

Zum Vater blickst du,
Und Seufzer schickst du
Hinauf um sein' und deine Noth.

Wer fühlet,
Wie wühlet
Der Schmerz mir im Gebein?
Was mein armes Herz hier banget,
Was es zittert, was verlanget,
Weißt nur du, nur du allein!

## "FAUST." Act IV. Scene VII.

*An enclosed area.*

(In a niche of the wall an image of the Mater dolorosa, with flower-jugs before it.)

MARGARET.

(Placing fresh flowers in the jugs.)

O mother rich in sorrows,
  Bend down to hear my cry!
O bend thee, gracious mother,
  To soothe mine agony!

Thy heart with swords is pierced,
  And tears are in thine eye,
Because they made thy dear Son
  A cruel death to die.

Thou lookest up to heaven,
  And deeply thou dost sigh;
His God and thine beholds thee
  And soothes thine agony.

Oh! who can know
  What bitter woe
Doth pierce me sharply now?
  The fear, the anguish of my heart,
Its every pang, its every smart,
  Know'st thou, and only thou.

Wohin ich immer gehe,
Wie weh, wie weh, wie wehe
Wird mir im Busen hier!
Ich bin, ach! kaum alleine,
Ich wein', ich wein', ich weine,
Das Herz zerbricht in mir.

Die Scherben vor meinem Fenster
Bethaut' ich mit Thränen, ach!
Als ich am frühen Morgen
Dir diese Blumen brach.

Schien hell in meine Kammer
Die Sonne früh herauf,
Saß ich in allem Jammer
In meinem Bett' schon auf.

Hilf! rette mich von Schmach und Tod!
Ach neige,
Du Schmerzenreiche,
Dein Antlitz gnädig meiner Noth!

And wheresoe'er I wend me,
  What woes, what woes attend me,
And how my bosom quakes!
  And when alone I find me,
With weeping, weeping, weeping,
  My heart for sorrow breaks.

These flowers, I pluck'd this morrow
  For thee, at break of day,
I dew'd with tears of sorrow,
  O wipe them thou away!

And ere the morn's first sunbeam
  Into my room was shed,
I sat in deepest anguish,
  And watch'd upon my bed.

O save me, Mother of Sorrows!
  Unto my prayer give heed,
By all the wounds that pierce thee,
  O save me in my need!

J. S. BLACKIE.

## Aus: „Faust."

Harzgebirg. Gegend von Schirke und Elend.

—·—  —  —  —  —  —
—  —  —  —·—  —

Faust, Mephistopheles, Irrlicht im Wechselgesang.

In die Traum- und Zaubersphäre
Sind wir, scheint es, eingegangen.
Führ' uns gut und mach' dir Ehre,
Daß wir vorwärts bald gelangen,
In den weiten, öden Räumen!


Seh' die Bäume hinter Bäumen,
Wie sie schnell vorüber rücken,
Und die Klippen, die sich bücken,
Und die langen Felsennasen,
Wie sie schnarchen, wie sie blasen!


Durch die Steine, durch den Rasen
Eilet Bach und Bächlein nieder.
Hör' ich Rauschen? hör' ich Lieder?
Hör' ich holde Liebesklage,

# "FAUST."

### Translated by Percy Bysshe Shelley.

*Scene. — May-Day-Night. The Hartz Mountain,*
*a desolate Country.* •

FAUST, MEPHISTOPHELES, *and* IGNIS-FATUUS *in alternate*
*Chorus.*

The limits of the sphere of dream,
  The bounds of true and false, are past.
Lead us on, thou wandering Gleam,
  Lead us onward far and fast,
To the wide, the desert waste.

But see, how swift advance and shift
Trees behind trees, row by row, —
  How, clift by clift, rocks bend and lift
Their frowning foreheads as we go.
  The giant-snouted crags, ho! ho!
How they snort, and how they blow!

Through the mossy sods and stones,
Stream and streamlet hurry down,
  A rushing throng! A sound of song
Beneath the vault of Heaven is blown!
Sweet notes of love, the speaking tones
  Of this bright day, sent down to say

Stimmen jener Himmelstage?
Was wir hoffen, was wir lieben!
Und das Echo, wie die Sage
Alter Zeiten, hallet wieder.

Uhu! Schuhu! tönt es näher;
Kauz und Kibitz und der Häher,
Sind sie alle wach geblieben?
Sind das Molche durchs Gesträuche?
Lange Beine, dicke Bäuche!
Und die Wurzeln, wie die Schlangen,
Winden sich aus Fels und Sande,
Strecken wunderliche Bande,
Uns zu schrecken, uns zu fangen;
Aus belebten derben Masern
Strecken sie Polypenfasern
Nach dem Wandrer. Und die Mäuse
Tausendfarbig, schaarenweise
Durch das Moos und durch die Haide!
Und die Funkenwürmer fliegen,
Mit gedrängten Schwärme=Zügen,
Zum verwirrenden Geleite.

That Paradise on Earth is known,
   Resound around, beneath, above;
All we hope and all we love
   Finds a voice in this blithe strain,
Which wakens hill and wood and rill,
   And vibrates far o'er field and vale,
And which Echo, like the tale
   Of old times, repeats again.

To-whoo! to-whoo! near, nearer now
   The sound of song, the rushing throng!
Are the screech, the lapwing, and the jay,
   All awake as if 'twere day?
See, with long legs and belly wide,     .
   A salamander in the brake!
Every root is like a snake,
   And along the loose hill side,
With strange contortions through the night,
   Curls, to seize or to affright;
And animated, strong, and many,
   They dart forth polypus-antennae,
To blister with their poison spume
   The wanderer. Through the dazzling gloom
The many-coloured mice that thread
   The dewy turf beneath our tread,
In troops each other's motions cross,
   Through the heath and through the moss;
And in legions intertangled,
   The fire-flies flit, and swarm, and throng,
Till all the mountain-depths are spangled.

J. W. von Goethe.

Aber sag' mir, ob wir stehen,
Oder ob wir weiter gehen?
Alles, alles scheint zu drehen,
Fels und Bäume, die Gesichter
Schneiden, und die irren Lichter,
Die sich mehren, die sich blähen.

— — — — — —
— — — — — —
— — — — — —

~~~~~~~~~~

.

Aus: „Faust."

— — — — — —
— — — — — —

Chor.

Wenn sich lau die Lüfte füllen
Um den grünumschränkten Plan,
Süße Düfte, Nebelhüllen
Senkt die Dämmerung heran:
Lispelt leise süßen Frieden,
Wiegt das Herz in Kindesruh',
Und den Augen dieses Müden
Schließt des Tages Pforte zu!

Tell me, shall we go or stay?
Shall we onward? Come along!
Everything around is swept
Forward, onward, far away!
Trees and masses intercept
The sight, and wisps on every side
Are puffed up and multiplied.

"FAUST." Part the 2nd. Act I.

Translated by Dr. J. Anster.

### CHORUS OF FAIRIES.

When the twilight mists of evening
Darken the encircling green,
Breezes come with balmy fragrance —
Clouds sink down with dusty screen;
And the heart — sweet whispers soothe it
Rocked to infant-like repose;
And the eyes of the o'er-wearied
Feel the gates of daylight close.

Nacht ist schon hereingesunken,
Schließt sich heilig Stern an Stern;
Große Lichter, kleine Funken
Glitzern nah und glänzen fern;
Glitzern hier im See sich spiegelnd,
Glänzen droben klarer Nacht;
Tiefsten Ruhens Glück besiegelnd,
Herrscht des Mondes volle Pracht.

Schon verloschen sind die Stunden,
Hingeschwunden Schmerz und Glück;
Fühl' es vor! Du wirst gesunden;
Traue neuem Tagesblick!
Thäler grünen, Hügel schwellen,
Buschen sich zu Schatten = Ruh;
Und in schwanken Silberwellen
Wogt die Saat der Ernte zu.

Wunsch um Wünsche zu erlangen,
Schaue nach dem Glanze dort!
Leise bist du nur umfangen,
Schlaf ist Schale, wirf sie fort!
Säume nicht, dich zu erdreisten,
Wenn die Menge zaudernd schweift;
Alles kann der Edle leisten,
Der versteht und rasch ergreift.

Night has now sunk down — and rising
Star comes close on holy star;
Sovereign splendours — tiny twinklers —
Sparkle near and shine from far:
Sparkle from the glassy waters —
Shine high up in the clear night;
While, of peace the seal and symbol,
Reigns the full moon's queenly light.

On have flown the hours — and sorrows
Vanish; nor can joy abide.
Feel through sleep the sense of healing!
In the purpling dawn confide!
Green vales brightening — hills out-swelling;
Flowering copses — budding tree —
In the young corn's silver wavelets
Bends the harvest soon to be.

Wake to Hope, and Hope's fulfilment;
In the sunrise see the day!
Thin the filmy bands that fold thee:
Fling the husk of sleep away!
Dare — determine — act. The many
Waver. Be not thou as these.
All things are the noble spirit's
Clear to see, and quick to seize.

—  —  —  —  —  —
—  —  —  —  —  —

## Aus: „Faust".

### II. Theil. Akt V.

—  —  —  —  —
—  —  —  —  —

#### Faust.

Ein Sumpf zieht am Gebirge hin,
Verpestet alles schon Errungne;
Den faulen Pfuhl auch abzuziehn,
Das Letzte wär' das Höchsterrungne.
Eröffn' ich Räume vielen Millionen,
Nicht sicher zwar, doch thätig frei, zu wohnen.
Grün das Gefilde, fruchtbar; Mensch und Heerde
Sogleich behaglich auf der neusten Erde,
Gleich angesiedelt an des Hügels Kraft,
Den aufgewälzt kühn-emsige Völkerschaft.
Im Innern hier ein paradiesisch Land,
Da rase draußen Fluth bis auf zum Rand,
Und wie sie nascht, gewaltsam einzuschießen,
Gemeindrang eilt, die Lücke zu verschließen.
Ja! diesem Sinne bin ich ganz ergeben,
Das ist der Weisheit letzter Schluß:
Nur der verdient sich Freiheit wie das Leben,
Der täglich sie erobern muß.
Und so verbringt, umrungen von Gefahr,
Hier Kindheit, Mann und Greis sein tüchtig Jahr.
Solch ein Gewimmel möcht' ich sehn,
Auf freiem Grund mit freiem Volke stehn.

## "FAUST." Part the 2nd. Act V.

### Translated by Dr. J. Anster.

— — — — — —
— — — — — —

FAUSTUS (*to himself*).

Along the mountain range a poisonous swamp
O'er what I've gained breathes pestilential damp.
To drain the fetid pool off, — were that done,
Then were indeed my greatest triumph won.
To many millions ample space 't would give,
Not safe, indeed, from inroad of the sea,
But yet, in free activity to live.
— Green fruitful fields, where man and beast are
                                    found
Dwelling contentedly on the new ground;
Homes, nestling in the shelter of the hill
Uprolled by a laborious people's skill;
A land like paradise within the mound,
Though the sea rave without to o'erleap its bound,
Or nibbling at it, sapping, plashing, win
Its way, impetuously to rush in.
All, with one impulse, haste to the sea wall,
Repel the mischief that endangers All.
For this one only object do I live,
To the absorbing thought myself I give.
Freedom like Life — the last best truth we learn —
Man still must conquer, and in conquering earn;
And girded thus by danger, Childhood here

Zum Augenblicke dürft' ich sagen:
Verweile doch, du bist so schön!
Es kann die Spur von meinen Erdetagen
Nicht in Aeonen untergehn. —
Im Vorgefühl von solchem hohen Glück
Genieß' ich jetzt den höchsten Augenblick.

(Faust sinkt zurück, die Lemuren fassen ihn auf und legen
ihn auf den Boden.)


### Mephistopheles.

Ihn sättigt keine Lust, ihm g'nügt kein Glück,
So buhlt er fort nach wechselnden Gestalten;
Den letzten, schlechten, leeren Augenblick,
Der Arme wünscht ihn fest zu halten.
Der mir so kräftig widerstand,
Die Zeit wird Herr, der Greis hier liegt im Sand.
Die Uhr steht still —


### Chor.

Steht still! Sie schweigt wie Mitternacht.
Der Zeiger fällt.


### Mephistopheles.

Er fällt, es ist vollbracht.

Gray Age and Man and Boy work out the year.
Oh! could I see such throngs, could I but stand
With a free people, and upon free land!
Then might I to such moment of delight
Say 'Linger with me, thou that art so bright!'
Ne'er shall the traces of my earthly day
Perish in lapsing centuries away.
Anticipating moment such as this,
Even now do I enjoy the highest bliss.

    (*Sinks back: Lemurs lay him on the ground.*)


### MEPHISTOPHELES.

— And this is the spirit that nothing can appease!
No joys give him content, no pleasures please —
Still hankering after strange stray phantasies.
The empty moment, that amused him last,
Infatuated, he would fain hold fast.
He, who against me made so stiff a stand,
Time is his master now — aye, there he is,
The gray old man stretched out upon the sand.
The Clock stands still.


### CHORUS.

    Stands still.
           Is silent as mid-night.
The Hand falls.


### MEPHISTOPHELES.

    Falls. 'T is finished: and all's right.

### Chor.

Es ist vorbei.

### Mephistopheles.

  Vorbei! ein dummes Wort.
Warum vorbei?
Vorbei und reines Nichts, vollkommnes Einerlei!
Was soll uns denn das ew'ge Schaffen!
Geschaffenes zu nichts hinwegzuraffen!
„Da ist's vorbei!" Was ist daran zu lesen!
Es ist so gut, als wär' es nicht gewesen,
Und treibt sich doch im Kreis, als wenn es wäre.
Ich liebte mir dafür das Ewig-Leere.

— — — — — —
— — — — — —

## Aus: „Iphigenie auf Tauris."

### Erster Aufzug.

### Iphigenie.

Heraus in eure Schatten, rege Wipfel
Des alten, heil'gen, dichtbelaubten Haines,
Wie in der Göttin stilles Heiligthum,
Tret' ich noch jetzt mit schauderndem Gefühl,
Als wenn ich sie zum erstenmal beträte,
Und es gewöhnt sich nicht mein Geist hierher.

CHORUS.

All's past away — gone by.

MEPHISTOPHELES.

Gone by! There is no meaning in the word!
Gone by? — All's over, then. Gone by? — absurd.
*Gone by* and utter *Nothing* are all one:
Why then does this Creating still go on?
Gone by? What means it? — What a sorry trade!
Making, and making nothing of what's made.
And then this nothing evermore we see
Making pretence a something still to be.
So on it goes, the same dull circle spinning —
'T were better with the Eternal Void beginning!

## "IPHIGENEIA IN TAURIS." Act I.

Translated by W. Taylor of Norwich.

IPHIGENEIA :

Beneath your waving shade, ye restless boughs
Of this long-hallow'd venerable wood,
As in the silent sanctuary's gloom,
I wander still with the same chilly awe
As when I enter'd first; in vain my soul
Attempts to feel itself no stranger to you.

So manches Jahr bewahrt mich hier verborgen
Ein hoher Wille, dem ich mich ergebe;
Doch immer bin ich, wie im ersten, fremd.
Denn, ach! mich trennt das Meer von den Geliebten,
Und an dem Ufer steh' ich lange Tage,
Das Land der Griechen mit der Seele suchend;
Und gegen meine Seufzer bringt die Welle
Nur dumpfe Töne brausend mir herüber.
Weh dem, der fern von Eltern und Geschwistern
Ein einsam Leben führt! Ihm zehrt der Gram
Das nächste Glück von seinen Lippen weg.
Ihm schwärmen abwärts immer die Gedanken
Nach seines Vaters Hallen, wo die Sonne
Zuerst den Himmel vor ihm aufschloß, wo
Sich Mitgeborne spielend fest und fester
Mit sanften Banden an einander knüpften.
Ich rechte mit den Göttern nicht; allein
Der Frauen Zustand ist beklagenswerth.
Zu Hauf' und in dem Kriege herrscht der Mann
Und in der Fremde weiß er sich zu helfen.
Ihn freuet der Besitz; ihn krönt der Sieg!
Ein ehrenvoller Tod ist ihm bereitet.
Wie eng=gebunden ist des Weibes Glück!
Schon einem rauhen Gatten zu gehorchen,
Ist Pflicht und Trost; wie elend, wenn sie gar
Ein feindlich Schicksal in die Ferne treibt!
So hält mich Thoas hier, ein edler Mann,
In ernsten, heil'gen Sklavenbanden fest.
O wie beschämt gesteh' ich, daß ich dir
Mit stillem Widerwillen diene, Göttin,

A mightier will, to whose behest I bow,
For years hath kept me here in deep concealment;
Yet now it seems as foreign as at first.
For, ah! the sea, from those I love, divides me:
And on its shore I stand the live-long day
Seeking, with yearning soul, the Grecian coast,
While the waves only echo back my sighs
In hoarser murmurs. O how luckless he,
Who from his parents and his brethren far
Lonesome abides! Th' approaching cup of joy
The hand of sorrow pushes from his lip.
His thoughts still hover round his father's hall,
When first the sun-beams to his infant eye
Unlock'd the gates of nature — where in sports
And games of mutual glee the happy brothers
Drew daily closer soft affection's bonds.
I would not judge the gods — but sure the lot
Of womankind is worthy to be pitied.
At home, at war, man lords it as he lists;
In foreign provinces he is not helpless;
Possession gladdens him; him conquest crowns;
E'en death to him extends a wreath of honour.
Confin'd and narrow'd is the womans' bliss:
Obedience to a rude imperious husband
Her duty and her comfort; and, if fate
On foreign shores have cast her, how unhappy!
So Thoas (yet I prize his noble soul)
Detains me here in hated hallow'd bondage.
For, tho' with shame I feel it, I acknowledge
It with secret loathness that I serve thee,

Dir, meiner Retterin! Mein Leben sollte
Zu freiem Dienste dir gewidmet sein.
Auch hab' ich stets auf dich gehofft und hoffe
Noch jetzt auf dich, Diana, die du mich,
Des größten Königes verstoßne Tochter,
In deinen heil'gen, sanften Arm genommen.
Ja, Tochter Zeus, wenn du den hohen Mann,
Den du, die Tochter fordernd, ängstigtest,
Wenn du den göttergleichen Agamemnon,
Der dir sein Liebstes zum Altare brachte,
Von Troja's umgewandten Mauern rühmlich
Nach seinem Vaterland zurückbegleitet,
Die Gattin ihm, Elektren und den Sohn,
Die schönen Schätze, wohl erhalten hast;
So gieb auch mich den Meinen endlich wieder,
Und rette mich, die du vom Tod' errettet,
Auch von dem Leben hier, dem zweiten Tode!

\*     \*     \*     \*

## Aus: „Goethe's Egmont."

### Die Trommel gerühret!

Die Trommel gerühret!
Das Pfeifchen gespielt!
Mein Liebster gewaffnet
Dem Haufen befiehlt,
Die Lanze hoch führet,
Die Leute regieret.

My great protectress, thee, to whom my life
'T were fitting I in gratitude devoted;
But I have ever hop'd and still I hope,
That thou, Diana, wilt not quite forsake
The banisht daughter of the first of Kings.
O born of Jove! if him, the mighty man
Whose soul thou woundest with unhealing pangs,
When thou didst ask his child in sacrifice —
If godlike Agamemnon, to thy altar
Who led his darling, from the fallen Troy
Thy hand hath to his country reconducted,
And on the hero hath bestow'd the bliss
To clasp his wife, Electra and his son —
Restore me also to my happy home;
And save me, whom thou hast from death preserv'd,
From worse than death, from banishment in Tauris.

\* \* \*

## FROM "EGMONT."

Translated by Arthur Duke Coleridge.

### The drums they are beating!

The drums they are beating!
The bugle is sounding!
My love, in full armour,
Commands in the van,
Waves gaily his pennon,
And marshals his clan. —

Wie klopft mir das Herze!
Wie wallt mir das Blut!
O hätt' ich ein Wämmslein
Und Hosen und Hut!

Ich folgt' ihm zum Thor 'naus
Mit muthigem Schritt,
Ging' durch die Provinzen,
Ging' überall mit.
Die Feinde schon weichen,
Wir schießen darein;
Welch Glück ohne Gleichen,
Ein Mannsbild zu sein!

## Zueignung.
### (Zu den Gedichten.)

Der Morgen kam; es scheuchten seine Tritte
Den leisen Schlaf, der mich gelind umfing,
Daß ich, erwacht, aus meiner stillen Hütte
Den Berg hinauf mit frischer Seele ging;
Ich freute mich bei einem jeden Schritte
Der neuen Blume, die voll Tropfen hing;
Der junge Tag erhob sich mit Entzücken,
Und alles ward erquickt mich zu erquicken.

Und wie ich stieg, zog von dem Fluß der Wiesen
Ein Nebel sich in Streifen sacht hervor,

How these pulses are bounding!
   This heart how it glows!
Oh! had I but doublet,'
   And helmet, and hose!

Through the gates with my lover
   Full boldly I'd ride,
And all, the world over
   Would march by his side.
Foes break at our volley,
   They waver and flee —
Oh! pleasure of pleasures,
   A soldier to be!

# INTRODUCTION [to the Poems].

Translated by Theodore Martin and W. E. Aytoun.

The morning came. Its footsteps scared away
The gentle sleep that hover'd lightly o'er me,
I left my quiet cot to greet the day,
And gaily climb'd the mountain-side before me.
The sweet young flowers! how fresh were they and
      tender,
Brimful with dew upon the sparkling lea;
The young day open'd in exulting splendour,
And all around seem'd glad to gladden me.
And as I mounted, o'er the meadow-ground
A white and filmy essence 'gan to hover;

Er wich und wechſelte mich zu umfließen,
Und wuchs geflügelt mir um's Haupt empor:
Des ſchönen Blicks ſollt' ich nicht mehr genießen,
Die Gegend deckte mir ein trüber Flor;
Bald ſah ich mich von Wolken wie umgoſſen,
Und mit mir ſelbſt in Dämmrung eingeſchloſſen.

Auf einmal ſchien die Sonne durchzudringen,
Im Nebel ließ ſich eine Klarheit ſehn.
Hier ſank er leiſe ſich hinabzuſchwingen,
Hier theilt' er ſteigend ſich um Wald und Höhn.
Wie hofft' ich, ihr den erſten Gruß zu bringen!
Sie hofft' ich nach der Trübe doppelt ſchön.
Der luft'ge Kampf war lange nicht vollendet,
Ein Glanz umgab mich und ich ſtand geblendet.

Bald machte mich, die Augen aufzuſchlagen,
Ein innrer Trieb des Herzens wieder kühn,
Ich konnt' es nur mit ſchnellen Blicken wagen,
Denn alles ſchien zu brennen und zu glühn.
Da ſchwebte mit den Wolken hergetragen
Ein göttlich Weib vor meinen Augen hin,
Kein ſchöner Bild ſah ich in meinem Leben,
Sie ſah mich an und blieb verweilend ſchweben.

Kennſt du mich nicht? ſprach ſie mit einem Munde,
Dem aller Lieb' und Treue Ton entfloß;
Erkennſt du mich, die ich in manche Wunde
Des Lebens dir den reinſten Balſam goß?
Du kennſt mich wohl, an die, zu ew'gem Bunde,

It sail'd and shifted till it hemm'd me round,
Then rose above my head, and floated over.
No more I saw the beauteous scene unfolded —
It lay beneath a melancholy shroud;
And soon was I, as if in vapour moulded,
Alone, within the twilight of the cloud.

At once, as though the sun were struggling through,
Within the mist a sudden radiance started.
Here sank the vapour, but to rise anew,
There on the peak, and upland forest parted.
O, how I panted for the first clear gleaming,
Made by the gloom it banish'd doubly bright!
It came not, but a glory round me beaming,
And I stood blinded by the gush of light.

A moment, and I felt enforc'd to look,
By some strange impulse of the heart's emotion;
But more than one quick glance I scarce could brook,
For all was burning like a molten ocean.
There, in the glorious clouds that seem'd to bear her,
A form angelic hover'd in the air;
Ne'er did my eyes behold a vision fairer,
And still she gazed upon me, floating there.

"Dost thou not know me?" and her voice was soft
As truthful love, and holy calm it sounded.
"Know'st thou not me, who many a time and oft
Pour'd balsam in thy hurts when sorest wounded?
Ah, well thou knowest her, to whom for ever

Dein strebend Herz sich fest und fester schloß.
Sah' ich dich nicht mit heißen Herzensthränen
Als Knabe schon nach mir dich eifrig sehnen?

Ja! rief ich aus, indem ich selig nieder
Zur Erde sank, lang' hab' ich dich gefühlt;
Du gabst mir Ruh', wenn durch die jungen Glieder
Die Leidenschaft sich rastlos durchgewühlt;
Du hast mir wie mit himmlischem Gefieder
Am heißen Tag die Stirne sanft gekühlt;
Du schenktest mir der Erde beste Gaben,
Und jedes Glück will ich durch dich nur haben!

Dich nenn' ich nicht. Zwar hör' ich dich von vielen
Gar oft genannt, und jeder heißt dich sein,
Ein jedes Auge glaubt auf dich zu zielen,
Fast jedem Auge wird dein Strahl zur Pein.
Ach, da ich irrte, hatt' ich viel Gespielen,
Da ich dich kenne, bin ich fast allein;
Ich muß mein Glück nur mit mir selbst genießen,
Dein holdes Licht verdecken und verschließen.

Sie lächelte, sie sprach: du siehst, wie klug,
Wie nöthig war's, euch wenig zu enthüllen!
Kaum bist du sicher vor dem gröbsten Trug,
Kaum bist du Herr vom ersten Kinderwillen,
So glaubst du dich schon Uebermensch genug,
Versäumst die Pflicht des Mannes zu erfüllen!
Wie viel bist du von andern unterschieden?
Erkenne dich, leb' mit der Welt in Frieden!

Thy heart in union pants to be allied!
Have I not seen the tears — the wild endeavour
That even in boyhood brought thee to my side?"

"Yes! I have felt thy influence oft," I cried,
And sank on earth before her, half-adoring;
"Thou brought'st me rest when Passion's lava-tide
Thro' my young veins like liquid fire was pouring.
And thou hast fann'd, as with celestial pinions,
In summer's heat, my parch'd and fever'd brow;     .
Gav'st me the choicest gifts of earth's dominions,
And, save through thee, I seek no fortune now.

"I name thee not, but I have heard thee named,
And heard thee styled their own ere now by many;
All eyes believe at thee their glance is aim'd,
Though thine effulgence is too great for any.
Ah! I had many comrades whilst I wander'd —
I know thee now, and stand almost alone:
I veil thy light, too precious to be squander'd,
And share the inward joy I feel with none."

Smiling she said — "Thou seest 't was wise from thee
To keep the fuller, greater revelation:
Scarce art thou from grotesque delusions free,
Scarce master of thy childish first sensation;
Yet deem'st thyself so far above thy brothers,
That thou hast won the right to scorn them! Cease,
Who made the yawning gulf 'twixt thee and others?
Know — know thyself — live with the world in peace."

Verzeih' mir, rief ich aus, ich meint' es gut;
Soll ich umsonst die Augen offen haben?
Ein froher Wille lebt in meinem Blut,
Ich kenne ganz den Werth von deinen Gaben!
Für andre wächst in mir das edle Gut,
Ich kann und will das Pfund nicht mehr vergraben!
Warum sucht' ich den Weg so sehnsuchtsvoll,
Wenn ich ihn nicht den Brüdern zeigen soll?

Und wie ich sprach, sah mich das hohe Wesen
Mit einem Blick mitleid'ger Nachsicht an,
Ich konnte mich in ihrem Auge lesen,
Was ich verfehlt und was ich recht gethan.
Sie lächelte, da war ich schon genesen,
Zu neuen Freuden stieg mein Geist heran;
Ich konnte nun mit innigem Vertrauen
Mich zu ihr nahn und ihre Nähe schauen.

Da reckte sie die Hand aus in die Streifen
Der leichten Wolken und des Dufts umher,
Wie sie ihn faßte, ließ er sich ergreifen,
Er ließ sich ziehn, es war kein Nebel mehr.
Mein Auge konnt' im Thale wieder schweifen,
Gen Himmel blickt' ich, er war hell und hehr.
Nun sah ich sie den reinsten Schleier halten,
Er floß um sie und schwoll in tausend Falten.

Ich kenne dich, ich kenne deine Schwächen,
Ich weiß, was Gutes in dir lebt und glimmt!
So sagte sie, ich hör' sie ewig sprechen,

"Forgive me!" I exclaim'd, "I meant no ill,
Else should in vain my eyes be disenchanted;
Within my blood there stirs a genial. will —
I know the worth of all that thou hast granted.
That boon I hold in trust for others merely,
Nor shall I let it rust within the ground;
Why sought I out the pathway so sincerely,
If not to guide my brothers to the bound?"

And as I spoke, upon her radiant face
Pass'd a sweet smile, like breath across a mirror;
And in her eyes' bright meaning I could trace
What I had answer'd well, and what in error.
She smiled, and then my heart regain'd its lightness,
And bounded in my breast with rapture high:
Then durst I pass within her zone of brightness,
And gaze upon her with unquailing eye.

Straightway she stretch'd her hand among the thin
And watery haze that round her presence hover'd;
Slowly it coil'd and shrank her grasp within,
And lo! the landscape lay once more uncover'd —
Again mine eye could scan the sparkling meadow,
I look'd to heaven, and all was clear and bright;
I saw her hold a veil without a shadow,
That undulated round her in the light.

"I know thee! — all thy weakness, all that yet
Of good within thee lives and glows, I've measured;"
She said — her voice I never may forget —

Empfange hier, was ich dir lang bestimmt,
Dem Glücklichen kann es an nichts gebrechen,
Der dieß Geschenk mit stiller Seele nimmt;
Aus Morgenduft gewebt und Sonnenklarheit,
Der Dichtung Schleier aus der Hand der Wahrheit.

Und wenn es dir und deinen Freunden schwüle
Am Mittag wird, so wirf ihn in die Luft!
Sogleich umsäuselt Abendwindeskühle,
Umhaucht euch Blumen= Würzgeruch und Duft.
Es schweigt das Wehen banger Erdgefühle,
Zum Wolkenbette wandelt sich die Gruft,
Besänftiget wird jede Lebenswelle,
Der Tag wird lieblich und die Nacht wird helle.

So kommt denn, Freunde, wenn auf euren Wegen
Des Lebens Bürde schwer und schwerer drückt,
Wenn eure Bahn ein frischerneuter Segen
Mit Blumen ziert, mit golduen Früchten schmückt,
Wir gehn vereint dem nächsten Tag entgegen!
So leben wir, so wandeln wir beglückt.
Und dann auch soll, wenn Enkel um uns trauern,
Zu ihrer Lust noch unsre Liebe dauern.

"Accept the gift that long for thee was treasur'd.
Oh! happy he, thrice-blest in earth and heaven,
Who takes this gift with soul serene and true,
The veil of song, by Truth's own fingers given,
Enwoven of sunshine and the morning-dew.

"Wave but this veil on high, whene'er beneath
The noonday fervour thou and thine are glowing,
And fragrance of all flowers around shall breathe,
And the cool winds of eve come freshly blowing.
Earth's cares shall cease for thee, and all its riot;
Where gloom'd the grave, a starry couch be seen;
The waves of life shall sink in halcyon quiet;
The days be lovely fair, the nights serene."

Come then, my friends, and whether 'neath the load
Of heavy griefs ye struggle on, or whether
Your better destiny shall strew the road
With flowers, and golden fruits that cannot wither,
United let us move, still forward striving;
So while we live shall joys our days illume,
And in our children's hearts our love surviving
Shall gladden them, when we are in the tomb.

J. W. von Goethe.

## Meeresstille.

———

Tiefe Stille herrscht im Wasser,
Ohne Regung ruht das Meer,
Und bekümmert sieht der Schiffer
Glatte Fläche rings umher.
Keine Luft von keiner Seite!
Todesstille fürchterlich!
In der ungeheuren Weite
Reget keine Welle sich.

————

## Wonne der Liebe.

———

Freudvoll
Und leidvoll,
Gedankenvoll sein,
Hangen
Und bangen
In schwebender Pein;
Himmelhoch jauchzend,
Zum Tode betrübt;
Glücklich allein
Ist die Seele, die liebt.

————

## OCEAN CALM.

Translated by Lady John Manners.

———

Deepest calm reigns on the water,
  Without movement rests the sea,
Which unto the troubled sailor
  Seems one smooth expanse to be;
Not a breath from any quarter,
  Fearful, silent as the grave;
In the mighty realm of water
  Motionless is every wave.

## CLÄRCHEN'S SONG.

Translated by Richard Garnett.

———

Cheerful,
And tearful,
And thoughtful to be;
Waiting,
Debating,
Irresolutely;
Cast into darkness,
Shouting above,
O! happy alone
Is the heart with its love.

### Zigeunerlied.

———

Im Nebelgeriesel, im tiefen Schnee,
Im wilden Wald, in der Winternacht,
Ich hörte der Wölfe Hungergeheul,
Ich hörte der Eulen Geschrei:
          Wille wau wau wau!
          Wille wo wo wo!
          Wito hu!




Ich schoß einmal eine Katz' am Zaun,
Der Anne, der Hex', ihre schwarze liebe Katz';
Da kamen des Nachts sieben Wehrwölf' zu mir,
Waren sieben Weiber vom Dorf.
          Wille wau wau wau!
          Wille wo wo wo!
          Wito hu!

## GIPSEY-SONG.

### Translated by Dr. J. Anster.

In foggy drizzle, in deep snow white,
In the wild wood wide, in a winternight,
I heard the hooting of the owls,
And I heard the wolves with their hungry howls.

> Wille wau wau wau,
> Wille wo wo wo,
> Tu-whit tu-whoo,
> Wille woo.

A cat came prowling down my ditch,
Anne's own black cat, the wicked witch;
I lifted my gun, and I fired for fun,
And I took good aim, and I cried fair game,
And cat or witch, I can't say which,
She uttered a scream, and she sputtered a scritch,
A scream of fright — and a scritch of spite,
And she cocked up her tail and took to flight.
In the night of that day, seven war-wolves gray
Came eyeing their prey,
    All eyeing me, — all hunger driven;
Eyeing their prey, seven war-wolves gray,
    Seven hags of the village were the seven.

> Wille wau wau wau,
> Wille wo wo wo,
> Tu-whit tu-whoo,
> Wille woo.

Ich kannte sie all',. ich kannte sie wohl,
Die Anne, die Ursel, die Käth',
Die Liese, die Barbe, die Ev', die Beth;
Sie heulten im Kreise mich an.
                    Wille wau wau wau!
                    Wille wo wo wo!
                    Wito hu!


Da nannt' ich sie alle bei Namen laut:
Was willst du, Anne? was willst du, Beth?
Da rüttelten sie sich, da schüttelten sie sich
Und liefen und heulten davon.
                    Wille wau wau wau!
                    Wille wo wo wo!
                    Wito hu!


## Mignon.

Kennst du das Land,. wo die Citronen blühn,
Im dunkeln Laub die Gold-Orangen glühn,
Ein sanfter Wind vom blauen Himmel weht,
Die Myrte still und hoch der Lorbeer steht?
    Kennst du es wohl?
                    Dahin! Dahin
Möcht' ich mit dir, o mein Geliebter, ziehn.

I knew them all and each, I guess,
There was Anne, and Ursula, and Bess,
And Lizzy and Barbara, Sue, and Kate,
And they circled me round, and howled for hate.
        Wille wau wau wau,
        Wille wo wo wo,
        Tu-whit tu-whoo,
        Wille woo.


I named their names, for my heart was stout,
What ails thee, Anne? — What is Bess about?
And they shook with fright, and shivered with fear,
And scudded away with howlings drear.
        Wille wau wau wau,
        Wille wo wo wo,
        Tu-whit tu-whoo,
        Wille woo.

## MIGNON.

Translated by Richard Garnett.

Know'st thou the land where flowers the citron-bloom,
And golden orange glows in leafy gloom?
A soft wind flutters from the fair blue sky,
Still stands the myrtle and the laurel high;
Know'st thou the land?
                O there, O there,
My Friend, my Love, might thou and I repair!

Kennst du das Haus? Auf Säulen ruht sein Dach,
Es glänzt der Saal, es schimmert das Gemach,
Und Marmorbilder stehn und sehn mich an:
Was hat man dir, du armes Kind, gethan?
     Kennst du es wohl?
                    Dahin! dahin
Möcht' ich mit dir, o mein Beschützer, ziehn.


Kennst du den Berg und seinen Wolkensteg?
Das Maulthier sucht im Nebel seinen Weg;
In Höhlen wohnt der Drachen alte Brut;
Es stürzt der Fels und über ihn die Fluth.
     Kennst du ihn wohl?
                    Dahin! Dahin
Geht unser Weg! o Vater, laß uns ziehn!

## Der Sänger.

Was hör' ich draußen vor dem Thor,
Was auf der Brücke schallen?
Laß den Gesang vor unserm Ohr
Im Saale wiederhallen!
Der König sprach's, der Page lief;
Der Knabe kam, der König rief:
Laßt mir herein den Alten!

Gegrüßet seid mir, edle Herrn,
Gegrüßt ihr, schöne Damen!

Know'st thou the house? on pillars rests its roof,
The high hall shines, the chamber gleams aloof,
And marble statues stand and gaze on me, —
What is·it they have done, poor child, to thee?
Know'st thou the house?

                   O there, O there,
My Friend, my Guide, might thou and I repair!


Know'st thou the mountain-path, in vapours grey
Immersed? the slow mule picks his foggy way;
In caves abide the dragon's ancient brood;
Crashes the rock, and over it the flood.
Know'st thou the path?

                   O there, O there,
My Friend, my Father, let us both repair!

## THE MINSTREL.

### Translated by James Clarence Mangan.

"What voice, what harp, are those we hear
    Beyond the gate in chorus?
Go, page! — the lay delights our ear,
    We'll have it sung before us!",
So speaks the king: the stripling flies —
He soon returns; his master cries —
    Bring in the hoary minstrel!"


"Hail, princes mine! Hail, noble knights!
    All hail, enchanting dames!

Welch reicher Himmel! Stern bei Stern!
Wer kennet ihre Namen?
Im Saal voll Pracht und Herrlichkeit
Schließt, Augen, euch; hier ist nicht Zeit
Sich staunend zu ergötzen.

Der Sänger drückt' die Augen ein,
Und schlug in vollen Tönen;
Die Ritter schauten muthig drein,
Und in den Schooß die Schönen.
Der König, dem das Lied gefiel,
Ließ ihm, zum Lohne für sein Spiel,
Eine goldne Kette bringen.

Die goldne Kette gieb mir nicht,
Die Kette gieb den Rittern,
Vor deren kühnem Angesicht
Der Feinde Lanzen splittern.
Gieb sie dem Kanzler, den du hast,
Und laß ihn noch die goldne Last
Zu andern Lasten tragen.

Ich singe, wie der Vogel singt,
Der in den Zweigen wohnet;
Das Lied, das aus der Seele dringt,
Ist Lohn, der reichlich lohnet;
Doch darf ich bitten, bitt' ich eins:
Laß mir den besten Becher Weins
In purem Golde reichen.

What starry heaven! What blinding lights!
  Whose tongue may tell their names?
In this bright hall, amid this blaze,
Close, close mine eyes! Ye may not gaze .
  On such stupendous glories!"


The Minnesinger closed his eyes;
  He struck his mighty lyre:
Then beauteous bosoms heaved with sighs,
  And warriors felt on fire;
The king, enraptured by the strain,
Commanded that a golden chain
  Be given the bard in guerdon.


"Not so! Reserve thy chain, thy gold,
  For those brave knights whose glances,
Fierce flashing through the battle bold,
  Might shiver sharpest lances!
Bestow it on thy Treasurer there —
The golden burden let him bear
  With other glittering burdens.


"I sing as in the greenwood bush
  The cageless wild-bird carols —
The tones that from the full heart gush
  Themselves are gold and laurels!
Yet, might I ask, then thus I ask,
Let one bright cup of wine in flask
  Of glowing gold be brought me!"

Er setzt' ihn an, er trank ihn aus;
O Trank voll süßer Labe!
O! dreimal hochbeglücktes Haus,
Wo das ist kleine Gabe!
Ergeht's euch wohl, so denkt an mich,
Und danket Gott so warm, als ich
Für diesen Trunk euch danke.

## Erlkönig.

Wer reitet so spät durch Nacht und Wind?
Es ist der Vater mit seinem Kind;
Er hat den Knaben wohl in dem Arm,
Er faßt ihn sicher, er hält ihn warm.

Mein Sohn, was birgst du so bang dein Gesicht? —
Siehst, Vater, du den Erlkönig nicht?
Den Erlenkönig mit Kron' und Schweif? —
Mein Sohn, es ist ein Nebelstreif. —

„Du liebes Kind, komm, geh mit mir!
„Gar schöne Spiele spiel' ich mit dir;
„Manch' bunte Blumen sind an dem Strand,
„Meine Mutter hat manch gülden Gewand." —

Mein Vater, mein Vater, und hörest du nicht,
Was Erlenkönig mir leise verspricht?
Sei ruhig, bleibe ruhig, mein Kind;
In dürren Blättern säuselt der Wind. —

They set it down: he quaffs it all —
   "O! draught of richest flavour!
O! thrice divinely happy hall,
   Where that is scarce a favour!
If Heaven shall bless ye, think on me,
And thank your God as I thank ye,
   For this delicious wine-cup!"

## THE ERL-KING.

### Translated by Peter Gardner.

Wha rides sae late through wind an' nicht?
   A faither it is wi' his bairn sae bricht;
The callan' he hauds wi' claspin' arm,
   He grips him sicker, he keeps him warm.

"Why hide ye yer face, son, tentily?"
   "The Erl-King, faither, div ye no see?
Erl-King, wi' croun an' train sweepin' far?"
   "My son, its just a streak i' the haar."

— "Thou winsome wean, come, gang wi' me,
   Siccan fine plays as I'll play wi' thee;
Bonny flow'rs mony are by the shore,
   My mither o' gowden dresses has store." —

"My faither, my faither, an' div ye no hear,
   Hoo Erl-King fleeches saft i' mine ear?"
"Be calm, keep calm, my bairn — its licht
   Thro' withered leaves whispers the wind o' nicht."

8 *

„Willst, feiner Knabe, du mit mir gehn?
„Meine Töchter sollen dich warten schön;
„Meine Töchter führen den nächtlichen Reihn,
„Und wiegen und tanzen und singen dich ein." —

Mein Vater, mein Vater, und siehst du nicht dort
Erlkönigs Töchter am düstern Ort? —
Mein Sohn, mein Sohn, ich seh' es genau:
Es scheinen die alten Weiden so grau. —

„Ich liebe dich, mich reizt deine schöne Gestalt;
„Und bist du nicht willig, so brauch' ich Gewalt." —
Mein Vater, mein Vater, jetzt faßt er mich an!
Erlkönig hat mir ein Leids gethan! —

Dem Vater grauset's, er reitet geschwind,
Er hält in den Armen das ächzende Kind,
Erreicht den Hof mit Müh' und Noth;
In seinen Armen das Kind war todt.

## Der Fischer.

Das Wasser rauscht', das Wasser schwoll,
Ein Fischer saß daran,
Sah nach dem Angel ruhevoll,
Kühl bis an's Herz hinan.

— "My bonnie boy, wilt gang wi' me?
  My dochters sall tent thee gentily;
My dochters sall nichtly lead dances o' glee,
  An' weel sall they cradle an' sweet sing to thee." —

"My faither, my faither, an' see ye no there
  Glint i' the mirk place his dochters sae fair?"
"My son, my son, I see it fine —
  Sae grey the auld saugh-trees seem to shine."

"I lo'e thee, thy beauty doth charm me sae,
  That gin thou's no willin', I'll gar thee gae."
"My faither, my faither, he grips me noo:
  Erl-King has wrocht me skaith, I trow."

Swift rides the faither, he groues forfairn,
  He hauds in his arms the moanin' bairn,
He reaches his ha' in dolour an' pain,
  The bairn in his arms was dead and gane!

---

## THE FISHER.

Translated by Theodore Martin.

The water plash'd, the water play'd,
  A fisher sat thereby,
And mark'd, as to and fro it sway'd,
  His float with dreamy eye;

Und wie er sitzt und wie er lauscht,
Theilt sich die Fluth empor;
Aus dem bewegten Wasser rauscht
Ein feuchtes Weib hervor.

Sie sang zu ihm, sie sprach zu ihm:
Was lockst du meine Brut
Mit Menschenwitz und Menschenlist
Hinauf in Todesgluth?
Ach wüßtest du, wie's Fischlein ist
So wohlig auf dem Grund,
Du stiegst herunter wie du bist
Und würdest erst gesund.

Labt sich die liebe Sonne nicht,
Der Mond sich nicht im Meer?
Kehrt wellenathmend ihr Gesicht
Nicht doppelt schöner her?
Lockt dich der tiefe Himmel nicht,
Das feuchtverklärte Blau?
Lockt dich dein eigen Angesicht
Nicht her in ew'gen Thau?

Das Wasser rauscht', das Wasser schwoll,
Netzt' ihm den nackten Fuß;
Sein Herz wuchs ihm so sehnsuchtsvoll,
Wie bei der Liebsten Gruß.
Sie sprach zu ihm, sie sang zu ihm;
Da war's um ihn geschehn:
Halb zog sie ihn, halb sank er hin,
Und ward nicht mehr gesehn.

And as he sits and watches there,
  He sees the flood unclose,
And from the parting waves a fair
  Mermaiden slowly rose.

She sang to him with witching wile,
  "My brood why wilt thou snare,
With human craft and human guile,
  To die in scorching air?
Ah! didst thou know how happy we,
  Who dwell in waters clear,
Thou wouldst come down at once to me,
  And rest for ever here.

"The sun and ladye-moon they lave
  Their tresses in the main,
And, breathing freshness from the wave,
  Come doubly bright again.
The deep-blue sky, so moist and clear,
  Hath it for thee no lure?
Does thine own face not woo thee down
  Unto our waters pure?"

The water plash'd, the water play'd —
  It lapp'd his naked feet;
He thrill'd as though he felt the touch
  Of maiden kisses sweet.
She spoke to him, she sang to him —
  Resistless was her strain —
Half-drawn, he sank beneath the wave,
  And ne'er was seen again.

## Der König in Thule.

Es war ein König in Thule,
Gar treu bis an das Grab,
Dem sterbend seine Buhle
Einen goldnen Becher gab.

Es ging ihm nichts darüber,
Er leert' ihn jeden Schmaus;
Die Augen gingen ihm über,
So oft er trank daraus.

Und als er kam zu sterben,
Zählt' er seine Städt' im Reich,
Gönnt' alles seinem Erben,
Den Becher nicht zugleich.

Er saß beim Königsmahle,
Die Ritter um ihn her,
Auf hohem Vätersaale,
Dort auf dem Schloß am Meer.

Dort stand der alte Zecher,
Trank letzte Lebensgluth,
Und warf den heil'gen Becher
Hinunter in die Fluth.

## THE KING IN THULE.

Translated by Lord Francis Leveson Gower.

———

There was a King in Thule,
  Was constant to the grave;
And she who loved him truly
  A goblet to him gave.

Alike the old man cherish'd
  Her memory and the cup;
And oft, to her who perish'd,
  He fill'd and drank it up.

Ere death had closed his pleasures,
  The states he summon'd all,
And portion'd out his treasures,
  The goblet not withal.

With all his knights before him
  He feasted royally,
In the hall of those who bore him,
  In his castle by the sea.

With closing life's emotion,
  He bade the goblet flow —
Then plunged it in the ocean,
  A hundred fathom low.

Er sah ihn stürzen, trinken
Und sinken tief in's Meer.
Die Augen thäten ihm sinken;
Trank nie einen Tropfen mehr.

―――――

## Der Schatzgräber.

―――――

Arm am Beutel, krank am Herzen,
Schleppt' ich meine langen Tage.
Armuth ist die größte Plage,
Reichthum ist das höchste Gut!
Und, zu enden meine Schmerzen,
Ging ich einen Schatz zu graben.
Meine Seele sollst du haben!
Schrieb ich hin mit eignem Blut.

Und so zog ich Kreis' um Kreise,
Stellte wunderbare Flammen,
Kraut und Knochenwerk zusammen:
Die Beschwörung war vollbracht.
Und auf die gelernte Weise
Grub ich nach dem alten Schatze
Auf dem angezeigten Platze:
Schwarz und stürmisch war die Nacht.

Und ich sah ein Licht von weiten,
Und es kam gleich einem Sterne

He saw it filling, drinking,
  And the calm sea closing o'er;
His eyes the while were sinking,
  No drop he e'er drank more.

## THE TREASURE-SEEKER.

Translated by the late Professor Aytoun.

Many weary days I suffer'd,
  Sick of heart and poor of purse;
Riches are the greatest blessing —
  Poverty the deepest curse!
Till at last to dig a treasure
  Forth I went into the wood —
'"Fiend! my soul is thine for ever!"
  And I sign'd the scroll with blood.

Then I drew the magic circles,
  Kindled the mysterious fire,
Placed the herbs and bones in order,
  Spoke the incantation dire.
And I sought the buried metal
  With a spell of mickle might —
Sought it as my master taught me;
  Black and stormy was the night.

And I saw a light appearing
  In the distance, like a star;

Hinten aus der fernsten Ferne
Eben als es zwölfe schlug.
Und da galt kein Vorbereiten.
Heller ward's mit einemmale
Von dem Glanz der vollen Schale,
Die ein schöner Knabe trug.

Holde Augen sah ich blinken
Unter dichtem Blumenkranze;
In des Trankes Himmelsglanze
Trat er in den Kreis herein.
Und er hieß mich freundlich trinken;
Und ich dacht': Es kann der Knabe
Mit der schönen lichten Gabe
Wahrlich nicht der Böse sein.

Trinke Muth des reinen Lebens!
Dann verstehst du die Belehrung,
Kommst, mit ängstlicher Beschwörung,
Nicht zurück an diesen Ort.
Grabe hier nicht mehr vergebens.
Tages Arbeit! Abends Gäste!
Saure Wochen! Frohe Feste!
Sei dein künftig Zauberwort.

When the midnight hour was tolling,
   Came it waxing from afar:
Came it flashing, swift and sudden,
   As if fiery wine it were,
Flowing from an open chalice,
   Which a beauteous boy did bear.

And he wore a lustrous chaplet,
   And his eyes were full of thought,
As he stepp'd into the circle
   With the radiance that he brought.
And he bade me taste the goblet;
   And I thought — "It cannot be,
That this boy should be the bearer
   Of the Demon's gifts to me!"

"Taste the draught of pure existence
   Sparkling in this golden urn,
And no more with baleful magic
   Shalt thou hitherward return.
Do not seek for treasures longer;
   Let thy future spellwords be,
Days of labour, nights of resting:
   So shall peace return to thee!"

# Friedrich von Schiller,

born 1759, died 1805.

„Körper und Stimme leiht die Schrift dem stummen Gedanken,
Durch der Jahrhunderte Strom trägt ihn das redende Blatt."

# Aus: „Wallensteins Lager."

## Achter Auftritt.

---

— Bergknappen treten auf und spielen einen Walzer, erst langsam und dann immer geschwinder. Der erste Jäger tanzt mit der Aufwärterin; die Marketenderin mit dem Rekruten; das Mädchen entspringt, der Jäger hinter ihr her, und bekommt den Kapuziner zu fassen, der eben hereintritt.

## Kapuziner.

Heisa, Juchheia, Dudeldumdei!
Das geht ja hoch her. Bin auch dabei!
Ist das eine Armee von Christen?
Sind wir Türken? sind wir Anabaptisten?
Treibt man so mit dem Sonntag Spott,
Als hätte der allmächtige Gott
Das Chiragra, könnte nicht drein schlagen?
Ist's jetzt Zeit zu Saufgelagen,
Zu Banketten und Feiertagen?
Quid hic statis otiosi?
Was steht ihr und legt die Hände in Schooß?
Die Kriegsfurie ist an der Donau los,

## "WALLENSTEIN'S CAMP." Scene VIII.

Translated by the late James Churchill.

———

*(Enter Miners and play a Waltz — at first slowly and afterwards quicker. — The first Yager dances with the Girl, the Sutler-woman with the Recruit. — The Girl springs away, and the Yager, pursuing her, seizes hold of a Capuchin Friar just entering.)*

### CAPUCHIN.

Hurrah! halloo! tol, lol, de rol, le!
The fun's at its height! I'll not be away!
Is't an army of Christians that joins in such works?
Or are we all turned Anabaptists and Turks?
Is the Sunday a day for this sport in the land,
As though the great God had the gout in his hand,
And thus couldn't smite in the midst of your band,
Say, is this a time for your revelling shouts,
For your banquetings, feasts, and your holiday bouts?
*Quid hic statis otiosi?* declare
Why, folding your arms, stand ye lazily there?
While the furies of war on the Danube now fare,

Das Bollwerk des Bayerlands ist gefallen,
Regensburg liegt in des Feindes Krallen,
Und die Armee liegt hier in Böhmen,
Pflegt den Bauch, läßt sich's wenig grämen,
Kümmert sich mehr um den Krug als den Krieg,
Wetzt lieber den Schnabel als den Säbel,
Hetzt sich lieber herum mit der Dirn',
Frißt den Ochsen lieber als den Oxenstirn.
Die Christenheit trauert in Sack und Asche,
Der Soldat füllt sich nur die Tasche.
Es ist eine Zeit der Thränen und Noth,
Am Himmel geschehen Zeichen und Wunder,
Und aus den Wolken, blutigroth,
Hängt der Herrgott den Kriegsmantel 'runter.
Den Kometen steckt er, wie eine Ruthe,
Drohend am Himmelsfenster aus,
Die ganze Welt ist ein Klagehaus,
Die Arche der Kirche schwimmt im Blute,
Und das römische Reich — daß Gott erbarm!
Sollte jetzt heißen römisch Arm;
Der Rheinstrom ist worden zu einem Peinstrom,
Die Klöster sind ausgenommene Nester,
Die Bisthümer sind verwandelt in Wüstthümer,
Die Abteien und die Stifter
Sind nun Raubteien und Diebesklüfter,
Und alle die gesegneten deutschen Länder
Sind verkehrt worden in Elender —
Woher kommt das? das will ich euch verkünden:
Das schreibt sich her von euern Lastern und Sünden,
Von dem Gräuel und Heidenleben,

And Bavaria's bulwark is lying full low,
And Ratisbon's fast in the clutch of the foe.
Yet, the army lies here in Bohemia still,
And caring for nought, so their paunches they fill!
Bottles far rather than battles you'll get,
And your bills than your broadswords more readily wet;
With the wenches, I ween, is your dearest concern;
And you'd rather roast oxen than Oxenstiern.
In sackcloth and ashes while Christendom's grieving,
No thought has the soldier his guzzle of leaving.
'Tis a time of misery, groans and tears!
Portentous the face of the heavens appears!
And forth from the clouds behold blood-red,
The Lord's war-mantle is downward spread —
While the comet is thrust as a threatening rod,
From the window of Heaven by the hand of God.
The world is but one vast house of woe,
The ark of the church stems a bloody flow,
The holy Empire — God help the same!
Has wretchedly sunk to a hollow name.
The Rhine's gay stream has a gory gleam,
The cloister's nests are now robbed by roysters,
The church-lands now are changed to lurch-lands;
Abbacies, and all other holy foundations
Now are but Robber-sees — rogues' habitations.
And thus is each once-blest German state
Deep sunk in the doom of the desolate!
Whence comes all this? O that will I tell —
It comes of your doings, of sin, and of hell;
Of the horrible, heathenish lives ye lead,

9*

Dem sich Officier' und Soldaten ergeben.
Denn die Sünd' ist der Magnetenstein,
Der das Eisen ziehet ins Land herein.
Auf das Unrecht, da folgt das Uebel,
Wie die Thrän' auf den herben Zwiebel,
Hinter dem U kommt gleich das Weh,
Das ist die Ordnung im A B C.

　　　Ubi erit victoriae spes,
Si offenditur Deus? Wie soll man siegen,
Wenn man die Predigt schwänzt und die Meß,
Nichts thut, als in den Weinhäusern liegen?
Die Frau in dem Evangelium
Fand den verlornen Groschen wieder,
Der Saul seines Vaters Esel wieder,
Der Joseph seine saubern Brüder;
Aber wer bei den Soldaten sucht
Die Furcht Gottes und die gute Zucht
Und die Scham, der wird nicht viel finden,
Thät' er auch hundert Laternen anzünden.
Zu dem Prediger in der Wüsten,
Wie wir lesen im Evangelisten,
Kamen auch die Soldaten gelaufen,
Thaten Buße und ließen sich taufen,
Fragten ihn: Quid faciemus nos?
Wie machen wir's, daß wir kommen in Abrahams Schooß?

　　　Et ait illis, und er sagt:
Neminem concutiatis,
Wenn ihr niemanden schindet und plackt.
Neque calumniam faciatis,
Niemand verlästert, auf niemand lügt.

Soldiers and officers all of a breed.
For sin is the magnet, on every hand,
That draws your steel throughout the land!
As the onion causes the tear to flow,
So Vice must ever be followed by Woe —
The W duly succeeds the V,
This is the order of A, B, C.
    *Ubi erit victoriae spes,*
*Si offenditur Deus?* which says,
How, pray ye, shall victory e'er come to pass,
If thus you play truant from sermon and mass,
And do nothing but lazily loll o'er the glass?
The woman, we're told in the Testament,
Found the penny, in search whereof she went.
Saul met with his father's asses again,
And Joseph his precious fraternal train,
But he who 'mong soldiers shall hope to see'
God's fear, or shame, or discipline — he
From his toil, beyond doubt, will baffled return,
Tho' a. hundred lamps in the search he_burn.
To the wilderness preacher, th'Evangelist says,
The soldiers, too, throng'd to repent of their ways,
And had themselves christen'd in former days.
*Quid faciemus nos?* they said:
Tow'rd Abraham's bosom what path must we tread?
    *Et ait illis*, and, said he,
*Neminem concutiatis;*
From bother and wrongs leave your neighbours free.
*Neque calumniam faciatis;*
And deal not in slander nor lies, d'ye see?

Contenti estote, euch begnügt,
Stipendiis vestris, mit eurer Löhnung
Und verflucht jede böse Angewöhnung.
Es ist ein Gebot: Du sollst den Namen
Deines Herrgotts nicht eitel auskramen!
Und wo hört man mehr blasphemiren,
Als hier in den Friedländischen Kriegsquartieren?
Wenn man für jeden Donner und Blitz,
Den ihr losbrennt mit eurer Zungenspitz',
Die Glocken müßt' läuten im Land umher,
Es wär' bald kein Meßner zu finden mehr.
Und wenn euch für jedes böse Gebet,
Das aus eurem ungewaschnen Munde geht,
Ein Härlein ausging aus eurem Schopf,
Ueber Nacht wär' er geschoren glatt,
Und wär' er so dick wie Absalon's Zopf.
Der Josua war doch auch ein Soldat,
König David erschlug den Goliath,
Und wo steht denn geschrieben zu lesen,
Daß sie solche Fluchmäuler sind gewesen?
Muß man den Mund doch, ich sollte meinen,
Nicht weiter aufmachen zu einem Helf Gott!
Als zu einem Kreuz-Sackerlot!
Aber wessen das Gefäß ist gefüllt,
Davon es sprudelt und überquillt.
     Wieder ein Gebot ist: Du sollst nicht stehlen.
Ja, das befolgt ihr nach dem Wort,
Denn ihr tragt alles offen fort.
Vor euren Klauen und Geiersgriffen,
Vor euren Praktiken und bösen Kniffen

*Contenti estote* — content ye, pray,
*Stipendiis vestris* — with your pay —
And curse for ever each evil way.

There is a command — thou shalt not utter
The name of the Lord thy God, in vain;
But where is it men most blasphemies mutter?
Why here, in Duke Friedland's headquarters, 'tis
                     plain.
If for every thunder! — and every blast!
Which blazing ye from your tongue points cast,
The bells were but rung, in the country round,
Not, a bellman, I ween, would there soon be found;
And if for each and ev'ry unholy prayer
Which to vent from your jabbering jaws you dare,
From your noddles were pluck'd but the smallest hair,
Ev'ry crop would be smooth'd e'er the sun went down.
Tho' at morn 'twere bushy as Absalom's crown.
Now Joshua, methinks, was a soldier as well —
By the arm of King David the Philistine fell;
But where do we find it written, I pray,
That they ever blasphemed in this villanous way?
One would think ye need stretch your jaws no more,
To cry, "God help us!" than "zounds!" to roar.
But, by the liquor that's pour'd in the cask, we know
With what it will bubble and overflow.

Again, it is written, thou shalt not steal,
And this you follow, i' faith, to the letter,
For open-faced robbery suits ye better.
The gripe of your vulture-claws you fix
On all — and your wiles and rascally tricks

Ist das Geld nicht geborgen in der Truh,
Das Kalb nicht sicher in der Kuh,
Ihr nehmt das Ei und das Huhn dazu.
Was sagt der Prediger? Contenti estote,
Begnügt euch mit eurem Commißbrote.
Aber wie soll man die Knechte loben,
Kommt doch das Aergerniß von oben!
Wie die Glieder, so auch das Haupt!
Weiß doch niemand, an wen der glaubt!

### Erster Jäger.

Herr Pfaff! uns Soldaten mag Er schimpfen,
Den Feldherrn soll Er uns nicht verunglimpfen.

### Kapuziner.

Ne custodias gregem meam!
Das ist so ein Ahab und Jerobeam,
Der die Völker von der wahren Lehren
Zu falschen Götzen thut verkehren.

### Trompeter und Rekrut.

Laß Er uns das nicht zweimal hören!

### Kapuziner.

So ein Bramarbas und Eisenfresser,
Will einnehmen alle festen Schlösser.
Rühmte sich mit seinem gottlosen Mund,
Er müsse haben die Stadt Stralsund,
Und wär' sie mit Ketten an den Himmel geschlossen.

Make the gold unhid in our coffers now,
And the calf unsafe while yet in the cow —
Ye take both the egg and the hen, I vow.
*Contenti estote* — the preacher said ;
Which means — be content with your army-bread.
But how should the slaves not from duty swerve?
The mischief begins with the lord they serve.
Just like the members so is the head.
I should like to know who can tell me *his* creed.

### FIRST YAGER.

Sir Priest, 'gainst ourselves rail on as you will —
Of the General we warn you to breathe no ill.

### CAPUCHIN.

*Ne custodias gregem meam !*
An Ahab is he and a Jeraboam,
Who the people from faith's unerring way,
To the worship of idols would turn astray.

### TRUMPETER and RECRUIT.

Let us not hear that again, we pray.

### CAPUCHIN.

Such a Bramarbas, whose iron tooth
Would seize all the strongholds of earth, forsooth ! —
Did he not boast, with ungodly tongue,
That Stralsund must needs to his grasp be wrung,
Though to heaven itself with a chain 'twere strung?

Trompeter.

Stopft ihm keiner sein Lästermaul?

Kapuziner.

So ein Teufelsbeschwörer und König Saul,
So ein Jehu und Holofern,
Verleugnet, wie Petrus, seinen Meister und Herrn,
Drum kann er den Hahn nicht hören krähn —

Beide Jäger.

Pfaffe! Jetzt ist's um dich geschehn!

Kapuziner.

So ein listiger Fuchs Herodes —

Trompeter und beide Jäger (auf ihn eindringend)

Schweig stille! Du bist des Todes!

Kroaten (legen sich drein).

Bleib da, Pfäfflein, fürcht' dich nit,
Sag' dein Sprüchel und theil's uns mit.

Kapuziner (schreit lauter).

So ein hochmüthiger Nebucadnezer,
So ein Sündenvater und mussiger Ketzer,
Läßt sich nennen den Wallenstein;
Ja freilich ist er uns allen ein Stein
Des Anstoßes und Aergernisses,
Und so lang der Kaiser diesen Friedeland
Läßt walten, so wird nicht Fried' im Land.

(Er hat nach und nach bei den letzten Worten, die er mit
erhobner Stimme spricht, seinen Rückzug genommen, indem die
Kroaten die übrigen Soldaten von ihm abwehren.)

TRUMPETER.

Will none put a stop to his slanderous bawl?

CAPUCHIN.

A wizard he is! — and a sorcerer Saul! —
Holofernes! — a Jehu! — denying we know,
Like St. Peter, his Master and Lord below;
And hence must he quail when the cock doth crow —

BOTH YAGERS.

Now, parson, prepare; for thy doom is nigh.

CAPUCHIN.

A fox more cunning than Herod, I trow —

TRUMPETER and both YAGERS (*pressing against him*).

Silence, again, — if thou wouldst not die!

CROATS (*interfering*).

Stick to it, father; we'll shield you, ne'er fear,
The close of your preachment now let's hear.

CAPUCHIN (still louder).

A Nebuchadnezzar, in towering pride!
And a vile and heretic sinner beside!
He calls himself rightly the stone of a wall;
For, faith! he's a stumbling-stone to us all.
And ne'er can the Emperor have peace indeed,
Till of Friedland himself the land is freed.

[*During the last passage, which he pronounces in an elevated
voice, he has been gradually retreating, the Croats keeping
the other soldiers off.*]

### Aus: „Die Piccolomini."
#### Erster Aufzug, vierter Auftritt.

##### Max Piccolomini.

O schöner Tag, wenn endlich der Soldat
Ins Leben heimkehrt, in die Menschlichkeit,
Zum frohen Zug die Fahnen sich entfalten,
Und heimwärts schlägt der sanfte Friedensmarsch.
Wenn alle Hüte sich und Helme schmücken
Mit grünen Maien, dem letzten Raub der Felder!
Der Städte Thore gehen auf von selbst,
Nicht die Petarde braucht sie mehr zu sprengen;
Von Menschen sind die Wälle rings erfüllt,
Von friedlichen, die in die Lüfte grüßen, —
Hell klingt von allen Thürmen das Geläut,
Des blut'gen Tages frohe Vesper schlagend.
Aus Dörfern und aus Städten wimmelnd strömt
Ein jauchzend Volk, mit liebend emsiger
Zudringlichkeit des Heeres Fortzug hindernd —
Da schüttelt, froh des noch erlebten Tags,
Dem heimgekehrten Sohn der Greis die Hände.
Ein Fremdling tritt er in sein Eigenthum,
Das längst verlaßne, ein; mit breiten Aesten
Deckt ihn der Baum bei seiner Wiederkehr,
Der sich zur Gerte bog, als er gegangen,
Und schamhaft tritt als Jungfrau ihm entgegen,
Die er einst an der Amme Brust verließ.
O! glücklich, wenn dann auch sich eine Thür,
Sich zarte Arme sanft umschlingend öffnen —

\*      \*      \*

## "THE PICCOLOMINI." Act I. Scene IV.

### Translated by Thomas Carlyle.

— — — — — —

### MAX PICCOLOMINI.

O blessed bright day, when at last the soldier
Shall turn back to life, and be again a man;
Through th' merry lines the colours are unfurl'd,
And homewards beats the thrilling soft peacemarch;
All hats and helmets deck'd with leafy sprays,
The last spoil of the fields! The city's gates
Fly up; now needs not the petard to burst them:
The walls are crowded with rejoicing people;
Their shouts ring through the air; from every tower
Blithe bells are pealing forth the merry vesper
Of that bloody day. From town and hamlet
Flow the jocund thousands; with their hearty
Kind impetuosity our march impeding.
The old man, weeping that he sees this day,
Embraces his long-lost son: a stranger
He revisits his old home; with spreading boughs
The tree o'ershadows him at his return,
Which waver'd as a twig when he departed;
And, modest blushing, comes a maid to meet him,
Whom on her nurse's breast he left. O happy!
For whom some kindly door like this, for whom
Soft arms to clasp him shall be open'd!

\*          \*          \*

## Aus: „Wallensteins Tod."

### Erster Aufzug, vierter Auftritt.

Wallenstein, mit sich selbst redend.

Wär's möglich? Könnt' ich nicht mehr, wie ich wollte?
Nicht mehr zurück, wie mir's beliebt? Ich müßte
Die That vollbringen, weil ich sie gedacht,
Nicht die Versuchung von mir wies — das Herz
Genährt mit diesem Traum, auf ungewisse
Erfüllung hin die Mittel mir gespart,
Die Wege bloß mir offen hab' gehalten? —
Beim großen Gott des Himmels! Es war nicht
Mein Ernst, beschlossne Sache war es nie:
In dem Gedanken bloß gefiel ich mir;
Die Freiheit reizte mich und das Vermögen.
War's Unrecht, an dem Gaukelbilde mich
Der königlichen Hoffnung zu ergötzen?
Blieb in der Brust mir nicht der Wille frei,
Und sah ich nicht den guten Weg zur Seite,
Der mir die Rückkehr offen stets bewahrte?
Wohin denn seh' ich plötzlich mich geführt?
Bahnlos liegt's hinter mir, und eine Mauer
Aus meinen eignen Werken baut sich auf,
Die mir die Umkehr thürmend hemmt!

(Er bleibt tiefsinnig stehen.)

# THE DEATH OF WALLENSTEIN.
## Act I. Scene IV.
### Translated by S. T. Coleridge.

WALLENSTEIN (in soliloquy).

Is it possible?

Is't so? I *can* no longer what I *would*?
No longer draw back at my liking? I
Must *do* the deed, because I *thought* of it,
And fed this heart here with a dream? Because
I did not scowl temptation from my presence,
Dallied with thoughts of possible fulfilment,
Commenced no movement, left all time uncertain,
And only kept the road, the access open?
By the great God of Heaven! It was not
My serious meaning, it was ne'er resolve.
I but amus'd myself with thinking of it.
The free-will tempted me, the power to do
Or not to do it. — Was it criminal
To make the fancy minister to hope,
To fill the air with pretty toys of air,
And clutch fantastic sceptres moving t'ward me?
Was not the will kept free? Beheld I not
The road of duty close beside me — but
One little step, and once more I was in it?
Where am I? Whither have I been transported?.
No road, no track behind me, but a wall
Impenetrable, insurmountable,
Rises obedient to the spells I mutter'd
And meant not — my own doings tower behind me.

*(Pauses and remains in deep thought.)*

Strafbar erschein' ich, und ich kann die Schuld,
Wie ich's versuchen mag, nicht von mir wälzen;
Denn mich verklagt der Doppelsinn des Lebens,
Und — selbst der frommen Quelle reine That
Wird der Verdacht, schlimmdeutend, mir vergiften.
War ich, wofür ich gelte, der Verräther,
Ich hätte mir den guten Schein gespart,
Die Hülle hätt' ich dicht um mich gezogen,
Dem Unmuth Stimme nie geliehn.   Der Unschuld,
Des unverführten Willens mir bewußt,
Gab ich der Laune Raum, der Leidenschaft — .
Kühn war das Wort, weil es die That nicht war.
Jetzt werden sie, was planlos ist geschehn,
Weitsehend, planvoll mir zusammenknüpfen,
Und was der Zorn, und was der frohe Muth
Mich sprechen ließ im Ueberfluß des Herzens,
Zu künstlichem Gewebe mir vereinen
Und eine Klage furchtbar draus bereiten,
Dagegen ich verstummen muß.   So hab' ich
Mit eignem Netz verderblich mich umstrickt,
Und nur Gewaltthat kann es reißend lösen.


                     (Wiederum still stehend.)



Wie anders! da des Muthes freier Trieb
Zur kühnen That mich zog, die rauh gebietend
Die Noth jetzt, die Erhaltung von mir heischt.
Ernst ist der Anblick der Nothwendigkeit.

A punishable man I seem; the guilt,
Try what I will, I cannot roll off from me:
The equivocal demeanour of my life
Bears witness on my prosecutor's party;
And even my purest acts from purest motives
Suspicion poisons with malicious gloss.
Were I that thing for which I pass, that traitor,
A goodly outside I had sure reserv'd,
Had drawn the cov'rings thick and double round me,
Been calm and chary of my utterance;
But being conscious of the innocence
Of my intent, my uncorrupted will,
I gave way to my humours, to my passion:
Bold were my words, because my deeds were *not*.
Now every planless measure, chance event,
The threat of rage, the vaunt and joy and triumph,
And all the May-games of a heart o'erflowing,
Will they connect, and weave them all together
Into one web of treason; all will be plain,
My eye ne'er absent from the far-off mark,
Step tracing step, each step a politic progress;
And out of all they'll fabricate a charge
So specious, that I must myself stand dumb.
I am caught in my own net, and only force,
Naught but a sudden rent can liberate me.

          *(Pauses again.)*

How else! since that the heart's unbias'd instinct
Impell'd me to the daring deed which now
Necessity, self-preservation, orders.
Stern is the on-look of necessity.

Nicht ohne Schauder greift des Menschen Hand
In des Geschicks geheimnißvolle Urne.
In meiner Brust war meine That noch mein;
Einmal entlassen aus dem sichern Winkel
Des Herzens, ihrem mütterlichen Boden,
Hinausgegeben in des Lebens Fremde,
Gehört· sie jenen tück'schen Mächten an,
Die keines Menschen Kunst vertraulich macht.

(Er macht heftige Schritte durchs Zimmer, dann bleibt er
wieder sinnend stehen.)

Und was ist dein Beginnen? Hast du dir's
Auch redlich selbst bekannt? Du willst die Macht,
Die ruhig, sicher thronende erschüttern,
Die in verjährt geheiligtem Besitz,
In der Gewohnheit festgegründet ruht,
Die an der Völker frommem Kinderglauben
Mit tausend zähen Wurzeln sich befestigt.
Das wird kein Kampf der Kraft sein mit der Kraft,
Den fürcht' ich nicht.  Mit jedem Gegner wag' ich's,
Den ich kann sehen und ins Auge fassen,
Der, selbst voll Muth, auch mir den Muth entflammt.
Ein unsichtbarer Feind ist's, den ich fürchte,
Der in der Menschen Brust mir widersteht,
Durch feige Furcht allein mir fürchterlich —
Nicht, was lebendig, kraftvoll sich verkündigt,
Ist das gefährlich Furchtbare.  Das ganz
Gemeine ist's, das ewig Gestrige,
Was immer war und immer wiederkehrt
Und morgen gilt, weil's heute hat gegolten!
Denn aus Gemeinem ist der Mensch gemacht,

Not without shudder may a human hand
Grasp the mysterious urn of destiny.
My deed was mine, remaining in my bosom.
Once suffer'd to escape from its safe corner
Within the heart, its nursery and birth-place,
Sent forth into the foreign, it belongs
For ever to those sly malicious powers
Whom never heart of man conciliated.

*(Paces in agitation through the chamber, then pauses, and,
after the pause, breaks out again into audible soliloquy.)*

What is thy enterprise? thy aim? thy object?
Hast honestly confess'd it to thyself?
Power seated on a quiet throne thou'dst shake,
Power on an ancient consecrated throne,
Strong in possession, founded in old custom;
Power by a thousand tough and stringy roots
Fix'd to the people's pious nursery-faith.
This, this will be no strife of strength with strength;
That I fear'd not. I brave each combatant,
Whom I can look on, fixing eye to eye,
Who, full himself of courage, kindles courage
In me too. 'Tis a foe invisible
The which I fear — a fearful enemy,
Which in the human heart opposes me,
By its coward fear alone made fearful to me.
Not that, which full of life, instinct with pow'r,
Makes known its present being; that is not
The true, the perilously formidable.
O no! it is the common, the quite common,
The thing of an eternal yesterday,

10 *

Und die Gewohnheit nennt er seine Amme.
Weh dem, der an den würdig alten Hausrath
Ihm rührt, das theure Erbstück seiner Ahnen!
Das Jahr übt eine heiligende Kraft;
Was grau vor Alter ist, das ist ihm göttlich.
Sei im Besitze, und du wohnst im Recht,
Und heilig wird's die Menge dir bewahren.

(Zu dem Pagen, der hereintritt.)

Der schwed'sche Oberst? Ist er's? Nun, er komme.

(Page geht: Wallenstein hat den Blick nachdenkend
auf die Thür geheftet.)

Noch ist sie rein — noch! das Verbrechen kam
Nicht über diese Schwelle noch — So schmal ist
Die Grenze, die zwei Lebenspfade scheidet!

Aus: „Wallenstein's Tod."

### Dritter Aufzug, dreizehnter Auftritt.

(Wallenstein im Harnisch.)

Du hast's erreicht, Octavio! — Fast bin ich
Jetzt so verlassen wieder, als ich einst
Vom Regensburger Fürstentage ging.
Da hatt' ich nichts mehr als mich selbst — doch was

What ever was, and ever more returns,
Sterling to-morrow, for to-day 'twas sterling!
For of the wholly common is man made,
And custom is his nurse! Woe then to them,
Who lay irreverent hands upon his old
House-furniture, the dear inheritance
From his forefathers. For time consecrates;
And what is grey with age becomes religion.
Be in possession, and thou hast the right,
And sacred will the many guard it for thee!

*(To the page, who enters.)*

The Swedish officer? — Well, let him enter.

*(The page exit; Wallenstein fixes his eye in deep thought on the door.)*

Yet is it pure — as yet! — the crime has come
Not o'er this threshold yet — so slender is
The boundary that divideth life's two paths.

---

# THE DEATH OF WALLENSTEIN.

### Act III. Scene XIII.

### Translated by S. T. Coleridge.

WALLENSTEIN (in armour; loquitur) :

Thou hast gained thy point, Octavio; once more am I
Almost as friendless as at Regensburg;
There I had nothing left me, but myself —
But what one man can do, you have now experience.
The twigs have you hew'd off, and here I stand
A leafless trunk. But in the sap within
Lives the creating power, and a new world
May sprout forth from it. Once already have I

Ein Mann kann werth sein, habt ihr schon erfahren.
Den Schmuck der Zweige habt ihr abgehauen,
Da steh' ich, ein entlaubter Stamm!  Doch innen
Im Marke lebt die schaffende Gewalt,
Die sprossend eine Welt aus sich geboren.
Schon einmal galt ich euch statt eines Heers,
Ich Einzelner. Dahingeschmolzen vor
Der schwed'schen Stärke waren eure Heere,
Am Lech sank Tilly, euer letzter Hort,
Ins Bayerland, wie ein geschwollner Strom,
Ergoß sich dieser Gustav, und zu Wien
In seiner Hofburg zitterte der Kaiser.
Soldaten waren theuer, denn die Menge
Geht nach dem Glück — Da wandte man die Augen
Auf mich, den Helfer in der Noth; es beugte sich
Der Stolz des Kaisers vor dem Schwergekränkten,
Ich sollte aufstehn mit dem Schöpfungswort
Und in die hohlen Läger Menschen sammeln.
Ich that's.  Die Trommel ward gerührt.  Mein Name
Ging, wie ein Kriegsgott, durch die Welt.  Der Pflug,
Die Werkstatt wird verlassen, alles wimmelt
Der altbekannten Hoffnungsfahne zu —
— Noch fühl' ich mich denselben, der ich war!
Es ist der Geist, der sich den Körper baut,
Und Friedland wird sein Lager um sich füllen.
Führt eure Tausende mir kühn entgegen,
Gewohnt wohl sind sie, unter mir zu siegen,
Nicht gegen mich — Wenn Haupt und Glieder sich trennen,
Da wird sich zeigen, wo die Seele wohnte.

                    (Illo und Terzky treten ein.)

Prov'd myself worth an army to you — I alone!
Before the Swedish strength your troops had melted;
Beside the Lech sunk Tilly, your last hope;
Into Bavaria, like a winter-torrent,
Did that Gustavus pour, and at Vienna
In his own palace did the Emperor tremble.
Soldiers were scarce, for still the multitude
Follow the luck: all eyes were turn'd on me,
Their helper in distress: the Emperor's pride
Bow'd itself down before the man he had injur'd.
'Twas I must rise, and with creative word
Assemble forces in the desolate camps.
I did it. Like a god of war, my name
Went thro' the world. The drum was beat — and lo!
The plough, the work-shop is forsaken; all
Swarm to the old familiar, long-lov'd banners;
And as the wood-choir, rich in melody,
Assemble quick around the bird of wonder,
When first his throat swells with his magic song,
So did the warlike youth of Germany
Crowd in, around the image of my eagle.
I feel myself the being that I was.
It is the soul that builds itself a body;
And Friedland's camp will not remain unfill'd.
Lead then your thousands out to meet me — true!
They are accustom'd under me to conquer,
But not against me. If the head and limbs
Separate from each other, 'twill be soon
Made manifest, in which the soul abode.

*(Illo and Tertsky enter.)*

Muth, Freunde, Muth! Wir sind noch nicht zu Boden.
Fünf Regimenter Terzky sind noch unser
Und Butler's wackre Schaaren — Morgen stößt
Ein Heer zu uns von sechzehntausend Schweden.
Nicht mächt'ger war ich, als ich vor neun Jahren
Auszog, dem Kaiser Deutschland zu erobern.

## Aus: „Wallenstein's Tod."
### Vierter Aufzug, zehnter Auftritt.

✳       ✳       ✳       ✳       ✳
   ✳       ✳       ✳       ✳

#### Der schwedische Hauptmann.

Wir standen, keines Ueberfalls gewärtig,
Bei Neustadt schwach verschanzt in unserm Lager,
Als gegen Abend eine Wolke Staubes
Aufstieg vom Wald her, unser Vortrab fliehend
Ins Lager stürzte, rief, der Feind sei da.
Wir hatten eben nur noch Zeit, uns schnell
Aufs Pferd zu werfen, da durchbrachen schon,
In vollem Rosseslauf daher gesprengt,
Die Pappenheimer den Verhack; schnell war
Der Graben auch, der sich ums Lager zog,
Von diesen stürm'schen Schaaren überflogen.
Doch unbesonnen hatte sie der Muth
Vorausgeführt den andern, weit dahinten
War noch das Fußvolk, nur die Pappenheimer waren
Dem kühnen Führer kühn gefolgt. —

(Thekla macht eine Bewegung. Der Hauptmann hält einen
  Augenblick inne, bis sie ihm einen Wink giebt, fortzufahren.)

Courage, friends! Courage! We are still unvanquish'd;
I feel my footing firm; five regiments, Tertsky,
Are still our own, and Butler's gallant troops;
And a host of sixteen thousand Swedes to-morrow.
I was not stronger, when nine years ago
I march'd forth, with glad heart and high of hope,
To conquer Germany for the Emperor.

## THE DEATH OF WALLENSTEIN.

### Act IV. Scene X.
### Translated by S. T. Coleridge.

\*     \*     \*     \*

#### THE SWEDISH CAPTAIN.

We lay, expecting no attack, at Neustadt,
Intrench'd but insecurely in our camp,
When towards evening rose a cloud of dust
From the wood thitherward; our vanguard fled
Into the camp, and sounded the alarm.
Scarce had we mounted, ere the Pappenheimers,
Their horses at full speed, broke thro' the lines,
And leap'd the trenches; but their heedless courage
Had borne them onward far before the others —
The infantry was still at distance; only
The Pappenheimers followed daringly
Their daring leader —

*(Thekla betrays agitation in her gestures. The Officer
pauses till she makes a sign to him to proceed.)*

Von vorn, und von den Flanken faßten wir
Sie jetzo mit der ganzen Reiterei
Und drängten sie zurück zum Graben, wo
Das Fußvolk, schnell geordnet, einen Rechen
Von Piken ihnen starr entgegenstreckte.
Nicht vorwärts konnten sie, auch nicht zurück,
Gekeilt in drangvoll fürchterliche Enge.
Da rief der Rheingraf ihrem Führer zu,
In guter Schlacht sich ehrlich zu ergeben;
Der Oberst Piccolomini —

        (Thekla, schwindelnd, faßt einen Sessel.)

                      Ihn machte
Der Helmbusch kenntlich und das lange Haar,
Vom raschen Ritte war's ihm losgegangen —
Zum Graben winkt er, sprengt, der Erste, selbst
Sein edles Roß darüber weg, ihm stürzt
Das Regiment nach — doch — schon war's geschehn!
Sein Pferd, von einer Partisan durchstoßen, bäumt
Sich wüthend, schleudert weit den Reiter ab,
Und hoch weg über ihn geht die Gewalt
Der Rosse, keinem Zügel mehr gehorchend.

(Thekla, welche die letzten Reden mit allen Zeichen wachsender
Angst begleitet, verfällt in ein heftiges Zittern, sie will sinken;
Fräulein Neubrunn eilt hinzu und empfängt sie in ihren Armen.)

              Neubrunn.
        Mein theures Fräulein —

          Hauptmann (gerührt).
           Ich entferne mich.

             Thekla.
Es ist vorüber — bringen Sie's zu Ende.

             Both in van and flanks
With our whole cavalry we now receiv'd them,
Back to the trenches drove them, where the foot
Stretch'd out a solid ridge of pikes to meet them.
They neither could advance, nor yet retreat;
And as they stood on every side wedg'd in,
The Rhinegrave to their leader call'd aloud,
Inviting a surrender; but their leader,
Young Piccolomini —

      *(Thekla, giddy, grasps a chair.)*

             Known by his plume,
And his long hair, gave signal for the trenches;
Himself leap'd first, the regiment all plung'd after. —
His charger, by an halbert gor'd, rear'd up,
Flung him with violence off, and over him,
The horses, now no longer to be curb'd —

*(Thekla, who has accompanied the last speech with all the marks of increasing agony, trembles through her whole frame, and is falling. The lady Neubrunn runs to her, and receives her into her arms.)*

LADY NEUBRUNN.

My dearest Lady —

CAPTAIN.

      I retire.

THEKLA.

             'Tis over.

Proceed to the conclusion.

#### Hauptmann.

Da ergriff, als sie den Führer fallen sahn,
Die Truppen grimmig wüthende Verzweiflung.
Der eignen Rettung denkt jetzt keiner mehr.
Gleich wilden Tigern fechten sie; es reizt
Ihr starrer Widerstand die Unsrigen,
Und eher nicht erfolgt des Kampfes Ende,
Als bis der letzte Mann gefallen ist.

#### Thekla (mit zitternder Stimme).

Und wo — wo ist — Sie sagten mir nicht alles.

#### Hauptmann (nach einer Pause).

Heut früh bestatteten wir ihn. Ihn trugen
Zwölf Jünglinge der edelsten Geschlechter,
Das ganze Heer begleitete die Bahre.
Ein Lorbeer schmückte seinen Sarg, drauf legte
Der Rheingraf selbst den eignen Siegerdegen.
Auch Thränen fehlten seinem Schicksal nicht,
Denn viele sind bei uns, die seine Großmuth
Und seiner Sitten Freundlichkeit erfahren,
Und alle rührte sein Geschick. Gern hätte
Der Rheingraf ihn gerettet, doch er selbst
Vereitelt' es; man sagt, er wollte sterben.

CAPTAIN.

Wild despair
Inspir'd the troops with frenzy when they saw
Their leader perish: every thought of rescue
Was spurn'd; they fought like wounded tigers; their
Frantic resistance rous'd our soldiery;
A murderous fight took place, nor was the contest
Finish'd before their last man fell.

THEKLA (*faltering*).

And where —
Where is — You have not told me all.

CAPTAIN (*after a pause*).

This morning
We buried him. Twelve youths of noblest birth
Did bear him to interment; the whole army
Follow'd the bier. A laurel deck'd his coffin;
The sword of the deceas'd was placed upon it,
In mark of honour, by the Rhinegrave's self.
Nor tears were wanting; for there are among us
Many, who had themselves experienced
The greatness of his mind, and gentle manners;
All were affected at his fate. The Rhinegrave
Would willingly have sav'd him; but himself
Made vain th' attempt — 'tis said he wish'd to die.

\* \* \* \*

\* \* \* \* \*

\* \* \* \*

## Prolog zur: „Jungfrau von Orleans."

### Vierter Auftritt.

—

(Johanna d'Arc, allein auf der Bühne, sagt ihrem Heimath-
Thale Lebewohl. Sie hat einen Helm auf dem Haupte, den sie
eben zuvor von Bertram empfangen.)

Lebt wohl, ihr Berge, ihr geliebten Triften,
Ihr traulich stillen Thäler, lebet wohl!
Johanna wird nun nicht mehr auf euch wandeln,
Johanna sagt euch ewig Lebewohl!
Ihr Wiesen, die ich wässerte, ihr Bäume,
Die ich gepflanzet, grünet fröhlich fort!
Lebt wohl, ihr Grotten und ihr kühlen Brunnen,
Du Echo, holde Stimme dieses Thals,
Die oft mir Antwort gab auf meine Lieder,
Johanna geht, und nimmer kehrt sie wieder!

Ihr Plätze alle meiner stillen Freuden,
Euch lass' ich hinter mir auf immerdar.
Zerstreuet euch, ihr Lämmer, auf den Heiden!
Ihr seid jetzt eine hirtenlose Schaar,
Denn eine andre Heerde muß ich weiden
Dort auf dem blut'gen Felde der Gefahr.
So ist des Geistes Ruf an mich ergangen,
Mich treibt nicht eitles, irdisches Verlangen.

## THE MAID OF ORLEANS. Prologue: Scene IV.

### Translated by the Rev. W. W. Skeat.

———

#### JOAN OF ARC,

*alone on the stage, is bidding farewell to her native valley.*
*She has upon her head a helmet, which she has just before*
*obtained from Bertram.*

Farewell! ye hills, and ye the haunts I love,
  Familiar dales, where silence still doth dwell;
No more Johanna through your shades will rove,
  Johanna bids you all a long farewell!
Ye meads I watered, and ye trees I planted,
  Still flourish fresh and fair, and still rejoice!
Farewell, cool streams, and grots like caves enchanted,
  And Echo, rolling through the glade thy voice,
Who often would'st repeat my plaintive strain;
Farewell! Johanna goes, and ne'er returns again.

Ye lovely spots, whereto my thoughts oft bend,
  For evermore I leave your calm delight;
Ye lambs, at will o'er wold and moorland wend,
  No shepherdess have ye to guide you right.
Henceforth I go another flock to tend,
  On yonder field, deepstained by gory fight,
I go, responsive to the Spirit's call,
No idle, earthly hopes my soaring soul enthral.

Denn der zu Mosen auf des Horebs Höhen
Im feur'gen Busch sich flammend niederließ
Und ihm befahl, vor Pharao zu stehen,
Der einst den frommen Knaben Isai's,
Den Hirten, sich zum Streiter ausersehen,
Der stets den Hirten gnädig sich bewies,
Er sprach zu mir aus dieses Baumes Zweigen:
„Geh hin! Du sollst auf Erden für mich zeugen."


„In rauhes Erz sollst du die Glieder schnüren,
Mit Stahl bedecken deine zarte Brust,
Nicht Männerliebe darf dein Herz berühren
Mit sünd'gen Flammen eitler Erdenlust.
Nie wird der Brautkranz deine Locke zieren,
Dir blüht kein lieblich Kind an deiner Brust;
Doch werd' ich dich mit kriegerischen Ehren,
Vor allen Erdenfrauen dich verklären."


„Denn wenn im Kampf die Muthigsten verzagen,
Wenn Frankreichs letztes Schicksal nun sich naht,
Dann wirst du meine Oriflamme tragen
Und, wie die rasche Schnitterin die Saat,
Den stolzen Ueberwinder niederschlagen;
Umwälzen wirst du seines Glückes Rad,
Errettung bringen Frankreichs Heldensöhnen
Und Rheims befrein und deinen König krönen!"


Ein Zeichen hat der Himmel mir verheißen,
Er sendet mir den Helm, er kommt von i h m,

For He who, at the bush by flames unbranded,
  On Horeb's mount His servant Moses chose,
And to be bold in Pharaoh's sight commanded —
  Yes! He who once, to scatter Israel's foes,
Made Jesse's son, the shepherd-lad, strong-handed,
  He who on shepherds favour still bestows,
Spake to me from the branches of this tree:
"Go forth! redeem the right! Go forth to witness me!"

"Henceforth in rugged armour-plates encase thee,
  Enclose thy breast, thy tender limbs, in steel:
No love for mortal man must e'er debase thee,
  Nor let thine heart love's softening transports feel.
No bridal wreath, twined round thy locks, shall grace
                      thee,
  Nor blooming child within thy lap shall kneel.
So shalt thou be with warlike honours crowned;
Above all earthly maids will I thy fame resound."

"For when the stoutest hearts their doom are dreading,
  When France's day of overthrow seems near;
Then thou, my sacred Oriflamme wide-spreading,
  Shalt, as the reaper crops the ripened ear,
Mow down the victors, all their pride down-treading,
  And all thy country's fame once more uprear.
To France's warrior-sons shalt safety bring,
Her foes from Rheims expel, and crown her lawful king."

And lo! a sign kind Providence hath given;
  It sends a helm, the gift I most require;

Mit Götterkraft berühret mich sein Eisen,
Und mich durchflammt der Muth der Cherubim;
Ins Kriegsgewühl hinein will es mich reißen,
Es treibt mich fort mit Sturmes Ungestüm,
Den Feldruf hör' ich mächtig zu mir dringen,
Das Schlachtroß steigt, und die Trompeten klingen.

Aus: „Die Braut von Messina."

Chor:

Durch die Straßen der Städte,
Vom Jammer gefolget,
Schreitet das Unglück —
Lauernd umschleicht es
Die Häuser der Menschen,
Heute an dieser
Pforte pocht es,
Morgen an jener,
Aber noch keinen hat es verschont.
Die unerwünschte,
Schmerzliche Botschaft,
Früher oder später,
Bestellt es an jeder
Schwelle wo ein Lebendiger wohnt.

Its iron touch bestows the might of Heaven,
  I feel its plates an angel-strength inspire :
Amidst the battle's tempest forward driven,
  I seem borne onward by some tempest dire.
Hark ! even now the warcry fierce is sounding,
Hark ! to the warsteed's tramp, the clarion's peal
                       rebounding !

# FROM "THE BRIDE OF MESSINA."

Translated by the late W. Taylor of Norwich.

### CHORUS.

Athwart the city's streets,
With wailing in her train,
Misfortune strides ;
Watchful she marks
The homes of men :
To-day at this,
To-morrow at yon other door, she knocks,
  · But misses none.
Sooner or later comes
Some messenger of woe
To every threshold, where the living dwell.

11 *

Wenn die Blätter fallen
In des Jahres Kreise,
Wenn zum Grabe wallen
Entnervte Greise,
Da gehorcht die Natur
Ruhig nur
Ihrem alten Gesetze,
Ihrem ewigen Brauch,
Da ist nichts, was den Menschen entsetze!
Aber das Ungeheure auch
Lerne erwarten im irdischen Leben!
Mit gewaltsamer Hand
Löset der Mord auch das heiligste Band.
In sein stygisches Boot
Raffet der Tod
Auch der Jugend blühendes Leben!

Wenn die Wolken gethürmt den Himmel schwärzen,
Wenn dumpftosend der Donner hallt,
Da, da fühlen sich alle Herzen
In des furchtbaren Schicksals Gewalt.
Aber auch aus entwölkter Höhe
Kann der zündende Donner schlagen,
Darum in deinen fröhlichen Tagen
Fürchte des Unglücks tückische Nähe!
Nicht an die Güter hänge dein Herz,
Die das Leben vergänglich zieren!
Wer besitzt, der lerne verlieren,
Wer im Glück ist, der lerne den Schmerz!

          *          *          *

When at the season's fall
The leaves decay,
When to the graves is borne
The hoary head,
Calm nature but obeys
Her ancient law,
And man respects her everlasting march.
But man must also learn,
To expect in earthly life
Unusual strokes of fate.
Murder, with violent hand,
May tear  the holiest bond,
And in his Stygian boat
Death may bear off the blooming form of youth.

When towering clouds o'erswarth the sky,
When loudly bellowing thunders roll,
Each heart in secret owns
The fearful might of fate.
But e'en from cloudless heights
Can kindling lightnings plunge;
E'en in the sunny day
Bale-breathing plagues may lurk.
Fix not on transient good
Thy trusty heart:
Let him who has, prepare to learn to lose;
Him who is happy, learn to bend to grief.

\*         \*         \*         \*         \*
       \*         \*         \*         \*

## Die unüberwindliche Flotte.

Sie kommt — sie kommt, des Mittags stolze Flotte,
    Das Weltmeer wimmert unter ihr,
Mit Kettenklang und einem neuen Gotte
    Und tausend Donnern naht sie dir —
Ein schwimmend Heer furchtbarer Citadellen
    (Der Ocean sah ihresgleichen nie).
Unüberwindlich nennt man sie,
Zieht sie einher auf den erschrocknen Wellen;
    Den stolzen Namen weiht
    Der Schrecken, den sie um sich speit.
Mit majestätisch stillem Schritte
    Trägt seine Last der zitternde Neptun;
Weltuntergang in ihrer Mitte,
    Naht sie heran, und alle Stürme ruhn.

    Dir gegenüber steht sie da,
Glücksel'ge Insel — Herrscherin der Meere!
Dir drohen diese Gallionenheere,
    Großherzige Britannia!
Weh' deinem freigebornen Volke!
Da steht sie, eine wetterschwangre Wolke.
Wer hat das hohe Kleinod dir errungen,
    Das zu der Länder Fürstin dich gemacht?
Hast du nicht selbst, von stolzen Königen gezwungen,
    Der Reichsgesetze weisestes erdacht?
Das große Blatt, das deine Könige zu Bürgern,

## THE ARMADA.

Translated by the late **Mr. Merivale**.

She comes, proud navy of the southern ocean,
  Beneath her foams the world-wide sea:
With clank of chains, and forms of strange devotion,
And thousand thunders, lo! she nears to thee —
A floating host of citadels tremendous —
Ne'er did the floods beneath so huge a monster swell,
  They call her name — "Invincible".
O'er the affrighted waves she moves stupendous;
    Terror, that round her waits,
    The proud name consecrates.
With silent sweep, majestic flowing,
Old Neptune trembling doth his burthen bear:
She, in her womb the World's destruction stowing,
While storms are lull'd around, moves on in full career.
  Thrice-happy Isle — queen of the sea!
There stands she now, thy bulwark's strength opposing—
  Magnanimous Britannia! — thee
They threat — these galleon-squadrons round thee
               closing.
  Woe to thy free-born sons! Descending
Swift on their heads, bursts the big cloud impending.
Who has that noblest jewel for thee wrested,
That o'er the nations sets thy conquering throne?
Say, was it not thyself the prize contested,
    From haughty monarchs greatly won,
  The wisest statute-law beneath the sun? —

Zu Fürsten deine Bürger macht?
Der Segel stolze Obermacht,
Haft du sie nicht von Millionen Würgern
   Erstritten in der Wasserschlacht?
Wem dankst du sie — erröthet, Völker dieser Erde —
Wem sonst, als deinem Geist und deinem Schwerte?
Unglückliche — blick' hin auf diese feuerwerfenden Kolossen,
   Blick' hin und ahnde deines Ruhmes Fall!
      Bang schaut auf dich der Erdenball,
Und aller freien Männer Herzen schlagen,
Und alle guten, schönen Seelen klagen
      Theilnehmend deines Ruhmes Fall.

      Gott, der Allmächt'ge, sah herab,
Sah deines Feindes stolze Löwenflaggen wehen,
   Sah drohend offen dein gewisses Grab —
Soll, sprach er, soll mein Albion vergehen,
   Erlöschen meiner Helden Stamm,
   Der Unterdrückung letzter Felsendamm
Zusammenstürzen, die Thyrannenwehre
Vernichtet sein von dieser Hemisphäre?
Nie, rief er, soll der Freiheit Paradies,
Der Menschenwürde starker Schirm verschwinden!
   Gott, der Allmächt'ge, blies,
Und die Armada flog nach allen Winden.

That great Land-charter, which to Kings thy burghers
          raises,
  To burghers lowers the regal height —
  And didst thou not thy navy's right
From bloody pirate bands, amidst the world's loud
          praises,
  Achieve in glorious Ocean-fight?
Who gave it thee? Blush, nations of the earth! —
Who else, but thy brave spirit, and thy good sword's
          worth?
Unhappy! — these colossal forms fire-sleeting
Survey — and thence presage thy glory's fall!
Gazes in sad suspense the earthly ball —
For thee the hearts of all free men are beating;
Whilst all that's good and beauteous mourns thy fleeting
  Splendours, and partakes thy funeral.
      But the Almighty God look'd down —
Saw where thy foe's proud lion-banners floated —
He saw thy yawning grave wide open frown.
"And shall my Albion (spake he) fall devoted? —
      My line of heroes thus expire?
The last rock-barrier 'gainst oppression dire
At once in ruins fall — the strong defence
That guards this Hemisphere be banish'd hence?
Ne'er be this Freedom's paradise o'erthrown —
This refuge tower of Human Virtue shatter'd!"
  — The Almighty God hath blown —
'And lo! to all the winds the Armada scatter'd!'

## Des Mädchens Klage.

Der Eichwald brauset, die Wolken ziehn,
Das Mägdelein sitzet an Ufers Grün,
Es bricht sich die Welle mit Macht, mit Macht,
Und sie seufzt hinaus in die finstre Nacht,
Das Auge von Weinen getrübet:

„Das Herz ist gestorben, die Welt ist leer,
Und weiter giebt sie dem Wunsche nichts mehr.
Du Heilige, rufe dein Kind zurück,
Ich habe genossen das irdische Glück,
Ich habe gelebt und geliebet!“

## Nadowessiers Todtenlied.

Seht, da sitzt er auf der Matte,
    Aufrecht sitzt er da,
Mit dem Anstand, den er hatte,
    Als er's Licht noch sah.
Doch, wo ist die Kraft der Fäuste,
    Wo des Athems Hauch,
Der noch jüngst zum großen Geiste

## THE MAIDEN'S LAMENT.
Translated by Charles Lamb.

The clouds are black'ning, the storms threat'ning,
  The cavern doth mutter, the greenwood moan;
Billows are breaking, the damsel's heart aching,
  Thus in the dark night she singeth alone,
        Her eye upward roving:

The world is empty, the heart is dead surely,
  In this world plainly all seemeth amiss;
To thy heaven, Holy One, take home thy little one,
  I have partaken of all earth's bliss,
        Both living and loving.

## THE INDIAN DEATH-DIRGE.
Translated by Lord Lytton.

See on his mat, as if of yore
  All life-like, sits he here!
With that same aspect which he wore
  When light to him was dear.
But where the right hand's strength? and where
  The breath that loved to breathe,
To the great Spirit aloft in air,

Blies der Pfeife Rauch?
Wo die Augen, falkenhelle,
    Die des Rennthiers Spur
Zählten auf des Grases Welle,
    Auf dem Thau der Flur?
Diese Schenkel, die behender
    Flohen durch den Schnee,
Als der Hirsch, der Zwanzigender,
    Als des Berges Reh?
Diese Arme, die den Bogen
    Spannten streng und straff?
Seht, das Leben ist entflogen!
    Seht, sie hängen schlaff!

Wohl ihm, er ist hingegangen,
    Wo kein Schnee mehr ist,
Wo mit Mais die Felder prangen,
    Der von selber sprießt;
Wo mit Vögeln alle Sträuche,
    Wo der Wald mit Wild,
Wo mit Fischen alle Teiche
    Lustig sind gefüllt.
Mit den Geistern speist er droben,
    Ließ uns hier allein,
Daß wir seine Thaten loben,
    Und ihn scharren ein.
Bringet her die letzten Gaben,
    Stimmt die Todtenklag'!
Alles sei mit ihm begraben,
    Was ihn freuen mag.
Legt ihm unter's Haupt die Beile,

The peace-pipe's  lusty wreath?
And where the hawk-like eye, alas!
   That wont the deer pursue,
Along the waves of rippling grass,
   Or fields that shone with dew?
Are these the limber, bounding feet,
   That swept the winter-snows?
What stateliest stag so fast and fleet?
   Their speed outstript the roe's!
These arms that then the sturdy bow
   Could supple from its pride,
How stark and helpless hang they now
   Adown the stiffen'd side!
Yet weal to him — at peace he strays
   Where never fall the snows;
Where o'er the meadows springs the maize
   That mortal never sows:
Where birds are blithe on every brake —
   Where forests teem with deer —
Where glide the fish through every lake —
   One chase from year to year!
With spirits now he feasts above;
   All left us — to revere
The deeds we honour with our love,
   The dust we bury here,
Here bring the last gifts! — loud and shrill
   Wail, death-dirge for the brave!
What pleased him most in life may still
   Give pleasure in the grave.
We lay the axe beneath his head

Die er tapfer schwang,
Auch des Bären fette Keule,
Denn der Weg ist lang;
Auch das Messer scharf geschliffen,
Das vom Feindeskopf
Rasch mit drei geschickten Griffen
Schälte Haut und Schopf;
Farben auch, den Leib zu malen,
Steckt ihm in die Hand,
Daß er röthlich möge strahlen
In der Seelen Land.

## Der Handschuh.

Vor seinem Löwengarten,
Das Kampfspiel zu erwarten,
Saß König Franz,
Und um ihn die Großen der Krone,
Und rings auf hohem Balcone
Die Damen in schönem Kranz.

Und wie er winkt mit dem Finger,
Auf thut sich der weite Zwinger,
Und hinein mit bedächtigem Schritt
Ein Löwe tritt,
Und sieht sich stumm

He swung, when life was strong —
The bear on which his banquets fed —
The way from earth is long!
And here, new-sharpen'd, place the knife
That sever'd from the clay,
From which the axe had spoil'd the life,
The conquer'd scalp away!
The paints that deck the Dead, bestow —
Yes, place them hand in hand —
That red the Kingly Shade may glow
Amidst the Spirit-Land!

## THE GLOVE.

Translated by Lord Lytton.

Before his lion-court,
To see the griesly sport,
Sate the king;
Beside him group'd his princely. peers,
And dames aloft, in circling tiers,
Wreath'd round their blooming ring.

King Francis, where he sate,
Raised a finger — yawn'd the gate,
And, slow from his repose
A lion goes!
Dumbly he gazed around

Rings um,
Mit langem Gähnen,
Und schüttelt die Mähnen,
Und streckt die Glieder,
Und legt sich nieder.

   Und der König winkt wieder,
Da öffnet sich behend
Ein zweites Thor,
Daraus rennt
Mit wildem Sprunge
Ein Tiger hervor.
Wie der den Löwen erschaut,
Brüllt er laut,
Schlägt mit dem Schweif
Einen furchtbaren Reif,
Und recket die Zunge,
Und im Kreise scheu
Umgeht er den Leu,
Grimmig schnurrend!
Drauf streckt er sich murrend
Zur Seite nieder.

   Und der König winkt wieder,
Da speit das doppelt geöffnete Haus
Zwei Leoparden auf einmal aus.
Die stürzen mit muthiger Kampfbegier
Auf das Tigerthier;
Das packt sie mit seinen grimmigen Tatzen,
Und der Leu mit Gebrüll

The foe-encircled ground;
And, with a lazy gape,
He stretch'd his lordly shape,
And shook his careless mane,
And — laid him down aga n!
   A finger raised the king —
And nimbly have the guard
A second gate unbarr'd;
Forth, with a rushing spring,
   A Tiger sprung!
   Wildly the wild one yell'd
   When the lion he beheld;
   And, bristling at the look,
   With his tail his sides he strook.
   And roll'd his rabid tongue.
In many a wary ring
He swept round the forest-king,
   With a fell and rattling sound; —
   And laid him on the ground,
   Grommelling.
The king raised his finger; then
Leap'd two leopards from the den
   With a bound;.
And boldly bounded they,
Where the crouching tiger lay,
   Terrible!
And he griped the beasts in his deadly hold';
In the grim embrace they grappled and roll'd;
   Rose the lion with a roar!
And stood the strife before;

Richtet sich auf, da wird's still;
Und herum im Kreis
Von Mordsucht heiß,
Lagern sich die gräulichen Katzen.

Da fällt von des Altans Rand
Ein Handschuh von schöner Hand
Zwischen den Tiger und den Leuen
Mitten hinein.

Und zu Ritter Delorges, spottender Weis',
Wendet sich Fräulein Kunigund:
„Herr Ritter, ist eure Lieb' so heiß,
Wie ihr mir's schwört zu jeder Stund',
Ei, so hebt mir den Handschuh auf!"

Und der Ritter, in schnellem Lauf,
Steigt hinab in den furchtbaren Zwinger
Mit festem Schritte,
Und aus der Ungeheuer Mitte
Nimmt er den Handschuh mit keckem Finger.

Und mit Erstaunen und mit Grauen
Sehen's die Ritter und Edelfrauen,
Und gelassen bringt er den Handschuh zurück.
Da schallt ihm sein Lob aus jedem Munde,
Aber mit zärtlichem Liebesblick —
Er verheißt ihm sein nahes Glück —
Empfängt ihn Fräulein Kunigunde.
Und er wirft ihr den Handschuh ins Gesicht:
„Den Dank, Dame, begehr' ich nicht,"
Und verläßt sie zur selben Stunde.

And the wild-cats, on the spot,
From the blood-thirst, wroth and hot,
    Halted still!
Now from the balcony above
A snowy hand let fall a glove: —
Midway between the beasts of prey,
Lion and tiger; there it lay,
    The winsome lady's glove.
    Fair Cunigonde said, with a lip of scorn,
To the knight Delorges — "If the love you have sworn
Were as gallant and leal as you boast it to be,
I might ask you to bring back that glove to me!"

The knight left the place where the lady sate;
The knight, he has pass'd thro' the fearful gate;
The lion and tiger he stoop'd above,
And his fingers have closed on the lady's glove!

All shuddering and stunn'd, they beheld him there,
The noble knights, and the ladies fair;
But loud was the joy and the praise, the while
He bore back the glove with his tranquil smile!

With a tender look in her softening eyes,.
That promised reward to his warmest sighs,
Fair Cunigonde rose her knight to grace,
— · He toss'd the glove in the lady's face!
"Nay, spare me the guerdon, at least" quoth he;
And he left for ever that fair ladye!

## Das Mädchen aus der Fremde.

In einem Thal bei armen Hirten
Erschien mit jedem jungen Jahr,
Sobald die ersten Lerchen schwirrten,
Ein Mädchen schön und wunderbar.

Sie war nicht in dem Thal geboren,
Man wußte nicht, woher sie kam;
Doch schnell war ihre Spur verloren,
Sobald das Mädchen Abschied nahm.

Beseligend war ihre Nähe,
Und alle Herzen wurden weit;
Doch eine Würde, eine Höhe
Entfernte die Vertraulichkeit.

Sie brachte Blumen mit und Früchte,
Gereift auf einer andern Flur,
In einem andern Sonnenlichte,
In einer glücklichern Natur.

Und theilte jedem eine Gabe,
Dem Früchte, jenem Blumen aus;
Der Jüngling und der Greis am Stabe,
Ein jeder ging beschenkt nach Haus.

Willkommen waren alle Gäste;
Doch nahte sich ein liebend Paar,
Dem reichte sie der Gaben beste,
Der Blumen allerschönste dar.

# THE MAIDEN FROM AFAR.
### Translated by the late Dr. Anster.

With peasants poor, in lowly glade,
  When the first larks were warbling there,
Came, with each coming year, a maid,
  Vision divinely fair!

Of that rough vale she was no child;
  She came, none knew from what far place:
She vanished, and the sylvan wild
  Retained of her no trace.

The bosoms of the savage race
  Expand; they see her and revere;
For round her dwells a lofty grace,
  That tempers love with fear.

And flowers she brought from that far land,
  Of happier suns and fruits mature,
From trees, by softer breezes fanned,
  Beneath a sky more pure.

She gives, and all receive with joy,
  To some rich fruits, gay flowers to some;
The grey-haired on his staff — the boy
  Alike went happy home.

Welcome were all that came, but when
  She saw two lovers fond and true,
Them gave she her best gifts, to them
  Her flowers of richest hue.

### Das Lied von der Glocke.

———

\* \* \* \* \*
\* \* \* \*

In die Erd' ist's aufgenommen,
Glücklich ist die Form gefüllt;
Wird's auch schön zu Tage kommen,
Daß es Fleiß und Kunst vergilt?
Wenn der Guß mißlang?
Wenn die Form zersprang?
Ach, vielleicht, indem wir hoffen,
Hat uns Unheil schon getroffen.

Dem dunkeln Schooß der heil'gen Erde
Vertrauen wir der Hände That,
Vertraut der Sämann seine Saat
Und hofft, daß sie entkeimen werde
Zum Segen, nach des Himmels Rath.
Noch köstlicheren Samen bergen
Wir trauernd in der Erde Schooß
Und hoffen, daß er aus den Särgen
Erblühen soll zu schönerm Loos.

Von dem Dome,
Schwer und bang,
Tönt die Glocke
Grabgesang.

## FROM "THE SONG OF THE BELL."

Translated by Lord Francis Leveson Gower.

\*      \*      \*      \*      \*
\*      \*      \*      \*

Through the moulded chambers gliding,
  Now the metal fills the soil;
May the fashion'd mass, subsiding,
  Prove deserving of our toil.
      Should our hopes be wreck'd!
      Should the stream be check'd!
  While in doubt we stand suspended,
  All our hopes perhaps are ended.

From earth, that now our work receives,
  We trust to reap our future meed,
  And he that sows his humbler seed,
Like us to reap his gain believes,
  If Heaven approve the deed.
But costlier seeds we now confide
  Deep to the all receiving earth,
And trust the harvest, in its pride,
  Will prove its nobler birth.

Hark! with sullen grate and swing,
Deeper, hollower murmurs ring;
Pealing o'er the cypress gloom,
'Tis the music of the tomb;

F. von Schiller.

Ernst begleiten ihre Trauerschläge
Einen Wandrer auf dem letzten Wege.

Ach! die Gattin ist's, die theure,
Ach! es ist die treue Mutter,
Die der schwarze Fürst der Schatten
Wegführt aus dem Arm des Gatten,
Aus der zarten Kinder Schaar,
Die sie blühend ihm gebar,
Die sie an der treuen Brust
Wachsen sah mit Mutterlust —
Ach! des Hauses zarte Bande
Sind gelöst auf immerdar;
Denn sie wohnt im Schattenlande,
Die des Hauses Mutter war;
Denn es fehlt ihr treues Walten,
Ihre Sorge wacht nicht mehr;
An verwaister Stätte schalten
Wird die Fremde, liebeleer.

\* \* \* \* \*
\* \* \* \*

And the solemn sounds attend
One who nears his journey's end.

Ah! 'tis she, the faithful wife,
'Tis the mother reft of life,
Whom the shadowy king, to-day,
In his cold arms bears away,
Tears her from the train of those
Who in her affection rose,
Whom her own parental breast
Pillow'd in their infant rest.
Ah! the tender ties that bound her,
    Now are burst for evermore;
Death has spread his pall around her,
    And the mother's race is o'er.
Her maternal reign has perish'd,
    Death has glazed her watchful eye —
Over those she loved and cherish'd
    Now the stranger's rule is high.

\*       \*       \*       \*       \*
    \*       \*       \*       \*

## Das Mädchen von Orleans.

Das edle Bild der Menschheit zu verhöhnen,
Im tiefsten Staube wälzte dich der Spott;
Krieg führt der Witz auf ewig mit dem Schönen,
Er glaubt nicht an den Engel und den Gott;
Dem Herzen will er seine Schätze rauben,
Den Wahn bekriegt er und verletzt den Glauben.

Doch, wie du selbst, aus kindlichem Geschlechte,
Selbst eine fromme Schäferin, wie du,
Reicht dir die Dichtkunst ihre Götterrechte,
Schwingt sich mit dir den ew'gen Sternen zu.
Mit einer Glorie hat sie dich umgeben;
Dich schuf das Herz, du wirst unsterblich leben.

Es liebt die Welt, das Strahlende zu schwärzen,
Und das Erhabne in den Staub zu ziehn;
Doch fürchte nicht! Es giebt noch schöne Herzen,
Die für das Hohe, Herrliche entglühn.
Den lauten Markt mag Momus unterhalten;
Ein edler Sinn liebt edlere Gestalten.

## JOAN D' ARC.

Translated by the late H. Merivale.

To heap man's godlike form with foul derision
  Hath mockery roll'd thee thro' the deepest dust.
With Beauty Wit for ever makes division,
  Nor God, nor Angel, holds in reverent trust:
The treasures of the heart it seeks to plunder,
  With Fancy wars, and rends pure Faith asunder.

Yet, like to thee, of childlike race descended,
  Herself a lowly shepherdess, like thee —
To thee her crown hath Poesy extended,
  And plac'd thee in the heavenly galaxy;
Thy brows hath circled with a wreath of glory,
  And given thine heart to live in deathless story.

The world delights to blot the daystar's splendour,
  To lay in dust the high, and lofty low;
Yet fear not! still are hearts that homage render
  To deed sublime, and feel heroic glow.
Momus may please the busy mart that courts him —
  The nobler soul in nobler forms disports him.

## Am Antritt des neuen Jahrhunderts.

Edler Freund! wo öffnet sich dem Frieden,
    Wo der Freiheit sich ein Zufluchtsort?
Das Jahrhundert ist im Sturm geschieden,
    Und das neue öffnet sich mit Mord.
Und das Band der Länder ist gehoben,
    Und die alten Formen stürzen ein;
Nicht das Weltmeer hemmt des Krieges Toben,
    Nicht der Nilgott und der alte Rhein.
Zwo gewalt'ge Nationen ringen
    Um der Welt alleinigen Besitz;
Aller Länder Freiheit zu verschlingen,
    Schwingen sie den Dreizack und den Blitz.
Gold muß ihnen jede Landschaft wägen,
    Und, wie Brennus in der rohen Zeit,
Legt der Franke seinen ehrnen Degen
    In die Wage der Gerechtigkeit.
Seine Handelsflotten streckt der Britte
    Gierig wie Polypenarme aus,
Und das Reich der freien Amphitrite
    Will er schließen, wie sein eignes Haus.
Zu des Südpols nie erblickten Sternen
    Dringt sein rastlos ungehemmter Lauf,
Alle Inseln spürt er, alle fernen
    Küsten — nur das Paradies nicht auf.

## THE COMMENCEMENT OF THE NINETEENTH CENTURY.

Translated by the late H. Merivale.

Noble friend! say where may Freedom banished,
   Where may stricken Peace a refuge find,
Now the century in storm has vanished,
   And the next in carnage stalks behind.
All old bonds of nations rent asunder;
   All old forms swift hastening to decline;
Nor can Ocean stay the battle's thunder,
   Nor the Nile-God, nor the ancient Rhine.
Two gigantic rival states, contending
   For the sole dominion of the world,
O'er all laws, all birthrights else, impending
   Have the trident and the lightning hurl'd.
Every land to them must mete its treasure;
   And, like Brennus in those ruder days, ·
Here the Frank his ponderous falchion's measure
   In the wavering scale of justice lays;
There his fleets the Briton, rich and mighty,
   Polypus-like, stretches o'er the deep,
And the kingdom of free Amphitrite
   Closes as his own peculiar keep.
To the South-pole's hidden ·constellations
   In his restless, boundless, course he flies,
To all isles, all coasts of furthest nations:
   All — but only those of Paradise.

Ach, umsonst auf allen Ländercharten
　　Spähst du nach dem seligen Gebiet,
Wo der Freiheit ewig grüner Garten,
　　Wo der Menschheit schöne Jugend blüht.
Endlos liegt die Welt vor deinen Blicken,
　　Und die Schifffahrt selbst ermißt sie kaum;
Doch auf ihrem unermess'nen Rücken
　　Ist für zehen Glückliche nicht Raum.
In des Herzens heilig stille Räume
　　Mußt du fliehen aus des Lebens Drang!
Freiheit ist nur in dem Reich der Träume,
　　Und das Schöne blüht nur im Gesang.

<hr />

## Sängers Abschied.

Die Muse schweigt; mit jungfräulichen Wangen,
Erröthen im verschämten Angesicht,
Tritt sie vor dich, ihr Urtheil zu empfangen;
Sie achtet es, doch fürchtet sie es nicht.
Des Guten Beifall wünscht sie zu erlangen,
Den Wahrheit rührt, den Flimmer nicht besticht;
Nur wem ein Herz, empfänglich für das Schöne,
Im Busen schlägt, ist werth, daß er sie kröne.

Nicht länger wollen diese Lieder leben,
Als bis ihr Klang ein fühlend Herz erfreut,
Mit schönern Phantasien es umgeben,

Vainly o'er the world's wide surface ranging,
   Would'st thou seek that blessed spot to know,
Where bright Freedom's verdure smiles unchanging,
   Where life's earliest flowers undying blow.
Endless lies the globe's huge, floating mansion,
   Scarce can sail its bulk enormous trace;
Yet not all throughout its vast expansion
   May ten happy beings find a place.
To the heart's still. chamber, deep and lonely,
   Must thou flee from life's tumultuous throng:
Freedom in the land of dreams is only,
   And the Beauteous blooms alone in song.

## FAREWELL TO THE READER.

### Translated by Lord Lytton.

The Muse is silent; with a virgin cheek,
   Bow'd with the blush of shame, she ventures near —
She waits the judgment that thy lips may speak,
   And feels the deference, but disowns the fear.
Such praise as Virtue gives, 'tis hers to seek —
   Bright Truth, not tinsel Folly to revere;
He only for her wreath the flowers should cull
Whose heart, with hers, beats for the Beautiful.

Nor longer yet these lays of mine would live,
   Than to one genial heart, not idly stealing.
There some sweet dreams and fancies fair to give,

Zu höheren Gefühlen es geweiht;
Zur fernen Nachwelt wollen sie nicht schweben,
Sie tönten, sie verhallen in der Zeit.
Des Augenblickes Lust hat sie geboren,
Sie fliehen fort im leichten Tanz der Horen.

Der Lenz erwacht, auf den erwärmten Triften
Schießt frohes Leben jugendlich hervor,
Die Staude würzt die Luft mit Nektardüften,
Den Himmel füllt ein muntrer Sängerchor,
Und Jung und Alt ergeht sich in den Lüften,
Und freuet sich und schwelgt mit Aug' und Ohr.
Der Lenz entflieht! Die Blume schießt in Samen,
Und keine bleibt von allen, welche kamen.

Some hallowing whispers of a loftier feeling.
Not for the far posterity they strive,
  Doom'd with the time, its impulse but revealing,
Born to record the Moment's smile or sigh,
And with the light dance of the Hours to fly.

Spring wakes — and life, in all its youngest hues,
  Shoots through the mellowing meads delightedly;
Air the fresh herbage scents with nectar-dews;
  Livelier the choral music fills the sky;
Youth grows more young, and age its youth renews,
  In that field-banquet of the ear and eye;
Spring flies — lo, seeds where once the flowers have
                                blush'd! —
And the last bloom is gone, and the last music hush'd.

# Ludwig Uhland,

born 1787, died 1862.

„Singe, wem Gesang gegeben,
In dem deutschen Dichterwald!"

13*

## Schäfers Sonntagslied.

———

Das ist der Tag des Herrn.
Ich bin allein auf weiter Flur;
Noch Eine Morgenglocke nur,
Nun stille nah und fern.

Anbetend knie' ich hier.
O süßes Graun, geheimes Wehn,
Als knieten viele ungesehn
Und beteten mit mir!

Der Himmel nah und fern
Er ist so klar und feierlich,
So ganz, als wollt' er öffnen sich,
Das ist der Tag des Herrn.

———————

## Würtemberg.

———

Was kann dir aber fehlen,
  Mein theures Vaterland?
Man hört ja weit erzählen
  Von deinem Segensstand.

## THE SHEPHERD'S SABBATH-SONG.

Translated by Lady John Manners.

It is the Sabbath of the Lord;
  In the wide plain I am alone,
  One morning bell chimes forth its tone,
Now perfect quiet reigns abroad.

Adoring, kneel I here:
  O secret awe! I thrill, and feel
  As if a multitude did kneel,
Unseen, and praying near.

The sky, so vast and broad,
  Is glorious on every side,
  Almost as if 'twould open wide —
It is the Sabbath of the Lord.


## WÜRTEMBERG.

Translated by the Rev. W. W. Skeat.

What is it that thou lackest,
  Mine own dear Fatherland?
The rumours of thy riches
  Are heard on every hand.

## Ludwig Uhland.

Man sagt, du seist ein Garten,
.Du seist ein Paradies;
Was kannst du mehr erwarten,
Wenn man dich selig pries?

Ein Wort, das sich vererbte,
Sprach jener Ehrenmann,
Wenn man dich gern verderbte,
Daß man es doch nicht kann.

Und ist denn nicht ergossen
Dein Fruchtfeld wie ein Meer?
Kommt nicht der Most geflossen
Von tausend Hügeln her?

Und wimmeln dir nicht Fische
In jedem Strom und Teich?
Ist nicht dein Waldgebüsche
An Wild nur allzu reich?

Treibt nicht die Wollenherde
Auf deiner weiten Alb,
Und nährest du nicht Pferde
Und Rinder allenthalb?

Hört man nicht fernhin preisen
Des Schwarzwalds stämmig Holz?
Hast du nicht Salz und Eisen
Und selbst ein Körnlein Golds?

They say thou art a garden,
  Where Eden's wealth is found;
What hast thou yet to wish for,
  When all thy praises sound?

We read, an ancient worthy
  Hath written thus of thee:
"Though men should seek thy ruin,
  Thou couldst not ruined be."

Do not thy fruitful cornfields
  Like some vast sea extend?
While from a thousand hill-tops
  Red streams of must descend?

And swarm not shoals of fishes
  In every dyke and stream?
Do not thy forest-copses
  With game exhaustless teem?

Roams not o'er every mountain
  The shepherd's fleecy care?
And hast thou not strong horses
  And heifers everywhere?

Is not Black-Forest timber
  In every land extolled?
Hast thou not salt and iron,
  And even grains of gold?

Und sind nicht deine Frauen
　　So häuslich, fromm und treu?
Erblüht in deinen Gauen
　　Nicht Weinsberg ewig neu?


Und sind nicht deine Männer
　　Arbeitsam, redlich, schlicht?
Der Friedenswerke Kenner
　　Und tapfer, wenn man ficht!


Du Land des Korns und Weines,
　　Du segenreich Geschlecht,
Was fehlt dir? All und eines,
　　Das alte gute Recht.


―――――

# Am achtzehnten October 1816.

―――――

(Dem dritten Jahrestage der Schlacht von Leipzig.)

Wenn heut ein Geist herniederstiege,
　　Zugleich ein Sänger und ein Held,
　Ein solcher, der im heilgen Kriege
Gefallen auf dem Siegesfeld,
Der sänge wohl auf deutscher Erde
Ein scharfes Lied wie Schwertesstreich.
Nicht so, wie ich es künden werde,
　Nein, himmelskräftig, donnergleich:

And are not all thy women
  Domestic, pure, and true?
Blooms not in every province
  A Weinsberg alway new?

And are not all thy yeomen
  Industrious, honest, blunt?
In arts of peace accomplished,
  And brave in battle's brunt?

Thou land of corn and vineyards,
  Whereon such blessings 'light,
What lack'st thou? *One*, yea, *all things* —
  Where's now the Good Old Right?

## ON THE 18th OF OCTOBER, 1816.

Translated by the Rev. W. W. Skeat.

(*The third anniversary of the battle of Leipsic.*)

Should now some spirit here alight,
  At once a bard and warrior brave,
Such as in Freedom's glorious fight
  His life to serve his country gave,
Wide through the German land should ring
  A stirring, sabre-edged song,
Not such as I, alas! shall sing,
  But thunder-loud, divinely strong: —

„Man sprach einmal von Festgeläute,
  Man sprach von einem Feuermeer;
  Doch, was das große Fest bedeute,
  Weiß es denn jetzt noch irgend wer?
  Wohl müssen Geister niedersteigen,
  Von heilgem Eifer aufgeregt,
  Und ihre Wundenmale zeigen,
  Daß ihr darein die Finger legt.

„Ihr Fürsten, seid zuerst befraget!
  Vergaßt ihr jenen Tag der Schlacht,
  An dem ihr auf den Knieen laget
  Und huldigtet der höhern Macht?
  Wenn eure Schmach die Völker löſten,
  Wenn ihre Treue sie erprobt,
  So iſt's an euch, nicht zu vertröſten,
  Zu leiſten jetzt, was ihr gelobt.

„Ihr Völker, die ihr viel gelitten,
  Vergaßt auch ihr den schwülen Tag?
  Das Herrlichste, was ihr erstritten,
  Wie kommt's, daß es nicht frommen mag?
  Zermalmt habt ihr die fremden Horden,
  Doch innen hat sich nichts gehellt,
  Und freier seid ihr nicht geworden,
  Wenn ihr das Recht nicht festgestellt.

„Ihr Weisen, muß man euch berichten,
  Die ihr doch Alles wissen wollt,
  Wie die Einfältigen und Schlichten
  Für klares Recht ihr Blut gezollt?

"Men speak of triumphs loud and gay,
  Of bonfires bright in years gone by,
But who is found to tell to-day
  What such rejoicings signify?
'Twould seem that spirits must descend,
  Raised from the dead by holy zeal,
To shew you where their wounds extend,
  That your own hands their depth may feel.

And first, ye dukes and princes, tell,
  Have ye forgot that battle-hour,
When on your knees ye humbly fell
  And magnified a Higher Power?
If for your fame the people fought,
  If ye have ever found them true,
'Tis yours, to vow no more for naught,
  But, what ye promised them, *to do!*

Ye people who have much endured,
  Have ye that day of toil forgot?
That day, that matchless fame procured —
  How comes it that it profits not?
The *foreign* hordes ye taught to flee,
  There shines *at home* no guiding light;
Ye are not free, ye are not free,
  Ye have not aye held fast the right.

Ye sages, must I hint to you
  In learned works so deeply read,
How well th' unlettered simple crew
  In Freedom's cause their life-blood shed?

# Ludwig Uhland.

Meint ihr, daß in den heißen Gluthen
Die Zeit, ein Phönix, sich erneut,
Nur um die Eier auszubruten,
Die ihr geschäftig unterstreut?

„Ihr Fürstenräth' und Hofmarschälle
  Mit trübem Stern auf kalter Brust,
  Die ihr vom Kampf um Leipzigs Wälle
  Wohl gar bis heute nichts gewußt,
  Vernehmt! an diesem heutgen Tage
  Hielt Gott der Herr ein groß Gericht.
  Ihr aber hört nicht, was ich sage,
  Ihr glaubt an Geisterstimmen nicht.

„Was ich gesollt, hab' ich gesungen
  Und wieder schwing' ich mich empor;
  Was meinem Blick sich aufgedrungen,
  Verkünd' ich dort dem sel'gen Chor:
  „„Nicht rühmen kann ich, nicht verdammen,
  Untröstlich ist's noch allerwärts;
  Doch sah ich manches Auge flammen
  Und klopfen hört' ich manches Herz.""

Think ye that in the flames of strife
    The age was, phoenix-like, re-made,
Only to bring the eggs to life
    That ye so busily have laid?

Ye councillors and courtiers all,
    With tarnished stars on breasts of stone,
Who of the fight by Leipsic's wall
    Till now, perchance, have never known,
Know that on this eventful day
    Did God His righteous dooms reveal;
But ah! — ye hear not what I say,
    Nor faith in Spirit-voices feel.

The lay I yearned to sing is o'er,
    I seek the skies from whence I came;
What here has come mine eyes before,
    I to the heavenly host proclaim.
'I scarce can praise, I will not blame,
    Small hope on every side is found;
Yet saw I many an eye aflame,
    And many a heart I heard to bound!'"

## Auf den Tod eines Landgeistlichen.

Bleibt abgeschiednen Geistern die Gewalt
Zu kehren nach dem irdschen Aufenthalt,
So kehrest du nicht in der Mondennacht,
Wenn nur die Sehnsucht und die Schwermuth wacht;
Nein, wann ein Sonnenmorgen niedersteigt,
Wo sich im weiten Blau kein Wölkchen zeigt,
Wo hoch und golden sich die Ernte hebt,
Mit rothen, blauen Blumen hell durchwebt,
Dann wandelst du, wie einst, durch das Gefild
Und grüßest jeden Schnitter freundlich mild.

## Aus: „Normännischer Brauch."

### Nordische Sage.
#### Thorilda singt:

Wohl sitzt am Meeresstrande
　Ein zartes Jungfräulein;
Sie angelt manche Stunde,
　Kein Fischlein beißt ihr ein.

Sie hat 'nen Ring am Finger
　Mit rothem Edelstein,
Den bind't sie an die Angel,
　Wirft ihn ins Meer hinein.

## ON THE DEATH OF A VILLAGE-PRIEST.
### Translated by the Rev. W. W. Skeat.

If with departed souls the power doth dwell
Again to visit scenes once loved so well,
Thou wilt not come when moonlight floods the skies,
When only sadness wakes, and passion sighs.
No! when the summer's morning softly breaks,
When the blue sky is free from cloudy flakes,
When wave the corn-fields high of golden hue,
Enwoven bright with flowerets red and blue,
Then through the fields thou'lt wander as erewhile,
Greeting each reaper with a friendly smile.

## FROM "A NORMAN CUSTOM; A DRAMATIC POEM."
### - Translated by W. Cullen Bryant.

**A northern legend.**

*(Thorilda's Song.)*

There sits a lovely maiden,
  The ocean murmuring nigh;
She throws the hook, and watches;
  The fishes pass it by.

A ring, with a red jewel,
  Is sparkling on her hand;
Upon the hook she binds it,
  And flings it from the land.

Da hebt sich aus der Tiefe
  'Ne Hand wie Elfenbein,
Die läßt am Finger blinken
  Das goldne Ringelein.

Da hebt sich aus dem Grunde
  Ein Ritter jung und fein,
Er prangt in goldnen Schuppen
  Und spielt im Sonnenschein.

Das Mädchen spricht erschrocken:
  „Nein, edler Ritter, nein.
Laß du mein Ringlein golden!
  Gar nicht begehrt' ich dein."

„Man angelt nicht nach Fischen
  Mit Gold und Edelstein;
Das Ringlein laß' ich nimmer,
  Mein eigen mußt du sein."

## Der blinde König.

Was steht der nordschen Fechter Schaar
  Hoch auf des Meeres Bord?
Was will in seinem grauen Haar
  Der blinde König dort?
Er ruft, in bittrem Harme
  Auf seinen Stab gelehnt,
Daß überm Meeresarme
  Das Eiland wiedertönt.

Uprises from the water
   A hand like ivory fair.
What gleams upon its finger?
   The golden ring is there.

Uprises from the bottom
   A young and handsome knight;
In golden scales he rises,
   That glitter in the light.

The maid is pale with terror —
   "Nay, Knight of Ocean, nay,
It was not thee I wanted;
   Let go the ring, I pray."

"Ah, maiden, not to fishes
   The bait of gold is thrown;
The ring shall never leave me,
   And thou must be my own."

## THE BLIND KING.

Translated by the Rev. W. W. Skeat.

Why hasten to the shining sands
   The warriors of the North?
Why, with white head uncovered, stands
   The blind old monarch forth?
Hark! o'er his staff low-bending,
   Loud shouts the anguished king,
Till, o'er the straits extending,
   The isle's loud echoes ring.

# Ludwig Uhland.

„Gieb, Räuber aus dem Felsverließ,
  Die Tochter mir zurück!
Ihr Harfenspiel, ihr Lied so süß
  War meines Alters Glück.
Vom Tanz auf grünem Strande
  Hast du sie weggeraubt;
Dir ist es ewig Schande,
  Mir beugt's das graue Haupt!"

Da tritt aus seiner Kluft hervor
  Der Räuber groß und wild,
Er schwingt sein Hünenschwert empor
  Und schlägt an seinen Schild:
„Du hast ja viele Wächter,
  Warum denn litten's die?
Dir dient so mancher Fechter,
  Und keiner kämpft um sie?"

Noch stehn die Fechter alle stumm,
  Tritt keiner aus den Reihn,
Der blinde König kehrt sich um:
  „Bin ich denn ganz allein?"
Da faßt des Vaters Rechte
  Sein junger Sohn so warm:
„Vergönn' mir's, daß ich fechte!
  Wohl fühl' ich Kraft im Arm."

„O Sohn, der Feind ist riesenstark,
  Ihm hielt noch keiner Stand,
Und doch, in dir ist edles Mark,
  Ich fühl's am Druck der Hand.

"Give, pirate! from thy rock-retreat,
  Give back my daughter dear!
Her sounding harp, her song so sweet
  My drooping age did cheer.
Here once she danced in gladness
  Thou stol'st my child away;
My head thou'st bowed with sadness,
  Thyself art shamed for aye!"

Then issues from his rocky cave
  The giant fierce and proud;
His giant sword behold him wave,
  His heavy shield clangs loud.
"Sure thou hadst guards unnumbered,
  But none would dare to stir;
With warriors *thou* art cumbered,
  Will no one fight for *her?*"

There steps no champion from the ring,
  But all are mute as stone;
Round turns in grief the aged king:
  "Why mourn I here alone?"
A hand his own is pressing,
  His son claims leave to fight:
"O father, grant thy blessing,
  I feel mine arm hath might."

"O son, a giant's strength hath he,
  Before him none may stand,
And yet — true courage reigns in thee,
  So firm thou hold'st my hand.

14*

Nimm hier die alte Klinge!
    Sie ist der Skalden Preis.
Und fällst du, so verschlinge
    Die Fluth mich armen Greis!"

Und horch! es schäumet, und es rauscht
    Der Nachen übers Meer,
Der blinde König steht und lauscht,
    Und alles schweigt umher,
Bis drüben sich erhoben
    Der Schild' und Schwerter=Schall
Und Kampfgeschrei und Toben
    Und dumpfer Wiederhall.

Da ruft der Greis so freudig bang:
    „Sagt an, was ihr erschaut!
Mein Schwert, ich kenn's am guten Klang,
    Es gab so scharfen Laut."
„Der Räuber ist gefallen,
    Er hat den blut'gen Lohn.
Heil dir, du Held vor Allen,
    Du starker Königssohn!"

Und wieder wird es still umher,
    Der König steht und lauscht:
„Was hör' ich kommen über's Meer?
    Es rudert und es rauscht."
„Sie kommen angefahren,
    Dein Sohn mit Schwert und Schild;
In sonnenhellen Haaren
    Dein Töchterlein Gunild."

Here, take my sword, for slaughter
  Renowned in minstrels' tale,
And let this surging water
  Receive me, should'st thou fail."

And hark! with keen and rushing prow
  The skiff skims o'er the deep;
The blind old king stands listening now,
  A silence spreads like sleep;
Soon o'er the straits the rattle
  Of sword and shield is sent,
And mingled cries of battle
  With echoes strangely blent.

With anxious glee the old man spoke,
  "Oh say, what have ye seen?
My sword — I know its grinding stroke,
  It sounds so sharp and keen!"
"The pirate's blood, out-welling,
  Is now his crime's reward.
Hail thou! in strength excelling,
  Brave prince, heroic lord!"

Once more o'er all doth silence reign,
  The King bends down to hark;
"What hear I come across the main,
  A rush of oars — a bark?"
"They come to thy caresses —
  Thy son with sword and shield,
And, crowned with sunbright tresses,
  Thy darling child Gunild!"

„Willkommen!" ruft vom hohen Stein
 Der blinde Greis herab,
„Nun wird mein Alter wonnig sein
 Und ehrenvoll mein Grab.
Du legst mir, Sohn, zur Seite
 Das Schwert von gutem Klang;
Gunilde, du Befreite,
 Singst mir den Grabgesang."

## Das Schloß am Meere.

Hast du das Schloß gesehen,
 Das hohe Schloß am Meer?
Golden und rosig wehen
 Die Wolken drüber her.

Es möchte sich niederneigen
 In die spiegelklare Fluth,
Es möchte streben und steigen
 In der Abendwolken Gluth.

„Wohl hab' ich es gesehen,
 Das hohe Schloß am Meer,
Und den Mond darüber stehen
 Und Nebel weit umher."

Der Wind und des Meeres Wallen,
 Gaben sie frischen Klang?
Vernahmst du aus hohen Hallen
 Saiten und Festgesang?

Blithe welcome from the cliff on high
  The blind old monarch gave;
"Now bliss shall crown me ere I die,
  And ·honour deck my grave.
My sword, renowned for slaughter,
  O son, beside me lay.
Gunild, my ransomed daughter,
  My dirge shall softly play!"

## THE CASTLE BY THE SEA.

Translated by Henry W. Longfellow.

"Hast thou seen that lordly castle,
  That Castle by the Sea?
Golden and red above it
  The clouds float gorgeously.

"And fain it would stoop downward
  To the mirror'd wave below;
And fain it would soar upward
  In the evening's crimson glow."

"Well have I seen that castle,
  That Castle by the Sea,
And the moon above it standing,
  And the mist rise solemnly."

"The winds and the waves of ocean,
  Had they a merry chime?
Didst thou hear, from those lofty chambers,
  The harp and the minstrel's rhyme?"

„Die Winde, die Wogen alle
    Lagen in tiefer Ruh';
Einem Klagelied aus der Halle
    Hört' ich mit Thränen zu."  .

Sahest du oben gehen
    Den König und sein Gemahl,
Der rothen Mäntel Wehen,
    Der goldnen Kronen Strahl?

Führten sie nicht mit Wonne
    Eine schöne Jungfrau dar,
Herrlich wie eine Sonne,
    Strahlend im goldnen Haar?

„Wohl sah' ich die Eltern beide
    Ohne der Kronen Licht
Im schwarzen Trauerkleide;
    Die Jungfrau sah' ich nicht."

## Das Ständchen.

Was wecken aus dem Schlummer mich
    Für süße Klänge doch?
O Mutter, sieh! wer mag es, sein
    In später Stunde noch?

„Ich höre nichts, ich sehe nichts,    .
    O schlummre fort so lind!
Man bringt dir keine Ständchen jetzt,
    Du armes krankes Kind!"

"The winds and the waves of ocean,
  They rested quietly;
But I heard, on the gale, a sound of wail,
  And tears came to mine eye."

"And sawest thou on the turrets
  The King and his royal bride?
And the wave of their crimson mantles?
  And the golden crown of pride?

"Led they not forth, in rapture,
  A beauteous maiden there?
Resplendent as the morning sun,
  Beaming with golden hair?"

"Well saw I the ancient parents,
  Without the crown of pride;
They were moving slow, in weeds of woe,
  `No maiden was by their side!"

## THE SERENADE.
### Translated by Lady John Manners.

"What from my slumber wakens me —
  What sweet tones echo near?
O mother, see, what can it be
  At this late hour I hear?"

"O slumber, slumber calmly still,
  Nothing I hear or see;
For now they bring no serenade,
  Poor suffering child, to thee."

Es ist nicht irdische Musik,
  Was mich so freudig macht,
Mich rufen Engel mit Gesang;
  O Mutter, gute Nacht!


## Des Sängers Wiederkehr.

Dort liegt der Sänger auf der Bahre,
  Deß bleicher Mund kein Lied beginnt;
Es kränzen Daphnes falbe Haare
  Die Stirne, die nichts mehr ersinnt.

Man legt zu ihm in schmucken Rollen
  Die letzten Lieder, die er sang;
Die Leier, die so hell erschollen,
  Liegt ihm in Armen, sonder Klang.

So schlummert er den tiefen Schlummer;
  Sein Lied umweht noch jedes Ohr,
Doch nährt es stets den herben Kummer,
  Daß man den Herrlichen verlor.

Wohl Monden, Jahre sind verschwunden,
  Cypressen wuchsen um sein Grab,
Die seinen Tod so herb empfunden,
  Sie sanken alle selbst hinab.

"It is no music of the earth
   That fills me with delight,
Angels are calling me with song;
   O, mother mine, good night!"

## THE MINSTREL'S RETURN.

Translated by the Rev. W. W. Skeat.

The minstrel on the bier reclines,
   His pallid lips no songs outpour;
Its faded leaves the laurel twines
   Around the brow that thinks no more.

And there, in scrolls rolled neatly round.
   Are laid the songs that last he sang;
His hands still touch, without a sound,
   The harp that once so blithely rang.

Tho' sleeping thus his last long sleep,
   Still sound his songs in every ear,
And feed men's sorrow keen and deep
   For loss of one sublime and dear. —

Now many a month and year have fled,
   Above him waves the cypress dim;
And they who mourned the minstrel dead,
   Themselves have sunk to sleep, like him.

Doch wie der Frühling wiederkehret
    Mit frischer Kraft und Regsamkeit,
So wandelt jetzt verjüngt, verkläret,
    Der Sänger in der neuen Zeit.


Er ist den Lebenden vereinet,
    Vom Hauch des Grabes keine Spur.
Die Vorwelt, die ihn todt gemeinet,
    Lebt selbst in seinem Liede nur.


## Der Student.


Als ich einst bei Salamanca
    Früh in einem Garten saß,
Und beim Schlag der Nachtigallen
    Emsig im Homerus las,


Wie in glänzenden Gewanden
    Helena zu Zinne trat,
Und so herrlich sich erzeigte
    Dem trojanischen Senat,


Daß vernehmlich der und jener
    Brummt in seinen grauen Bart:
„Solch ein Weib ward nie gesehen,
    Traun, sie ist von Götterart,"

Yet as the spring returns, endued
   With verdure fresh and quickening power;
So lives, with fame and youth renewed,
   The minstrel — to this latest hour.

Unblighted by the grave's cold breath,
   To living men he yet belongs;
The age, that once bemoaned his death,
   Survives but in his deathless songs.

## THE STUDENT.

(From Blackwood's Magazine. May 1846.)

As by Salamanca's city,
   Once I sate within the vale,
And while birds were round me singing,
   Read in Homer's master tale;

How, in gay and rich apparel,
   Helen mounted Ilion's wall:
And so wondrous seemed her beauty
   To the Trojan elders all,

"That each greybeard to his neighbour
   Muttered, gazing on her face:
Trust me, never was there woman
   Seen so fair of earthly race!"

Als ich so mich ganz vertiefet,
 Wußt' ich nicht, wie mir geschah,
In die Blätter fuhr ein Wehen,
 Daß ich staunend um mich sah.


Auf benachbartem Balkone
 Welch ein Wunder schaut' ich da!
Dort in glänzenden Gewanden
 Stand ein Weib wie Helena,


Und ein Graubart ihr zur Seite,
 Der so seltsam freundlich that,
Daß ich schwören mocht', er wäre
 Von der Troer hohem Rath.


Doch ich selbst ward ein Achäer,
 Der ich nun seit jenem Tag
Vor dem festen Gartenhause,
 Einer neuen Troja, lag.


Um es unverblümt zu sagen,
 Manche Sommerwoch' entlang
Kam ich dorthin jeden Abend
 Mit der Laut' und mit Gesang,


Klagt' in mannigfachen Weisen
 Meiner Liebe Qual und Drang,
Bis zuletzt vom hohen Gitter
 Süße Antwort niederklang.

And I deeper read and deeper,
  Marking nought that passed around,
Till the leaves beside me rustled,
  Then I started at the sound.

On a neighbouring balcony,
  What a wonder there I saw!
There in gay and rich apparel
  Stood a maid like Helena.

And an old man was behind her,
  With so strange, yet kind a mien,
That I could have sworn — the elder
  Had of Priam's counsel been.

Then was I a bold Achaian,
  For from that remember'd day,
Ever near the haunted dwelling,
  Like another Troy, I lay.

Simply to relate my story —
  Many a week of summer long,
Came I every evening thither,
  With my lute and with my song,

Told in many a mournful ditty
  All my love and all my pain,
Till from out the lofty lattice
  Came a sweet response again.

Solches Spiel mit Wort und Tönen
   Trieben wir ein halbes Jahr,
Und auch dies war nur vergönnet,
   Weil halb taub der Vormund war.


Hub er gleich sich oft vom Lager
   Schlaflos, eifersüchtig bang,
Blieben doch ihm unsre Stimmen
   Ungehört wie Sphärenklang.


Aber einst (die Nacht war schaurig,
   Sternlos, finster wie das Grab)
Klang auf das gewohnte Zeichen
   Keine Antwort mir herab;


Nur ein alt zahnloses Fräulein
   Ward von meiner Stimme wach,
Nur das alte Fräulein Echo
   Stöhnte meine Klagen nach:


Meine Schöne war verschwunden,
   Leer die Zimmer, leer der Saal,
Leer der blumenreiche Garten,
   Rings verödet Berg und Thal.


Ach, und nie hatt' ich erfahren
   Ihre Heimath, ihren Stand,
Weil sie, beides zu verschweigen,
   Angelobt mit Mund und Hand.

Thus exchanging word and music
    Passed we half the fleeting year; —
Even this was only granted
    While the dotard did not hear.


Often from his couch he wandered,
    Restless, jealous, and awake;
But unheard by him our voices,
    As the songs the planets make. .


But at last — the night was fearful,
    Starless, gloomy as the grave —
To my well-accustomed signal
    No response the loved one gave;


Only one old toothless lady
    Heard me evermore complain —
Only that old maiden, Echo,
    Sent me back my call again.


Vanished was my love — my beauty —
    Empty chamber, room, and hall;
Empty was the blooming garden —
    Cold and desolate were all!


Ah! and ne'er had I discover'd,
    Where her home, or what her name;
For by word and sign she threaten'd
    Never to disclose the same.

Da beschloß ich, sie zu suchen
　　Nah und fern, auf irrer Fahrt;
Den Homerus ließ ich liegen,
　　Nun ich selbst Ulysses ward,

Nahm die Laute zur Gefährtin
　　Und vor jeglichem Altan,
Unter jedem Gitterfenster
　　Frag' ich leis' mit Tönen an,

Sing' in Stadt und Feld das Liedchen,
　　Das im Salamanker Thal
Jeden Abend ich gesungen
　　Meiner Liebsten zum Signal;

Doch die Antwort, die ersehnte,
　　Tönet nimmermehr, und, ach,
Nur das alte Fräulein Echo
　　Reist zur Qual mir ewig nach.

## Harald.

Vor seinem Heergefolge ritt
　　Der kühne Held Harald;
Sie zogen in des Mondes Schein
　　Durch einen wilden Wald.

Then I went about to seek her,
  Far and near, my lot to try;
Homer's tale I left behind me,
  For Ulysses self was I!

But I took my lute to guide me,
  And beside each castle-door,
Under every lattice window,
  Made I music as before;

Sang the strain in field and city
  Which, in Salamanca's grove,
Every evening I had chanted
  As a signal to my love;

But the hoped-for, longed-for answer
  Came not back to bless my ear,
Only that old lady, Echo,
  Travelled with me, ever near.

## HAROLD.

Imitated by the Rev. W. W. Skeat.

Heading his heroes
  Hardy king Harold,
Marching by moonlight
  Moved through the forest.

15 *

Sie tragen manch' erkämpfte Fahn',
   Die hoch im Winde wallt,
   Sie singen manches Siegeslied,
   Das durch die Berge hallt.


Was rauschet, lauschet im Gebüsch?
   Was wiegt sich auf dem Baum?
   Was senket aus den Wolken sich
   Und taucht aus Stromes Schaum?


Was wirft mit Blumen um und um?
   Was singt so wonniglich?
   Was tanzet durch der Krieger Reihn,
   Schwingt auf die Rosse sich?


Was kost so sanft und küßt so süß
   Und hält so lind umfaßt
   Und nimmt das Schwert und zieht vom Roß
   Und läßt nicht Ruh' noch Rast?


Es ist der Elfen leichte Schaar;
   Hier hilft kein Widerstand,
   Schon sind die Krieger all' dahin,
   Sind all' im Feenland.


Nur er, der Beste, blieb zurück,
   Der kühne Held Harald;
   Er ist vom Wirbel bis zur Sohl'
   In harten Stahl geschnallt.

Banners their hands bare
  Taken in battle;
Wildly their war-flags
  Waved in the wind;
Wildly their war-songs
  Rang through the woodland.
What bodeth yon bustle
  That's heard in the brushwood?
What swings there, close-swarming,
  And sways in the tree-tops?
What drops from the dark cloud,
  And darts from the fountain?
What flings to them flowers,
  While fluently singing?
What whirls round each warrior,
  And leaps on each war-horse?
What clasps them so closely,
  And clings to their armour?
Draweth their daggers,
  And drags them from horseback,
Conquers their calmness,
  And keeps them unquiet?

'Tis the army of Elfins!
  No aid can avail them;
The fairies have found them,
  And force them to Fay-land!

But hardy king Harold,
  Brave hero, was left there;

All seine Krieger sind entrückt,
    Da liegen Schwert und Schild;
    Die Rosse, ledig ihrer Herrn,
    Sie gehn im Walde wild.


In großer Trauer ritt von dann
    Der stolze Held Harald;
    Er ritt allein im Mondenschein
    Wohl durch den weiten Wald.


Vom Felsen rauscht es frisch und klar;
    Er springt vom Rosse schnell,
    Er schnallt vom Haupte sich den Helm
    Und trinkt vom kühlen Quell.


Doch, wie er kaum den Durst gestillt,
    Versagt ihm Arm und Bein;
    Er muß sich setzen auf den Fels,
    Er nickt und schlummert ein.


Er schlummert auf demselben Stein
    Schon manche hundert Jahr',
    Das Haupt gesenket auf die Brust,
    Mit grauem Bart und Haar.

From steel-cap to stirrup
  In steel was he cased.
Shields sees he and swords,
  Tho' the swordsmen have vanished;
Bereft of their riders
  Steeds rush thro' the forest.
Heavy at heart
  The hardy king Harold
Mused as he moved
  Through the forest by moonlight.

Down from a dark cleft
  A fountain is dashing,
Lightly down-leaping
  He loosens his helmet;
Lightly down-leaping
  He lappeth the cool wave.
He feels that his forces
  Wax faint as he drinketh;
He slumbers and sleeps
  As he sinks on the boulders.
He rests on his rock-bed,
  Naught recking, for ages;
His head, with his hoar locks,
  Still heaves with his breathing.

When flameth and flasheth
  The flare of the lightning;
When rustle the rain-drops
  And rolleth the thunder,

Wann Blitze zucken, Donner rollt,
   Wann Sturm erbraust im Wald,
Dann greift er träumend nach dem Schwert,
   Der alte Held Harald.

---

## König Karls Meerfahrt.

Der König Karl fuhr über Meer
   Mit seinen zwölf Genossen,
Zum heil'gen Lande steuert' er
   Und ward vom Strom verstoßen.

Da sprach der kühne Held Roland:
   „Ich kann wohl fechten und schirmen,
Doch hält mir diese Kunst nicht Stand
   Vor Wellen und vor Stürmen."

Dann sprach Herr Holger aus Dänemark:
   „Ich kann die Harfe schlagen;
Was hilft mir das, wenn also stark
   Die Wind' und Wellen jagen?"

Herr Oliver war auch nicht froh;
   Er sah auf seine Wehre:
„Es ist mir um mich selbst nicht so,
   Wie um die Alte Clere."

Lo! Harold the hero
   Still handles his sword-hilt,
Seeking to seize it
   Though sunk in his slumber.

## KING CHARLES'S SEA-VOYAGE.

Translated by the Rev. W. W. Skeat.

King Charles with all his doucĕperes
   Across the ocean sailed;
Towards the Holy Land he steers —
   A dreadful storm prevailed.

Out spake Sir Roland, hero brave:
   "I well can fence and fight;
Yet little may such arts avail
   Against the tempest's might."

Next spake Sir Holgar, Denmark's pride:
   "I've skill with harp and song;
What 'vails me this, when thus contends
   The blast with billows strong?"

Sir Oliver felt little cheer;
   He viewed his weapons keen:
"It is not for my life I fear,
   But Alta Clara's sheen!".

Dann sprach der schlimme Ganelon,
(Er sprach es nur verstohlen):
„Wär' ich mit guter Art davon,
Möcht' euch der Teufel holen."

Erzbischof Turpin seufzte sehr:
„Wir sind die Gottesstreiter;
Komm, liebster Heiland, über das Meer
Und führ' uns gnädig weiter."

Graf Richard Ohnefurcht hub an:
„Ihr Geister aus der Hölle,
Ich hab' euch manchen Dienst gethan;
Jetzt helft mir von der Stelle!"

Herr Naimes diesen Ausspruch that:
„Schon Vielen rieth ich heuer,
Doch süßes Wasser und guter Rath
Sind oft zu Schiffe theuer."

Da sprach der graue Herr Riol:
„Ich bin ein alter Degen,
Und möchte meinen Leichnam wohl
Dereinst ins Trockne legen."

Es war Herr Gui, ein Ritter fein,
Der fing wohl an zu singen!
„Ich wollt', ich wär' ein Vögelein;
Wollt' mich zu Liebchen schwingen."

Next spake the treach'rous Ganelon —
  In undertone he spake : —
"Were I but far from hence on land,
  The rest the fiend might take!"

Archbishop Turpin sighed aloud:
  "God's champions stout are we;
Come, Saviour dear, and walk the waves,
  And speed us o'er the sea."

Next Richard — Dauntless named — 'gan say:
  "Ye powers and imps of hell;
Now help me in my need, I pray,
  I oft have served you well."

Sir Naimé next his rede began : —
  "I've counselled much this year;
But water sweet and counsel good
  On shipboard oft are dear."

Then spake Rioul, a veteran brave: —
  "A warrior old am I,
And fain would hope my corse at last
  In good dry ground may lie."

Sir Guy, a young and gallant knight,
  Right gaily 'gan to sing:
"I would I were a lightsome bird,
  I'd to my love take wing!

Da sprach der edle Graf Garein:
  „Gott helf' uns aus der Schwere!
Ich trink viel lieber den rothen Wein,
  Als Wasser in dem Meere."

Herr Lambert sprach, ein Jüngling frisch:
  „Gott woll' uns nicht vergessen!
Äß' lieber selbst 'nen guten Fisch,
  Statt daß mich Fische fressen."

Da sprach Herr Gottfried lobesan:
  „Ich laß' mir's halt gefallen;
Man richtet mir nichts anders an,
  Als meinen Brüdern allen."

Der König Karl am Steuer saß;
  Der hat kein Wort gesprochen,
Er lenkt das Schiff mit festem Maß,
  Bis sich der Sturm gebrochen.

## Des Sängers Fluch.

Es stand in alten Zeiten ein Schloß so hoch und hehr,
Weit glänzt es über die Lande bis an das blaue Meer,
Und rings von duft'gen Gärten ein blüthenreicher Kranz,
D'rin sprangen frische Brunnen in Regenbogenglanz.

Then spake Guarine, that noble knight:
  "May God our succour be!
I'd rather drink the good red wine
  Than water in the sea."

Sir Lambert next, brave youngster, cried:
  "God our protection be!
I'd rather eat the dainty fish
  Than that the fish ate me!"

Last spake Sir Godfrey, far renowned:
  "What matters what befall?
Whatever fate myself o'ertakes
  Shall whelm my brethren all."

King Charles beside the rudder sat,
  No word his lips would vent;
With sure control the ship he steered
  Until the storm was spent.

## THE MINSTREL'S CURSE.

Translated by the Rev. W. W. Skeat.

There stood in former ages a castle high and large,
Above the slope it glistened far down to ocean's marge;
Around it like a garland bloomed gardens of delight,
Where sparkled cooling fountains, with sunbow-glories
                dight.

Dort saß ein stolzer König, an Land und Siegen reich,
Er saß auf seinem Throne so finster und so bleich;
Denn was er sinnt, ist Schrecken, und was er blickt, ist Wuth,
Und was er spricht, ist Geißel, und was er schreibt, ist Blut.


Einst zog nach diesem Schlosse ein edles Sängerpaar,
Der Ein' in goldnen Locken, der Andre grau von Haar;
Der Alte mit der Harfe, der saß auf schmuckem Roß,
Es schritt ihm frisch zur Seite der blühende Genoß.


Der Alte sprach zum Jungen: „Nun sei bereit, mein Sohn!
Denk' unsrer tiefsten Lieder, stimm' an den vollsten Ton!
Nimm alle Kraft zusammen, die Lust und auch den Schmerz!
Es gilt uns heut, zu rühren des Königs steinern Herz."


Schon stehn die beiden Sänger im hohen Säulensaal
Und auf dem Throne sitzen der König und sein Gemahl;
Der König, furchtbar prächtig, wie blut'ger Nordlichtschein,
Die Königin süß und milde, als blickte Vollmond drein.

There sat a haughty monarch, who lands in war had won;
With aspect pale and gloomy he sat upon the throne;
His thoughts are fraught with terrors, his glance of
fury blights;
His words are galling scourges, with victims' blood he
writes.

Once moved towards this castle a noble minstrel-pair,
The one with locks all-golden, snow-white the other's
hair;
With harp in hand, the gray-beard a stately courser rode,
In flower of youth beside him his tall companion strode.

Then spake the gray-haired father — "Be well pre-
pared, my son,
Think o'er our loftiest ballads, breathe out thy fullest
tones;
Thine utmost skill now summon, joy's zest and sorrow's
smart,
'Twere well to move with music the monarch's stony
heart."

Now in the spacious chamber the minstrels twain are
seen,
High on the throne in splendour are seated king and
queen;
The king with terrors gleaming — a ruddy Northern
Light
The queen all grace and sweetness — a full moon
soft and bright.

Da schlug der Greis die Saiten, er schlug sie wundervoll,
Daß reicher, immer reicher der Klang zum Ohre schwoll,
Dann strömte himmlisch helle des Jünglings Stimme vor,
Des Alten Sang dazwischen, wie dumpfer Geisterchor.


Sie singen von Lenz und Liebe, von sel'ger gold'ner Zeit,
Von Freiheit, Männerwürde, von Treu' und Heiligkeit.
Sie singen von allem Süßen, was Menschenbrust durchbebt,
Sie singen von allem Hohen, was Menschenherz erhebt.


Die Höflingschaar im Kreise verlernet jeden Spott,
Des Königs trotz'ge Krieger, sie beugen sich vor Gott;
Die Königin, zerflossen in Wehmuth und in Lust,
Sie wirft den Sängern nieder die Rose von ihrer Brust.


„Ihr habt mein Volk verführet; verlockt ihr nun mein Weib?"
Der König schreit es wüthend, er bebt am ganzen Leib;
Er wirft sein Schwert, das blitzend des Jünglings Brust
                              durchdringt,
Draus statt der gold'nen Lieder ein Blutstrahl hoch aufspringt.


Und wie vom Sturm zerstoben ist all der Hörer Schwarm;
Der Jüngling hat verröchelt in seines Meisters Arm,

The gray-beard swept the harp-strings, they sounded
         wondrous clear:
The notes with growing fulness thrilled through the lis-
         tening ear;
Pure as the tones of angels the young man's accents
         flow,
The old man's gently murmur, like spirit-voices low.

They sing of love and springtime, of happy golden days —
Of manly worth and freedom, of truth and holy ways;
They sing of all things lovely, that human hearts delight,
They sing of all things lofty, that human souls excite.

The courtier-train around them forget their jeerings now,
The king's defiant soldiers in adoration bow;
The queen, to tears now melted, with rapture now
         possessed,
Throws down to them in guerdon a rosebud from her
         breast.

"Have ye misled my people, and now my wife suborn?"
Shouts out the ruthless monarch, and shakes with wrath
         and scorn;
He whirls his sword, like lightning the young man's
         breast it smote,
That, 'stead of golden legends, bright life-blood filled
         his throat.

Dispersed, as by a tempest, was all the listening swarm;
The youth sighs out his spirit upon his master's arm,

Der schlägt um ihn den Mantel und setzt ihn auf das Roß,
Er bind't ihn aufrecht feste, verläßt mit ihm das Schloß.


Doch vor dem hohen Thore, da hält der Sängergreis,
Da faßt er seine Harfe, sie aller Harfen Preis,
An einer Marmorsäule, da hat er sie zerschellt;
Dann ruft er, daß es schaurig durch Schloß und Gärten gellt:


„Weh' euch, ihr stolzen Hallen! nie töne süßer Klang
Durch eure Räume wieder, nie Saite, noch Gesang,
Nein! Seufzer nur und Stöhnen und scheuer Sklavenschritt,
Bis euch zu Schutt und Moder der Rachegeist zertritt!


„Weh' euch, ihr duft'gen Gärten im holden Maienlicht!
Euch zeig' ich dieses Todten entstelltes Angesicht,
Daß ihr darob verdorret, daß jeder Quell versiegt,
Daß ihr in künft'gen Tagen versteint, verödet liegt.


„Weh' dir, verruchter Mörder! Du Fluch des Sängerthums!
Umsonst sei all dein Ringen nach Kränzen blut'gen Ruhms!
Dein Name sei vergessen, in ew'ge Nacht getaucht,
Sei, wie ein letztes Röcheln, in leere Luft verhaucht!"

Who round him wraps his mantle, and sets him on the
steed,
There tightly binds him upright, and from the court
doth speed.

Before the olden gateway — there halts the minstrel old
His golden harp he seizes, above all harps extolled :
Against a marble-pillar he snaps its tuneful strings ;
Through castle and through garden his voice of menace
rings.

"Wo, wo to thee, proud castle! ne'er let sweet tones
resound
Henceforward through thy chambers, nor harp's nor
voice's sound ;
Let sighs and tramp of captives and groans dwell here
for aye,
Till retribution sink thee in ruin and decay.

Wo, wo to you, fair gardens, in summerlight that glow,
To you this pallid visage, deformed by death, I shew,
That every leaf may wither, and every fount run dry,
That ye in future ages a desert heap may lie.

Wo, wo to thee, curst tyrant! that art the minstrel's bane;
Be all thy savage strivings for glory's wreath in vain !
Be soon thy name forgotten, sunk deep in endless
night,
Or, like a last death-murmur, exhaled in vapour
light!"

16*

Der Alte hat's gerufen, der Himmel hat's gehört!
Die Mauern liegen nieder, die Hallen sind zerstört;
Noch eine hohe Säule zeugt von verschwundner Pracht;
Auch diese, schon geborsten, kann stürzen über Nacht.

Und rings, statt duft'ger Gärten, ein ödes Haideland,
Kein Baum verstreuet Schatten, kein Quell durchdringt
                                den Sand.
Des Königs Name meldet kein Lied, kein Heldenbuch!
Versunken und vergessen! Das ist des Sängers Fluch.

The graybeard's curse was uttered; heav'n heard his
bitter cry;
The walls are strewn in fragments, the halls in ruins
lie!
Still stands one lofty column to witness olden might,
E'en this, already shivered, may crumble down to-
night.

Where once were pleasant gardens, is now a wasted
land;
No tree there lends its shadow, nor fount bedews the
sand;
The monarch's name recordeth no song, nor lofty verse:
'Tis wholly sunk — forgotten! Such is the *Minstrel's
Curse!*

# Theodor Körner,

born 1791, died 1813.

„Denn was, berauscht, die Leyer vorgesungen,
Das hat des Schwertes freie Kraft errungen."

## Die Eichen.

---

Abend wird's, des Tages Stimmen schweigen,
　Röther strahlt der Sonne letztes Glühn;
Und hier sitz' ich unter euren Zweigen,
　Und das Herz ist mir so voll, so kühn!
Alter Zeiten alte treue Zeugen,
　Schmückt euch doch des Lebens frisches Grün,
Und der Vorwelt kräftige Gestalten
Sind uns noch in eurer Pracht erhalten.


Viel des Edlen hat die Zeit zertrümmert,
　Viel des Schönen starb den frühen Tod,
Durch die reichen Blätterkränze schimmert
　Seinen Abschied dort das Abendroth.
Doch, um das Verhängniß unbekümmert,
　Hat vergebens euch die Zeit bedroht,
Und es ruft mir aus der Zweige Wehen:
Alles Große muß im Tod bestehen! —

# THE FIVE OAKS OF DALLWITZ.

Translated by the late John Anster.

———

'Tis evening : in the silent west,
  The rosy hues of daylight fade,
And here I lay me down to rest,
  Beneath your venerable shade,
Bright records of a better day,
Aged, — but sacred from decay —
Still in your stately form reside,
Of ages past the grace and pride!


The brave hath died — the good hath sunk,
  The beautiful hath past away —
Yet green each bough and strong each trunk
  That smiles in evening's farewell ray!
Storm blew in vain — the leaves still spread
A bright crown on each aged head —
And yet, methinks the branches sigh :
"Farewell, the Great of Earth must die!"

Und ihr habt bestanden! — Unter allen
   Grünt ihr frisch und kühn mit starkem Muth;
Wohl kein Pilger wird vorüberwallen,
   Der in eurem Schatten nicht geruht.
Und wenn herbstlich eure Blätter fallen,
   Todt auch sind sie euch ein köstlich Gut:
Denn, verwesend, werden eure Kinder
Eurer nächsten Frühlingspracht Begründer.

Schönes Bild von alter deutscher Treue,
   Wie sie bess're Zeiten angeschaut,
Wo in freudig kühner Todesweihe
   Bürger ihre Staaten festgebaut. —
Ach, was hilft's, daß ich den Schmerz erneue?
   Sind doch Alle diesem Schmerz vertraut!
Deutsches Volk, du herrlichstes von allen,
Deine Eichen steh'n, du bist gefallen!

## Aufruf.

Frisch auf, mein Volk! Die Flammenzeichen rauchen,
   Hell aus dem Norden bricht der Freiheit Licht.
Du sollst den Stahl in Feindesherzen tauchen;
Frisch auf, mein Volk! — die Flammenzeichen rauchen,
   Die Saat ist reif; ihr Schnitter, zaudert nicht!

But ye have stood! still bold and high,
  And fresh and strong, and undecayed,
When hath the pilgrim wandered by,
  Nor rested in your quiet shade; —
Ye mourn not when the sore leaves fall
At coming Winter's icy call! —
They perish in their parent earth,
They nurse the tree that gave them birth!

Emblems of ancient Saxon faith!
  Our fathers in our country's cause,
Thus died the patriot's noble death,
  Died for her freedom and her laws!
In vain they died! — the storm hath past
O'er Germany: — her oaks stand fast —
Her people perished in the blast!

## SUMMONS TO ARMS.

Translated by Madame Davies De Pontes.

Brothers, arise! the beacon fires are blazing,
Clear from the north breaks freedom's glorious ray.
Brothers, arise! the beacon fires are blazing.
Arise! her lofty standard proudly raising;
The seed is ripe; ye reapers, why delay?

Das höchste Heil, das letzte, liegt im Schwerte!
  Drück' dir den Speer in's treue Herz hinein:
Der Freiheit eine Gasse! — Wasch' die Erde,
Dein deutsches Land, mit deinem Blute rein!


Es ist kein Krieg, von dem die Kronen wissen;
  Es ist ein Kreuzzug, 's ist ein heil'ger Krieg!
Recht, Sitte, Tugend, Glauben und Gewissen
Hat der Tyrann aus deiner Brust gerissen;
  Errette sie mit deiner Freiheit Sieg!
Das Winseln deiner Greise ruft: „Erwache!"
  Der Hütte Schutt verflucht die Räuberbrut,
Die Schande deiner Töchter schreit um Rache,
  Der Meuchelmord der Söhne schreit nach Blut.


Zerbrich die Pflugschaar, laß den Meißel fallen,
  Die Leyer still, den Webstuhl ruhig stehn!
Verlasse deine Höfe, deine Hallen: —
Vor dessen Antlitz deine Fahnen wallen,
  Er will sein Volk in Waffenrüstung sehn,
Denn einen großen Altar sollst du bauen
  In seiner Freiheit ew'gem Morgenroth;
Mit deinem Schwert sollst du die Steine hauen,
  Der Tempel gründe sich auf Heldentod. —


Was weint ihr, Mädchen, warum klagt ihr, Weiber,
  Für die der Herr die Schwerter nicht gestählt,
Wenn wir entzückt die jugendlichen Leiber
Hinwerfen in die Schaaren eurer Räuber,
  Daß euch des Kampfes kühne Wollust fehlt?

Our soul's salvation on the sword is resting,
Then up, true steel, our refuge sure and good!
With fearless hand our sacred rights contesting,
We'll purify our native soil with blood.

This is no war for empire, wealth, or fame,
'Tis a crusade which every heart should thrill.
Of right and honour, conscience, faith, and name,
Of *these* to rob us is the tyrant's aim,
And victory alone can save us still.
Our aged men would rouse thee, faintly sighing —
Our ruined hamlets curse the robber brood,
Our daughters' shame for full revenge in crying —
Our murdered sons demand the assassin's blood.

Break, break the ploughshare, let the chisel fall,
Hush'd be the lyre, and silent stand the wheel!
Let the hind leave his cot, the prince his hall,
The Lord of battles doth his people call,
And bids them boldly don the avenging steel!
For by his mighty aid our foes subduing,
Fair freedom's sacred temple shall we rear,
The mighty stones with our good falchions hewing,
And raise the structure on our martyrs' bier.

Why should your tears, ye maid and matrons, flow?
E'en tho' denied our proudly cherished right!
And while our souls with patriot ardour glow,
And we rush boldly on the invading foe,
Ye may not share the glories of the fight.

Ihr könnt ja froh zu Gottes Altar treten!
   Für Wunden gab er zarte Sorgsamkeit,
Gab euch in euern herzlichen Gebeten
   Den schönen, reinen Sieg der Frömmigkeit.


So betet, daß die alte Kraft erwache,
   Daß wir dastehn, das alte Volk des Siegs!
Die Märtyrer der heil'gen deutschen Sache,
O ruf't sie an als Genien der Rache,
   Als gute Engel des gerechten Kriegs!
Louise, schwebe segnend um den Gatten:
   Geist unsers Ferdinand, voran dem Zug!
Und all' ihr deutschen, freien Heldenschatten,
   Mit uns, mit uns und unsrer Fahnen Flug!


Der Himmel hilft, die Hölle muß uns weichen!
   Drauf, wackres Volk! Drauf! ruft die Freiheit, drauf!
Hoch schlägt dein Herz, hoch wachsen deine Eichen,
Was kümmern dich die Hügel deiner Leichen?
   Hoch pflanze da die Freiheitsfahne auf! —
Doch stehst du dann, mein Volk, bekränzt vom Glücke,
   In deiner Vorzeit heilgem Siegerglanz:
Vergiß die treuen Todten nicht und schmücke
   Auch unsre Urne mit dem Eichenkranz!

Before his shrine, in meek submission bending,
While unto Heaven your supplications soar,
With gentle hand the sick and wounded tending,
*This* is your province, can you wish for more?

Pray, then, our ancient courage may awake,
To guard at once our country and our laws,
What, tho' we perish for their holy sake?
Spirit of vengeance, oh! our fetters break,
And stand forth guardian of our sacred cause.
Louisa, on thy lord thy blessing cast!
Spirit of Ferdinand, our cause befriend!
Arise, ye shadows of the mighty past,
And on our *banner* bid success attend.

With heaven to aid us hell must fly before us,
Up, gallant brothers, freedom calls the brave!
High beat our hearts, our oaks are waving o'er us,
Bid freedom flourish, though upon our grave.
And when the hour of thy regeneration,
Oh, Fatherland, once more beholds thee bloom,
Then think of those who died for thy salvation,
And lay the wreath upon thy martyrs' tomb!

## An die Königin Louise.

———

Du Heilige! hör' Deiner Kinder Flehen,
    Es dringe mächtig auf zu Deinem Licht.
Kannst wieder freundlich auf uns niedersehen,
    Verklärter Engel! Länger weine nicht!

Denn Preußens Adler soll zum Kampfe wehen,
    Es drängt Dein Volk sich jubelnd zu der Pflicht,
Und jeder wählt, und Keinen siehst Du beben,
    Den freien Tod für ein bezwung'nes Leben.

Wir lagen noch in feige Schmach gebettet;
    Da rief nach Dir dein besseres Geschick.
An die unwürd'ge Zeit warst Du gekettet,
    Zur Rache mahnte Dein gebrochner Blick.

So hast Du uns den deutschen Muth gerettet. —
    Jetzt sieh' auf uns, sieh' auf dein Volk zurück,
Wie alle Herzen treu und muthig brennen,
    Nun woll' uns auch die Deinen wieder nennen.

Und wie einst, alle Kräfte zu beleben,
    Ein Heilgenbild, für den gerechten Krieg
Dem Heeresbanner schützend zugegeben
    Als Oriflamme in die Lüfte stieg:

# TO THE MEMORY OF QUEEN LOUISE.

Translated by Madame Daviès de Pontès.

Oh! to thy children's prayers incline thine ear,
  Thou sainted spirit! from yon realms of light
Look down upon us! dry each lingering tear,
  Look down rejoicing in the glorious sight!

For Prussia's eagle shall in battle wave,
  And with exulting spirit to the strife
Thy people rush; all perils will they brave;
  Better to perish free than live a slave.

Long we lay dead to honour and to fame,
  Then thy good angel to a better shore
Bore thy pure spirit, and each spark of shame
  Roused by thy parting glance awoke once more.

Thus hast thou saved thy country; thou alone:
  Behold us now more worthy of thy name.
And every German heart is fearless grown:
  Now wilt thou deign to call us all thine own.

And as to nerve each breast, of old, full oft
  Before the host, some pictured saint so fair
Was borne, as their banner high aloft
  Floated, a conquering oriflamme in air,

So soll Dein Bild auf unsern Fahnen schweben,
  Und soll uns leuchten durch die Nacht zum Sieg.
Louise sei der Schutzgeist deutscher Sache,
Louise sei das Losungswort zur Rache!

Und wenn wir dann dem Meuter=Heer begegnen,
  Wir stürzen uns voll Zuversicht hinein!
Und mögen tausend Flammenblitze regnen,
  Und mögen tausend Tode uns umdräu'n:

Ein Blick auf Deine Fahne wird uns segnen;
  Wir stehen fest, wir müssen Sieger sein! —
Wer dann auch fällt für Tugend, Recht und Wahrheit,
  Du trägst ihn sanft zu Deiner ew'gen Klarheit.

## Bundeslied vor der Schlacht.

### Am Morgen des Gesechts bei Dannenberg.

Ahnungsgrauend, todesmuthig
  Bricht der große Morgen an,
Und die Sonne kalt und blutig
  Leuchtet unsrer blut'gen Bahn.
In der nächsten Stunde Schooße
  Liegt das Schicksal einer Welt,
Und es zittern schon die Loose,
  Und der eh'rne Würfel fällt.
Brüder! euch mahne die dämmernde Stunde,
Mahne euch ernst zu dem heiligsten Bunde:
  Treu, so zum Tod', als zum Leben gesellt!

E'en thus shall guide us still thine image bright;
    And light us 'mid the gloom of dark despair.
Louise! the guardian angel of our right!
    Louise! the watchword of the avenging fight!

And when we meet the foe, all risk disdaining;
    Onward we'll rush as strangers to dismay,
And though a thousand fires were on us raining,
    And though a thousand deaths before us lay,

That banner with sweet hopes of vict'ry rife
    Shall marshal us upon our glorious way;
And those who perish in the avenging strife,
    Thou'lt bear to realms of endless light and life!

## WAR SONG.

Written before the battle of Dannenberg.
Translated by the late Earl of Ellesmere.

Fraught with battles to be won,
    Dawning breaks the eventful day;
And the red and misty sun
    Lights us on our gory way.
In a few approaching hours
    Europe's doubtful fortunes lie,
While upon her banded powers
    Thundering falls the iron die.
Brothers and comrades, on you it is falling —
On you the proud voice of your country is calling,
    While the lot of the balance is trembling on high!

17 *

Hinter uns, im Grau'n der Nächte,
 Liegt die Schande, liegt die Schmach,
Liegt der Frevel fremder Knechte,
 Der die deutsche Eiche brach.
Unsre Sprache ward geschändet,
 Unsre Tempel stürzten ein;
Unsre Ehre ist verpfändet:
 Deutsche Brüder, lös't sie ein.
Brüder, die Rache flammt! Reicht euch die Hände,
Daß sich der Fluch der Himmlischen wende!
 Lös't das verlorne Palladium ein!


Vor uns liegt ein glücklich Hoffen,
 Liegt der Zukunft goldne Zeit,
Steht ein ganzer Himmel offen,
 Blüht der Freiheit Seligkeit.
Deutsche Kunst und deutsche Lieder,
 Frauenhuld und Liebesglück,
Alles Große kommt uns wieder,
 Alles Schöne kehrt zurück.
Aber noch gilt es ein gräßliches Wagen,
Leben und Blut in die Schanze zu schlagen:
 Nur in dem Opfertod reift uns das Glück.


Nun, mit Gott! wir wollen's wagen,
 Fest vereint dem Schicksal stehn,
Unser Herz zum Altar tragen
 Und dem Tod' entgegen gehn.
Vaterland! dir woll'n wir sterben,
 Wie dein großes Wort gebeut!

In the night we leave behind us,
    Lies the shame and lies the yoke —
Chains of him who once could bind us,
    Him who spoil'd the German oak.
E'en our native speech was slighted;
    Ruin smote our holy fanes:
Now revenge's oath is plighted,
    The redeeming task remains.
For honour and vengeance then join we our hands,
That the curses of Heaven may pass from our lands,
    And the foe be expell'd from our native domains.

Hope and better days before us,
    To a happier lot invite;
All the heavens expanding o'er us,
    Freedom greets our longing sight.
German arms again caress us,
    German muses wake the strain;
All that's great again shall bless us,
    All that's fair shall bloom again.
But a game must be play'd of destruction and strife:
There is freedom to win, but the venture is life!
    And thousands must die ere that freedom shall reign.

Now, by heaven! we will not falter,
    But united firm to stand,
Lay our hearts upon the altar
    Offer'd to our native land.
Yes, my country, take the spirit
    Which I proudly give to thee;

Unsre Lieben mögen's erben,
        Was wir mit dem Blut befreit.
Wachse, du Freiheit der deutschen Eichen,
Wachse empor über unsre Leichen! —
        Vaterland, höre den heiligen Eid! —


Und nun wendet eure Blicke
        Noch einmal der Liebe nach;
Scheidet von dem Blüthenglücke,
        Das der gift'ge Süden brach.
        Wird euch auch das Auge trüber —
        Keine Thräne bringt euch Spott.
        Werft den letzten Kuß hinüber,
        Dann befehlt sie eurem Gott!
Alle die Lippen, die für uns beten,
Alle die Herzen, die wir zertreten,
        Tröste und schütze sie, ewiger Gott!


Und nun frisch zur Schlacht gewendet,
        Aug' und Herz zum Licht hinauf!
Alles Ird'sche ist vollendet,
        Und das Himmlische geht auf.
        Faßt euch an, ihr deutschen Brüder!
        Jede Nerve sei ein Held!
        Treue Herzen sehn sich wieder;
        Lebewohl für diese Welt!
Hört ihr's? schon jauchzt es uns donnernd entgegen!
Brüder! hinein in den blitzenden Regen!
        Wiedersehn in der besseren Welt!

Let my progeny inherit,
    What his father's blood could free.
And the oaks of my country their branches shall wave,
Whose roots are entwined in the patriot's grave —
    The grave which the foeman has destined for me.


Bend your looks of parting sorrow
    On the friends you leave to-day;
On the widows of to-morrow
    Look your last, and turn away.
Should the silent tear be starting,
    Those are drops to be forgiven;
Give your last fond kiss of parting,
    Give them to the care of heaven.
Thou God of the orphan, oh! grant thy protection,
To the lips which are pouring the prayer of affection,
    And comfort the bosoms which sorrow has riven!


Freshly, as the foe advances,
    Now we turn us to the fray;
Heavenly radiance o'er us glances,
    Earth and darkness pass away.
Yes! the oath we now have plighted
    Joins us in a world of bliss —
There the free shall be united —
    Brothers! fare ye well for this!
Hark! 'tis the thunder, where banners are streaming,
Where bullets are whistling, and sabres are gleaming!
    Forward! — to meet in the mansions of bliss!

## Gebet während der Schlacht.

Vater, ich rufe Dich!
Brüllend umwölkt mich der Dampf der Geschütze,
Sprühend umzucken mich rasselnde Blitze.
Lenker der Schlachten, ich rufe Dich;
Vater Du, führe mich!

Vater Du, führe mich!
Führ' mich zum Siege, führ' mich zum Tode!
Herr, ich erkenne Deine Gebote!
Herr, wie Du willst, so führe mich.
Gott, ich erkenne Dich!

Gott, ich erkenne Dich!
So im herbstlichen Rauschen der Blätter,
Als im Schlachtendonnerwetter,
Urquell der Gnade, erkenn' ich Dich.
Vater Du, segne mich!

Vater Du, segne mich!
In Deine Hand befehl' ich mein Leben,
Du kannst es nehmen, Du hast es gegeben;
Zum Leben, zum Sterben segne mich!
Vater, ich preise Dich!

Vater, ich preise Dich!
's ist ja kein Kampf für die Güter der Erde;
Das Heiligste schützen wir mit dem Schwerte;
Drum, fallend und siegend, preis ich Dich,
Gott, Dir ergeb' ich mich!

## PRAYER DURING THE BATTLE.

Translated by the late G. F. Richardson.

Father, I call on thee!
While the smoke of the firing envelops my sight,
And the lightnings of slaughter are wing'd on their flight,
Leader of battles, I call on thee!
Father, oh lead me!

Father, oh lead me!
Lead me to vict'ry, or lead me to death!
Lord, I yield to thee my breath!
Lord, as thou wilt, so lead me!
God, I acknowledge thee!

God, I acknowledge thee!
In the grove where the leaves of the autumn are fading,
As here 'mid the storms of the loud cannonading,
Fountain of love, I acknowledge thee!
Father, oh bless me!

Father, oh bless me!
I commit my life to the will of Heaven,
For thou canst take it as thou hast given.
In life and death, oh bless me!
Father, I praise thee!

Father, I praise thee!
This is no strife for the goods of this world;
For Freedom alone is our banner unfurl'd.
Thus, falling or conqu'ring, I praise thee!
God, I yield myself to thee!

Gott, Dir ergeb' ich mich!
Wenn mich die Donner des Todes begrüßen,
Wenn meine Adern geöffnet fließen:
    Dir, mein Gott, Dir ergeb' ich mich!
    Vater, ich rufe Dich!

## Zur Nacht.

Gute Nacht!
Allen Müden sei's gebracht.
Neigt der Tag sich schnell zum Ende,
Ruhen alle fleiß'gen Hände,
Bis der Morgen neu erwacht.
    Gute Nacht!

Geht zur Ruh',
Schließt die müden Augen zu!
Stiller wird es auf den Straßen
Und den Wächter hört man blasen,
Und die Nacht ruft Allen zu:
    Geht zur Ruh'!

Schlummert süß!
Träumt euch euer Paradies.
Wem die Liebe raubt den Frieden,
Sei ein schöner Traum beschieden,
Als ob Liebchen ihn begrüß'.
    Schlummert süß!

God, I yield myself to thee!
When the thunders of battle are loud in their strife,
And my opening veins pour forth my life,
God, I yield myself to thee!
Father, I call on thee!

## GOOD NIGHT!

Translated by "M. T." for the Feast of the Poets, Tait's
Magazine. Sept. 1846.

Good night.
Let troubles pass away with light,
Day declineth, fades away:
Till breaks forth the new morn's ray
Busy hands shall cease their toil:
Good night.

Go to rest;
Let the eyes in sleep be press'd.
All is silent in the streets,
The watchman alone the hour repeats,
And stilly night doth beckon all,
Go to rest.

Slumber light;
Of Paradise your dreams be bright;
Let glorious visions gild thy dreams;
Fancy thou feelest love's warm beams,
'Tho' waking love is cold to thee,
Slumber light.

Theodor Körner.

Gute Nacht!
Schlummert, bis der Tag erwacht,
Schlummert, bis der neue Morgen
Kommt mit seinen neuen Sorgen,
Ohne Furcht, der Vater wacht!
Gute Nacht.

Good night;
Slumber till the day is bright;
Slumber till the morning fair
Brings its trouble and its care;
Fearless slumber — God is watching.
Good night.

# Heinrich Heine,

born 1799, died 1856.

„Und als ich euch meine Schmerzen geklagt,
Da habt ihr gegähnt und Nichts gesagt;
Doch als ich sie zierlich in Verse gebracht,
Da habt ihr mir große Elogen gemacht.“

# Zwei Brüder.

---

Oben auf der Bergesspitze
Liegt das Schloß in Nacht gehüllt;
Doch im Thale leuchten Blitze,
Helle Schwerter klirren wild.

Das sind Brüder, die dort fechten
Grimmen Zweikampf, wuthentbrannt.
Sprich, warum die Brüder rechten
Mit dem Schwerte in der Hand?

Gräfin Laura's Augenfunken
Zündete den Brüderstreit;
Beide glühen liebestrunken
Für die adlig holde Maid.

Welchem aber von den Beiden
Wendet sie ihr Herze zu?
Kein Ergrübeln kann's entscheiden, —
Schwert heraus, entscheide du!

# THE TWO BROTHERS.

Translated by Edgar Alfred Bowring.

On the mountain summit darkling
  Lies the castle, veil'd in night;
Lights are in the valley sparkling,
  Clashing swords are gleaming bright.

Brothers 'tis who in fierce duel
  Fight with wrath to fury fann'd;
Tell me, why these brothers cruel
  Strive thus madly, sword in hand?

By the eyes of Countess Laura
  Were they thus in strife array'd;
Both with glowing love adore her. —
  Her, the noble, beauteous maid.

Unto which now of the brothers
  Is her heart the most inclined?
She her secret feelings smothers, —
  Out, then, sword, the truth to find!

Und sie fechten kühn verwegen,
Hieb' auf Hiebe niederkracht's.
Hütet euch, ihr wilden Degen,
Böses Blendwerk schleicht des Nachts.

Wehe! Wehe! blut'ge Brüder!
Wehe! Wehe! blut'ges Thal!
Beide Kämpfer stürzen nieder,
Einer in des andern Stahl. —

Viel' Jahrhunderte verwehen,
Viel' Geschlechter deckt das Grab;
Traurig von des Berges Höhen
Schaut das öde Schloß herab.

Aber Nachts, im Thalesgrunde,
Wandelt's heimlich, wunderbar;
Wenn da kommt die zwölfte Stunde,
Kämpfet dort das Brüderpaar.

## Die Grenadiere.

Nach Frankreich zogen zwei Grenadier',
Die waren in Rußland gefangen.
Und als sie kamen in's deutsche Quartier,
Sie ließen die Köpfe hangen,

And they fight with rage despairing,
  Blows exchange with savage might;
Take good heed, ye gallants daring, —
  Mischief walks abroad by night.

Woe, O woe, ye brothers cruel!
  Woe, O woe, thou vale abhorr'd!
Both fall victims in the duel,
  Falling on each other's sword.

Races are to dust converted,
  Many centuries have flown,
And the castle, now deserted,
  Sadly from the mount looks down.

But at night-time in the valley
  Wondrous forms appear again;
At the stroke of twelve, forth sally
  To the fight the brothers twain.

## THE GRENADIERS.

Translated by Edgar Alfred Bowring.

Two grenadiers travell'd tow'rds France one day,
  On leaving their prison in Russia,
And sadly they hung their heads in dismay
  When they reach'd the frontiers of Prussia.

Da hörten sie Beide die traurige Mähr:
Daß Frankreich verloren gegangen,
Besiegt und zerschlagen das tapfere Heer, —
Und der Kaiser, der Kaiser gefangen.


Da weinten zusammen die Grenadier'
Wohl ob der kläglichen Kunde:
Der Eine sprach: „Wie weh wird mir,
Wie brennt meine alte Wunde."


Der Andre sprach: „Das Lied ist aus,
Auch ich möcht' mit dir sterben,
Doch hab' ich Weib und Kind zu Haus,
Die ohne mich verderben."


„Was schert mich Weib, was schert mich Kind,
Ich trage weit beß'res Verlangen;
Laß sie betteln gehn, wenn sie hungrig sind, —
Mein Kaiser, mein Kaiser gefangen!


„Gewähr' mir, Bruder, eine Bitt':
Wenn ich jetzt sterben werde,
So nimm meine Leiche nach Frankreich mit,
Begrab' mich in Frankreichs Erde.


„Das Ehrenkreuz am rothen Band
Sollst du auf's Herz mir legen;
Die Flinte gieb mir in die Hand,
Und gürt' mir um den Degen.

For there they first heard the story of woe,
   That France had utterly perish'd,
The grand army had met with an overthrow,
   They had captured their Emperor cherish'd.

Then both of the grenadiers wept full sore
   At hearing the terrible story;
And one of them said: "Alas! once more
   "My wounds are bleeding and gory."

The other one said: "The game's at an end,
   "With thee I would die right gladly,
"But I've wife and child, whom at home I should tend,
   "For without me they'll fare but badly."

"What matters my child, what matters my wife?
   "A heavier care has arisen;
"Let them beg, if they're hungry, all their life, —
   "My Emperor sighs in a prison!"

"Dear brother, pray grant me this one last prayer:
   "If my hours I now must number,
"O take my corpse to my country fair,
   "That there it may peacefully slumber."

"The legion of honour, with ribbon red,
   "Upon my bosom place thou,
"And put in my hand my musket dread,
   "And my sword around me brace thou."

„So will ich liegen und horchen still
　　Wie eine Schildwach', im Grabe,
Bis einst ich höre Kanonengebrüll
　　Und wiehernder Rosse Getrabe.

„Dann reitet mein Kaiser wohl über mein Grab,
　　Viel Schwerter klirren und blitzen;
Dann steig ich gewaffnet hervor aus dem Grab, —
　　Den Kaiser, den Kaiser zu schützen!"

## An meine Mutter.

Ich bin's gewohnt, den Kopf recht hoch zu tragen,
　　Mein Sinn ist auch ein bischen starr und zähe;
　　Wenn selbst der König mir in's Antlitz sähe,
Ich würde nicht die Augen niederschlagen.
Doch, liebe Mutter, offen will ich's sagen:
　　Wie mächtig auch mein stolzer Muth sich blähe,
　　In deiner selig süßen, trauten Nähe
Ergreift mich oft ein demuthvolles Zagen.
Ist es dein Geist, der heimlich mich bezwinget,
　　Dein hoher Geist, der alles kühn durchdringet,
　　Und blitzend sich zum Himmelslichte schwinget?
Quält mich Erinnerung, daß ich verübet
　　So manche That, die dir das Herz betrübet,
　　Das schöne Herz, das mich so sehr geliebet!

"And so in my grave will I silently lie
  "And watch like a guard o'er the forces,
"Until the roaring of cannon hear I,
  "And the trampling of neighing horses."

"My Emperor then will ride over my grave,
  "While the swords glitter brightly and rattle ;
"Then arm'd to the teeth will I rise from the grave,
  "For my Emperor hasting to battle !"

## TO MY MOTHER.

Translated by Edgar Alfred Bowring.

I have been wont to bear my head right high,
  My temper too is somewhat stern and rough ;
  Even before a monarch's cold rebuff
  I would not timidly avert mine eye.
Yet, mother dear, I'll tell it openly :
  Much as my haughty pride may swell and puff,
  I feel submissive and subdued enough,
  When thy much-cherished, darling form is nigh.
Is it thy spirit that subdues me then,
  Thy spirit, grasping all things in its ken,
  And soaring to the light of heaven again?
By the sad recollection I'm oppress'd
  That I have done so much that griev'd thy breast,
  Which loved me, more than all things else, the best.

# Heinrich Heine.

## „Ein Fichtenbaum steht einsam.“

Ein Fichtenbaum steht einsam
Im Norden auf kahler Höh'.
Ihn schläfert; mit weißer Decke
Umhüllen ihn Eis und Schnee.

Er träumt von einer Palme,
Die fern im Morgenland
Einsam und schweigend trauert
Auf brennender Felsenwand.

## „Ich hab' im Traum geweinet.“

Ich hab' im Traum geweinet,
Mir träumte, du lägest im Grab.
Ich wachte auf, und die Thräne
Floß noch von der Wange herab.

Ich hab' im Traum geweinet,
Mir träumt', du verließest mich.
Ich wachte auf, und ich weinte
Noch lange bitterlich.

Ich hab' im Traum geweinet,
Mir träumte, du bliebest mir gut.
Ich wachte auf, und noch immer
Strömt meine Thränenfluth.

## "A PINE-TREE STANDS IN THE NORLAND!"
### Translated by Dr. James Steele.

A pine-tree stands in the Norland
　Alone on a desolate hill;
He slumbers beneath his mantle
　Of snow fleece, icy-chill.

He dreams of his cousin the palm-tree,
　Who, far amid tropical sand,
In silence and solitude shrivels
　'Neath the vertical noonday brand.

## "I WEPT AS I SLUMBERED AT NIGHT."
### Translated by "J. H."

I wept as I slumbered at night,
For I saw thy grave in my dream;
I awoke — it had taken to flight,
But tears down my wasted checks stream.

I wept in a dream of the night!
I dreamt thou hadst left me and gone;
I awoke — the morning was bright,
But bitterly wept I alone!

I wept in a dream of the night!
Thou wert true, I thought in my sleep.
I awoke, but what brought the light
But to weep, aye, ever to weep?

## Lorelei.

Ich weiß nicht, was soll es bedeuten,
Daß ich so traurig bin;
Ein Mährchen aus alten Zeiten,
Das kommt mir nicht aus dem Sinn.

Die Luft ist kühl und es dunkelt,
Und ruhig fließt der Rhein;
Der Gipfel des Berges funkelt
Im Abendsonnenschein.

Die schönste Jungfrau sitzet
Dort oben wunderbar,
Ihr gold'nes Geschmeide blitzet,
Sie kämmt ihr goldenes Haar.

Sie kämmt es mit goldenem Kamme,
Und singt ein Lied dabei;
Das hat eine wunderfame,
Gewaltige Melodei.

Den Schiffer im kleinen Schiffe
Ergreift es mit wildem Weh;
Er schaut nicht die Felsenriffe,
Er schaut nur hinauf in die Höh'.

Ich glaube, die Wellen verschlingen
Am Ende Schiffer und Kahn;
Und das hat mit ihrem Singen
Die Lorelei gethan.

# LORELEY.

### Translated by Dr. James Steele.

I know not how it befalleth
  That all so sad am I:
And strangely my mind recalleth
  A tale of years gone by.

The dewy eve advances,
  And tranquil flows the Rhine;
The rock's bold forehead glances
  In daylight's parting shine.

There sits the wondrous sitter,
  The beautiful girl, up there;
Her golden jewels glitter.
  She combs her golden hair.

A madrigal she singeth.
  As her golden comb she plies;
The music wildly ringeth
  Adown the river, and dies.

In his little boat the rower
  Is caught with a pang of love;
He sees not the rock below her,
  He sees but the girl above.

And there where the wavelets are dancing
  He sank, with the setting sun;
And this with her music entrancing
  The Loreley hath done.

## „Mein Herz, mein Herz ist traurig."

Mein Herz, mein Herz ist traurig,
Doch lustig leuchtet der Mai;
Ich stehe, gelehnt an der Linde,
Hoch auf der alten Bastei.

Da drunten fließt der blaue
Stadtgraben in stiller Ruh';
Ein Knabe fährt im Kahne,
Und angelt und pfeift dazu.

Jenseits erheben sich freundlich,
In winziger, bunter Gestalt,
Lusthäuser und Gärten und Menschen,
Und Ochsen und Wiesen und Wald.

Die Mägde bleichen Wäsche,
Und springen im Gras herum;
Das Mühlrad stäubt Diamanten,
Ich höre sein fernes Gesumm'.

Am alten grauen Thurme
Ein Schilderhäuschen steht;
Ein rothgeröckter Bursche
Dort auf und nieder geht.

Er spielt mit seiner Flinte,
Die funkelt im Sonnenroth,
Er präsentiert und schultert —
Ich wollt', er schösse mich todt.

## 'MY HEART, MY HEART IS SINKING."

Translated by Dr. James Steele.

My heart, my heart is sinking,
  As the May awakes in glee;
I stand high up on the rampart,
  With my back to a linden-tree.

Below me crawls in silence
  The city's broad blue moat;
Where a boy is singing and angling
  As he veers about in his boat.

Far over, by distance mellowed,
  The landscape lies unrolled:
Wayfarer, garden and villa,
  And kine and meadow and wold.

On the green the linen is bleaching
  While gambol the girls around;
The mill-wheel scatters its diamonds;
  I hear its monotonous sound.

Upon the old gray tower
  There stands a sentry-box;
I see the guard, red-coated,
  As up and down he walks.

I see him play with his musket,
  Which gleams in the morning-red;
He shoulders it and levels it; —
  I would he shot me dead!

„Wenn ich an deinem Hause."

————

Wenn ich an deinem Hause
Des Morgens vorüber geh',
So freut's mich, du liebe Kleine,
Wenn ich dich am Fenster seh'.

Mit deinen schwarzbraunen Augen
Siehst du mich forschend an:
„Wer bist du, und was fehlt dir,
Du fremder, kranker Mann?"

Ich bin ein deutscher Dichter,
Bekannt im deutschen Land;
Nennt man die besten Namen,
So wird auch der meine genannt.

Und was mir fehlt, du Kleine,
Fehlt Manchem im deutschen Land;
Nennt man die schlimmsten Schmerzen,
So wird auch der meine genannt.

## "I LIKE, WHEN IN THE MORNING."
### Translated by Dr. James Steele.

I like, when in the morning
    Your cottage door I pass,
To see you at the window,
    You pretty little lass.

Your dark brown eyes with wonder
    Are filled, as I go on; —
"Who are you and what ails you,
    You stranger, woe—begone?"

"I am a German poet,
    In Germany renowned,
And high among the best ones
    My name is to be found.

And that which ails me, darling,
    Ails Germans many a one;
But where their sorrow endeth,
    Mine only hath begun."

„Wie der Mond sich leuchtend dränget."

———

Wie der Mond sich leuchtend dränget
Durch den dunkeln Wolkenflor,
Also taucht aus dunkeln Zeiten
Mir ein lichtes Bild hervor.

Saßen all' auf dem Verdecke,
Fuhren stolz hinab den Rhein
Und die sommergrünen Ufer
Glühn im Abendsonnenschein.

Sinnend saß ich zu den Füßen
Einer Dame, schön und hold;
In ihr liebes, bleiches Antlitz
Spielt' das rothe Sonnengold.

Lauten klangen, Buben sangen,
Wunderbare Fröhlichkeit!
Und der Himmel wurde blauer,
Und die Seele wurde weit.

Märchenhaft vorüberzogen
Berg' und Burgen, Wald und Au; —
Und das Alles sah' ich glänzen
In dem Aug' der schönen Frau.

## "AS THE MOON'S FAIR FACE APPEARS."
Translated by Miss M. Hutchison.

As the Moon's fair face appears,
  Smiling through the clouds of night,
So mid dark of vanished years
  Gleams a memory of light.

Down the Rhine, the proudly flowing,
  Merry voyagers sailing on;
Banks of summer-greenness glowing
  In the glare of evening sun.

At the foot of a dear maiden,
  Dear and sweet, I musing lay,
On her pale and lovely features
  Flashed the light of fading day.

Music ringing, voices singing,
  Wondrous rapture, strange and new!
Far and high the soul's swift winging
  Through the broader deeper blue!

Like a dream of shifting splendour,
  Mount and tower and tree went by,
Glancing in the radiance tender
  Of the darling maiden's eye!

Heinrich Heine.

## Du bist wie eine Blume.

Du bist wie eine Blume,
So hold und schön und rein;
Ich schau' dich an und Wehmuth
Schleicht mir ins Herz hinein.

Mir ist, als ob ich die Hände
Aufs Haupt dir legen sollt',
Betend, daß Gott dich erhalte
So rein und schön und hold.

## Sturm.

Es wüthet der Sturm,
Und er peitscht die Wellen,
Und die Well'n, wuthschäumend und bäumend,
Thürmen sich auf, und es wogen lebendig
Die weißen Wasserberge,
Und das Schifflein erklimmt sie,
Hastig, mühsam,
Und plötzlich stürzt es hinab
In schwarze, weitgähnende Fluthabgründe. —

Vergebens mein Bitten und Flehn!
Mein Rufen verhallt im tosenden Sturm,
Im Schlachtlärm der Winde.
Es braust und pfeift und prasselt und heult,

## "E'EN AS A BEAUTEOUS FLOWER."

Translated by Mrs. E. Kroeker, née Freiligrath.

E'en as a beauteous Flower
 So fair and pure thou art,
I gaze on thee and sadness
 Comes stealing o'er my heart.

My hands I fain had folded
 Upon thy soft brown hair,
Praying that God would keep thee
 Thus lovely, pure and fair.

## THE TEMPEST.

Translated by Richard Garnett.

Fierce streams the blast — in anguish coils
The wave beneath it, gleams and boils,
And soars with many a foaming fountain,
A white and living water-mountain.
The bark the waves in mockery fling
Forth from their foamy ravening,
A moment gleams — and instant is
Lost in a yawning black abyss.

In vain my prayer and deprecation;
Drown'd in the shock and agitation
Of the wild winds that raving battle,
And roar, and shriek, and howl, and rattle,

19*

Wie ein Tollhaus von Tönen!
Und zwischendurch hör' ich vernehmbar
Lockende Harfenlaute,
Sehnsuchtwilden Gesang,
Seelenschmelzend und seelenzerreißend,
Und ich erkenne die Stimme.

Fern an schottischer Felsenküste,
Wo das graue Schlößlein hinausragt
Ueber die brandende See,
Dort am hochgewölbten Fenster,
Steht eine schöne, kranke Frau,
Zartdurchsichtig und marmorblaß,
Und sie spielt die Harfe und singt,
Und der Wind durchwühlt ihre langen Locken,
Und trägt ihr dunkles Lied
Ueber das weite, stürmende Meer.

## Seegespenst.

Ich aber lag am Rande des Schiffes,
Und schaute, träumenden Auges,
Hinab in das spiegelklare Wasser,
Und schaute tiefer und tiefer —
Bis tief im Meeresgrunde,
Anfangs wie dämmernde Nebel,
Jedoch allmählig farbenbestimmter,
Kirchenkuppel und Thürme sich zeigten,

Like one vast cell of maniac sound —
Yet hear I 'mid the broil resound
The gusty accents of a lyre,
And twanging chords, and voice of fire
That tear the shuddering soul along
And hearkening know whence comes the song.

Far on the rugged Scottish shore,
Where the old castle gazes o'er
The frantic waters in amazement —
There, at the lofty vaulted casement,
A pallid lovely woman stands,
Tender of glance and frail, her hands
Clang on the harp, and wild she sings,
And wild the storm her tresses flings,
And bears the voice of her emotion
Far o'er the roaring wastes of Ocean.

## SEA VISION.

Translated by Mrs. E. Kroeker. née Freiligrath.

But I lay at the edge of the vessel,
And gazed with eye that was dreaming
Down into the clear crystal water,
And gazed down deeper and deeper
Till far on the ground of the Ocean,
At first like mists of twilight,
But soon more defined in colour and substance,
Domes of churches appeared and steeples,

Und endlich, sonnenklar, eine ganze Stadt.
Alterthümlich niederländisch,
Und menschenbelebt.
Bedächtige Männer, schwarzbemäntelt,
Mit weißen Halskrausen und Ehrenketten,
Und langen Degen und langen Gesichtern,
Schreiten über den wimmelnden Marktplatz
Nach dem treppenhohen Rathhaus,
Wo steinerne Kaiserbilder
Wacht halten mit Zepter und Schwert.
Unferne, vor langen Häuser-Reihn,
Wo spiegelblanke Fenster
Und pyramidisch beschnittene Linden,
Wandeln seidenrauschende Jungfern,
Schlanke Leibchen, die Blumengesichter
Sittsam umschlossen von schwarzen Mützchen
Und hervorquellendem Goldhaar.
Bunte Gesellen, in spanischer Tracht,
Stolzieren vorüber und nicken.
Bejahrte Frauen,
In braunen, verschollnen Gewändern,
Gesangbuch und Rosenkranz in der Hand,
Eilen, trippelnden Schritts,
Nach dem großen Dome,
Getrieben von Glockengeläute
Und rauschendem Orgelton.


Mich selbst ergreift des fernen Klangs
Geheimnißvoller Schauer!
Unendliches Sehnen, tiefe Wehmuth

And at length, clear as day, an entire town,
Antiquated, Netherlandish,
And thronging with people.
Solemn men, clothed in black mantles,
With snow-white ruffs, and chains of honour,
Wearing long swords, and long stiff faces,
Stalk gravely across the busy market
To the Town Hall, ascended by flights of steps,
Where imperial statues of stone
Guard entrance, with sceptre and sword.
Not far off, before long rows of houses —
The windows glittering like polished mirrors —
Before lindens clipt into pyramids quaintly,
Maidens are walking, with rustling silk garments,
Slim little waists, their fair blooming faces
Modestly peering out forth from their tresses,
Golden tresses all gloriously flowing.
Gay young fellows in Spanish costume
Pass by, haughtily nodding.
Aged women
In brown old-fashioned dresses,
Bearing in hand their rosary and prayer-books,
Hasten with feeble steps
To the great Cathedral,
Urged thither by clanging of bells,
And the deep-thrilling tones of the organ.

Myself am moved by the secret
Mysterious power of the distant sound.
An infinite yearning, deep melancholy

Beschleicht mein Herz,
Mein' kaum geheiltes Herz; —
Mir ist, als würden seine Wunden
Von lieben Lippen aufgeküßt,
Und thäten wieder bluten, —
Heiße, rothe Tropfen,
Die lang und langsam niederfall'n
Auf ein altes Haus, dort unten
In der tiefen Meerstadt,
Auf ein altes, hochgegiebeltes Haus,
Das melancholisch menschenleer ist,
Nur daß am untern Fenster
Ein Mädchen sitzt,
Den Kopf auf den Arm gestützt,
Wie ein armes, vergessenes Kind —
Und ich kenne dich, armes, vergessenes Kind.

So tief, meertief also
Versteckst du dich vor mir
Aus kindischer Laune,
Und konntest nicht mehr herauf,
Und saßest fremd unter fremden Leuten,
Jahrhunderte lang,
Derweilen ich, die Seele voll Gram,
Auf der ganzen Erde dich suchte,
Und immer dich suchte,
Du Immergeliebte,
Du Längstverlorene,
Du Endlichgefundene —
Ich hab' dich gefunden und schaue wieder

Comes creeping o'er my heart,
My scarcely healed heart; —
I feel as though its wounds were kissed open
Once more again, by beloved lips,
And that again they were bleeding,
Hot drops of blood,
Which downwards fall slowly
Upon an old house below,
Far in the depths of the Ocean,
Upon an old house and lofty-gabled,
Which stands in sad drear solitude,
But that at one window
Sits, forlorn, a maiden,
Supporting her head on her arm,
Like a poor forgotten child,
And I know thee, thou poor and forgotten child!

Thus deep then, even as deep as the Ocean
Didst thou hide away from me
In childish caprice,
And could'st return again never,
And didst remain as a stranger among strange people,
For centuries,
While I, with grieving soul,
The whole earth over have sought thee,
Aye without ceasing have sought thee,
Thou ever loved one,
Oh thou long lost one,
At length found again!
But now I have found thee — once more I behold

Dein süßes Gesicht,
Die klugen, treuen Augen,
Das liebe Lächeln —
Und nimmer will ich dich wieder verlassen
Und ich komme hinab zu dir,
Und mit ausgebreiteten Armen
Stürz' ich hinab an dein Herz. —

Aber zur rechten Zeit noch
Ergriff mich beim Fuß der Kapitän
Und zog mich vom Schiffsrand,
Und rief, ärgerlich lachend:
„Doctor, sind Sie des Teufels?"

## Frühlingslied.

Leise zieht durch mein Gemüth
Liebliches Geläute.
Klinge, kleines Frühlingslied,
Kling' hinaus in's Weite!

Kling' hinaus bis in das Haus
Wo die Blumen sprießen!
Wenn du eine Rose schau'st,
Sag', ich laß' sie grüßen!

Thy sweet, sweet face,
And those kind faithful eyes
And that dear sad smile. —
And never, never again will I leave thee,
I am coming to thee,
And with arms outspread
Let me down to thy heart! —

But just in the nick of time
My foot was grasped by the Captain,
Who pulled me away from the edge of the vessel
And cried half vexed, and half laughing,
"Sir! what the Deuce, are you up to?" —

## SPRING SONG.

Translated by Mrs. E. Kroeker, née Freiligrath.

Soft and gently through my soul
    Sweetest bells are ringing,
Speed you forth, my little song
    Of spring-time gaily singing!

Speed you onward, to a house
    Where sweet flowers are fleeting,
If perchance a Rose you see,
    Say, I send her greeting.

## Der Runenstein.

———

Es ragt ins Meer der Runenstein,
Da sitz' ich mit meinen Träumen;
Es pfeift der Wind — die Möwen schrei'n,
Die Wellen, sie wandern und schäumen.

Ich habe geliebt manch schönes Kind,
Und manchen guten Gesellen;
Wo sind sie hin? Es pfeift der Wind,
Es wandern und schäumen die Wellen!

## Die Weber.

———

Im düstern Auge keine Thräne,
Sie sitzen am Webstuhl und fletschen die Zähne:
„Deutschland, wir weben dein Leichentuch,
Wir weben hinein den dreifachen Fluch —
        Wir weben, wir weben!

„Ein Fluch dem Götzen, zu dem wir gebeten
In Winterskälte und Hungersnöthen;
Wir haben vergebens gehofft und geharrt,
Er hat uns geäfft und gefoppt und genarrt —
        Wir weben, wir weben!

## THE RUNIC STONE.

Translated by Edgar Alfred Bowring.

The Runic stone 'mongst the waves stands high,
  There sit I, with thoughts far roaming;
The wind pipes loudly, the seamews cry,
  The billows are curling and foaming.

I've loved full many a charming girl,
  Loved many a comrade proudly —
Where are they now? The billows curl
  And foam, and the wind pipes loudly.

## THE SILESIAN WEAVERS.

Translated by Edgar Alfred Bowring.

No tears from their gloomy eyes are flowing.
They sit at the loom, their white teeth showing:
"Thy shroud, O Germany, now weave we,
"A threefold curse we're weaving for thee, —
      "We're weaving, we're weaving!"

"A curse on the God to whom our petition
"We've vainly adress'd when in starving condition;
"In vain did we hope, and in vain did we wait,
"He only derided and mock'd our sad fate. —
      "We're weaving, we're weaving!

„Ein Fluch dem König, dem König der Reichen,
Den unfer Elend nicht konnte erweichen,
Der den letzten Groschen von uns erpreßt,
Und uns wie Hunde erschießen läßt —
　　Wir weben, wir weben!

„Ein Fluch dem falschen Vaterlande,
Wo nur gedeihen Schmach und Schande,
Wo jede Blume früh geknickt,
Wo Fäulniß und Moder den Wurm erquickt —
　　Wir weben, wir weben!

„Das Schiffchen fliegt, der Webstuhl kracht,
Wir weben emsig Tag und Nacht —
Altdeutschland, wir weben dein Leichentuch,
Wir weben hinein den dreifachen Fluch.
　　Wir weben, wir weben!"

"A curse on the King of the wealthy, whom often
"Our misery vainly attempted to soften;
"Who takes away e'en the last penny we've got,
"And lets us like dogs in the highway be shot, —
    "We're weaving, we're weaving!

"A curse on our fatherland false and contriving,
"Where shame and disgrace alone are seen thriving,
"Where flowers are pluck'd before they unfold,
"Where batten the worms on corruption and mould, —
    "We're weaving, we're weaving!

"The shuttle is flying, the loom creaks away,
"We're weaving busily night and day;
"Thy shroud, Old Germany, now weave we,
"A threefold curse we're weaving for thee, —
    "We're weaving, we're weaving!"

# Ferdinand Freiligrath,

born 1810.

„Laß braufen deiner Sagen Quell!
O, laß mich hören dein Gedicht!"

# Die Auswanderer.

Ich kann den Blick nicht von euch wenden;
Ich muß euch anschau'n immerdar:
Wie reicht ihr mit geschäft'gen Händen
Dem Schiffer eure Habe dar!

Ihr Männer, die ihr von dem Nacken
Die Körbe langt, mit Brod beschwert,
Das ihr, aus deutschem Korn gebacken,
Geröstet habt auf deutschem Herd;

Und ihr, im Schmuck der langen Zöpfe,
Ihr Schwarzwaldmädchen, braun und schlank
Wie sorgsam stellt ihr Krüg' und Töpfe
Auf der Schaluppe grüne Bank!

Das sind dieselben Töpf' und Krüge,
Oft an der Heimath Born gefüllt;
Wenn am Missouri Alles schwiege,
Sie malten euch der Heimath Bild;

# THE EMIGRANTS.

## Translated by Dr. Alfred Baskerville.

I cannot turn my look aside,
But ling'ring watch ye on the strand,
As to the sailor ye confide
Your wealth, your all, with busy hand.

Men, from your shoulders placing round,
Bread laden baskets on the earth;
The meal of German corn was ground,
And baked upon a German hearth.

And ye, adorned with braided hair,
Black-Forest maidens, slender, brown,
How on the shallop's bench with care
Ye lay your jugs and pitchers down!

How oft have flown those pitchers o'er
With water from your native spring;
When silent is Missouri's shore
Sweet dreams of home to you they'll bring.

20*

Des Dorfes steingefaßte Quelle,
Zu der ihr schöpfend euch gebückt;
Des Herdes traute Feuerstelle,
Das Wandgesims, das sie geschmückt,

Bald zieren sie im fernen Westen
Des leichten Bretterhauses Wand;
Bald reicht sie müden, braunen Gästen,
Voll frischen Trunkes, eure Hand.

Es trinkt daraus der Tscherokese,
Ermattet, von der Jagd bestaubt;
Nicht mehr von deutscher Rebenlese
Tragt ihr sie heim, mit Grün belaubt.

O sprecht! warum zogt ihr von dannen?
Das Neckarthal hat Wein und Korn,
Der Schwarzwald steht voll finst'rer Tannne
Im Spessart klingt des Älplers Horn.

Wie wird es in den fremden Wäldern
Euch nach der Heimathberge Grün,
Nach Deutschlands gelben Weizenfeldern,
Nach seinen Rebenhügeln ziehn!

Wie wird das Bild der alten Tage
Durch eure Träume glänzend wehn!
Gleich einer stillen, frommen Sage
Wird es euch vor der Seele stehn.

The stone-encircled village well,
Where ye to draw the water bent;
The hearth, where soft affections dwell,
The mantle-piece, its ornament;

Soon will they, in the distant west,
Adorn the log-hut's wooden side,
Soon to the red-skinned weary guest
Ye'll hand their clear refreshing tide.

The Cherookees will drink their flood,
Who in the chase exhausted roam;
No more, filled with the grape's red blood,
Nor hung with wreaths, ye'll bear them home.

Say! why seek ye a distant land?
The Neckar-vale has wine and corn;
Dark pines in your Black-Forest stand,
In Spessart sounds the Alpine horn.

How, when in distant woods, forlorn,
Ye for your native hills will pine,
For Deutschland's golden fields of corn
And verdant hills of clust'ring vine;

How will the image of the past
Through all your dreams in brightness roll,
And, like some pious legend, cast
A veil of sadness o'er your soul!

Der Bootsman winkt! — Zieht hin in Frieden!
Gott schütz' euch, Mann und Weib und Greis!
Sei Freude eurer Brust beschieden,
Und euren Feldern Reis und Mais!

## Meersabel.

Ebbetrocken auf dem Strande
Lag die unbeholfne Kof;
Schwärzlich hing am Mast das Zugnetz
Das vom letzten Fange troff.

Tastend prüfte seine Maschen
Ein barfüßiger Gesell;
Fische dorrten in der Sonne
An dem hölzernen Gestell.

Heiß und durstig sah die Dirne
Auf das Meer, ein Tantalus;
Wie ein großer Silberhalbmond
Blitzte der Oceanus.

Jede Welle, grau und salzig,
Die sich an dem Ufer brach,
Wie zum Gruße mit dem Haupte
Nickte brandend sie, und sprach:

The boatman beckons — go in peace!
May God preserve you, man and wife,
Your fields of rice and maize increase
And with his blessings crown your life!

## SEA FABLE.

Translated by Mrs. E. Kroeker, née Freiligrath.

High and dry upon the sea-shore
　　Lies the helpless fishing-smack,
From the mast the net is hanging,
　　Dripping still all wet and black.

Yon bare-footed youth is trying
　　All its meshes o'er with care;
Fishes in the sun are drying
　　On the wooden framework there.

Parched, the arid plain is gazing
　　On the sea, like Tantalus,
As a mighty silver Crescent
　　Flashes great Oceanus.

Every billow, gray and salty,
　　As upon the beach it broke,
As if greeting with its crested
　　Head, it nodded, and then spoke:

Am Gestade rausch' ich gerne,
Lecke gern den harten Sand;
Bunte Muscheln, Meeressterne
Schleudre gern ich an das Land.

Gerne seh' ich Haid' und Ginster
Wuchern um die Dünen her.
Hier vergeß' ich, wie so finster
Draußen ist das hohe Meer,

Das die kalten Stürme peitschen,
Wo der Normann Fische fängt,
Wo das Eismeer mit des deutschen
Meers Gewässern sich vermengt.

Keine Tonn' und keine Bake
Schwimmt und flammt dort auf der See
Und allnächtlich steigt der Krake
Aus den Tiefen in die Höh'.

Eine Insel, starr von Schuppen,
Rudert dort das Ungethüm.
Aengstlich flüchten die Schaluppen,
Und der Fischer greift zum Riem.

———————

„Aehnlich einer großen schwarzen -
Fläche liegt er, kampfbereit,
Und sein Rücken ist mit Warzen,
Wie mit Hügeln überstreut.

On the beach I love to murmur,
    Love to lick the firm hard sand,
Coloured shells and starfish gladly
    Do I fling upon the strand.

Much I love to see the wild gorse
    Straggling grow about the plain;
Here do I forget how gloomy
    Is, without, the boundless main,

Which the stormy tempest lashes,
    Where the Norsemen fishing go,
Where the Arctic and the German
    Oceans both together flow.

Neither buoy nor blazing beacon
    Watch upon the sea there keep,
And the kraken rises nightly
    From his caverns in the deep.

Stiff with scales, a rigid island,
    See him steer along the shore,
Terrified the skiffs seek safety
    And the fisher grasps his oar.

———————

"A huge plain doth he resemble —
    Combat-ready lies he now,
And his back with warts is covered
    As with hillocks — high and low.

Ruhig schwimmt er — doch nicht lange! —
Auf dem Haupte grünes Moos,
Zischend zuckt die Meeresschlange,
Die gewalt'ge, auf ihn los.

Wenn sie blutend sich umklaftern,
Wenn die rothen Kämme wehn,
Kann man keinen fabelhaftern
Anblick auf dem Meere sehn.

Einsam, schauerlich und finster
Ist das ferne, hohe Meer!
Gerne seh' ich Haid' und Ginster
Wuchern um die Dünen her."

## Die Bilderbibel.

Du Freund aus Kindertagen,
Du brauner Foliant,
Oft für mich aufgeschlagen
Von meiner Lieben Hand;
Du, dessen Bildergaben
Mich Schauenden ergötzten,
Den spielvergeßnen Knaben
Nach Morgenland versetzten.

"Calmly floats he — on a sudden,
  With a hissing fierce and dread,
Darts on him the great sea-serpent —
  Moss is growing on its head.

"When the two are struggling, when their
  Gory crests do wave, I ween,
Ne'er more wondrous and more fearful
  Sight on Ocean yet was seen.

"Lonely, horrible and gloomy
  Is the distant dreary main;
Much I love to see the wild gorse
  Straggling grow about the plain,"

## THE ILLUSTRATED BIBLE.

Translated by "S. M."

Thou old and time-worn volume,
  Thou friend of childhood's age,
How frequently dear hands for me
  Have turned the pictured page!
How oft, his sports forgetting,
  The gazing boy was borne
With joyous heart, by the sweet art,
  To tread the land of morn.

Du schobst für mich die Riegel
    Von ferner Zone Pforten,
Ein kleiner, reiner Spiegel
    Von dem, was funkelt dorten!
Dir Dank! durch dich begrüßte
    Mein Aug' eine fremde Welt,
Sah Palm', Kameel und Wüste,
    Und Hirt und Hirtenzelt.

Du brachtest sie mir näher,
    Die Weisen und die Helden,
Wovon begeisterte Seher
    Im Buch der Bücher melden:
Die Mädchen, schön und bräutlich,
    So ihre Worte schildern,
Ich sah sie alle deutlich
    In deinen feinen Bildern.

Der Patriarchen Leben,
    Die Einfalt ihrer Sitte,
Wie Engel sie umschweben
    Auf jedem ihrer Schritte,
Ihr Ziehn und Heerdentränken,
    Das hab' ich oft gesehn,
Konnt' ich mit stillem Denken
    Vor deinen Blättern stehn:

Mir ist, als lägst du prangend
    Dort auf dem Stuhle wieder;
Als beugt' ich mich verlangend
    Zu deinen Bildern nieder;

Thou didst fling wide the portals
  Of many a distant zone;
As in a glass I saw them pass,
  Faces and forms unknown!
For a new world I thank thee! —
  The camel wandering free,
The desert calm, and the stately palm.
  And the Bedouin's tent, I see.

And thou didst bring them near me,
  Hero, and saint, and sage,
Whose deeds were told by the seers of old
  On the book of books' dread page:
And the fair and bride-like maidens
  Recorded in thy lines —
Well could I trace each form of grace
  Amid thy rich designs.

And I saw the hoary patriarchs
  Of old and simple days,
An angel-band, on either hand,
  Kept watch upon their ways:
I saw their meek herds drinking
  By fount or river-shore,
When mute I stood, in thoughtful mood,
  Thine open page before.

Methinks I see thee lying
  Upon thy well-known chair;
Mine eager gaze once more surveys
  The scenes unfolded there;

Als stände, was vor Jahren
Mein Auge staunend sah,
In frischen, wunderbaren,
Erneuten Farben da;

Als säh' ich in grotesken,
Verworrenen Gestalten,
Auf's Neue die Moresken,
Die bunten, mannigfalten,
Die jedes Bild umfaßten,
Bald Blumen, bald Gezweig,
Und zu dem Bilde paßten,
An sinniger Deutung reich!

Als trät' ich, wie vor Zeiten,
Zur Mutter bittend hin,
Daß sie mir sollte deuten
Jedweden Bildes Sinn;
Als lehrte zu jedem Bilde
Sie Sprüche mich und Lieder;
Als schaute sanft und milde
Der Vater auf uns nieder.

O Zeit, du bist vergangen!
Ein Mährchen scheinst du mir!
Der Bilderbibel Prangen,
Das gläub'ge Aug' dafür,
Die theuren Eltern beide,
Der stillzufriedne Sinn,
Der Kindheit Lust und Freude —
Alles dahin, dahin!

As, years ago, I saw them
  With wonder and delight,
Each form renews its faded hues,
  Fresh, beautiful, and bright.

Again I see them twining
  In ceaseless shapes of change;
Bright and grotesque each arabesque,
  Mazy, and wild, and strange:
Each fair design encircling
  In varied shape and dress,
A blossom now, and then a bough,
  But never meaningless.

As in old times, entreating,
  I seek my mother's knee,
That she may teach the name of each,
  And what their meanings be;
I learn, for every picture,
  A text, a verse, a psalm;
With tranquil smile, my sire the while
  Watches, well pleased, and calm.

Ye seem but as a fable,
  O days that are gone by!
That Bible old, with clasps of gold —
  That young, believing eye —
Those loved and loving parents —
  That childhood blithe and gay —
That calm content, so innocent —
  All, all are past away!

# Ferdinand Freiligrath.

## Ammonium.

---

„Fremdling, laß deine Stute grasen,
O, zieh' nicht weiter diese Nacht!
Dies ist die grünste der Oasen;
Im gelben Sandmeer glänzt ihr Rasen,
Gleichwie inmitten von Topasen
Ein grüner, funkelnder Smaragd."

Er sprach: „Gern will ich mich entgürten!"
Und nahm dem Pferde das Gebiß.
Er setzte sich zu seinen Wirthen;
Des Wüstengeiers Flügel schwirrten
An ihm vorüber nach den Syrten,
Zu ruhn in der Pentapolis.

Die Lieder und die Cymbeln klangen,
Die Mappe lag auf seinen Knien.
Die Rosse mit den blanken Stangen,
Die finstern Reiter mit den langen
Gewanden und den bärt'gen Wangen,
Die Zelte — fremd ergriff es ihn.

Mit farb'gen Stiften schuf er glühend
Ein Bildniß dieser Wüstenrast.
Die Dromedare lagen knieend
Am Quell; des Wirthes Töchter, blühend
Und schlank, bald nahend und bald fliehend,
Umtanzten singend ihren Gast:

## AMMONIUM.

### Translated by Richard Garnett.

—

"Rest, stranger, while thy courser grazes;
O travel on no more this night!
Stay by the greenest of oases,
That shines amid the sandy places
As when a topaz-wreath enchases
An emerald's pure, refreshing light!"

"Thanks for your hospitable proffer!"
He said and lighted down from his
Steed on the grass, and sat down over
Against his hosts, while past did hover
The vulture, flying to recover
His eyrie in Pentapolis.

A sound of song and joyous dances;
Wide on his knees he spreads his book:
The tents, the fires, the steeds, the lances,
The swart Arabian countenances,
The beards, the shields — like wild romances
These things his ardent fancy took.

He sat with busy pencil stealing
An image of his desert rest;
By the clear spring were camels kneeling;
The lissom Arab maids, revealing
Their features half, and half concealing,
Sang, fleeting round their Christian guest: —

„Fremdling, laß deine Stute grasen!
O, zieh nicht weiter diese Nacht!
Dies ist die grünste der Oasen,
Im gelben Sandmeer glänzt ihr Rasen,
Gleichwie inmitten von Topasen
Ein grüner, funkelnder Smaragd!"

## Löwenritt.

Wüstenkönig ist der Löwe; will er sein Gebiet durchfliegen,
Wandelt er nach der Lagune, in dem hohen Schilf zu liegen.
Wo Gazellen und Giraffen trinken, kauert er im Rohre;
Zitternd über dem Gewalt'gen rauscht das Laub der Sy-
camore.

Abends, wenn die hellen Feuer glühn im Hottentottenkraale,
Wenn des jähen Tafelberges bunte, wechselnde Signale
Nicht mehr glänzen, wenn der Kaffer einsam schweift durch
die Karroo
Wenn im Busch die Antilope schlummert, und am Strom
das Gnu:

Sieh', dann schreitet majestätisch durch die Wüste die Giraffe,
Daß mit der Lagune trüben Fluthen sie die heiße, schlaffe

"Rest, stranger, while thy courser grazes;
O travel on no more this night!
Stay by the greenest of oases,
That shines amid the sandy places
As when a topaz-wreath enchases
An emerald's pure, refreshing light!"

## THE LION'S RIDE.

### Translated by Dr. Alfred Baskerville.

From his lair the desert king arose through his domain
to fly,
To the far lagoon he wanders, in the lofty reeds to lie;
Where gazelles drink and giraffes, he lurks upon the
rushy shore;
Trembling o'er the mighty monarch, waves the shady
sycamore.

When at eve the blazing fire crackles in the Caffre's
kraal,
When on Table-Mount no more the signal flutters
in the gale,
When the solitary Hottentot sweeps o'er the wide karroo,
When the antelope sleeps 'neath the bush, and by
the stream the gnu;

Lo! then stalks majestically through the desert the giraffe,
There to lave the stagnant waters, there the slimy
draught to quaff;

21 *

Zunge kühle; lechzend eilt sie durch der Wüste nackte Strecken,
Knieend schlürft sie langen Halses aus dem schlammgefüllten
　　　　　　　　Becken.


Plötzlich regt es sich im Rohre; mit Gebrüll auf ihren
　　　　　　　　Nacken
Springt der Löwe; welch ein Reitpferd! sah man reichere
　　　　　　　　Schabracken
In den Marstallkammern einer königlichen Hofburg liegen,
Als das bunte Fell des Renners, den der Thiere Fürst be=
　　　　　　　　stiegen!


In die Muskeln des Genickes schlägt er gierig seine Zähne;
Um den Bug des Riesenpferdes weht des Reiters gelbe
　　　　　　　　Mähne.
Mit dem dumpfen Schrei des Schmerzes springt es auf und
　　　　　　　　flieht gepeinigt;
Sieh', wie Schnelle des Kameeles es mit Pardelhaut vereinigt.


Sieh', die mondbestrahlte Fläche schlägt es mit den leichten
　　　　　　　　Füßen!
Starr aus ihrer Höhlung treten seine Augen; rieselnd fließen
An dem braungefleckten Halse nieder schwarzen Blutes Tropfen,
Und das Herz des flücht'gen Thieres hört die stille Wüste
　　　　　　　　klopfen.

Parched with thirst, he skims the naked plain his burning
  tongue to cool,
  Kneeling, with extended neck, he drinks from out
  the miry pool.

Suddenly the rushes quiver; on his back with fearful roar,
  Springs the lion ; what a steed ! were richer housings
  e'er before
Seen in knight's or prince's stall, or on the champing
  war-steed's sides
Than the spotted charger's trappings, which the desert
  king bestrides ?

In the muscles of the neck he digs his greedy fangs
  amain,
  O'er the giant courser's shoulder waves the rider's
  yellow mane ;
With the hollow shriek of pain, he starts, and, mad
  with fury, flies ;
  See ! the spotted leopard's skin, how with the camel's
  speed it vies !

Hark ! he strikes the moon-illumined plain with foot
  swift as the roe's,
  Staring from their sockets start his bloodshot eyes,
  and trickling flows
O'er the brown bespotted neck the gory torrent's purple
  stain,
  And the victim's beating heart resounds along the
  silent plain.

Gleich der Wolke, deren Leuchten Israel im Lande Yemen
Führte, wie ein Geist der Wüste, wie ein fahler, luft'ger
        Schemen,
Eine sandgeformte Trombe in der Wüste sand'gem Meer,
Wirbelt eine gelbe Säule Sandes hinter ihnen her.


Ihrem Zuge folgt der Geier; krächzend schwirrt er durch
        die Lüfte;
Ihrer Spur folgt die Hyäne, die Entweiherin der Grüfte;
Folgt der Panther, der des Caplands Hürden räuberisch
        verheerte;
Blut und Schweiß bezeichnen ihres Königs grausenvolle
        Fährte.


Zagend auf lebend'gem Throne sehn sie den Gebieter sitzen,
Und mit scharfer Klaue seines Sitzes bunte Polster ritzen,
Rastlos, bis die Kraft ihr schwindet, muß ihn die Giraffe
        tragen,
Gegen einen solchen Reiter hilft kein Bäumen und kein
        Schlagen.


Taumelnd an der Wüste Saume stürzt sie hin, und röchelt
        leise.
Todt, bedeckt mit Staub und Schaume, wird das Roß des
        Reiters Speise.

Like the cloud which guided Israel to Yemen's promised
    land,
    Like a genius of the waste, a phantom riding o'er
        the strand,   ·
Whirling on, a sandy column, like a vortex in the skies,
    Through the desert's sandy sea, behind the horse and
        rider, flies.


Whirring in their wake, the vulture pierces with his
        shriek the gloom,
    And the fell hyena follows, desecrator of the tomb;
And the panther, dread destroyer of the Capeland's herds,
        gives chace;
    Drops of sweat and gore point out their grisly monarch's
        fearful trace.


Trembling they beheld their lord, as on his living
        throne he stood,
    Tearing with his grisly fangs the chequered cushion,
        stained with blood.
Onwards, till his strength's exhausted, must the steed
        his burden bear,
    'Gainst a rider such as this, 'twere vain indeed to
        plunge and rear!


Stagg'ring, on the desert's brink the victim falls and
        ·    gurgling lies;
    Dead, besmeared with froth and gore, the steed
        becomes the rider's prize.

Über Madagaskar, fern im Osten, sieht man Frühlicht
glänzen —
So durchsprengt der Thiere König nächtlich seines Reiches
Grenzen.

### Gesicht des Reisenden.

Mitten in der Wüste war es, wo wir Nachts am Boden
ruhten;
Meine Beduinen schliefen bei den abgezäumten Stuten.
In der Ferne lag das Mondlicht auf der Nilgebirge Jochen;
Rings im Flugsand umgekommner Dromedare weiße
Knochen!

Schlaflos lag ich; statt des Pfühles diente mir mein leichter
Sattel,
Dem ich unterschob den Beutel mit der dürren Frucht der
Dattel;
Meinen Kaftan ausgebreitet hatt' ich über Brust und Füße;
Neben mir mein bloßer Säbel, mein Gewehr und meine
Spieße.

Tiefe Stille, nur zuweilen knistert das gesunkne Feuer;
Nur zuweilen knirscht verspätet ein vom Horst verirrter Geier;

Over Madagascar, in the east, the, morning glimmers
          grey, —
O'er the frontiers of his realm the king of beasts
          pursues his way.

# THE SPECTRE-CARAVAN.

Translated by the late James Clarence Mangan.

'Twas at midnight, in the Desert, where we rested on
          the ground;
There my Beddaweens were sleeping, and their steeds
          were stretched around;
In the farness lay the moonlight on the Mountains of
          the Nile,
And the camel-bones that strewed the sands for many
          an arid mile.

With my saddle for a pillow did I prop my weary head.
And my kaftan-cloth unfolded o'er my limbs was lightly
          spread,
While beside me as the Kapitaun and watchman of my
          band,
Lay my Bazra sword and pistols twain a-shimmering
          on the sand.

And the stillness was unbroken, save at moments by a cry
From some stray belated vulture, sailing blackly down
          the sky,

Nur zuweilen stampft im Schlafe eins der angebundnen Rosse;
Nur zuweilen fährt ein Reiter träumend nach dem Wurf-
　　　　geschosse.


Da auf einmal bebt die Erde; auf den Mondschein folgen
　　　　trüber
Dämmrung Schatten; Wüstenthiere jagen aufgeschreckt
　　　　vorüber.
Schnaubend bäumen sich die Pferde; unser Führer greift
　　　　zur Fahne;
Sie entsinkt ihm, und er murmelt: Herr, die Geisterkara-
　　　　vane! —


Ja, sie kommt! vor den Kameelen schweben die gespenst'schen
　　　　Treiber,
Ueppig in den hohen Sätteln lehnen schleierlose Weiber;
Neben ihnen wandeln Mädchen, Krüge tragend, wie Rebekka
Einst am Brunnen; Reiter folgen — sausend sprengen sie
　　　　nach Mekka.


Mehr noch! — nimmt der Zug kein Ende? — immer mehr!
　　　　wer kann sie zählen?
Weh', auch die zerstreuten Knochen werden wieder zu Ka-
　　　　meelen,
Und der braune Sand, der wirbelnd sich erhebt in dunklen
　　　　Massen,
Wandelt sich zu braunen Männern, die der Thiere Zügel
　　　　fassen.

Or the snortings of a sleeping steed at waters fancy-seen,
Or the hurried warlike mutterings of some dreaming
Beddaween.


When, behold! — a sudden sandquake — and atween
the earth and moon
Rose a mighty Host of Shadows, as from out some dim
lagoon :
Then our coursers gasped with terror, and a thrill shook
every man !
And the cry was : "*Allah Akbar!* — 'tis the Spectre-
Caravan !"


On they came, their hueless faces toward Mecca evermore ;
On they came, long files of camels, and of women whom
they bore,
Guides and merchants, youthful maidens, bearing
pitchers in their hands,
And behind them troops of horsemen following, sumless
as the sands !


More and more ! the phantom-pageant overshadowed all
the plains,
Yea, the ghastly camel-bones arose, and grew to camel-
trains ;
And the whirling column-clouds of sand to forms in
dusky garbs,
Here, afoot as Hadjee pilgrims — there, as warriors
on their barbs !

Denn dies ist die Nacht, wo Alle, die das Sandmeer schon
                    verschlungen,
Deren sturmverwehte Asche heut' vielleicht an unsern Zungen
Klebte, deren mürbe Schädel unsrer Rosse Huf zertreten,
Sich erheben und sich schaaren, in der heil'gen Stadt zu beten.


Immer mehr! — noch sind die Letzten nicht an uns vorbei-
                    gezogen,
Und schon kommen dort die Ersten schlaffen Zaums zurück-
                    geflogen.
Von dem grünen Vorgebirge nach der Babelmandeb=Enge
Saus'ten sie, eh' noch mein Reitpferd lösen konnte seine
                    Stränge.


Haltet aus, die Rosse schlagen! jeder Mann zu seinem Pferde!
Zittert nicht, wie vor dem Löwen die verirrte Widderheerde!
Laßt sie immer euch berühren mit den wallenden Talaren!
Rufet: Allah! — und vorüber ziehn sie mit den Drome-
                    daren.


Harret, bis im Morgenwinde eure Turbanfedern flattern!
Morgenwind und Morgenröthe werden ihnen zu Bestattern.

Whence we knew the Night was come, when all whom
     Death had sought and found,
Long ago amid the sands whereon their bones yet
     bleach around,
Rise by legions from the darkness of their prisons low
     and lone,
And in dim procession march to kiss the Kaaba's Holy
     Stone.

And yet more and more for ever! — still they swept
     in pomp along,
Till I asked me, Can the Desert hold so vast a muster
     throng?
Lo! the Dead are here in myriads! the whole World
     of Hades waits,
As with eager wish to press beyond the Babelmandeb
     Straits!

Then I spake: "Our steeds are frantic: To your saddles,
     every one!
Never quail before these Shadows! You are children
     of the Sun!
If their garments rustle past you, if their glances reach
     you here,
Cry *Bismillah!* — and that mighty Name shall banish
     every fear".

"Courage, comrades! Even now the moon is waning
     far a–west,
Soon the welcome Dawn will mount the skies in gold
     and crimson vest,

Mit dem Tage wieder Asche werden diese nächt'gen Zieher! —
Seht, es dämmert schon! ermuth'gend grüßt ihn meines
        Thiers Gewieher.

## Mirage.

Mein Auge mustert unruhvoll des Hafens wimpelreich Revier,
Doch deines richtet lächelnd sich auf meines Hutes Federzier:
„Von deinen Wüsten hör' ich gern in einer meerumrauschten
        Jacht;
Ein Bild aus dem Gebiete drum, das diesen Schmuck her-
        vorgebracht!"


Wohlan! ich lege meine Stirn in's Hohle meiner rechten
        Hand!
Die Wimper fällt, die Schläfe fliegt — sieh' da, der Oede
        glüh'nder Sand!
Die Lagerplätze grüßen dich des Volks, dem ich entsprossen
        bin;
In ihrer brand'gen Wittwentracht tritt die Sahara vor dich
        hin.


Wer trabte durch das Löwenland? von Klaun und Hufen
        zeugt der Kies.
Tombuktu's Karavanenzug! — am Horizonte blitzt der Spieß!

And in thinnest air will melt away those phantom shapes
        forlorn,
When again upon your brows you feel the odour-winds
        of Morn !"

## MIRAGE.

### (From Tait's Edinburgh Magazine, April 1845.)

All o'er the harbour gay with flags, my restless eyes
        a-wandering go ;
But thine, with laughing glances, seek the plume that
        droops across my brow !
"Fain of thy deserts would I hear, while waves are
        gurgling round the boat ;
Come, paint me something of the land from whence
        that ostrich-tuft was brought."

Thou wilt ? I shade my brow awhile beneath the hollow
        of my hand :
Let fall the curtain of thine eyes : Lo ! there the desert's
        glowing sand :
The camping places of the tribe that gave me birth,
        thine eye discerns ;
Bare in her sun-scorched widow's weed around thee
        now Zahara burns.

Who travelled through the Lion-land? Of hoofs and
        claws ye see the prints ;
Tombuctoo's caravan ! the spear far on the horizon,
        yonder, glints ;

Die Banner wehn, im Staube schwimmt des Emirs pur-
    purn Ehrenkleid,
Und des Kameeles Haupt entragt dem Knäul mit ernster
    Stattlichkeit.

Sie reiten im gedrängten Troß, wo sich vermengen Sand
    und Luft;
Sieh' da, verschlungen hat sie schon der Ferne schwefel-
    farbner Duft!
Allein verfolgen ohne Müh' kannst du der Flücht'gen breite
    Spur:
Was sie verloren, Mal an Mal durchschimmert es die
    Körnerflur.


Das erste — wie zum Meilenstein da liegt's: ein todtes
    Dromedar!
Auf dem Gestürzten, federlos die Hälse, sitzt ein Geierpaar;
Sie ziehn das lang entbehrte Mahl dem prächt'gen Turban
    drüben vor,
Den in des Rittes wilder Hast ein junger Araber verlor.


Und nun: Schabrackenstoff umfliegt der Tamariske dorn'gen
    Strauch;
Daneben, staubig und geleert, ein jähgeborstner Wasser-
    schlauch: —
Wer ist es, der den klaffenden wahnsinn'gen Blicks mit
    Füßen tritt?
Es ist der dunkelhaar'ge Scheik des Landes Biledulgerid.

Wave banners; purple through the dust streams out
        the Emir's princely dress;
And grave, with sober statelihood, the camels'head o'er-
        looks the press.

In serried troop, where sand and sky together melt,
        they hurry on;
Already in the sulphurous mist, the lurid distance
        gulps them down;
Yet, by the riders' track, too well ye trace the flying
        onward host;
Full thickly marked, the sand is strewn with many a
        thing their speed has lost.

The first — a dromedary, dead — a ghastly milestone
        marks their course;
Perched on the bulk, with naked throats, two vultures
        revel, shrieking hoarse;
And eager for the meal delayed, yon costly turban little
        heed,
Lost by an Arab youth, and left in their wild journey's
        desperate speed.

Now bits of rich caparisons the thorny tamarisk bushes
        strew;
And, nearer, drained, and white with dust, a water-
        skin rent through and through:
Who's he that kicks the gaping thing, and furious stares,
        with quivering lid?
It is the black-haired Sheik, who rules the land of
        Biledulgerid.

Die Nachhut schließend, fiel sein Roß; er blieb zurück,
           er ward versprengt.
Verlechzend hat sein Lieblingsweib an seinen Gürtel sich
           gehängt.
Wie blitzte jüngst ihr Auge noch, als er sie vor sich hob auf's
           Pferd!
Nun schleift er durch die Wüste sie, wie man am Gurte
           schleift ein Schwert.


Der heiße Sand, den Nächtens nur der zottige Schweif des
           Löwen schlägt,
Er wird vom flutenden Gelock der Regungslosen nun gefegt!
Er fängt sich in der Haare Schwall, er sengt der Lippe
           würz'gen Thau;
Mit seinen Kieseln röthet er die Knöchel der erschöpften Frau.


Und auch der Emir wankt; das Blut in seinen Pulsen
           quillt und kocht,
Sein Auge strotzt, und seiner Stirn blau schimmerndes
           Geäder pocht.
Mit einem letzten brennenden Kuß erweckt er die Fezzanerin,
Und plötzlich dann mit wildem Fluch in's Unwirthbare stürzt
           er hin.


Sie aber sieht sich wundernd um. — Ha, was ist das? —
           „Du schläfst, Gemahl?
Der Himmel, der von Erze schien — sieh' da, er kleidet
           sich in Stahl!

He closed the rear; the courser fell, and cast him off
and fled away;
All panting to his girdle hangs his favourite wife, in
wild deray;
How flashed her eye, as, raised to selle, at dawn she
smiled upon her lord!
Now through the waste he drags her on, as from a
baldric trails a sword!

The sultry sand that but by night the lion's shaggy
tail beats down
The hair of yonder helpless thing now sweeps, in
tangled tresses strown;
It gathers in her flow of locks, burns up her sweet
lips' spicy dew;
Its cruel flints, with sanguine streaks, her tender drag-
ging limbs embrew.

And now the stronger Emir fails! with boiling blood
his pulses strain;
His eye is gorged, and on his brow, blue glistening,
beats the throbbing vein;
With one devouring kiss, his last, he wakes the drooping Moorish child;
Then flings himself with furious curse down on the red
unsheltered wild.

But she, amazed, looks round her: — Ha! what sight?
My lord, awake! behold,
The Heaven, that seemed all brazen, how, like steel,
it glimmers, clear and cold!

22 *

Wo blieb der Wüste lodernd Gelb? — wohin ich schaue,
　　　　　　　　blendend Licht!
Es ist ein Schimmern, wie des Meers, das sich an Algiers
　　　　　　　　Küste bricht!

Es blitzt und brandet wie ein Strom; es leckt herüber feucht
　　　　　　　　und kühl!
Ein ries'ger Spiegel funkelt es; wach' auf, es ist vielleicht
　　　　　　　　der Nil!
Doch nein, wir zogen südwärts ja; — so ist es wohl der
　　　　　　　　Senegal?
Wie, oder wär' es gar das Meer mit seiner Wasser sprüh'n=
　　　　　　　　dem Schwall?

Gleichviel! 's ist Wasser ja! Wach auf! Am Boden schon
　　　　　　　　liegt mein Gewand.
Wach' auf, o Herr, und laß uns ziehn, und löschen unsrer
　　　　　　　　Leiber Brand!
Ein frischer Trunk, ein stärkend Bad, und uns durchsiedet
　　　　　　　　neue Kraft!
Die Veste drüben, hochgethürmt, beschließe bald die Wander=
　　　　　　　　schaft!

Um ihre grauen Thore fliegt scharlachner Fahnen trotzig
　　　　　　　　Wehn:
Von Lanzen starrt ihr schart'ger Rand, und ihre Mitte von
　　　　　　　　Moskeen;
Auf ihrer Rhede tummelt sich hochmast'ger Schiffe stolze
　　　　　　　　Reih',
Und jene Pilger füllen ihr Bazar und Karavanserai.

The desert's yellow glare is lost! all round the dazzling
       light appears, —
It is a glitter like the sea's, that with its breakers
       rocks Algiers!

It surges, sparkles, like a stream! I scent its moisture
       cool from hence;
A wide-spread mirror yonder gleams! awake! it is the
       Nile, perchance.
Yet no! we travelled south, indeed: — then surely
       'tis the Senegal, —
Or, can it be the ocean free, whose billows yonder rise
       and fall?

What matter? Still 'tis water! Wake! My cloak's al-
       ready flung away, —
Awake, my lord! and let us on, — this deadly scorch-
       ing to allay!
A cooling draught, a freshening bath, with life anew
       will nerve our limbs,
To reach yon fortress towering high, that distance
       now with rack bedims.

I see around its portals gray the crimson banners,
       waving, set;
Its battled ramparts rough with spears; its hold with
       mosque and minaret;
All in its roads, with lofty masts, slow rocking, many
       a galley lies;
Our travellers crowd its rich bazaars, and fill its
       caravanscrais.

Geliebter, meine Zunge lechzt! wach' auf, schon naht die
      Dämmerung!" —
Noch einmal hob er seinen Blick; dann sagt' er dumpf:
      „die Spiegelung!
Ein Blendwerk, ärger als der Smum! bösart'ger Geister
      Zeitvertreib." —
Er schwieg — das Meteor verschwand — auf seine Leiche
      sank das Weib!

— Im Hafen von Venedig so von seiner Heimath sprach der
      Mohr;
Des Feldherrn Rede strömte süß in Desdemonens gierig Ohr.
Auffuhr sie, als das Fahrzeug nun an's Ufer stieß mit
      jähem Stoß —
Er führte schweigend zum Palast das einz'ge Kind Braban-
      tio's.

## Der Liebe Dauer.

O lieb', so lang du lieben kannst!
   O lieb', so lang du lieben magst!
   Die Stunde kommt, die Stunde kommt,
   Wo du an Gräbern stehst und klagst!

Und sorge, daß dein Herze glüht
   Und Liebe hegt und Liebe trägt,
   So lang' ihm noch ein ander Herz
   In Liebe warm entgegenschlägt!

Beloved! I am faint with thirst! wake up! the twilight
nears. Alas!
He raised his eye once more, and groaned, — It is the
desert's mocking glass!
A cheat, the play of spiteful fiends, more cruel than
the Smoom. — All hoarse,
He stopped: — the vision fades! she sank, — the
dying girl, upon his corse!

— Thus of his native land the Moor in Venice haven
oft would tell:
On Desdemona's eager ear, the Captain's story thrilling
fell.
She started, as the gondola jarred on the quay with
trembling prow:
He, silent, to her palace led the Heiress of Brabantio.

## LOVE'S DURATION.

(From the "Hermann," of June 15th. 1868.)

O love, as long as love thou canst!
As long as love's pure flame will burn!
The hour will come, the hour will come,
When, bent o'er graves, thou'lt weep and mourn.

Thy heart — O let it ever feel
Love's sweetest tendrils round it twine,
As long as on the earth one heart
Responsive beats with love to thine!

Und wer dir seine Brust erschließt,
   O thu' ihm, was du kannst, zu lieb!
   Und mach' ihm jede Stunde froh,
   Und mach' ihm keine Stunde trüb!

Und hüte deine Zunge wohl,
   Bald ist ein böses Wort gesagt!
   O Gott, es war nicht bös gemeint, —
   Der Andre aber geht und klagt.

O lieb', so lang du lieben kannst!
   O lieb', so lang du lieben magst!
   Die Stunde kommt, die Stunde kommt,
   Wo du an Gräbern stehst und klagst!

Dann kniest du nieder an der Gruft,
   Und birgst die Augen, trüb und naß
   — Sie sehn den Andern nimmermehr —
   In's lange, feuchte Kirchhofsgras.

Und sprichst: O schau' auf mich herab,
   Der hier an deinem Grabe weint!
   Vergib, daß ich gekränkt dich hab'!
   O Gott, es war nicht bös gemeint!

Er aber sieht und hört dich nicht,
   Kommt nicht, daß du ihn oft umfängst,
   Der Mund, der oft dich küßte, spricht
   Nie wieder: ich vergab dir längst!

For him, who opes his breast to thee,
O let thy heart with kindness glow!
Turn every hour of his to joy —
Nor for a moment cloud his brow.


Guard still thy tongue; a thoughtless word
Oft leaves a sting — a bitter smart;
For, though perchance no harm is meant,
Thy friend may leave with wounded heart.


O love, as long as love thou canst!
As long as love's pure flame will burn!
The hour will, come, the hour will come,
When, bent o'er graves, thou'lt weep and mourn.


With downcast eyes, bedimm'd with tears —
Thy friend they ne'er will look upon —
Thou'lt kneel upon the grassy mound
Beside the cold, cold lifeless stone,


And cry: on him who prostrate lies
Look loving down from realms above!
Forgive, if e'er I gave thee pain!
I did not mean to slight thy love.


He cannot see thee—cannot hear —
To meet thy fond embrace comes not —.
The lips, so often pressed to thine,
Will never say: 'tis long forgot.

Er that's, vergab dir lange schon,
  Doch manche heiße Thräne fiel
Um dich und um dein herbes Wort —
  Doch still — er ruht, er ist am Ziel!

O lieb', so lang du lieben kannst!
  O lieb', so lang du lieben magst!
Die Stunde kommt, die Stunde kommt,
  Wo du an Gräbern stehst und klagst!

## Westfälisches Sommerlied.
### — 1866. —

Bei Wetterschein und Regenguß,
  Und in der Sonne Strahlen,
Wie thust du freudig, Schuß auf Schuß
  Du Saat im Land Westfahlen!
Du Hellwegsroggen schlank und schwank,
Korn sieben Fuß und drüber lang,
  Wie herrlich stehst und reifst du!

„Ich reif' und wachse mit Gewalt;
  Es trieft das Jahr von Segen;
Vollauf zu sätt'gen Jung und Alt
  Reif' ich an allen Wegen.
Doch weißt du nicht, o Wandersmann,
Daß heuer mich nicht ernten kann,
  Wer frohen Muths mich sä'te?

He did forgive thee — years have passed —
Yet many a sigh burst from his breast
O'er thee and o'er thy thoughtless word —
But hush! he sleeps, he is at rest!

O love, as long as love thou canst!
As long as love's pure flame will burn!
The hour will come — the hour will come,
When, bent o'er graves, thou'lt weep and mourn!

## WESTPHALIAN SUMMER SONG.
### — 1866. —

Translated by Mrs. E. Kroeker, née Freiligrath.

In lightning and in summer's rain,
In noon-sun hot and glowing,
Full gaily, O Westphalia's grain
Art shooting up and growing!
Old Hellweg's rye, so lithe and strong,
Seven feet and more thy stems are long,
How gloriously dost ripen!

"I grow and ripen fast and strong,
The year with gifts is mellow,
To satisfy both old and young
I ripen rich and yellow.
But dost thou not, O wanderer! know
That he who joyfully did sow
Can never cut and reap me?'

„Hinaus durch meiner Aehren Rauch,
Hinaus .in Reih'n und Rotten,
Die Faust geballt, die Thrän' im Aug',
Zog er von Kamp uns Kotten;
Die Trommel rief ihn und das Horn:
Er soll des deutschen Bruders Korn
Im Bruderkrieg zerstampfen.

„Wer holt denn nun zum Erntetanz
Die schmucken Dirnen heuer?
O weh! wer schwingt den Erntekranz,
Wer pflanzt ihn auf die Scheuer?
Es ist ein Schnitter, der heißt Tod,
Der mäht dies Jahr mit Kraut und Loth —
Ich weiß, wer ihn gedungen!

„Es singt ein Vöglein auf der Haar:
Am Elbstrom und am Maine,
Da liegt, der hier ein Pflüger war,
Erschlagen auf dem Raine;
Er war der Seinen Stolz und Lust,
Ein Bruder schoß ihn durch die Brust! —
Ich rausche leis im Winde!"

"Forth through my swaying ears he went,
    In rank and order starting,
With clenched fist and head low bent
    From house and home departing;
Loud summoned by the drum and horn
He goes to crush his brother's corn
    In brother-war unhallowed.

"Who, then, for this year's harvest-home
    Will fetch the girls to foot it?
Alas! who'll wave the harvest-wreath?
    Upon the barn who'll put it?
The reaper's name is Death, I wot,
He mows this year with grape and shot;
    Well know I who has hired him.

"A little bird sings on the Haar:
    Where Elbe and Maine are hieing,
There he who was a ploughboy here
    All stiff and stark is lying.
His homestead's pride, forth did he go;
A brother's bullet laid him low! —
    I rustle to the breezes."

# MISCELLANEOUS AUTHORS.

---

# Vermisches.

# Aennchen von Tharau.

## Simon Dach.

Aennchen von Tharau ist's, die mir gefällt,
Sie ist mein Leben, mein Gut und mein Geld.

Aennchen von Tharau hat wieder ihr Herz
Auf mich gerichtet in Lieb' und in Schmerz.

Aennchen von Tharau, mein Reichthum, mein Gut,
Du meine Seele, mein Fleisch und mein Blut!

Käm' alles Wetter gleich auf uns zu schlahn,
Wir sind gesinnt, bei einander zu stahn.

Krankheit, Verfolgung, Betrübniß und Pein
Soll unsrer Liebe Verknotigung sein.

Recht als ein Palmbaum hoch über sich steigt,
Je mehr ihn Hagel und Regen ansicht;

So wird die Lieb' in uns mächtig und groß,
Durch Kreuz, durch Leiden, durch allerlei Noth.

# ANNIE OF THARAW.

Translated by Henry W. Longfellow.

Annie of Tharaw, my true love of old,
She is my life, and my goods, and my gold.

Annie of Tharaw, her heart once again
To me has surrendered in joy and in pain.

Annie of Tharaw, my riches, my good,
Thou, O my soul, my flesh and my blood!

Then come the wild weather, come sleet or come snow,
We will stand by each other, however it blow.

Oppression, and sickness, and sorrow, and pain
Shall be to our true love as links to the chain.

As the palm-tree standeth so straight and so tall,
The more the hail beats, and the more the rains fall, —

So love in our hearts shall grow mighty and strong,
Through crosses, through sorrows, through manifold
wrong.

Würdeſt du gleich einmal von mir getrennt,
Lebteſt da, wo man die Sonne kaum kennt:

Ich will dir folgen durch Wälder und Meer,
Durch Eis, durch Eiſen, durch feindliches Heer.

Aennchen von Tharau, meine Luſt, meine Sonn',
Mein Leben ſchließ' ich um deines herum.

---

## Arion.

### A. W. von Schlegel
geboren 1767; geſtorben 1845.

Arion war der Töne Meiſter,
Die Cither lebt' in ſeiner Hand!
Damit ergötzt' er alle Geiſter,
Und gern empfing ihn jedes Land.
　　Er ſchiffte goldbeladen
　　Jetzt von Tarents Geſtaden,
Zum ſchönen Hellas heimgewandt.

Zum Freunde zieht ihn ſein Verlangen,
Ihn liebt der Herrſcher von Korinth.
Eh' in die Fremd' er ausgegangen,
Bat er ihn, brüderlich geſinnt:
　　Laß dir's in meinen Hallen
　　Doch ruhig wohlgefallen,
Viel kann verlieren, wer gewinnt.

Should'st thou be torn from me to wander alone
In a desolate land where the sun is scarce known, —

Through forests I'll follow, and where the sea flows,
Through ice, and through iron, through armies of foes.

Annie of Tharaw, my light and my sun,
The threads of our two lives are woven in one.

## ARION.

Translated by D. F. Maccarthy.

A master of melodious sound
   Arion was, and in his hand
The cithern lived: joy scattering round
   Him warmly welcomed every land.
      A thousand golden gifts he bore,
      And now from fair Tarentum's shore
Hies home to Hellas' lovelier strand.

Friends charmed him back, for he was loved
   By Corinth's prince, its noblest son,
Who, ere to stranger lands he roved,
   Had done what brother might have done,
      Had said, "within my royal halls
      Here take thy rest, whate'er befalls,
He much may lose, who much hath won."

23*

Arion sprach: „Ein wandernd Leben
Gefällt der freien Dichterbrust.
Die Kunst, die mir ein Gott gegeben,
Sie sei auch vieler Tausend Lust.
　　An wohlerworbnen Gaben
　　Wie werd' ich einst mich laben,
Des weiten Ruhmes froh bewußt!"

Er steht im Schiff am zweiten Morgen,
Die Lüfte wehen lind und warm,
„O Periander, eitle Sorgen!
Vergiß sie nun in meinem Arm!
　　Wir wollen mit Geschenken
　　Die Götter reich bedenken,
Und jubeln in der Gäste Schwarm."

Es bleiben Wind und See gewogen,
Auch nicht ein fernes Wölkchen graut;
Er hat nicht allzuviel den Wogen,
Den Menschen allzuviel vertraut.
　　Er hört die Schiffer flüstern,
　　Nach seinen Schätzen lüstern;
Doch bald umringen sie ihn laut.

„Du darfst, Arion, nicht mehr leben:
Begehrst du auf dem Land ein Grab,
So mußt du hier den Tod dir geben,
Sonst wirf dich in das Meer hinab." —
　　So wollt ihr mich verderben?
　　Ihr mögt mein Gold erwerben,
Ich kaufe gern mein Blut euch ab. —

Arion spoke: "A wandering fate
　　Best suits the poet's free-born breast,
The art, a god hath delegate
　　To me, may make even myriads blest.
　　　　Oh! how shall I enjoy one day
　　　　The well-won gifts: for then I may,
　　Of glory and the crown possest."

He stands on deck the second morn,
　　The air blows round him soft and warm;
"O Periander! cares vain-born
　　Of fear forget within my arm.
　　　　We to the gods with offerings rare
　　　　Will show our gratitude, and share
　　Our joy with guests in countless swarm."

The wind and wave fraternal touch
　　Each other, even the clouds look gay;
The waves he trusteth not too much,
　　'Tis men he trusts too much to-day.
　　　　He hears the seamen whispering low —
　　　　With greedy eyes that gloat and glow,
　　They round him come, and loudly say;

"No longer hast thou got to live,
　　Arion; if an earthly grave
Thou car'st for, here thy death-blow give,
　　Else plunge thee headlong in the wave."
　　　　"And will ye thus my life destroy?
　　　　My gold ye freely may enjoy.
　　My blood I'll buy with all I have".

„Nein, nein, wir lassen dich nicht wandern,
Du wärst ein zu gefährlich Haupt.
Wo blieben wir vor Periandern,
Verriethst du, daß wir dich beraubt?
　　　　Uns kann dein Gold nicht frommen,
　　　　Wenn wieder heimzukommen
Uns nimmermehr die Furcht erlaubt." —

„Gewährt mir dann noch eine Bitte,
Gilt, mich zu retten, kein Vertrag,
Daß ich nach Citherspieler-Sitte,
Wie ich gelebet, sterben mag.
　　　　Wann ich mein Lied gesungen,
　　　　Die Saiten ausgeklungen,
Dann fahre hin des Lebens Tag."

Die Bitte kann sie nicht beschämen,
Sie denken nur an den Gewinn,
Doch solchen Sänger zu vernehmen,
Das reizet ihren wilden Sinn.
　　　　„Und wollt ihr ruhig lauschen,
　　　　Laßt mich die Kleider tauschen:
Im Schmuck nur reißt Apoll mich hin." —

Der Jüngling hüllt die schönen Glieder
In Gold und Purpur wunderbar.
Bis auf die Sohlen wallt hernieder
Ein leichter, faltiger Talar;
　　　　Die Arme zieren Spangen,
　　　　Um Hals und Stirn und Wangen
Fliegt duftend das bekränzte Haar.

"No, no, we cannot let thee wander,
  Thou hast too dangerous a soul;
How would we fare with Periander,
  If thou couldst say, my gold they stole?
    The pleasure of our promised joy
    The fear of that would all destroy,
  When anchored we had reached the goal."

"Then grant to me one boon, I pray,
  Since I cannot my ransom buy;
'Tis this, that as I've lived, I may
  A simple cithern-player die:
    When I my farewell-song have sung,
    And left the silent chords unstrung,
  Then life, and light, and love, good-bye".

Through shame they grant so slight a thing,
  Sure of the gain of their offence;
To hear so sweet a singer sing
  Seems even to charm their savage sense.
    "And would you hear my song with ease,
    Oh! let me change such clothes as these,
  For robed the god would snatch me hence."

The youth his limbs of loveliest mould
  Enwraps in gold and purple fair,
Even to his feet falls fold on fold
  A robe as light as summer air;
    His arms rich golden bracelets deck,
    And round his brow, and cheeks, and neck
In fragrance floats the leaf-crowned hair.

Die Cither ruht in seiner Linken,
Die Rechte hält das Elfenbein;
Er scheint erquickt die Luft zu trinken,
Er strahlt im Morgensonnenschein.
　　Es staunt der Schiffer Bande;
　　Er schreitet vorn zum Rande,
Und sieht in's blaue Meer hinein.

Er sang: „Gefährtin meiner Stimme!
Komm, folge mir in's Schattenreich!
Ob auch der Höllenhund ergrimme,
Die Macht der Töne zähmt ihn gleich.
　　Elysiums Heroen,
　　Dem dunkeln Strom entflohen,
Ihr friedlichen, schon grüß' ich euch!

Doch könnt ihr mich des Grams entbinden?
Ich lasse meinen Freund zurück,
Du gingst Eurydicen zu finden;
Der Hades barg dein süßes Glück.
　　Da wie ein Traum zerronnen
　　Was dir dein Lied gewonnen,
Verfluchtest du der Sonne Blick.

Ich muß hinab, ich will nicht zagen!
Die Götter schauen aus der Höh'.
Die ihr mich wehrlos habt erschlagen,
Erblasset, wenn ich untergeh'!
　　Den Gast, zu euch gebettet,
　　Ihr Nereiden, rettet!"
So sprang er in die tiefe See.

His left hand doth the cithern bear,
  His right the plectrum's ivory key;
He seems revived to drink the air,
  In morning's sunshine fair to see.
    The sailor-band with wonder stare,
    He to the stern strides on, and there
Looks down upon the dark blue sea.

He sang, "Companion of my voice,
  Down to the shade-world follow me,
For even the hell-hound hath no choice
  But charmed by music's power must be;
    Elysium's heroes, who have fled
    Enfranchised o'er the field of dread,
Ye calm, already greet I ye.

"But can ye not this coil unbind?
  I leave my friend and plunge in night,
Thou wentst Eurydice to find,
  For Hades held thy soul's delight,
    There as a dream whose course is run
    Was lost the prize thy song had won,
How cursed thou then the sunshine's light!"

"Down must I go, I'll tremble not,
  The gods are looking from on high,
Me here defenceless ye have caught,
  But ye will pale to see me die.
    O Nereids of the dark blue sea,
    Protect the guest who trusteth ye!"
Then sprang he mid the deep sea nigh.

Ihn decken alsobald die Wogen;
Die sichern Schiffer segeln fort.
Delphine waren nachgezogen,
Als lockte sie ein Zauberwort:
    Eh' Fluthen ihn ersticken,
    Beut einer ihm den Rücken
Und trägt ihn sorgsam hin zum Port.

Des Meers verworrenes Gebrause
Ward stummen Fischen nur verliehn;
Doch lockt Musik aus salz'gem Hause
Zu frohen Sprüngen den Delphin.
    Sie konnt' ihn oft bestricken,
    Mit sehnsuchtsvollen Blicken
Dem falschen Jäger nachzuziehn.

So trägt den Sänger mit Entzücken
Das menschenliebend sinn'ge Thier.
Er schwebt auf dem gewölbten Rücken,
Hält im Triumph der Leier Zier;
    Und kleine Wellen springen
    Wie nach der Saiten Klingen
Rings in dem bläulichen Revier.

Wo der Delphin sich sein entladen,
Der ihn gerettet uferwärts,
Da wird dereinst in Felsgestaden
Das Wunder aufgestellt in Erz.
    Jetzt, da sich jeder trennte
    Zu seinem Elemente,
Grüßt ihn Arions volles Herz.

The waves closed o'er him blue and black,
  The crew breathed free, the wind blew fair,
But dolphins followed in his track
  As if a spell had fixed them there,
    And ere the flood had gulped him down
    One bore him on his broad back brown
Safe towards the port with tender care.

The roaring sea, the rushing wave,
  Are given to silent fish for aye;
Still music from his salt sea cave
  Can lure the dolphin up to play —
    Can lure him oft with longing eyes
    To follow where the false ship flies,
Swift-speeding on its homeward way.

And so the gentle brute and wise,
  The singer bears in joyful trance,
Upon his vaulted back he lies,
  The cithern proudly in advance,
    And little waves in widening rings
    Arise beneath the twinkling strings,
Outspreading o'er the blue expanse.

The dolphin the dear weight it bore
  Safe landed from the rocks apart,
'Twas where, years after, on that shore
  In bronze this tale was told by Art.
    And as they each asunder went
    Back to their separate element,
Thus spoke Arions grateful heart:

„Leb' wohl und könnt' ich dich belohnen,
Du treuer, freundlicher Delphin!
Du kannst nur hier, ich dort nur wohnen:
Gemeinschaft ist uns nicht verliehn.
　　　Dich wird auf feuchten Spiegeln
　　　Noch Galatea zügeln,
Du wirst sie stolz und heilig ziehn."


Arion eilt nun leicht von hinnen,
Wie einst er in die Fremde fuhr;
Schon glänzen ihm Korinthus Zinnen,
Er wandelt sinnend durch die Flur.
　　　Mit Lieb' und Lust geboren,
　　　Vergißt er, was verloren,
Bleibt ihm der Freund, die Cither nur.


Er tritt hinein: „Vom Wanderleben
Nun ruh' ich, Freund, an deiner Brust.
Die Kunst, die mir ein Gott gegeben,
Sie wurde vieler Tausend Lust.
　　　Zwar falsche Räuber haben
　　　Die wohlerworbnen Gaben;
Doch bin ich mir des Ruhms bewußt."


Dann spricht er von den Wunderdingen,
Daß Periander staunend horcht:
„Soll Jenen solch ein Raub gelingen?
Ich hätt' umsonst die Macht geborgt.
　　　Die Thäter zu entdecken,
　　　Mußt du dich hier verstecken,
So nahn sie sich wohl unbesorgt." —

"Thee can I not reward! Farewell,
  Farewell, thou dolphin true and kind,
Thou here, I there could never dwell;
  No life in common could we find,
    Thee still upon the glassy main
    Will Galatea gently rein,
  Thou her wilt draw through wave and wind."

Arion, lightly as in hours
  When hence he roamed, returns again.
Already glisten Corinth's towers,
  He wanders singing o'er the plain;
    The child of love and pleasure,
    He heeds not his lost treasure,
  His friend, his cithern still remain.

He steppeth on. "No longer driven
  World-wandering, friend, I seek thy breast,
The art, to me a god hath given,
  Hath made a many a thousand blest.
    True, robbers rapine-swollen
    The well won gifts have stolen,
  Still of my fame am I possest."

Then tells he the astounding story
  In Periander's wandering ear —
"In vain were all my power and glory,
  If theft like this should prosper here;
    The guilty to discover
    Here rest thee under cover,
  For sure of safety they'll draw near."

Und als im Hafen Schiffer kommen,
Bescheidet er sie zu sich her.
„Habt vom Arion ihr vernommen?
Mich kümmert seine Wiederkehr."
     „Wir ließen recht im Glücke
     Ihn zu Tarent zurücke." —
Da, siehe! tritt Arion her.

Gehüllt sind seine schönen Glieder
In Gold und Purpur wunderbar,
Bis auf die Sohlen wallt hernieder
Ein leichter faltiger Talar;
     Die Arme zieren Spangen,
     Um Hals und Stirn und Wangen
Fliegt duftend das bekränzte Haar.

Die Cither ruht in seiner Linken,
Die Rechte hält das Elfenbein,
Sie müssen ihm zu Füßen sinken,
Es trifft sie wie des Blitzes Schein.
     „Ihn wollten wir ermorden;
     Er ist zum Gotte worden:
O schläng' uns nur die Erd' hinein!" —

„Er lebet noch, der Töne Meister,
Der Sänger steht in heil'ger Hut.
Ich rufe nicht der Rache Geister,
Arion will nicht euer Blut.
     Fern mögt ihr zu Barbaren,
     Des Geizes Knechte, fahren;
Nie labe Schönes euren Muth."

Full soon in port the bark is lying,
  He bids the crew before him come :
"What tidings have ye of Arion?
  I long for his returning home."
    "In luck the gods have sent him ;
    We left him at Tarentum."
Forth steps Arion,—they are dumb.

He hides his limbs of loveliest mould
  In gold and purple wondrous fair ;
Even to his feet falls fold on fold
  A robe as light as summer air ;
    His arms rich golden bracelets deck,
    And round his brow, and cheeks, and neck
In fragrance floats the leaf-crowned hair.

His left hand holds the cithern sweet,
  The ivory bow is in his right ;
They must fall down before his feet
  As strucken, by the lightning's light.
    "A god ! we thought to slay him —
    A god ! for waves obey him —
O Earth ! conceal us from his sight."

"The minstrel lives, nor think it strange —
  The singer stands in holy care ;
Not his the spirit of revenge,
  Your lives Arion deigns to spare.
    To Barbary's congenial clay
    Ye slaves of Avarice, away !
And ne'er may Beauty be your share."

## Des Schiffers Traum.

Ernst Moritz Arndt
geboren 1769; gestorben 1860.

Es heult der Sturm, die Woge schäumt,
　Und durch die Wolken fahren Blitze,
Der alte Schiffer nickt und träumt
　Gar ruhig auf dem nassen Sitze:
Wie wild um ihn die Woge schlägt,
　Wie auf und ab das Schifflein schaukelt,
Ein Traum, der süße Bilder trägt,
　Umspielt sein Haupt und scherzt und gaukelt.

Ein Eiland hebt er hell und schön
　Mit reichen Fluren aus den Wogen,
Ein wundervolles Lenzgetön
　Aus Blüthenhainen kommt's geflogen —
Der Alte ruft: „Hier legt an's Land,
　Hier in die Bucht, den stillen Hafen!
O kommst du endlich, Friedensstand?
　Wie will ich süß nach Stürmen schlafen"

Da schießt aus schwarzer Nacht ein Strahl,
　Ein glühnder Gottespfeil, von oben,
Der Schiffer und das Schiff zumal
　Mit Mann und Maus sie sind zerstoben;
Die wilde Woge treibt zum Strand,
　Treibt Trümmer und Leichen treu zum Hafen.
Glückseliger Träumer! du hast Land,
　Nun kannst du süß nach Stürmen schlafen.

# THE SEAMAN'S DREAM.

### Translated by the Rev. W. W. Skeat.

Foam crests the waves, the storm-cloud lowers,
  Athwart dark skies the lightning gleams;
Yet, stretched on deck 'mid spray and showers,
  An aged seaman nods and dreams.
Tho' wildly round the waters swell,
  Tho' to and fro the vessel rocks,
A dream with sweet alluring spell,
  Too bright for truth, his vision mocks.

He marks, from out the foaming seas,
  An island rise, with verdure crowned;
From flowery groves sweet melodies
  Burst forth with soul-entrancing sound.
"Behold", he cries, "the happy shore!
  Our port, our long-wished haven see!
At length comes rest; wild storms no more
  Shall rage, and sweet my sleep shall be!"

Thro' night's thick gloom a lightning-flash,
  God's flaming dart, shoots down from heaven;
'Mid anguished cries, with deafening crash,
  The gallant ship in twain is riven.
Black spars and corpses high on shore
  Are scattered by the rolling sea —
Thy port is gained, storms rage no more:
  Fond dreamer, sweet thy sleep shall be!

## Frauen-Liebe und Leben.
### Adalbert von Chamisso
geboren 1781; gestorben 1833.

### 1.

Seit ich ihn gesehen,
Glaub' ich blind zu sein.
Wo ich hin nur blicke,
Seh' ich ihn allein.
Wie in wachem Traume
Schwebt sein Bild mir vor,
Taucht aus tiefstem Dunkel
Heller nur empor.

Sonst ist licht und farblos
Alles um mich her,
Nach der Schwestern Spiele
Nicht begehr' ich mehr,
Möchte lieber weinen
Still im Kämmerlein;
Seit ich ihn gesehen,
Glaub' ich blind zu sein

### 2.

Er der herrlichste von allen,
Wie so milde, wie so gut!
Holde Lippen, klares Auge,
Hellen Sinn und festen Muth.

## WOMAN'S LOVE AND LIFE.

Translated by Dr. Alfred Baskerville.

### 1.

Since mine eyes beheld him,
　Blind I seem to be:
Wheresoe'er they wander,
　Him alone they see.
Round me glows his image,
　In a waking dream,
From the darkness rising,
　Brighter doth it beam.

All is drear and gloomy
　That around me lies,
Now my sisters' pastimes
　I no longer prize;
In my chamber rather
　Would I weep alone;
Since mine eyes beheld him,
　Blind methinks I'm grown.

### 2.

He, the best of all, the noblest,
　O how gentle! O how kind!
Lips of sweetness, eyes of brightness,
　Steadfast courage, lucid mind!

24 *

So wie dort in blauer Tiefe,
Hell und herrlich, jener Stern,
Also er an meinem Himmel
Hell und herrlich, hoch und fern.

Wandle, wandle deine Bahnen;
Nur betrachten deinen Schein;
Nur in Demuth ihn betrachten,
Selig nur und traurig sein.

Höre nicht mein stilles Beten,
Deinem Glücke nur geweiht;
Darfst mich, niedre Magd, nicht kennen,
Hoher Stern der Herrlichkeit!

Nur die Würdigste von allen
Soll beglücken deine Wahl,
Und ich will die Hohe segnen,
Segnen viele tausend Mal.

Will mich freuen dann und weinen,
Selig, selig bin ich dann,
Sollte mir das Herz auch brechen,
Brich, o Herz, was liegt daran!


### 3.

Ich kann's nicht fassen, nicht glauben,
Es hat ein Traum mich berückt;
Wie hätt' er doch unter allen
Mich Arme erhöht und beglückt?

As on high, in Heaven's azure,
  Bright and splendid, beams yon star,
Thus he in my heaven beameth,
  Bright and splendid, high and far.

Wander, wander where thou listest:
  I will gaze but on thy beam,
With humility behold it,
  In a sad, yet blissful dream.

Hear me not thy bliss imploring
  With prayer's silent eloquence!
Know me not, a lowly maiden,
  Star of proud magnificence!

May thy choice be rendered happy
  By the worthiest alone!
And I'll call a thousand blessings
  Down on her exalted throne.

Then I'll weep with tears of gladness,
  Happy, happy then my lot!
If my heart should rive asunder,
  Break, O heart, it matters not!


### 3.

Is it true? O, I cannot believe it,
  A dream doth my senses enthrall;
O can he have made me so happy,
  And exalted me thus above all?

Mir war's, er habe gesprochen:
„Ich bin auf ewig dein" —
Mir war's — ich träume noch immer,
Es kann ja nimmer so sein.

O laß im Traume mich sterben,
Gewieget an seiner Brust,
Den seligsten Tod mich schlürfen
In Thränen unendlicher Lust.

### 4.

Helft mir, ihr Schwestern,
Freundlich mich schmücken,
Dient der Glücklichen heute mir.
Windet geschäftig
Mir um die Stirne
Noch der blühenden Myrte Zier.

Als ich befriedigt,
Freudiges Herzens,
Dem Geliebten im Arme lag,
Immer noch rief er,
Sehnsucht im Herzen,
Ungeduldig den heutigen Tag.

Helft mir, ihr Schwestern,
Helft mir verscheuchen
Eine thörichte Bangigkeit!
Daß ich mit klarem
Aug' ihn empfange,
Ihn, die Quelle der Freudigkeit.

Meseems as if he had spoken,
  "I am thine, ever faithful and true!"
Meseems — O still am I dreaming,
  It cannot, it cannot be true!

O fain would I, rocked on his bosom,
  In the sleep of eternity lie,
That death were indeed the most blissful,
  In the rapture of weeping to die.

### 4.

  Help me, ye sisters,
  Kindly to deck me,
Me, O the happy one, aid me this morn!
  Let the light finger
  Twine the sweet myrtle's
Blossoming garland, my brow to adorn!

  As on the bosom
  Of my beloved one,
Wrapt in the bliss of contentment, I lay,
  He, with soft longing
  In his heart thrilling.
Ever impatiently sighed for to-day.

  Aid me, ye sisters,
  Aid me to banish
Foolish anxieties, timid, and coy,
  That I with sparkling
  Eye may receive him,
Him the bright fountain of rapture and joy.

Bist, mein Geliebter,
Du mir erschienen
Gibst du, Sonne, mir deinen Schein?
Laß mich in Andacht,
Laß mich in Demuth
Mich verneigen dem Herren mein.


Streuet ihm, Schwestern,
Streuet ihm Blumen,
Bringt ihm knospende Rosen dar;
Aber euch, Schwestern,
Grüß' ich mit Wehmuth,
Freudig scheidend aus eurer Schaar.


### 5.

Süßer Freund, du blickest
Mich verwundert an;
Kannst es nicht begreifen,
Wie ich weinen kann!
Laß der feuchten Perlen
Ungewohnte Zier
Freudenhell erzittern
In den Wimpern mir.


Wie so bang mein Busen,
Wie so wonnevoll!
Wüßt' ich nur mit Worten
Wie ich's sagen soll!

Do I behold thee,
Thee, my beloved one,
Dost thou, O´sun, shed thy beams upon me?
Let me devoutly,
Let me in meekness
Bend to my lord and my master the knee!

Strew, ye fair sisters,
Flowers before him,
Cast budding roses around at his feet!
Joyfully quitting
Now your bright circle,
You, lovely sisters, with sadness I greet.


5.

Dearest friend, thou lookest
On me with surprise,
Dost thou wonder, wherefore
Tears suffuse mine eyes?
Let the dewy pearl-drops
Like rare gems appear,
Trembling, bright with gladness,
In their crystal sphere.


With what anxious raptures
Doth my bosom swell!
O had I but language
What I feel to tell!

Komm und birg dein Antlitz
Hier an meiner Brust;
Will in's Ohr dir flüstern
Alle meine Lust.

Weißt du nun die Thränen,
Die ich weinen kann,
Sollst du nicht sie sehen,
Du geliebter Mann;
Bleib an meinem Herzen,
Fühle dessen Schlag,
Daß ich fest und fester
Nur dich drücken mag.

Hier an meinem Bette
Hat die Wiege Raum,
Wo sie still verberge
Meinen holden Traum;
Kommen wird der Morgen,
Wo der Traum erwacht,
Und daraus dein Bildniß
Mir entgegenlacht.


### 6.

An meinem Herzen, an meiner Brust,
Du meine Wonne, du meine Lust!
Das Glück ist die Liebe, die Lieb' ist das Glück.
Ich hab' es gesagt und nehm's nicht zurück.
Hab' überglücklich mich geschätzt,
Bin überglücklich aber jetzt.

Come and hide thy face, love,
  Here upon my breast,
In thine ear I'll whisper
  Why I am so blest.

Now the tears thou knowest
  Which my joy confessed,
Thou shalt not behold them,
  Thou, my dearest, best;
Linger on my bosom,
  Feel its throbbing tide.
Let me press thee firmly,
  Firmly to my side!

Here may rest the cradle,
  Close my couch beside,
Where it may in silence
  My sweet vision hide;
Soon will come the morning,
  When my dream will wake,
And thy smiling image
  Will to life awake.

## 6.

Upon my heart, and upon my breast,
  Thou joy o all joys, my sweetest, best!
Bliss, thou art love, O love, thou art bliss,
  I've said it, and seal it here with a kiss.
I thought no happiness mine could exceed,
  But now I am happy, O happy indeed!

Nur die da säugt, nur die da liebt
Das Kind, dem sie die Nahrung giebt.
Nur eine Mutter weiß allein,
Was lieben heißt und glücklich sein.
O wie bedaur' ich doch den Mann,
Der Mutterglück nicht fühlen kann!
Du schaust mich an und lächelst dazu,
Du lieber, lieber Engel du!
An meinem Herzen, an meiner Brust,
Du meine Wonne, du meine Lust.

### 7.

Nun hast du mir den ersten Schmerz gethan,
    Der aber traf.
Du schläfst, du harter, unbarmherz'ger Mann,
    Den Todesschlaf.

Es blicket die Verlassene vor sich hin,
    Die Welt ist leer.
Geliebet hab' ich und gelebt, ich bin
    Nicht lebend mehr.

Ich zieh' mich in mein Inn'res still zurück,
    Der Schleier fällt;
Da hab' ich dich und mein vergangnes Glück,
    Du meine Welt.

### 8.

Traum der eignen Tage,
Die nun ferne sind,

She only, who to her bosom hath pressed
   The babe who drinketh life at her breast;
'Tis only a mother the joys can know
   Of love, and real happiness here below.
How I pity man, whose bosom reveals
   No joy like that which a mother feels!
Thou look'st on me, with a smile on thy brow,
   Thou dear, dear little angel, thou!
Upon my heart, and upon my breast,
   Thou joy of all joys, my sweetest, best!

### 7.

Ah! thy first wound hast thou inflicted now,
        But Oh! how deep!
Hard-hearted cruel man, now sleepest thou
        Death's long, long sleep.

I gaze upon the void in silent grief,
        The world is drear,
I've lived and loved, but now the verdant leaf
        Of life is sere.

I will retire within my soul's recess,
        The veil shall fall;
I'll live with thee and my past happiness,
        O thou my all!

### 8.

Dream of days now distant,
Which on me have smiled;

Tochter meiner Tochter,
Du mein süßes Kind,
Nimm, bevor die Müde
Deckt das Leichentuch,
Nimm in's frische Leben
Meinen Segensspruch.

Siehst mich grau von Haaren,
Abgezehrt und bleich,
Bin, wie du, gewesen
Jung und wonnereich;
Liebte wie du liebtest,
Ward, wie du, auch Braut,
Und auch du wirst altern,
So wie ich ergraut.

Laß die Zeit im Fluge
Wandeln fort und fort,
Nur beständig wahre
Deines Busens Hort;
Hab' ich's einst gesprochen,
Nehm' ich's nicht zurück:
Glück ist nur die Liebe,
Liebe nur ist Glück.

Als ich, den ich liebte,
In das Grab gelegt,
Hab' ich meine Liebe
Treu in mir gehegt;

Daughter of my daughter,
Thou, my dearest child.
Ere these weary members
Rest upon the bier,
Take my blessing with thee
On thy young career.

Now thou seest me hoary,
Worn, and wan, and pale,
But I've been as thou art,
Lovely, young, and hale.
Loved, as thou now lovest,
Was a bride, as thou;
Thou, too, wilt grow older,
Grey, as I am now.

Let time ever onwards,
Onwards ever sweep,
But thy bosom's treasure
In thy bosom keep.
Once have I confessed it,
And again I own,
Bliss is only love, and
Love is bliss alone.

When the grave received him,
Over whom I wept,
Faithful in my bosom
E'er my love I kept.

War mein Herz gebrochen,
Blieb mir fest der Muth,
Und des Alters Asche
Wahrt die heil'ge Gluth.

Nimm, bevor die Müde
Deckt das Leichentuch,
Nimm in's frische Leben
Meinen Segensspruch:
Muß das Herz dir brechen,
Bleibe fest dein Muth;
Sei der Schmerz der Liebe
Dann dein höchstes Gut!

## Das Schloß Boncourt.
### Adalbert von Chamisso.

Ich träum' als Kind mich zurücke,
Und schüttle mein greises Haupt!
Wie sucht ihr mich heim, ihr Bilder,
Die lang ich vergessen geglaubt?

Hoch ragt aus schatt'gen Gehegen
Ein schimmerndes Schloß hervor,
Ich kenne die Thürme, die Zinnen,
Die steinerne Brücke, das Thor.

Though my heart was broken,
Faith did not expire,
Still in Age's embers
Glows the sacred fire.

Ere these weary members
Rest upon the bier,
Take my blessing with thee
On thy young career.
Must thy heart be broken,
Let not courage flee;
Be the pain of love then
All in all to thee.

## CHATEAU BONCOURT.

Translated by "G. E. H."

Sadly I shake my hoary head,
  And muse upon the days of yore,
Images I thought long dead,
  Must ye haunt me thus once more?

O'er woods and blossoming hedges
  A castle rises on high;
I see its glittering turrets,
  And pass them with a sigh.

Es schauen vom Wappenschilde
Die Löwen so traulich mich an,
Ich grüße die alten Bekannten
Und eile den Burghof hinan.

Dort liegt die Sphinx am Brunnen,
Dort grünt der Feigenbaum,
Dort hinter diesen Fenstern
Verträumt' ich den ersten Traum.

Ich tret' in die Burgkapelle
Und suche des Ahnherrn Grab,
Dort ist's, dort hängt vom Pfeiler
Das alte Gewaffen herab.

Noch lesen umflort die Augen
Die Züge der Inschrift nicht,
Wie hell durch die bunten Scheiben
Das Licht darüber auch bricht.

So stehst du, o Schloß meiner Väter,
Mir treu und fest in dem Sinn,
Und bist von der Erde verschwunden,
Der Pflug geht über dich hin.

Sei fruchtbar, o theurer Boden,
Ich segne dich mild und gerührt,
Und segn' ihn zwiefach, wer immer
Den Pflug nun über dich führt.

I know the ancient gateway,
   The lions towering above,
And a mournful smile flits o'er me,
   As I think of my youth, my love.


The Sphinx lies by the fountain,
   The summer-air is mild,
The glorious trees are waving —
   Here I was once a child.


I enter the grand old chapel,
   And seek my forefather's grave.
His arms hang from the pillar —
   I think of my sire so brave.


The sun breaks through the colour'd panes,
   Dispels the gath'ring gloom,
My eyes, bedimm'd with gushing tears,
   Light on his marbletomb.


Thus, castle old, thou standest
   Fix'd firmly in my mind —
The ploughshare now goes o'er thee,
   A stranger walks behind.


May ample harvests crown thee,
   Dear soil I love so well;
Joy be with those and blessings,
   Who on thy grounds now dwell.

Ich aber will auf mich raffen,
Mein Saitenspiel in der Hand,
Die Weiten der Erde durchschweifen,
Und singen von Land zu Land.

- - - - - - - - - -

## Der reichste Fürst.
### Justinus Kerner
geboren 1786, gestorben 1862.

Preisend mit viel schönen Reden
Ihrer Länder Werth und Zahl,
Saßen viele deutsche Fürsten
Einst zu Worms im Kaisersaal.

„Herrlich," sprach der Fürst von Sachsen,
„Ist mein Land und seine Macht:
Silber hegen seine Berge
Wohl in manchem tiefen Schacht."

„Seht mein Land in üpp'ger Fülle,"
Sprach der Kurfürst von dem Rhein,
„Gold'ne Saaten in den Thälern,
Auf den Bergen edlen Wein!"

„Große Städte, reiche Klöster,"
Ludwig, Herr zu Baiern, sprach,
„Schaffen, daß mein Land den euren
Wohl nicht steht an Schätzen nach."

I rise in earnest prayer —
  My harp is in my hand —
Far, far off will I wander,
  And sing in many a land.

## THE RICHEST PRINCE.

Translated by Lady John Manners.

In the Hall at Worms were sitting
  ('Tis a tale of bygone days)
Many noble German princes —
  Each his own domains did praise.

Spake the Saxon Prince: "Right noble
  Is the country I call mine;
In the caverns of its mountains
  Ores of precious silver shine."

"See my country's rich abundance,"
  Spake the Palsgrave of the Rhine;
"Golden harvests bear the valleys,
  And the mountains generous wine."

"Stately cities, wealthy cloisters"
  Ludwig of Bavaria cried,
"Make my land so rich, your countries
  Cannot rival it in pride."

Eberhard, der mit dem Barte,
Würtembergs geliebter Herr,
Sprach: „Mein Land hat kleine Städte,
Trägt nicht Berge, silberschwer;

„Doch ein Kleinod hält's verborgen:
Daß in Wäldern, noch so groß,
Ich mein Haupt kann kühnlich legen
Jedem Unterthan in Schooß."

Und es rief der Herr von Sachsen,
Der von Baiern, der vom Rhein:
„Graf im Bart, Ihr seid der Reichste,
Euer Land trägt Edelstein."

<hr>

## Die sterbende Blume.
### Friedrich Rückert
geboren 1789, gestorben 1866.

Hoffe! du erlebst es noch,
Daß der Frühling wiederkehrt.
Hoffen alle Bäume doch,
Die des Herbstes Wind verheert,
Hoffen mit der stillen Kraft
Ihrer Knospen winterlang,
Bis sich wieder regt der Saft;
Und ein neues Grün entsprang. —

Wurtemberg's beloved master,
   Bearded Eberhardt, replies,
"But small towns can boast my country,
   In its caves no silver lies."

"Yet a jewel there is hidden:
   I can boldly lay my head
On the lap of every subject
   In its woods, nor treason dread."

Then the Saxon Prince, the Palsgrave,
   And Bavaria's ruler, cried,
"Count, thy land is far the richest,
   Precious gems thy forests hide."

## THE DYING FLOWER.

### Translated by Professor Blackie.

"Have hope, why shouldst thou not? — the trees
   Have hope and not in vain,
Stripped by the rough unfriendly breeze,
   That spring shall come again;
Thou too, within whose secret bud
   A life hath lurked unseen,
Shalt wait till spring revive thy blood,
   And renovate thy green."

„Ach, ich bin kein starker Baum,
   Der ein Sommertausend lebt,
   Nach verträumtem Wintertraum
   Neue Lenzgedichte webt!
   Ach, ich bin die Blume nur,
   Die des Maies Kuß geweckt,
   Und von der nicht bleibt die Spur,
   Wenn das weiße Grab sie deckt!" —

Wenn du denn die Blume bist,
   O bescheidenes Gemüth,
   Tröste dich, beschieden ist
   Samen Allem, was da blüht.
   Laß den Sturm des Todes doch
   Deinen Lebensstaub verstreu'n;
   Aus dem Staube wirst du noch
   Hundertmal dich selbst erneu'n. —

„Ja, es werden nach mir blüh'n
   Andre, die mir ähnlich sind;
   Ewig ist das ganze Grün,
   Nur das Einzge welkt geschwind.
   Aber, sind sie, was ich war,
   Bin ich selber es nicht mehr;
   Jetzt nur bin ich ganz und gar,
   Nicht zuvor und nicht nachher.

„Wenn einst sie der Sonne Blick
   Wärmt, der jetzt noch mich durchflammt,
   Lindert das nicht mein Geschick,
   Das mich nun zur Nacht verdammt.

—"Alas! no stately tree am I,
  No oak, no forest king,
Whose dreams of winter prophesy
  A speedy day of spring.
A daughter of an humble race,
  A flower of yearly blow,
Of what I was remains no trace,
  Beneath my tomb of snow."

—"And if thou wert the frailest reed,
  The weakest herb that grows,
Thou needst not fear; God gave a seed
  To everything that blows.
Although the winter's stormy strife
  A thousand times bestrew
The sod with thee, thou canst thy life
  A thousand times renew."

—"Yes, thousands after me will blow
  As fair — more fair than I;
No end can earth's green virtue know,
  But each green thing must die.
Though they shall share in mine, no share
  In their life waits for me,
Myself have changed — the things that were,
  Are not, nor more may be.

"And when the sun shall shine on them,
  That shines on me so bright,
What boots their coloured diadem,
  To me sunk deep in night?

Sonne, ja du äugelst schon
Ihnen in die Fernen zu;
Warum noch mit frost'gem Hohn
Mir aus Wolken lächelst du?

„Weh' mir, daß ich dir vertraut,
Als mich wach geküßt dein Strahl;
Daß in's Aug' ich dir geschaut,
Bis es mir das Leben stahl!
Dieses Lebens armen Rest
Deinem Mitleid zu entziehn,
Schließen will ich krankhaft fest
Mich in mich, und dir entfliehn!

„Doch du schmelzest meines Grimms
Starres Eis in Thränen auf;
Nimm mein fliehend Leben, nimm's
Ewige, zu dir hinauf!
Ja, du sonnest noch den Gram
Aus der Seele mir zuletzt;
Alles, was von dir mir kam,
Sterbend dank' ich es dir jetzt:

„Aller Lüfte Morgenzug,
Dem ich sommerlang gebebt,
Aller Schmetterlinge Flug,
Die um mich im Tanz geschwebt;
Augen, die mein Glanz erfrischt,
Herzen, die mein Duft erfreut;
Wie aus Duft und Glanz gemischt
Du mich schufst, dir dank' ich's heut'.

Thou sun, whose cold and frosty smile
   Mocks at my honours brief,
Seemst thou not beckoning the while
   A future summer's chief?

"Alas! why did my leaves incline
   Unto thy faithless ray?
For while mine eye looked into thine,
   Thou filchd my life away.
Thou shalt not triumph o'er my death,
   My parting leaves I close
Upon myself — receive my breath
   Not thou that caused my woes!

—"Yet dost thou melt my pride away,
   Change into tears my stone! —
Receive my fleet life of a day,
   Thou endless one alone!
Yes! thou hast made my pride to pass,
   Mine ire hast sunn'd away,
All that I am, all that I was,
   I owe it to thy ray.

"Each zephyr of each balmy morn
   That made me breathe perfume,
Each sportive moth on bright wing borne
   That danced around my bloom,
Each shining eye that brighter shone
   My magic hues to see;
These purest joys I owe alone,
   Eternal One, to thee!

„Eine Zierde deiner Welt,
   Wenn auch eine kleine nur,
Ließest du mich blühn im Feld,
   Wie die Stern' auf höh'rer Flur.
Einen Odem hauch' ich noch,
   Und er soll kein Seufzer sein;
Einen Blick zum Himmel hoch
   Und zur schönen Welt hinein.

„Ew'ges Flammenherz der Welt,
   Laß verglimmen mich an dir!
Himmel, spann' dein blaues Zelt,
   Mein vergrüntes sinket hier.
Heil, o Frühling, deinem Schein!
   Morgenluft, Heil deinem Wehn!
Ohne Kummer schlaf' ich ein,
   Ohne Hoffnung, aufzustehn.

---

## „Wenn du willst im Menschenherzen.“
### Friedrich Rückert.

Wenn du willst im Menschenherzen
   Alle Saiten rühren an,
Stimme du den Ton der Schmerzen,
   Nicht den Klang der Freuden an.
Mancher ist wohl, der erfahren
   Hat auf Erden keine Lust;
Keiner, der nicht stillbewahren
   Wird ein Weh in seiner Brust.

"As with thy stars thou didst begirth
  The never fading blue,
So didst thou gem thy green of earth
  With bright flowers ever new.
One breath I have not drawn in vain
  For thee — be it no sigh!
One look I have for earth's fair plain,
  One for the welkin high.

"Thou world's warm-glowing heart, be spent
  My life's last pulse on thee!
Receive me, heaven's bright azure tent,
  My green tent breaks with me.
Hail! to thee, Spring, in glory bright!
  Morn with thy thousand dyes!
Without regret I sink in night,
  Though without hope to rise."

## TO THE MINSTREL.

Translated by the Rev. W. W. Skeat.

Wouldst thou seek, within man's heart
  To strike each secret string?
To thy song sad tones impart,
  Not strains of gladness sing.
Many a man hath lived on earth
  Whom joy hath seldom blessed;
None, but bears, from earliest birth,
  Some grief within his breast.

## Reue.

### August Graf von Platen
geboren 1796, gestorben 1835.

Wie rafft' ich mich auf in der Nacht, in der Nacht,
Und fühlte mich fürder gezogen!
Die Gassen verließ ich, vom Wächter bewacht,
Durchwandelte sacht
In der Nacht, in der Nacht
Das Thor mit dem gothischen Bogen.

Der Mühlbach rauschte durch felsigen Schacht,
Ich lehnte mich über die Brücke;
Tief unter mir nahm ich der Wogen in Acht,
Die wallten so sacht
In der Nacht, in der Nacht,
Doch wallte nicht eine zurücke.

Es drehte sich oben, unzählig entfacht,
Melodischer Wandel der Sterne,
Mit ihnen der Mond in beruhigter Pracht,
Sie funkelten sacht
In der Nacht, in der Nacht
Durch lauschend entlegene Ferne.

Ich blickte hinauf in der Nacht, in der Nacht,
Ich blickte hinunter aufs Neue:
O wehe, wie hast du die Tage verbracht,
Nun stille du sacht
In der Nacht, in der Nacht
Im pochenden Herzen die Reue!

# IN THE NIGHT.

### Translated by Richard Garnett.

How started I up in the night, in the night,
  A moody dissatisfied mortal!
The street left behind me, the watch and his light,
Went through in my flight,
In the night, in the night,
  The Gothic old arch and its portal.

The rillet ran on, coming down from the height,
  I bent o'er the hand-rail with yearning,
And watched the bright ripples, as, clear as the sight,
They fleeted so light,
In the night, in the night,
  With never a thought of returning.

Above, in the blue inaccessible height,
  The stars' multitudinous splendour
Burn'd round the clear moon, that with purity bright
Made even their light,
In the night, in the night,
  More chaste and more tranquilly tender.

I look'd up aloft to the night, to the night,
  And downward again to the chasm:
O woe! thou hast wasted the day and its light,
And now thou must fight
In the night, in the night,
  With grief and a sorrowful spasm!

## Der Ring.
### Anastasius Grün
geboren 1806.

Ich saß auf einem Berge
Gar fern dem Heimathland,
Tief unter mir Hügelreihen,
Thalgründe, Saatenland!

In stillen Träumen zog ich
Den Ring vom Finger ab,
Den sie, ein Pfand der Liebe,
Beim Lebewohl mir gab.

Ich hielt ihn vor das Auge,
Wie man ein Fernrohr hält,
Und guckte durch das Reifchen
Hernieder auf die Welt.

Ei, lustiggrüne Berge
Und goldnes Saatgefild,
Zu solchem schönen Rahmen
Fürwahr ein schönes Bild!

Hier schmucke Häuschen schimmernd
Am grünen Bergeshang,
Durch Sicheln und Sensen blitzend
Die reiche Flur entlang!

## THE GOLDEN RING.

Translated by "S. S."; contributed to the Feast of the Poets
in "Tait's Mag." September 1843.

An exile from my native land,
  I sat upon a mountain high;
Below me valleys, hills, and plains,
  Above me an autumnal sky.

Then gentle thoughts of bygone times
  Came gushing up from Mem'ry's spring,
And from my hand her farewell pledge
  Of faith I took — a golden ring.

Like to a telescope I raised
  Unto mine eyes that ring of gold,
And, looking down upon the earth,
  Beheld it like a map unrolled.

The fields all rich with yellow corn,
  The groves of shaded green, I found
More beautiful a thousand times,
  When in my golden circlet bound.

And huts, "where poor men lie," shone white
  Upon the hills of sloping green;
And in the sun the mowers' scythes
  Threw back a flickering silver sheen.

Und weiterhin die Ebne,
Die stolz der Sturm durchzieht,
Und fern die blauen Berge,
Gränzwächter von Granit.

Und Städte mit blanken Kuppeln,
Und frisches Wäldergrün,
Und Wolken, die zur Ferne,
Wie meine Sehnsucht, ziehn!

Die Erde und den Himmel,
Die Menschen und ihr Land,
Dies Alles hielt als Rahmen
Mein goldner Reif umspannt.

O schönes Bild, zu sehen
Vom Ring der Lieb' umspannt:
Die Erde und den Himmel,
Die Menschen und ihr Land.

# Die beiden Engel.

### Emanuel Geibel
geboren 1815.

O kennst du, Herz, die beiden Schwesterengel,
Herabgestiegen aus dem Himmelreich:
Stillsegnend Freundschaft mit dem Lilienstengel,
Entzündend Liebe mit dem Rosenzweig?

And high-piled rocks of granite grey,
  Like battlements of antique mould,
Bounded the plain where, serpent-like,
  A noble river winding roll'd.

And there were dark primeval woods,
  And towers, and towns, whence the smoke curl'd
Unto the clouds, and seem'd to fly
  Where I would fain, o'er half the world.

All these were framed within my ring,
  And lands, and men, and sea, and skies;
A wondrous halo round them thrown —
  I gazed on them with wond'ring eyes.

And thence I learned: all God hath made —
  The earth beneath, the skies above,
And all that breathes is beautified,
  When framed within the Ring of Love.

## THE TWO ANGELS.

### Translated by Lady John Manners.

Know'st thou, O heart! the two fair sister-angels
  That have descended to us from above;
Friendship, with her pale lilies, peace bestowing,
  And, with her branch of roses, glowing Love?

26 *

Schwarzlockig ist die Liebe, feurig glühend,
　　Schön wie der Lenz, der hastig sprossen will;
　　Die Freundschaft blond, in sanftern Farben blühend,
　　Und wie die Sommernacht, so mild und still.

Die Lieb' ein brausend Meer, wo im Gewimmel
　　Vieltausendfältig Wog' an Woge schlägt;
　　Freundschaft ein tiefer Bergsee, der den Himmel
　　Klar wiederspiegelnd in den Fluten trägt.

Die Liebe bricht herein wie Wetterblitzen,
　　Die Freundschaft kommt wie dämmernd Mondenlicht;
　　Die Liebe will erwerben und besitzen,
　　Die Freundschaft opfert, doch sie fordert nicht.

Doch dreimal selig, dreimal hoch zu preisen
　　Das Herz, wo beide freundlich eingekehrt,
　　Und wo die Glut der Rose nicht dem leisen,
　　Geheimnißvollen Blühn der Lilie wehrt!

*＊＊＊＊＊＊＊*

## Der deutsche Rhein.
### Nicolaus Becker
geboren 1810, gestorben 1845.

Sie sollen ihn nicht haben,
Den freien, deutschen Rhein,
Ob sie wie gier'ge Raben
Sich heiser darnach schrein;

Dark are Love's locks, her eyes with lustre glowing,
   Lovely as spring, dawning in golden light;
Friendship is fair, in softer colours blooming,
   And mild and tranquil as a summer-night.

Love is a tossing sea, where, in the tumult,
   Thousands of dashing billows foaming rise;
Friendship a mountain-lake, whose limpid waters
   In their clear depths do mirror back the skies.

Love enters like a flash of gleaming lightning;
   Friendship steals in like threads by moonlight spun.
Love is resolved to win, and keep for ever;
   Friendship makes offerings, but she asks for none.

But, ah! thrice blessed, thrice blessed the happy bosom,
   Where both the sister-angels may abide;
Where the bright glowing rose and gentle lily
   Dwell ever in sweet concord, side by side.

## THE GERMAN RHINE.

### Translated by Dr. James Steele.

It never shall be France's
   The free, the German Rhine,
Tho' raven-like she glances
   And croaks her foul design.

So lang' er ruhig wallend
Sein grünes Kleid noch trägt,
So lang' ein Ruder schallend
In seine Woge schlägt! —

Sie sollen ihn nicht haben,
Den freien, deutschen Rhein,
So lang' sich Herzen laben
An seinem Feuerwein;

So lang' in seinem Strome
Noch fest die Felsen stehn!
So lang' sich hohe Dome
In seinem Spiegel sehn!

Sie sollen ihn nicht haben,
Den freien, deutschen Rhein,
So lang' dort kühne Knaben
Um schlanke Dirnen frei'n;

So lang' die Flosse hebet
Ein Fisch auf seinem Grund,
So lang' ein Lied noch lebet
In seiner Sänger Mund!

Sie sollen ihn nicht haben,
Den freien, deutschen Rhein,
Bis seine Fluth begraben
Des letzten Manns Gebein.

So long as calmly gliding
   It wears its mantle green,
So long as oar, dividing
   Its mirrored wave, is seen.

It never shall be France's
   The free, the German Rhine;
So long as youth enhances
   His fervour with its wine.

So long as, sentry keeping,
   The rocks its margin stud,
So long as spires are steeping
   Their image in its flood;

It never shall be France's
   The free, the German Rhine,
So long as festive dances
   Its lover-groups combine.

So long as angler bringeth
   Its lusty trout to shore,
So long as minstrel singeth
   Its praise from door to door;

It never shall be France's
   The free, the German Rhine,
Until its broad expanse is
   Its last defender's shrine.

## Das Grab.
### Johann Gaudenz von Salis
#### geboren 1762, gestorben 1834.

Das Grab ist tief und stille
    Und schauderhaft sein Rand;
Es deckt mit schwarzer Hülle
    Ein unbekanntes Land.

Das Lied der Nachtigallen
    Tönt nicht in seinen Schooß,
Der Freundschaft Rosen fallen
    Nur auf des Hügels Moos.

Verlaß'ne Bräute ringen
    Umsonst die Hände wund;
Der Waisen Klagen dringen
    Nicht in der Tiefe Grund.

Doch sonst an keinem Orte
    Wohnt die ersehnte Ruh';
Nur durch die dunkle Pforte
    Geht man der Heimath zu.

Das arme Herz, hienieden
    Von manchem Sturm bewegt,
Erlangt den wahren Frieden
    Nur wo es nicht mehr schlägt.

## THE GRAVE.

Translated by "T." (Tait's Magazine 1843).

The grave is deep, and stern, and still,
  And terrors round its margin stand:
It with a veil of darkness hides
  The Undiscover'd Land.

A silent realm, where never sounds
  The voice of bird in flowing song;
There friendship's roses, fallen away,
  Are strewed in dust along.

The bride bereaved may mourn in vain,
  And wring her hands in deep despair;
Loud may the cry of orphans be; —
  No sorrow reacheth there!

Yet weary hearts that here below
  Have struggled with the storms of life,
Long for its everlasting Peace,
  Untroubled more with strife.

For to us in no other place
  That welcome, looked-for, rest can come;
And only through that Portal dark
  Man goeth to his Home.

# HYMNS.

---

## Erbauliches.

# Ein' feste Burg.

### Dr. Martin Luther
geboren 1483, gestorben 1546.

Ein' feste Burg ist unser Gott,
Ein' gute Wehr und Waffen,
Er hilft uns frei aus aller Noth,
Die uns jetzt hat betroffen.
Der alte böse Feind
Mit Ernste er's jetzt meint:
Groß' Macht und viele List
Sein' grausam' Rüstung ist.


Mit unsrer Macht ist nichts gethan,
Wir sind gar bald verloren,
Es streit't für uns der rechte Mann,
Den Gott selbst hat erkoren.
Fragst du, wer er ist?
Er heißet Jesus Christ,
Der Herre Zebaoth,
Und ist kein andrer Gott,
Das Feld muß er behalten.

# "A TOWER OF STRENGTH."

Translated by Dr. Alford, Dean of Canterbury.

A Tower of strength is God our Lord,
A sure defence and trusty guard:
His help as yet in every need
From danger hath our spirit freed:
    Our ancient foe in rage
      May all his spite display:
    May war against us wage,
      And arm him for the fray,
      He that can keep all earth at bay.

Weak is our unassisted power,
Defeated soon in peril's hour:
But on our side, and for the right,
The man of God's own choice doth fight:
    Jesus, the Christ, whose Name
      Exalted is on high,
    The Lord of Hosts, the same
      That reigneth in the sky,
      He giveth us the victory.

## Die Güte Gottes.

C. F. Gellert
geboren 1717, gestorben 1769.

Wie groß ist des Allmächt'gen Güte!
Ist der ein Mensch, den sie nicht rührt,
Der mit verhärtetem Gemüthe
Den Dank erstickt, der ihm gebührt?
Nein, seine Liebe zu ermessen,
Sei ewig meine größte Pflicht!
Der Herr hat mein noch nicht vergessen;
Vergiß, mein Herz, auch seiner nicht!

Wer hat mich wunderbar bereitet?
Der Gott, der meiner nicht bedarf.
Wer hat mit Langmuth mich geleitet?
Er, dessen Rath ich oft verwarf.
Wer stärkt den Frieden im Gewissen?
Wer giebt dem Geiste neue Kraft?
Wer läßt mich so viel Heil genießen?
Ist's nicht sein Arm, der alles schafft?

Schau', o mein Geist! in jenes Leben,
Zu welchem du geschaffen bist;
Wo du, mit Herrlichkeit umgeben,
Gott ewig sehn wirst, wie er ist.
Du hast ein Recht zu diesen Freuden;
Durch Gottes Güte sind sie dein.
Sieh, darum mußte Christus leiden,
Damit du könntest selig sein.

## GRATITUDE.

### Translated by * *

How great Jehovah's love, how tender!
   He hath no heart who sits unmoved,
Stifling the thanks he ought to render,
   Nor ever thinks that he is loved.
Yes! and that love to fathom, ever
   Shall be my first, my earnest thought.
This mighty Lord forgets me never:
   Oh, then, my soul, forget Him not!

Who has my wondrous lot provided?
   The Lord, who had no need of me.
Who has my stumbling footsteps guided?
   He whom I tried to shun and flee.
Who with new strength revived my spirit?
   And who this inward peace has given?
Who gives me all things to inherit?
   Who, but the Lord of earth and heaven!

Above this life in spirit bounding,
   Behold, my soul, the heavenly bliss,
Where thou, God's glory all surrounding,
   Shalt ever see Him as He is!
These joys thou shalt be soon possessing,
   Thy right shall never be denied;
For, lo! to win for thee the blessing,
   The Saviour came, and lived, and died.

Und diesen Gott sollt' ich nicht ehren?
Und seine Güte nicht verstehn?
Er sollte rufen, ich nicht hören?
Den Weg, den er mir zeigt, nicht gehn?
Lebt seine Lieb' in meiner Seele,
So treibt sie mich zu jeder Pflicht;
Und ob ich schon aus Schwachheit fehle,
Herrscht doch in mir die Sünde nicht.

O Gott, laß deine Güt' und Liebe
Mir immerdar vor Augen sein!
Sie stärk' in mir die guten Triebe,
Mein ganzes Leben dir zu weihn;
Sie tröste mich zur Zeit der Schmerzen,
Sie leite mich zur Zeit des Glücks;
Und sie besieg' in meinem Herzen
Die Furcht des letzten Augenblicks!

#### „O Haupt voll Blut und Wunden!"
##### Paul Gerhard
###### geboren 1606, gestorben 1675.

O Haupt voll Blut und Wunden,
Voll Schmerz und voller Hohn!
O Haupt zum Spott gebunden
Mit einer Dornenkron'!
O Haupt, das sonst getragen
Die höchste Ehr' und Zier,
Doch schimpflich nun geschlagen,
Gegrüßest seist du mir!

Then shall I not, in glad allegiance,
   To God the Lord my homage pay;
And when He calls, with swift obedience,
   Go where I see Him point the way?
His love, within my heart now reigning,
   Leads me to duties hid before;
And though I fail, through sin remaining,
   It shall not have dominion more.

Here, then, my Saviour, let me ever
   More of Thy love and goodness see,
To strengthen every weak endeavour
   That dedicates my life to Thee;
To cheer when sorrow clouds my dwelling,
   To keep me safe in joy's bright day,
And all my fears of guilt dispelling,
   To take the sting of death away.

## "AH WOUNDED HEAD".

Translated by Miss Catherine Winkworth.

Ah wounded Head! Must Thou
   Endure such shame and scorn!
The blood is trickling from Thy brow,
   Pierced by the crown of thorn,
   Thou who wast crowned on high
   With light and majesty,
In deep dishonour here must die,
   Yet here I welcome Thee.

Du edles Angesichte,
　　Das sonst, der Sonne gleich,
　　Gestrahlt im hellsten Lichte,
　　Wie bist du nun so bleich;
　　Dein Blick mit Kraft gefüllet,
　　Der sonst die Welt geschreckt,
　　Wie ist er jetzt verhüllet,
　　Mit Dunkel ganz bedeckt.

Die Farbe deiner Wangen
　　Und deiner Lippen Roth
　　Ist hin, und ganz vergangen
　　In deiner Todesnoth.
　　Was hat dem Tod gegeben,
　　O Jesu, diese Macht,
　　Daß er dein heilig Leben
　　Versenkt in seine Nacht?

O Herr, was du erduldet,
　　Ist Alles meine Last:
　　Ich, ich hab' es verschuldet,
　　Was du getragen hast.
　　Schau her, hier steh' ich Armer,
　　Der Zorn verdienet hat!
　　Gieb mir, o mein Erbarmer,
　　Den Anblick deiner Gnad'!

Erkenne mich, mein Hüter,
　　Mein Hirte, nimm mich an.
　　Du hast, Quell aller Güter,
　　Viel Gutes mir gethan.

Thou noble countenance!
All earthly lights are pale
Before the brightness of that glance,
At which a world shall quail.
How is it quenched and gone!
Those gracious eyes how dim!
Whence grew that cheek so pale and wan?
Who dared to scoff at Him!

All hues of lovely life,
That glowed on lip and cheek,
Have vanished in that awful strife;
The mighty One is weak,
Pale Death has won the day.
He triumphs in this hour
When Strength and Beauty fade away,
And yield them to his power.

Ah Lord, Thy woes belong,
Thy cruel pains, to me,
The burden of my sin and wrong
Hath all been laid on Thee.
Behold me where I kneel,
Wrath were my rightful lot,
One glance of love yet let me feel!
Redeemer! spurn me not!

My Guardian, own me Thine;
My Shepherd, bear me home;
O Fount of mercy, Source Divine,
From Thee what blessings come!

27 *

Oft hast du mich gelabet,
Mit Himmels=Brod gespeist,
Mit Trost mich reich begabet
Durch deinen freud'gen Geist.

Es dient zu meinen Freuden
Und thut mir herzlich wohl,
Daß ich mich in dein Leiden,
Mein Heil, versenken soll.
Ach könnt' ich, o mein Leben,
An deinem Kreuze hier
Mein Leben von mir geben,
Wie wohl geschähe mir!

Ich danke dir von Herzen,
O Jesu, liebster Freund,
Für deine Todesschmerzen,
Da du's so gut gemeint.
O gieb, daß ich mich halte
Zu dir und deiner Treu',
Und wenn ich einst erkalte,
In dir mein Ende sei.

Wenn ich einmal soll scheiden,
So scheide nicht von mir,
Wenn ich den Tod soll leiden,
So tritt du dann herfür;
Wenn mir am allerbängsten
Wird um das Herze sein,
So reiß mich aus den Aengsten,
Kraft deiner Angst und Pein.

How oft Thy mouth has fed
  My soul with Angels' food,
How oft Thy Spirit o'er me shed
  His stores of heavenly Good.

Ah would that I could share
  Thy cross, Thy bitter woes!
All true delight lies hidden there,
  Thence all true comfort flows.
  Ah well were it for me
  That I could end my strife,
And die upon the cross with Thee,
  Who art my Life of life!

My soul is still o'erfraught,
  O Jesus, dearest Friend,
With thankful love to Him who sought
  Such woe, for such an end.
  Grant me as true a faith,
  As Thou art true to me,
That so the icy sleep of Death
  Be but a rest in Thee.

Yes, when I must depart,
  Depart Thou not from me;
When Death is creeping to my heart,
  Bear Thou mine agony.
  When faith and courage sink,
  O'erwhelmed with dread dismay,
Come Thou who ne'er from pain didst shrink,
  And chase my fears away.

Erscheine mir zum Schilde,
  Zum Trost in meinem Tod,
  Und laß mich sehn dein Bilde
  In deiner Kreuzesnoth:
  Da will ich nach dir blicken,
  Da will ich glaubensvoll
  Fest an mein Herz dich drücken:
  Wer so stirbt, der stirbt wohl.

## „Nun ruhen alle Wälder."
### Paul Gerhard.

Nun ruhen alle Wälder,
Vieh, Menschen, Städt' und Felder,
  Es schläft die ganze Welt;
Ihr aber, meine Sinnen,
Auf, auf! ihr sollt beginnen,
  Was eurem Schöpfer wohlgefällt.

Wo bist du, Sonne, blieben?
Die Nacht hat dich vertrieben,
  Die Nacht, des Tages Feind.
Fahr' hin, ein' and're Sonne,
Mein Jesus, meine Wonne,
  Gar hell in meinem Herzen scheint.

Der Tag ist nun vergangen,
Die güld'nen Sternlein prangen
  Am blauen Himmelssaal;

Come to me ere I die,
My comfort and my shield;
And gazing on Thy cross can I
Calmly my spirit yield.
On Thee when life is past,
My darkening eyes shall dwell,
My heart in faith shall hold Thee fast;
Who dieth thus, dies well.

## EVENING HYMN.

Translated by " * * "

Quietly rest the woods and dales,
Silence round the hearth prevails,
The world is all asleep:
Thou, my soul, in thought arise,
Seek thy Father in the skies,
And holy vigils with Him keep.

Sun, where hidest thou thy light?
Art thou driven hence by Night,
Thy dark and ancient foe?
Go! another Sun is mine,
Jesus comes with light divine,
To cheer my pilgrimage below.

Now that day has past away,
Golden stars in bright array
Bespangle the blue sky:

Also werd' ich auch stehen,
Wenn mich wird heißen gehen
   Mein Gott aus diesem Jammerthal.

Der Leib eilt nun zur Ruhe,
Legt ab das Kleid und Schuhe,
   Das Bild der Sterblichkeit;
Die zieh' ich aus, dagegen
Wird Christus mir anlegen
   Den Rock der Ehr' und Herrlichkeit.

Das Haupt, die Füß' und Hände
Sind froh, daß nun zu Ende
   Die Arbeit kommen sei.
Herz, freu' dich, du sollst werden
Vom Elend dieser Erden
   Und von der Sünden-Arbeit frei.

Nun geht, ihr matten Glieder,
Geht hin und legt euch nieder,
   Der Betten ihr begehrt.
Es kommen Stund' und Zeiten,
Da man euch wird bereiten
   Zur Ruh' ein Bettlein in der Erd'.

Mein' Augen steh'n verdrossen,
Im Hui sind sie geschlossen;
   Wo bleibt dann Leib und Seel'?
Nimm sie zu deinen Gnaden,
Sei gut für allen Schaden,
   Du Aug' und Wächter Israel.

. Bright and clear, so would I stand,
When I hear my Lord's command
To leave this earth, and upward fly.

Now this body seeks for rest,
From its vestments all undrest,
   Types of mortality:
Christ shall give me soon to wear
Garments beautiful and fair, —
White robes of glorious majesty.

Head, and feet, and hands, once more
Joy to think of labour o'er,
   And night with gladness see.
Oh, my heart, thou too shalt know
Rest from all thy toil below,
And from earth's turmoil soon be free.

Weary limbs, now rest ye here,
Safe from danger and from fear,
   Seek slumber on this bed:
Deeper rest ere long to share,
Other hands shall soon prepare
My narrow couch among the dead.

While my eyes I gently close,
Stealing o'er me soft repose,
   Who shall my guardian be?
Soul and body now I leave,
And Thou wilt the trust receive,
O Israel's Watchman! unto Thee.

Auch euch, ihr meine Lieben,
Soll heute nicht betrüben
    Ein Unfall noch Gefahr;
Gott laß euch selig schlafen,
Stell' euch die güldnen Waffen
    Um's Bett und seiner Engel Schaar.

<div align="center">~~~~~~~~~~~~</div>

# „Liebe, die du mich zum Bilde."
### Johann Scheffler
geboren 1624, gestorben 1677.

Liebe, die du mich zum Bilde
    Deiner Gottheit hast gemacht;
Liebe, die du mich so milde
    Nach dem Fall mit Heil bedacht;
Liebe, dir ergeb' ich mich,
Dein zu bleiben ewiglich.

Liebe, die mich hat erkoren,
    Eh' ich noch in's Leben kam;
Liebe, welche Menschgeboren
    Meine Schwachheit an sich nahm;
Liebe, dir ergeb' ich mich,
Dein zu bleiben ewiglich.

Liebe, die durch Tod und Leiden
    Für mich hat genug gethan;
Liebe, die mir ew'ge Freuden,

O my friends, from you this day
May all ill have fled away,
  No danger near have come;
Now, my God, these dear ones keep,
Give to my beloved sleep,
And angels send to guard their home!

## MY BELOVED IS MINE, AND I AM HIS.

Translated by * *

Loved One! who, by grace, hast wrought me
  Somewhat to thy likeness pure;
Loved One! who, in mercy, sought me.
  Lost and wretched, blind and poor;
Loved One! hear me vow, this day,
To be Thine eternally.

Loved One! who, in heaven, chose me
  Ere creation found me here, —
Loved One! who once stooped so lowly,
  As among us to appear;
Loved One! hear me vow, this day,
To be thine eternally.

Loved One! who endured such anguish,
  Who for man so toiled and bled;
Loved One! who by death did vanquish

Heil und Seligkeit gewann;
Liebe, dir ergeb' ich mich,
Dein zu bleiben ewiglich.


Liebe, die mit Kraft und Leben
    Mich erfüllet durch das Wort;
Liebe, die den Geist ergeben
    Mir zum Trost und Seelenhort;
Liebe, dir ergeb' ich mich,
Dein zu bleiben ewiglich.


Liebe, die, zu Gott erhöhet,
    Mir erhält, was sie erstritt;
Liebe, die stets für mich flehet
    Und mich kräftiglich vertritt;
Liebe, dir ergeb' ich mich,
Dein zu bleiben ewiglich.


Liebe, die mich schützend decket,
    Wenn des Todes Macht mir dräut;
Liebe, die mich auferwecket
    Und mich führt zur Herrlichkeit;
Liebe, dir ergeb' ich mich,
Dein zu bleiben ewiglich.

All my foes, and in my stead;
Loved One! hear me vow, this day,
To be Thine eternally.

Loved One! who art now bestowing
  Light and knowledge, truth and grace —
Loved One! who Thyself art showing
  As the sinner's hiding-place;
Loved One! hear me vow, this day,
To be Thine eternally.

Loved One! who for ever loves me,
  Still for me in heaven prays, —
Loved One! who my freedom gives me,
  And the mighty ransom pays;
Loved One! hear me vow, this day,
To be Thine eternally.

Loved One! who, ere long, wilt wake me
  From the grave, where I shall lie;
Loved One! who, ere long, wilt make me
  Sharer of Thy bliss on high;
Loved One! hear me vow, this day,
To be Thine eternally.

## „Es ist noch eine Ruh' vorhanden dem Volke Gottes."

Hebräer IV, 9.

### Johann Sigmund Kunth
geboren 1700, gestorben 1779.

Es ist noch eine Ruh' vorhanden,
    Auf, müdes Herz, und werde Licht!
    Du seufzest hier in deinen Banden,
    Und deine Sonne scheinet nicht.
    Sieh' auf das Lamm, das dich mit Freuden
    Dort wird vor seinem Stuhle weiden,
    Wirf hin die Last und eil' herzu.
    Bald ist der schwere Kampf geendet,
    Bald ist der saure Lauf vollendet,
    So gehst du ein zu deiner Ruh'.

Gott hat dir diese Ruh' erkoren,
    Die Ruh', so nie ein Ende nimmt;
    Eh' noch ein Menschenkind geboren,
    Hat sie die Lieb' uns schon bestimmt.
    Das Lämmlein wollte darum sterben,
    Uns diese Ruhe zu erwerben,
    Es ruft, es locket weit und breit:
    Ihr müden Seelen und ihr Frommen,
    Versäumt nicht, heute noch zu kommen
    Zu meiner Ruhe Lieblichkeit.

So kommet denn, ihr matten Seelen,
    Die manche Last und Bürde drückt,

## "THERE REMAINETH THEREFORE A REST FOR THE PEOPLE OF GOD."

Hebr. IV, 9.

Translated by H. L. L.

Yes, still for us a rest remaineth, —
  Arise, sad heart! let there be light!
Thou sighest here in gloomy bondage,
  Thou canst not see the sunshine bright.
Look up to Him, who longs to lead thee
Where with His own flock He may feed thee;
  Cast all thy burdens on His breast.
Soon shall the conflict cease, so weary, —
Soon shall the journey end, so dreary, —
  And thou shalt enter into rest.

God has for us the rest provided,
  The perfect, everlasting bliss.
Before mankind were here created
  His love divine had planned for this.
And Christ our Lord, the cross enduring,
A full salvation thus procuring,
  Now calls, inviting all around, —
"O come to Me! make no delaying,
But prove, my gentle call obeying,
  What rest and love with Me are found!"

Come then, ye weary, heavy laden,
  By many burdens long oppressed,

Eilt, eilt aus euren Kummerhöhlen,
Geht nicht mehr krumm und sehr gebückt.
Ihr habt des Tages Last getragen,
Dafür läßt Euch das Lämmlein sagen:
Ich will selbst eure Ruhe sein.
Ihr seid sein Volk, ihr Jacobiten,
Ob Sünde, Welt und Teufel wüthen,
Seid nur getrost und gehet ein.

Was mag wohl einen Kranken laben,
Was stärkt den müden Wandersmann?
Wo jener nur ein Bettlein haben
Und sanft auf solchem ruhen kann;
Wenn dieser sich darf niedersetzen,
An einem frischen Brunn' ergetzen,
So sind sie beide höchst vergnügt.
Doch dies sind kurze Ruhestunden;
Es ist noch eine Ruh' erfunden,
Wo man in Christi Armen liegt.

Da wird man Freudengarben bringen,
Denn unsre Thränensaat ist aus;
O welch ein Jubel wird erklingen,
Und süßer Ton im Vaterhaus!
Schmerz, Seufzen, Leid, Tod und dergleichen
Wird müssen fliehn und von uns weichen;
Wir werden auch das Lämmlein sehn.
Es wird beim Brünnlein uns erfrischen,
Die Thränen von den Augen wischen:
Wer weiß, was sonst noch soll geschehn.

Come from your cells of lonely sorrow,
   And Christ himself shall give you rest.
Hear His own loving invitation,
Accept His full and free salvation, —
   Himself hath vanquished all your foes;
Now for His people He will take you,
Nor ever will your King forsake you,
   Though Satan and his hosts oppose.

Where does the sick man find refreshment?
   Where does the wanderer seek repose?
On his low couch, in peaceful slumber,
   The sufferer may forget his woes, —
Beneath a tree the weary stranger
In the cool shadow, safe from danger,
   With thankful heart may rest awhile; —
But brief the solace both are sharing;
Ah! nought on earth is worth comparing
   With rest in Jesu's love and smile!

The year of jubilee approaches,
   When tearful sowing-time is past, —
Oh! what shall be "the joy of harvest"
   Within the Father's house at last!
When sighing, pain, and death are banished,
When all our griefs and tears have vanished,
   When our own eyes our Lord behold!
In pastures green the Lamb shall feed us,
Beside the living waters lead us, —
   Ah! who can now the joys unfold?

Kein Durst noch Hunger wird uns schwächen,
Denn die Erquickungszeit ist da.
Die Sonne wird uns nicht mehr stechen,
Das Lamm ist seinem Volke nah.
Es will selbst unter ihnen wohnen,
Und ihre Treue wohl belohnen
Mit Licht und Trost, mit Ehr' und Preis.
Es werden die Gebeine grünen,
Der große Sabbath ist erschienen,
Da man von keiner Arbeit weiß.

Da ruhen wir, und sind in Frieden,
Und leben ewig sorgenlos.
Ach, fasset dieses Wort, ihr Müden,
Legt euch dem Lamm in seinen Schooß.
Ach, Flügel her! Wir müssen eilen
Und uns nicht länger hier verweilen,
Dort wartet schon die frohe Schaar.
Fahr hin, mein Geist, zum Jubiliren,
Begürte dich zum Triumphiren,
Auf, auf, es kommt das Ruhejahr!

Hunger and thirst shall pain no longer,
  When life undying is our own.
No burning noonday-sun shall smite us,
  Where Christ the Light of all is known.
He dwells among His flock for ever,
Of every good the bounteous Giver,
  Repaying all their toils and care;
From earth's dark graves to heaven ascending,
They find a Sabbath never ending,
  A rest eternal, waits them there.

In full, unbroken peace reposing, —
  All sin and sorrow left behind, —
Hear, weary souls, the word of promise,
  The balm for wounded heart and mind!
Ah! lend me wings! Were faith but stronger,
How could we bear to linger longer,
  While dear ones call us from above?
Arise, my soul! begin preparing
To join their songs, their triumphs sharing,
  The jubilee of rest and love!

## Abendlied.
### Matthias Claudius
geboren 1740, gestorben 1815.

Der Mond ist aufgegangen,
Die goldnen Sternlein prangen
Am Himmel hell und klar;
Der Wald steht schwarz und schweiget,
Und aus den Wiesen steiget
Der weiße Nebel wunderbar.

Wie ist die Welt so stille,
Und in der Dämm'rung Hülle
So traulich und so hold,
Als eine stille Kammer,
Wo ihr des Tages Jammer
Verschlafen und vergessen sollt.

Seht ihr den Mond dort stehen?
Er ist nur halb zu sehen,
Und ist doch rund und schön!
So sind wohl manche Sachen,
Die wir getrost verlachen,
Weil unsre Augen sie nicht seh'n.

Wir stolzen Menschenkinder
Sind doch recht arme Sünder,
Und wissen gar nicht viel;
Wir spinnen Luftgespinnste
Und suchen viele Künste
Und kommen weiter von dem Ziel.

# EVENING HYMN.

Translated by Miss Catherine Winkworth.

The moon hath risen on high
And in the clear dark sky
The golden stars all brightly glow;
　And black and hush'd the woods
　While o'er the fields and floods
The white mists hover to and fro.

　How still the earth! how calm!
　What dear and homelike charm
From gentle twilight doth she borrow!
　Like to some quiet room,
　Where wrapt in still soft gloom,
We sleep away the daylight's sorrow.

　Look up; the moon to-night,
　Shows us but half her light,
And yet we know her round and fair;
　At other things how oft
　We in our blindness scoff'd,
Because we saw not what was there.

　We haughty sons of men
　Have but a narrow ken,
We are but sinners poor and weak.
　Yet many dreams we build
　And deem us wise and skilled,
And come not nearer what we seek.

Gott, laß dein Heil uns schauen,
Auf nichts Vergänglich's bauen,
Nicht Eitelkeit uns freu'n!
Laß uns einfältig werden,
Und vor dir hier auf Erden
Wie Kinder fromm und fröhlich sein.

Wollst endlich sonder Grämen
Aus dieser Welt uns nehmen
Durch einen sanften Tod!
Und wenn du uns genommen,
Laß uns in Himmel kommen,
Du lieber, treuer, frommer Gott!

So legt euch denn, ihr Brüder!
In Gottes Namen nieder,
Kühl ist der Abendhauch.
Verschon' uns, Gott, mit Strafen
Und laß uns ruhig schlafen,
Und unsern kranken Nachbar auch!

### „Wem sein nahes Ende."
Aus de la Motte Fouqué's: Sintram und seine Gefährten,
geboren 1777, gestorben 1843.

Wem sein nahes Ende
Durch Herz und Glieder ahnend schleicht,
Der wende,
Der wende Sinn und Hände
Zum Gnadenthor
Vertrau'nd empor,
So macht's der Herr ihm leicht.

Thy mercy let us see,
Nor find in vanity
Our joy; not trust in what departs;
But true and simple grow,
And live to Thee below
With sunny, pure, and childlike hearts.

Let Death all gently come
At last to take us home,
And let us meet him fearlessly;
And when these bonds are riven,
Oh take us to Thy heaven,
Our Lord and God, to dwell with Thee.

Now in his Name most blest
My brethren, sink to rest,
The wind is cold, chill falls the dew.
Spare us, O God, and keep
Us safe in quiet sleep,
And all the sick and suffering too.

## "WHEN DEATH IS DRAWING NEAR."

Translated from "Sintram and his companions".

When death is drawing near,
When thy heart shrinks in fear,
And thy limbs fail,
Then raise thy hands and pray
To him who smoothes thy way
Through the dark vale.

Seht Ihr's im Osten funkeln?
  Hört Ihr die Eng'lein singen,
  Durch's junge Morgenroth?
  Ihr war't so lang im Dunkeln,
  Nun will Euch Hülfe bringen
  Der gnadenreiche Tod.
  Den müßt Ihr freundlich grüßen,
  Dann wird er freundlich auch,
  Und kehrt in Lust das Büßen;
  So ist sein alter Brauch.

Wem sein nahes Ende
  Durch Herz und Glieder ahnend schleicht,
  Der wende,
  Der wende Sinn und Hände
  Zum Gnadenthor
  Vertrau'nd empor,
  So macht's der Herr ihm leicht.

***

„Lobe den Herren, den mächtigen König der Ehren.
Joachim Neander
geboren 1640, gestorben 1680.

Lobe den Herren, den mächtigen König der Ehren,
Meine geliebete Seele, das ist mein Begehren.
  Kommet zu Hauf,
  Psalter und Harfe, wacht auf,
  Lasset die Musikam hören!

See'st thou the Eastern dawn?
Hearest thou in the red morn
The angel's song?
O lift thy drooping head,
Thou who in gloom and dread
Hast lain so long!

Death comes to set thee free!
O, meet him cheerily,
As thy true friend —
And all thy fears shall cease,
And in eternal peace
Thy penance end!

When death is drawing near,
When thy heart shrinks in fear,
And thy limbs fail,
Then raise thy hands and pray
To him who smoothes thy way
Through the dark vale.

## PRAISE.
Translated by H. L. L.

Praise to Jehovah! the almighty king of Creation!
Swell Heaven's chorus, chime in every heart, every.
nation!
Oh, my soul, awake!
Harp, lute, and psaltery take,
Sound forth in glad adoration!

Lobe den Herren, der künstlich und fein dich bereitet,
Der dir Gesundheit verliehen, dich freundlich geleitet
    In wie viel Noth;
    Hat nicht der gnädige Gott
    Ueber dir Flügel gebreitet?

Lobe den Herren, der deinen Stand sichtbar gesegnet,
Der aus dem Himmel mit Strömen der Liebe geregnet;
    Denke daran,
    Was der Allmächtige kann,
    Der dir mit Liebe begegnet.

Lobe den Herren, was in mir ist, lobe den Namen!
Alles, was Odem hat, lobe mit Abrahams Samen.
    Er ist dein Licht,
    Seele, vergiß es ja nicht!
    Lobende, schließe mit Amen.

### Behüt' dich Gott!
#### Psalm 121.
#### Karl Gerok.

Behüt' dich Gott, geliebtes Kind,
In deinen Locken spielt der Wind,
Das Hündlein wedelt, springt und bellt,
Dein Muth ist frisch und schön die Welt!
Behüt' dich Gott!

Praise to Jehovah! whose love o'er thy course is attending,
Redeeming thy life, and thee from all evil defending.
    Through all the past,
  O my soul, over thee cast,
His sheltering wings were bending!

Praise to Jehovah! whose fence has been planted
                            around thee,
Who, from His heavens, with blessing and mercy
                            has crowned thee.
    Think, happy One!
  What He can do, and has done,
Since in His pity He found thee.

Praise to Jehovah! all that hath breath praise Him,
                            sing praises!
Bless God, O my soul, and all that is in me, sing
                            praises!
    In him rejoice,
  Until for ever thy voice
The hymn of eternity raises!

## GOD KEEP MY CHILD!
### Psalm CXXI.
### Translated by "H. L. L."

God keep my child! the hour has come,
  Thou goest forth from friends and home,
  While life and love and hope are new
And all seems bright that meets the view, —
    God keep my child!

Behüt' dich Gott, mein Herz ist schwer,
　Ich kann dich hüten nimmermehr,
　Doch send' ich dir als Engelwach'
　Geflügelte Gebete nach:
　　　　Behüt' dich Gott!


Behüt' dich Gott an Seel' und Leib,
　Daß Noth und Schmerz dir ferne bleib';
　Des Vaters Aug', der Mutter Hand,
　Sie reichen nicht ins fremde Land;
　　　　Behüt' dich Gott!


Behüt' dich Gott an Leib und Seel',
　Vor Sünd' und Schand', vor Fall und Fehl;
　Dein kindlich Herz, vom Argen rein,
　O hüt' es wohl wie Edelstein;
　　　　Behüt' dich Gott!


Behüt' dich Gott, die Welt ist schlimm,
　Verderblich ist ihr Haß und Grimm,
　Verderblicher ihr Glanz und Glück;
　Vor des Verführers goldnem Strick
　　　　Behüt' dich Gott!


Behüt' dich Gott, dein Herz ist schwach,
　Hab' Gott vor Augen, bet' und wach';
　Sein guter Geist, o ruf' ihn an,
　Er führe dich auf ebner Bahn;
　　　　Behüt' dich Gott!

God keep my child! the world is wide,
   I may not hold thee at my side,
   But strong as angel guards shall be
The earnest prayers that follow thee, —
     God keep my child!


A father's eye, a mother's hand,
   They cannot reach the stranger land,
   But One is ever present there,
I give my treasure to His care, —
     God keep my child!


From all the tempters varied wiles,
   Temptations veiled in frowns or smiles, —
   From evil men and evil ways,
Perils of dark or joyous days, —
     God keep my child!


Thy heart is weak, thy strength is small, —
   Ready to stumble or to fall;
   Oh, seek the Lord's upholding power,
His Spirit's help in danger's hour!
     God keep my child!

Behüt' dich Gott, ein starker Hort,
		Sein Scepter reicht von Ort zu Ort,
		Sein Arm gebeut, sein Auge schaut,
		So weit der weite Himmel blaut;
				Behüt' dich Gott!

Behüt' dich Gott, ein guter Hirt,
		Sein Schäflein hat sich nie verirrt,
		Mit Jacob zog er schützend aus,
		Tobiam bracht' er froh nach Haus;
				Behüt' dich Gott!

Behüt' dich Gott — und nun zum Schluß,
		Von Mund zu Mund den letzten Kuß,
		Von Herz zu Herz das letzte Wort,
		Auf Wiedersehn hier oder dort;
				Behüt" dich Gott!

## Am Bache Krith.
1 Könige 17, 5. 6.
### Karl Gerok.

Elias haust als stiller Eremit
Am Bache Krith,
Hier birgt er sich am frischen Waldesborn
Vor Ahabs Zorn,
Hier spottet er am kühlen Wüstenquell
Des heißen Grimms der stolzen Isebel.

His sceptre all creation sways,
His will the universe obeys,
Within His arm, before His sight,
We stand, in darkness or in light, —
God keep my child!

Yet the Good Shepherd's tender care
The feeblest of his flock shall share.
He who led Jacob in the way,
Still guides and guards, by night or day, —
God keep my child!

The signal waves, — the hour has come,
Thou must go forth from friends and home.
Now let the last fond kiss be given,
And "au revoir" in earth or heaven!
God keep my child!

## BY THE BROOK CHERITH.
**I Kings XVII. 5. 6.**
Translated by "H. L. L."

By the brook Cherith, in the evil hour
Of Ahab's power,
The great Elijah finds a safe retreat,
A refuge sweet;
When at the tyrant's fury he can smile,
And from his toil and dangers rest awhile.

Die Sonne glüht, es dorrt im Sommerbrand
Ringsum das Land;
Kein Regen fällt, es labt kein Tropfen Thau
Die dürre Au',
Kein Brünnlein fließt, kein Bäumlein kann mehr blühn,
Am Krith allein da rauscht's noch kühl und grün.

\* \* \* \*

Ringsum im Lande schreien sie nach Brod,
Er hat nicht Noth;
Die Raben bringen täglich mit Gekreisch
Ihm Brod und Fleisch;
Ein lichter Engel wie ein schwarzer Rab'
Steht Gott dem Herrn zu Dienst als Edelknab'.

Am Bache Krith da ist es still genug —
Ein Vogelflug,
Ein Rabenschrei, des Löwen fern Gebrüll, —
Sonst Alles still;
O heil'ge Stille, hehre Einsamkeit:
Dem Manne Gottes ist's um dich nicht leid.

Hier fühlt er sich im unerforschten Hain
Mit Gott allein;
Hier weht in jedem Baum, in jedem Strauch
Des Schöpfers Hauch:
Das Felsenthal, der hohe Wald ringsum
Verklärt sich ihm zum hehren Heiligthum.

\* \* \* \*

Die Morgenwinde rauschen ihren Psalm
In Laub und Halm,

The noontide sun flames like a burning brand
   O'er the parched land,
All nature faints, — the flowers forget to blow,
   The streams to flow; —
But here the prophet views another scene —
By the brook Cherith all is cool and green.

   &ast;  &ast; &ast;  &ast;  &ast;

Through all the land resounds a cry for bread, —
   *He* is well fed;
Each morn and eve the ravens as they fly,
   Bring full supply;
All creatures are God's messengers; His will
Ravens or angels can alike fulfil.

By the brook Cherith all is still and lone —
   A dove's soft moan,
The raven's call, the distant lion's roar —
   These and no more,
Save summer breezes sighing through the wood,
Disturb the calm and holy solitude.

But to the man of God how sweet the rest,
   The calm how blest!
To hear, remote from strife and folly's noise
   Jehovah's voice;
Deep full communion with Himself to hold,
In the great temple He had built of old.

   &ast;  &ast; &ast;  &ast;  &ast;

Like sacred anthems sounds among the trees
   The morning breeze;

Die Abendröthe flammt als Opferbrand
Am Felsenrand,
Als Fackelträger halten in der Nacht
Die Sterne Gottes stille Tempelwacht.


Des Tages Lärm, der Menschen Lust und Pein
Wird hier so klein;
Vergessen ist, was sonst das Herz berückt,
Den Geist umstrickt;
Ich steige nieder in der Wesen Grund
Und bad' im Quell der Wahrheit mich gesund.


Drum, wenn auch dich dein Gott in Wüsten weist
Und ruhen heißt,
Wenn dir die Welt oft kalt und liebelos
Die Thür verschloß,
Dann baue du als stiller Eremit
Dein Hüttlein dir, o Freund, am Bache Krith.


Dir fließt ein Krith im grünen Waldesschoß
Bei Fels und Moos,
Dir fließt ein Krith im stillen Kämmerlein
Bei Lampenschein;
Wo sich ein Herze still in Gott versenkt,
Da wird es aus dem Bache Krith getränkt.


Und wenn das Bächlein, das dich still vergnügt,
Zuletzt versiegt,

The western skies glow as the sun retires,
     Like altar fires;
The stars look down through the long silent night,
Like holy watchers with their torches bright.

Oh, happy still the prophet's lot to share,
     And place of prayer!
By a vain world forgot, alone with Thee,
     Our God, to be!
Beside the fountains of all truth to go
And bathe the soul where living waters flow!

Then in the wilderness, when called from toil,
     To rest awhile —
When the world turns away with closing door,
     And smiles no more —
Then, brother, hear the Master's kind command,
By the brook Cherith meekly take thy stand.

In nature's solitudes — the forest glade,
     The mountain's shade, —
In the lone chamber, by the lamp's pale light,
     Or moonbeams bright, —
Wherever God is sought in lowly prayer,
By the brook Cherith He can meet thee there.

And when the ravens fail to bring supply,
     The stream is dry,

Und wenn der Herr aus deinem Friedenszelt
Dich ruft ins Feld,
Dann steh' als Gottes Knecht mit Freuden auf
Und richte stracks gen Zarpat deinen Lauf.

## Morija.
### 1 Moses 29.
### Karl Gerok.

Zwei Pilger gehn im Dämmergrau
Geheimnißvoll durch Feld und Au'.

Am Himmel glänzt der Morgenstern,
Noch schweigt die Erde nah und fern.

Und schweigend gehn die Wandrer fort,
Und keiner spricht ein lautes Wort.

Der Eine wie der Morgen klar,
Mit rosigen Wangen und goldenem Haar.

Der Andre würdig von Gestalt,
Von silberweißem Bart umwallt.

So fromm und fröhlich blickt das Kind,
Es spielt sein Haar im Morgenwind.

Der Alte geht so tief gebückt,
Als ob ihn schwere Bürde drückt.

Der Knabe auf den Schultern trägt
Das Holz, zum Opferbrand zerlegt.

And to the battle-field, or harvest plain,
    Christ calls again —
Then the new summons with new strength obey,
And to Zarephath gladly take thy way.

## MORIAH.
### Gen. XXIX.
#### Translated by H. L. L.

Two pilgrims journey along the way,
Far in the East, by the twilight gray.

Faintly above shines the morning star;
Earth is in silence, near and far.

Silent the voices of breeze or bird;
Silent the pilgrims — they speak no word.

One is a youth, like the morning fair,
With rosy cheeks and with golden hair;

The other of aspect calm and high
A snow-white beard, and an eagle eye.


Lightly the boy gazes all around,
Sadly the man's eyes seek the ground.


On the lad's shoulder wood is laid,
(Of such is the fire on the altar made);

Der Alte trägt den Opferstahl,
Der funkelt roth im Frühlichtstrahl.

Der Knabe zu dem Vater spricht,
Und hebt empor sein hold Gesicht:

„Das Holz zum Opfer hab' ich hier,
Sag, Vater, wo das Opferthier?"

Der Vater zu dem Knaben spricht,
Und wendet ab sein trüb Gesicht:

„Das Lämmlein wird ihm Gott ersehn,
Mein Sohn, laß du uns fürbaß gehn.'

Und schweigend gehn die Pilger fort,
Und keiner spricht ein lautes Wort.

Das ist der Vater Abraham
Mit Isaak, seinem Opferlamm;

Mit Isaak, seinem einz'gen Sohn,
Mit seines Alters Lust und Kron'.

Manch schweren Gang hat er gethan,
Doch keiner kam so schwer ihm an.

Doch will er auch noch diesen gehn,
Was Gott gebeut, das muß geschehn.

Zum Berg Morija steigt er auf,
Das ist des Glaubens Pilgerlauf.

————————

Wohl wallen noch zum gleichen Ziel,
Zum Opferberg der Pilger viel;

The father carries a dagger bright;
It glimmers red in the morning light.

Now to his father speaks the boy,
Lifting his face of light and joy:

"Father, we carry the wood and knife;
Where is the lamb that must yield its life?"

Then to the son does the father say,
Turning his sorrowful face away, —

"God will provide Him a lamb, my son."
So in the silence they journey on.

This is Abraham, the saint of old;
That is his Isaac, long foretold —

Isaac, the joy of his heart and eyes,
Claimed by his God for a sacrifice!

Abraham knows many a weary way,
But none like this which he takes to-day,

Yet will he tread it, faltering not,
On to the heaven-appointed spot.

See in the distance Moriah rise!
There is the mount of sacrifice!

Up its steep places the pair ascend;
There shall Faith's journey find an end.

———

Still the procession moveth on —
Many in Abraham's steps have gone;

Sie gehn alleine, Paar und Paar,
In braunen Locken, grauem Haar.

Dort geht mit seines Herzens Kron'
Ein Vater mit dem einz'gen Sohn.

Da trägt die Mutter, bleich von Harm,
Ihr weißes Lämmlein in dem Arm.

Und jener trägt ein Kreuz mit Schmerz,
Und dieser trägt ein schweres Herz.

Sie wandern still des Weges fort,
Und keiner spricht ein frohes Wort.

Und fraget eins: wie und warum?
So bleibet Erd' und Himmel stumm.

Was Gott gebeut, das muß geschehn,
Das Andre wird der Herr versehn.

Drum bringe du dein Opfer still,
Und füge dich, wie Gott es will.

Drum trage nur und frage nicht,
Drum wage nur und zage nicht.

Und wär's auch dunkel nah und fern
Am Himmel glänzt ein Morgenstern,

Golden ringlets and locks of snow,
Still together we see them go,

With weary footsteps and weeping eyes,
Up to the mount of sacrifice.

Yonder a father, with silver-hair,
Leading his Isaac, young and fair;

Yonder a mother, sad and pale,
Hushing her infant's feeble wail;

Silent and slow their treasures they bear,
To lay them bound on the altar there,

And if one questions, how or why?
Heaven nor earth will make reply.

What thou demandest, Father, see!
We bring it — and leave the rest to thee.

Onward, sad pilgrims! surrender all;
Question not at the Master's call.

See in the distance Moriah rise!
There is the mount of sacrifice!

Der führt zum Opferberg hinauf;
Das ist des Glaubens Pilgerlauf.

———

Wer steigt vom Opferberg herab?
Ein sel'ger Greis, ein froher Knab'.

Das ist der Vater Abraham
Mit Isaak, seinem Opferlamm,

Mit Isaak, seinem einz'gen Sohn,
Mit seines Alters Lust und Kron'.

Er führt den Knaben an der Hand,
Gen Himmel ist sein Blick gewandt.

Der Ausgang war so trüb und schwer,
So fröhlich ist die Wiederkehr.

Der Morgen graut in Sorg' und Noth,
So selig glüht das Abendroth.

Der ew'ge Gott ist fromm und gut,
Er dürstet nicht nach Menschenblut.

Er hat sein Opfer schon ersehn,
Du Menschenkind sollst frei ausgehn,

Und wer sein Liebstes nicht verschont,
Sieht himmlisch seine Treu' belohnt.

So viel am Himmel Sterne stehn,
So viel soll Abram Kinder sehn. —

———

Up its steep places by faith ascend;
There shall the journey find an end.

---

Who are descending the mountain-way?
A smiling youth and a patriarch gray.

This is Abraham, the saint of old;
That is his Isaac, long foretold —

Isaac, the joy of his heart and eyes,
Claimed by his God for a sacrifice.

The father holds by the hand his boy,
And looks up to heaven in speechless joy.

Sad was their upward path at morn,
Light are their steps as they now return;

Darkly and sadly the morning rose,
Joyful and bright will the evening close.

Still and for ever the Lord is good;
He asks for faith, and not for blood.

God for himself does the lamb supply;
One mighty victim *shall* bleed and die.

And he who his dearest gave to the Lord,
An hundred-fold shall receive reward:

Countless the stars that in heaven we see,
So shall the children of Abraham be!

---

Drum trage du und frage nicht,
Drum wage du und zage nicht.

Der ew'ge Gott ist fromm und gut,
Er will dein Herz und nicht dein Blut.

Das Gotteslamm ist schon ersehn
Und du sollst frei und ledig gehn.

Sein Todesgang und Opferblut
Macht all dein Kreuz und Schaden gut.

Und wenn dein Herz vor Jammer brach
Der Herr vergilt dir's tausendfach.

Da droben glänzet Stern an Stern,
Das sind die Tröstungen vom Herrn.

Hier ist des Glaubens Pilgerlauf
Und droben geht das Schauen auf.

Tremble not — doubt not — venture all ;
Question not at the Master's call.

Still and for ever the Lord is good —
He asks our heart, and not our blood,

One mighty victim by faith we see,
So may the children of men go free.

With breaking hearts to the mount we come ;
With strange, deep joy He can send us home, —

Yes, and an hundred-fold repay
All He has asked for and called away.

Countless the stars in the heaven above ;
Countless the comforts of Jesus' love !

## Der Herr kennet die Seinen.
### Carl Johann Philipp Spitta
geboren 1801, gestorben 1859.

Es kennt der Herr die Seinen
Und hat sie stets gekannt,
Die Großen und die Kleinen
In jedem Volk und Land,
Er läßt sie nicht verderben,
Er führt sie aus und ein;
Im Leben und im Sterben
Sind sie und bleiben sein.

Er kennet seine Schaaren
Am Glauben, der nicht schaut,
Und doch dem Unsichtbaren,
Als säh' er ihn, vertraut;
Der aus dem Wort gezeuget,
Und durch das Wort sich nährt,
Und vor dem Wort sich beuget,
Und mit dem Wort sich wehrt.

Er kennt sie als die Seinen
An ihrer Hoffnung Muth,
Die fröhlich auf dem Einen,
Daß er der Herr ist, ruht,
In seiner Wahrheit Glanze
Sich sonne frei und kühn
Die wunderbare Pflanze,
Die immerdar ist grün.

# THE LITTLE FLOCK.

### Translated by X. X.

He knoweth all His people, —
From everlasting knew, —
The greatest and the smallest,
The many and the few.
Not one of them shall perish;
He guardeth each alone:
In living and in dying
They shall remain His own.

The little flock He knoweth, —
Who, though by faith, not sight
Th' Invisible are seeing,
And trusting in His might.
Born by His word of power,
And nourished by that word;
Within His storehouse finding
The armour of their Lord.

And thus He knows His people, —
By hope so bright and blest,
By faith that can its burden
Upon the Saviour rest;
And by the look of gladness,
Where truth shines forth serene,
That plant that ever weareth
An amaranthine green.

Er kennt sie an der Liebe,
Die seiner Liebe Frucht,
Und die mit lautrem Triebe
Ihm zu gefallen sucht;
Die Andren so begegnet,
Wie er das Herz bewegt;
Die segnet, wie er segnet,
Und trägt, wie er sie trägt.

So kennt der Herr die Seinen,
Wie er sie stets gekannt,
Die Großen und die Kleinen,
In jedem Volk und Land;
Am Werk der Gnadentriebe
Durch seines Geistes Stärk',
An Glauben, Hoffnung, Liebe,
Als seiner Gnade Werk.

So hilf uns, Herr, zum Glauben
Und halt' uns fest dabei;
Laß nichts die Hoffnung rauben;
Die Liebe herzlich sei.
Und wird der Tag erscheinen,
Da dich die Welt wird sehn,
So laß uns als die Deinen
Zu deiner Rechten stehn.

He knows them by their loving —
    The fruit of His own love,
And by their earnest longing
    To please their Lord above;
By their long-suffering patience,
    When others work them ill;
By blessing as He blesseth,
    And bearing all His will.

And thus He knows His people, —
    From everlasting knew, —
The greatest and the smallest,
    The many and the few.
Where His own spirit's working
    In gracious power is seen;
By faith, hope, love abounding,
    Where'er His step has been.

So help us, Lord, we pray Thee,
    Our goings thus uphold,
That none of glory rob us,
    Nor make our love grow cold;
That when the day of wonder
    Reveals Thy judgment throne,
We may look up rejoicing,
    Since numbered with Thine own.

## Geduld.
### Carl Johann Philipp Spitta.

Es zieht ein stiller Engel
Durch dieses Erdenland,
Zum Trost für Erdenmängel
Hat ihn der Herr gesandt.
In seinem Blick ist Frieden,
Und milde, sanfte Huld,
O folg' ihm stets hienieden,
Dem Engel der Geduld!

Er führt dich immer treulich
Durch alles Erdenleid,
Und redet so erfreulich
Von einer schönern Zeit.
Denn willst du ganz verzagen,
Hat er doch guten Muth;
Er hilft das Kreuz dir tragen,
Und macht noch Alles gut.

Er macht zu linder Wehmuth
Den herbsten Seelenschmerz,
Und taucht in stille Demuth
Das ungestüme Herz.
Er macht die finstre Stunde
Allmälig wieder hell,
Er heilet jede Wunde
Gewiß, wenn auch nicht schnell.

## THE ANGEL OF PATIENCE.
### Translated by H. L. L.

A gentle angel walketh
Throughout a world of woe,
With messages of mercy
To mourning hearts below,
His peaceful smile invites them
To love and to confide,
O follow in His footsteps,
Keep closely by His side!

So gently will He lead thee
Through all the cloudy day,
And whisper of glad tidings,
To cheer the pilgrim's way,
*His* courage never failing,
When thine is almost gone,
He takes thy heavy burden,
And helps to bear it on.

To soft and tearful sadness
He changes dumb despair,
And soothes to deep submission
The storm of grief and care;
Where midnight shades are brooding,
He pours the light of noon,
And every wound He healeth,
Most surely, if not soon.

30*

Er zürnt nicht deinen Thränen,
Wenn er dich trösten will;
Er tadelt nicht dein Sehnen,
Nur macht er's fromm und still.
Und wenn im Sturmestoben
Du murrend fragst: warum?
So deutet er nach oben,
Mild lächelnd, aber stumm.

Er hat für jede Frage
Nicht Antwort gleich bereit,
Sein Wahlspruch heißt: ertrage,
Die Ruhstatt ist nicht weit!
So geht er dir zur Seite,
Und redet gar nicht viel,
Und denkt nur in die Weite,
An's schöne, große Ziel.

## Das Lied der Lieder.
### Carl Johann Philipp Spitta.

Es giebt ein Lied der Lieder,
Das singst du immer wieder,
Wenn du es einmal singen lernst;
Kein Mensch hat es ersonnen,
Das Lied so reich an Wonnen,
Und doch so lehrreich, tief und ernst.

He will not blame thy sorrows,
While He brings the healing balm,
He does not chide thy longings,
While He soothes them into calm;
And when thy heart is murmuring,
And wildly asking, why?
He, smiling, beckons forward,
Points upward to the sky.

He will not always answer
Thy questions and thy fear,
His watchword is, "Be patient,
The journey's end is near!"
And ever through the toilsome way,
He tells of joys to come,
And points the pilgrim to his rest,
The wanderer to his home.

## THE SONG OF SONGS.
### Translated by X. X.

There is a song now singing,
Catch but its sweet beginning,
And you will still its notes prolong:
For ever, ever learning,
Yet never quite discerning
The deep, full meaning of the song!

Es singt von einer Liebe,
Vor der des Lebens Trübe
Wie Nebel vor der Sonne flieht.
Wie weichen alle Schmerzen,
Wenn man so recht von Herzen
Anstimmen kann das schöne Lied!

It tells of love undying,
Before which grief is flying,
Like mists swept by the sun along.
Oh! how earth's sorrow leaveth
The heart that here receiveth
The holy music of that song!

# NOTES.

Lenore (Ellenore), by *G. A. Buerger*, translated by W i l-
   l i a m  T a y l o r, of Norwich.

   This translation was first published in the second number
of the M o n t h l y  M a g a z i n e for 1796. Mr. Taylor wrote,
with regard to the deviations from the original which cannot
fail to strike the Reader, as follows: "In the original the
emperor and empress have made peace, which places the
scene in southern Germany; and the army in returning home
triumphant. By shifting the scene to England and making
William a soldier of Richard Lionheart, it becomes necessary
that the ghost of Ellenore, whom Death, in the form of her
lover, conveys to William's grave, should cross the sea.
Hence the splash of the XXXIX and other stanzas, of which
there is no trace in the original; of the tramp! tramp! there
is. I could not prevail on myself to efface these words, which
have been gotten by heart, and which are quoted even in
Don Juan; but I am aware that the translation is in some
respects too free for a history of poetry etc. etc." [Historic
Survey of German Poetry, interspersed with various Translations, by W. Taylor, of Norwich. 3 vols. London, 1829.]
The following anecdote, referring to Taylor's "Ellenore" is
told in a letter from Miss A i k i n to Mr. M u r c h, dated:

Hampstead, December 20th 1841.

\* , \* \* \* \* \* \*
\* \* \* \* \* \* \*
\* \* \* \* \* \* \*

"A remarkable anecdote belongs to his (Taylor's) incomparable version of "Lenora" which I heard from the lips of Sir Walter Scott himself, as he was relating it to Mrs. Barbauld. After reminding her that long before the ballad was printed she had carried it with her to Edinburgh, and read it to Mr. Dugald Stewart. 'He', said Scott, 'repeated all he could remember of it to me, and this, Madam, was what made me a poet. I had several times attempted the more regular kinds of poetry without success, but here was something that I thought I could do.' — A translation capable of lighting up such a flame, certainly deserves all the praise of an original; indeed no one could guess it to be any other; so racy and idiomatical in the old English in which he has clothed it." [A memoir of the life and writings of the late William Taylor, of Norwich, etc., compiled and edited by T. W. Roberts, F. G. S., of Norwich. 2 Vols, London, 1843].

p. 94. **Zueignung** (zu Goethe's Gedichten); translated by Theodore Martin and the late Prof. Aytoun.

The Reader is asked to compare the cold verdict of the accomplished Translators, as recorded in the Book from which the Translation is taken, with the eloquent praises of Adolf Stahr, who \* likens the introductory poem to a lofty vestibule leading to some glorious temple, and impressing every one who enters at once with a sense of awe-inspiring perfect grandeur.

---

\* Goethe's Frauengestalten. Berlin, 1869.

p. 106. **Zigeunerlied** (*Goethe*), translated by the late Dr. Anster.

This translation appeared, in 1837, in Xeniola, under the title "Nursery Rhymes." It is somewhat free, but very spirited. "Wehrwölf'", is, oddly enough, translated by war-wolves, instead of werewolves. Goethe, of course, alludes to that terrible superstition — Lycanthropy: according to which human beings could change, or be changed, into wolves, and would assume not only the shape, but the lust and rapacity of these animals. I beg to refer any Reader who is interested in the subject to the Reprint, by the Early English Text Society, of William of Palerne, or William and the Werewolf, edited by Mr. Skeat; or to Mr. S. Baring-Gould's "Book on Werewolves."

p. 114. **Erlkönig** (*Goethe*), translated by Peter Gardner.

The simple, homely beauty of Mr. Gardner's version, which appeared some years ago in the Scotsman, and was largely re-printed in the United States, reproduces the German tone with wonderful accuracy. Mr. Theodore Martin's matchless Translation, as well as Sir Walter Scott's version, are, without doubt, known to the Reader. M. Émile Deschamps, deservedly famous for his translation of "Romeo and Juliet", has written the following fine imitation:

> Qui donc passe à cheval dans la nuit et le vent?
> 　　C'est le père avec son enfant.
> De son bras crispé de tendresse
> Contre sa poitrine il le presse,
> 　　Et de la bise il le défend.
>
> Mon fils, d'où vient qu'en mon sein tu frissonnes?
> Mon père - - là - - vois-tu le roi des aunes,
> Couronne au front, en long manteau? —
> Mon fils, c'est un brouillard sur l'eau.

»Viens, cher enfant, suis-moi dans l'ombre,
»Je t'apprendrai des jeux sans nombre ;
»J'ai de magiques fleurs et des perles encore,
»Ma mère a de beaux habits d'or.« —

N'entends-tu point, mon père (oh! que tu te dépêches)
Ce que le roi murmure et me promet tout bas?
Endors-toi, mon cher fils, et ne t'agite pas :
C'est le vent qui bruit parmi les feuilles sèches.

»Veux-tu venir, mon bel enfant? Oh! ne crains rien,
»Mes filles, tu verras, te soigneront si bien!
    »La nuit mes filles blondes
    »Mènent les molles rondes,
    »Elles te berceront,
    »Danseront, chanteront!«

Mon père, dans les brumes grises
Vois ses filles en cercle assises!
Mon fils, mon fils, j'aperçois seulement
Les saules gris au bord des flots dormant.

»Je t'aime, toi, je suis attiré par ta grace,
»Viens, viens donc, un refus pourrait t'être fatal!«
Ah! mon père! mon père! il me prend — il m'embrasse —
    Le roi des aunes m'a fait mal!

Et le père frémit et galope plus fort,
Il serre entre ses bras son enfant qui sanglotte,
Il touche à sa maison : son manteau s'ouvre et flotte,
    Dans son bras l'enfant était mort!

  . . . .

p. 166. **Die unüberwindliche Flotte** (*Schiller*), translated by the late C. H. Merivale, F. S. A.

The two concluding lines of this poem allude to the modest inscription: 'Afflavit Deus, et dissipati sunt' on the medal, struck, by Queen Elizabeth's command, to commemorate the marvellous victory of the English over the Armada.

p. 186. **Das Mädchen von Orleans** (*Schiller*), translated by C. H. Merivale.

This is a poetic protest against the foul and hollow ribaldry of Voltaire's Pucelle d'Orléans.

p. 196. **Würtemberg** (*Uhland*), translated by W. W. Skeat.

'Blooms not in every province
A Weinsberg alway new?'⁻

Allusion is here made to the story that the duke of Bavaria, being besieged in the castle of Weinsberg by Conrad III, was obliged to surrender at discretion. "The emperor granted the duke and his chief officers permission to retire unmolested; but the duchess, suspecting Conrad, begged that she and the other women in the castle might be allowed to come out with as much as each of them could carry, to be conducted to a place of safety. The request was granted, and, to the surprise of the emperor and his army, the duchess and her fair companions staggered forth, each carrying her husband. A.D. 1140." Epitome of Russell's Modern Europe.

p. 208. **Der blinde König** (*Uhland*), translated by W. W. Skeat.

A sad misprint has crept in here, p. 213, line 15 — viz.

'My sword — I know its grinding stroke.'

What was meant, is, of course, the fine, expressive word: griding. — See Milton's . . . . . . . "So sore

The griding sword with discontinuous wound
Pass'd through him: etc."

Paradise Lost, Book VI, line 329 &c.

p. 220. **Der Student** (*Uhland*), from Blackwood's Magazine.

This translation, which appeared in the May No. 1836 (not, as erroneously printed in May 1846, when a story,

entitled "The student of Salamanca" appeared in the Magazine) is from the pen — now, alas, still for ever — of Professor
Aytoun, and was one of his first contributions to Blackwood's, for whose pages "Bon Gaultier" afterwards wrote so
much and so well. — The Compiler is indebted to Mr. John
Blackwood, the present Editor, for this information, and
for permission to reprint the translation.

p. 232. **König Karl's Meerfahrt** (*Uhland*), translated by
W. W. Skeat.

'King Charles with all his doucëperes' etc.

The twelve peers of France were called sometimes
"doucëperes", from the French: les douze paires. Thus
Spencer: —

'Big-looking like a haughty doucëpere.'

Faerie Queene. III, 10. 31.

Stanza IV: "But Alta Clara's sheen."

Alta Clara, i. e. "tall and bright", was the name of
Oliver's battle-sword. Roland's sword was named Durin-
dana, and King Charles's Joyeuse. W. W. S.

p. 354. **Arion** (*Schlegel*), translated by D. J. Mac Carthy.

The late Dr. Anster, in the notes to his unique translation of the second part of Faust (Faustus: The second
part. From the German of Goethe, etc., London, 1864),
in reference to the dialogue between the Herold and the
Knabenlenker, and, especially, in reference to the lines:

»Und welch ein zierliches Gewand
Fliesst dir von Schultern zu den Socken,
Mit Purpursaum und Glitzertand!«

explains, that this is the dress of Apollo Musagetes,
and quotes this translation of his friend's, Mr. Mac Carthy,

which is dated "November 1863", and which was then
published for the first time. I have taken the liberty of
extending Mrs. Anster's kind permission to avail myself of
the late Dr. Anster's Translation 'ad libitum' to quote
this version of one of the most melodious poems in the
German Language — and I throw myself on the Translator's
courtesy.

p. 370. **Frauen-Liebe und Leben** (*Chamisso*), translated
   by Dr. A. Baskerville.

The Translator, Author of "The Poetry of Germany",
and Headmaster of the International College at Godesberg,
near Bonn on the Rhine, writes, in reference to No. 8 of the
(English) series of poems, which form the charming, truly
German, whole: ***** "Your letter caused me to resume,
for a moment, a once favourite occupation, now for many
years put aside. I have translated for you the poem you
wished to have. . . . . . . . You are aware that I have also
omitted the fourth of the original series, beginning:

   'Du Ring an meinem Finger',

which I did because the exchange of rings in betrothment
is unknown in England." — — — —

p. 430. „**Es ist noch eine Ruh' vorhanden**" (*Kunth*),
   translated by H. L. L.

This hymn, in which the Compiler feels peculiarly interested (because it was composed by one of his maternal
ancestors), has been, at his special request, translated by
"H. L. L.", a lady who has often enriched the pages of
certain Periodicals by her sweet renderings of sacred German Poetry. Mr. Theodore Kübler, in his deeply
interesting "Historical Notes to the Lyra Germanica"
says, with regard to the poem itself: "... It was written

under the following peculiar circumstances. Kunth travelled
with his pious patron, Count von Henkel, to some estates in
Silesia, belonging to the Count. * On the journey the coach
broke down, which caused considerable delay. The Count
was vexed and irritated, and bitterly complained of the
various troubles man had to undergo on earth. "Yes",
replied Kunth; "but there remaineth yet a rest for the people
of God." These words had the desired effect: the pious
Count's irritation was at once dispelled. Kunth, soon afterwards, took a walk, and composed, in the open air, this
hymn, which after his return he read aloud to the edification
and delight of his fellow-travellers. It was first printed in
1733. Subsequently Kunth became superintendent pastor in
Baruth, in Upper Lusatia, where he died in 1779. He composed only three hymns, of which the above is the best
known. It has often cheered weary Christians on their
pilgrimage. It was a favourite hymn of the late Dr. Barth,
in Calw (known in England through his Church History, his
children's stories, and other works); and his most intimate
friend, Dr. Zeller, in Nagold, a most excellent Christian,
died on the 12th February, 1864, just as the last verse of
this hymn was being sung by a few Christian friends. Möwes,
the author of several beautiful hymns, was, after fearful
sufferings, comforted in his last moments by his wife reading
this hymn."

---

* He had just inherited those estates.                    H. E. G.

Printed by Breitkopf and Härtel, Leipzig.

14, *Henrietta Street, Covent Garden, London;* and
20, *South Frederick Street, Edinburgh.*

# WILLIAMS AND NORGATE'S

LIST OF

## 𝕱rench, German, Italian, Latin and Greek,

AND OTHER

## SCHOOL BOOKS AND MAPS.

### French.

FOR PUBLIC SCHOOLS WHERE LATIN IS TAUGHT.

**Eugène (G.) The Student's Comparative Grammar of the French Language,** with an Historical Sketch of the Formation of French. For the use of Public Schools. With Exercises. By G. Eugène-Fasnacht, French Master, Westminster School. 12th Edition, thoroughly revised. Square crown 8vo, cloth. 5s.

Or Grammar, 3s. ; Exercises, 2s. 6d.

"The appearance of a Grammar like this is in itself a sign that great advance is being made in the teaching of modern languages. . . . . The rules and observations are all scientifically classified and explained."—*Educational Times.*

"In itself this is in many ways the most satisfactory Grammar for beginners that we have as yet seen."—*Athenæum.*

**Eugène's French Method.** Elementary French Lessons. Easy Rules and Exercises preparatory to the "Student's Comparative French Grammar." By the same Author. 9th Edition. Crown 8vo, cloth. 1s. 6d.

"Certainly deserves to rank among the best of our Elementary French Exercise-books."—*Educational Times.*

**Delbos. Student's Graduated French Reader,** for the use of Public Schools. I. First Year. Anecdotes, Tales, Historical Pieces. Edited, with Notes and a complete Vocabulary, by Leon Delbos, M.A., of King's College, London. 3rd Edition. Crown 8vo, cloth. 2s.

—————— The same. II. Historical Pieces and Tales. 3rd Edition. Crown 8vo, cloth. 2s.

**Little Eugène's French Reader.** For Beginners. Anecdotes

**Krueger (H.) Short French Grammar.** 6th Edition. 180 pp.
12mo, cloth. *2s.*

**Victor Hugo. Les Misérables, les principaux Episodes.** With
Life and Notes by J. Boïelle, Senior French Master,
Dulwich College. 2 vols. Crown 8vo, cloth. Each 3s. 6d.

——— **Notre-Dame de Paris.** Adapted for the use of Schools
and Colleges, by J. Boïelle, B.A., Senior French Master,
Dulwich College. 2 vols. Crown 8vo, cloth. Each 3s.

**Boïelle. French Composition through Lord Macaulay's English.**
Edited, with Notes, Hints, and Introduction, by James
Boïelle, B.A. (Univ. Gall.), Senior French Master,
Dulwich College, &c. &c. Crown 8vo, cloth.

1. Frederic the Great. 3s.
2. Warren Hastings. 3s. 6d.
3. Lord Clive. *In the Press.*

**Foa (Mad. Eugen.) Contes Historiques.** With Idiomatic Notes
by G. A. Neveu. 3rd Edition. Crown 8vo, cloth. 2s.

**Larochejacquelein (Madame de) Scenes from the War in the**
Vendée. Edited from her Mémoirs in French, with
Introduction and Notes, by C. Scudamore, M.A. Oxon,
Assistant Master, Forest School, Walthamstow. Crown
8vo, cloth. *2s.*

**French Classics for English Schools.** Edited, with Introduction
and Notes, by Leon Delbos, M.A., of King's College.
Crown 8vo, cloth.

No. 1. Racine's Les Plaideurs. 1s. 6d.
No. 2. Corneille's Horace. 1s. 6d.
No. 3. Corneille's Cinna. 1s. 6d.
No. 4. Molière's Bourgeois Gentilhomme. 1s. 6d.
No. 5. Corneille's Le Cid. 1s. 6d.
No. 6. Molière's Précieuses Ridicules. 1s. 6d.
No. 7. Chateaubriand's Voyage en Amérique. 1s. 6d.
No. 8. De Maistre's Prisonniers du Caucase and Lepreux
d'Aoste. 1s. 6d.
No. 9. Lafontaine's Fables Choisies. 1s. 6d.

**Lemaistre (J.) French for Beginners.** Lessons Systematic, Practical and Etymological. By J. Lemaistre. 2nd Edition.
Crown 8vo, cloth. 2s.

**Boget (F. F.) Introduction to Old French.** History, Grammar,
Chrestomathy, Glossary. 400 pp. Crown 8vo, cl. 6s.

**Kitchin.** Introduction to the Study of Provençal. By Darcy B. Kitchin, B.A. [Literature—Grammar—Texts—Glossary.] Crown 8vo, cloth. 4s. 6d.

**Tarver.** Colloquial French, for School and Private Use. By H. Tarver, B.-ès-L., late of Eton College. 328 pp., crown 8vo, cloth. 5s.

**Ahn's French Vocabulary and Dialogues.** 2nd Edition. Crown 8vo, cloth. 1s. 6d.

**Delbos (L.) French Accidence and Minor Syntax.** 2nd Edition. Crown 8vo, cloth. 1s. 6d.

—— Student's French Composition, for the use of Public Schools, on an entirely new Plan. 250 pp. Crown 8vo, cloth. 3s. 6d.

**Vinet (A.) Chrestomathie Française** ou Choix de Morceaux tirés des meilleurs Écrivains Français. 11th Edition. 358 pp., cloth. 3s. 6d.

**Roussy.** Cours de Versions. Pieces for Translation into French. With Notes. Crown 8vo. 2s. 6d.

**Williams (T. S.) and J. Lafont.** French Commercial Correspondence. A Collection of Modern Mercantile Letters in French and English, with their translation on opposite pages. 2nd Edition. 12mo, cloth. 4s. 6d.
For a German Version of the same Letters, vide p. 4.

**Fleury's Histoire de France,** racontée à la Jeunesse, with Grammatical Notes, by Auguste Beljame, Bachelier-ès-lettres. 3rd Edition. 12mo, cloth boards. 3s. 6d.

**Mandrou (A.) French Poetry for English Schools.** Album Poétique de la Jeunesse. By A. Mandrou, M.A. de l'Académie de Paris. 2nd Edition. 12mo, cloth. 2s.

## German.

**Schlutter's German Class Book.** A Course of Instruction based on Becker's System, and so arranged as to exhibit the Self-development of the Language, and its Affinities with the English. By Fr. Schlutter, Royal Military Academy, Woolwich. 5th Edition. 12mo, cloth. 5s. (Key, 5s.)

Möller (A.) A German Reading Book. A Companion to Schlutter's German Class Book. With a complete Vocabulary.
150 pp. 12mo, cloth.                                      2s.

Ravensberg (A. v.) Practical Grammar of the German Language.
Conversational Exercises, Dialogues and Idiomatic Ex-
pressions. 3rd Edition. Cloth. (Key, 2s.)                5s.

—————— English into German. A Selection of Anecdotes,
Stories, &c., with Notes for Translation. Cloth. (Key,
5s.)                                                   4s. 6d.

—————— German Reader, Prose and Poetry, with copious Notes
for Beginners. 2nd Edition. Crown 8vo, cloth.           3s.

Weisse's Complete Practical Grammar of the German Language,
with Exercises in Conversations, Letters, Poems and
Treatises, &c. 4th Edition, very much enlarged and
improved. 12mo, cloth.                                   6s.

—————— New Conversational Exercises in German Composition,
with complete Rules and Directions, with full Refer-
ences to his German Grammar. 2nd Edition. 12mo,
cloth. (Key, 5s.)                                      3s. 6d.

Wittich's German Tales for Beginners, arranged in Progressive
Order. 26th Edition. Crown 8vo, cloth.                  4s.

—————— German for Beginners, or Progressive German Exercises. 8th Edition. 12mo, cloth. (Key, 5s.)             4s.

—————— German Grammar. 10th Edition. 12mo, cloth. 4s. 6d.

Hein. German Examination Papers. Comprising a complete
Set of German Papers set at the Local Examinations in
the four Universities of Scotland. By G. Hein, Aberdeen
Grammar School. Crown 8vo, cloth.                      2s. 6d.

Schinzel (E.) Child's First German Course; also, A Complete
Treatise on German Pronunciation and Reading. Crown
8vo, cloth.                                            2s. 6d.

—————— German Preparatory Course. 12mo, cloth.        2s. 6d.

—————— Method of Learning German. (A Sequel to the Preparatory Course.) 12mo, cloth.                         3s. 6d.

Apel's Short and Practical German Grammar for Beginners, with
copious Examples and Exercises. 3rd Edition. 12mo,
cloth.                                                 2s. 6d.

Sonnenschein and Stallybrass. German for the English. Part I.
First Reading Book. Easy Poems with interlinear Trans-
lations, and illustrated by Notes and Tables, chiefly
Etymological. 4th Edition. 12mo, cloth.               4s. 6d.

Williams (T. S.) Modern German and English Conversations and Elementary Phrases, the German revised and corrected by A. Kokemueller. 21st enlarged and improved Edition. 12mo, cloth. 3s. 6d.

—— and O. Cruse. German and English Commercial Correspondence. A Collection of Modern Mercantile Letters in German and English, with their Translation on opposite pages. 2nd Edition. 12mo, cloth. 4s. 6d.

For a French Version of the same Letters, vide p. 2.

Apel (H.) German Prose Stories for Beginners (including Lessing's Prose Fables), with an interlinear Translation in the natural order of Construction. 12mo, cloth. 2s. 6d.

——— German Prose. A Collection of the best Specimens of German Prose, chiefly from Modern Authors. 500 pp. Crown 8vo, cloth. 3s.

German Classics for English Students. With Notes and Vocabulary. Crown 8vo, cloth.

Schiller's Lied von der Glocke (the Song of the Bell), and other Poems and Ballads. By M. Förster. 2s.
——— Maria Stuart. By M. Förster. 2s. 6d.
——— Minor Poems and Ballads. By Arthur P. Vernon. 2s.
Goethe's Iphigenie auf Tauris. By H. Attwell. 2s.
——— Hermann und Dorothea. By M. Förster. 2s. 6d.
——— Egmont. By H. Apel. 2s. 6d.
Lessing's Emilia Galotti. By G. Hein. 2s.
——— Minna von Barnhelm. By J. A. F. Schmidt. 2s. 6d.
Chamisso's Peter Schlemihl. By M. Förster. 2s.
Andersen's Bilderbuch ohne Bilder. By Alphons Beck. 2s.
Nieritz. Die Waise, a German Tale. By E. C. Otte. 2s. 6d.
Hauff's Mærchen. A Selection. By A. Hoare. 3s. 6d.

Carové (J. W.) Mærchen ohne Ende (The Story without an End). 12mo, cloth. 2s.

Fouque's Undine, Sintram, Aslauga's Ritter, die beiden Hauptleute. 4 vols. in 1. 8vo, cloth. 7s. 6d.

Undine. 1s. 6d.; cloth, 2s.    Aslauga. 1s. 6d.; cloth, 2s.
Sintram. 2s. 6d.; cloth, 3s.    Hauptleute. 1s. 6d.; cloth, 2s.

## Latin and Greek.

**Cæsar de Bello Gallico.** Lib. I. Edited, with Introduction, Notes and Maps, by Alexander M. Bell, M.A., Ball. Coll. Oxon. Crown 8vo, cloth. . *2s. 6d.*

**Euripides' Medea.** The Greek Text, with Introduction and Explanatory Notes for Schools, by J. H. Hogan. 8vo, cloth. *3s. 6d.*

———— **Ion.** Greek Text, with Notes for Beginners, Introduction and Questions for Examination, by Dr. Charles Badham, D.D. 2nd Edition. 8vo. *3s. 6d.*

**Æschylus. Agamemnon.** Revised Greek Text, with literal line-for-line Translation on opposite pages, by John F. Davies, B.A. 8vo, cloth. *3s.*

**Platonis Philebus.** With Introduction and Notes by Dr. C. Badham. 2nd Edition, considerably augmented. 8vo, cloth. *4s.*

———— **Euthydemus et Laches.** With Critical Notes and an Epistola critica to the Senate of the Leyden University, by Dr. Ch. Badham, D.D. 8vo, cloth. *4s.*

———— **Symposium,** and Letter to the Master of Trinity, "De Platonis Legibus,"—Platonis Convivium, cum Epistola ad Thompsonum edidit Carolus Badham. 8vo, cloth. *4s.*

**Sophocles. Electra.** The Greek Text critically revised, with the aid of MSS. newly collated and explained. By Rev. H. F. M. Blaydes, M.A., formerly Student of Christ Church, Oxford. 8vo, cloth. *6s.*

———— **Philoctetes.** Edited by the same. 8vo, cloth. *6s.*

———— **Trachiniæ.** Edited by the same. 8vo, cloth. *6s.*

———— **Ajax.** Edited by the same. 8vo, cloth. *6s.*

**Dr. D. Zompolides.** A Course of Modern Greek, or the Greek Language of the Present Day. I. The Elementary Method. Crown 8vo. *5s.*

**Kiepert's New Atlas Antiquus.** Maps of the Ancient World, for Schools and Colleges. 6th Edition. With a complete Geographical Index. Folio, boards. *7s. 6d.*

**Kampen.** 15 Maps to illustrate Cæsar's De Bello Gallico. 15 coloured Maps. 4to, cloth. *3s. 6d.*

# Italian.

Volpe (Cav. G.) Eton Italian Grammar, for the use of Eton College. Including Exercises and Examples. New Edition. Crown 8vo, cloth. *4s. 6d.*

———— Key to the Exercises. *1s.*

Rossetti. Exercises for securing Idiomatic Italian by means of Literal Translations from the English, by Maria F. Rossetti. 12mo, cloth. *3s. 6d.*

———— Aneddoti Italiani. One Hundred Italian Anecdotes, selected from "Il Compagno del Passeggio." Being also a Key to Rossetti's Exercises. 12mo, cloth. *2s. 6d.*

Venosta (F.) Raccolta di Poesie tratti dai piu celebri autori antichi e moderni. Crown 8vo, cloth. *5s.*

Christison (G.) Racconti Istorici e Novelle Morali. Edited for the use of Italian Students. 12th Edition. 18mo, cloth. *1s. 6d.*

# Danish—Dutch.

Bojesen (Mad. Marie) The Danish Speaker. Pronunciation of the Danish Language, Vocabulary, Dialogues and Idioms for the use of Students and Travellers in Denmark and Norway. 12mo, cloth. *4s.*

Williams and Ludolph. Dutch and English Dialogues, and Elementary Phrases. 12mo. *2s. 6d.*

# Wall Maps.

Sydow's Wall Maps of Physical Geography for School-rooms, representing the purely physical proportions of the Globe, drawn in a bold manner. An English Edition, the Originals with English Names and Explanations. Mounted on canvas, with rollers :

1. The World. 2. Europe. 3. Asia. 4. Africa. 5. America (North and South). 6. Australia and Australasia.
Each *10s.*

———— Handbook to the Series of Large Physical Maps for School Instruction, edited by J. Tillcard. 8vo. *1s.*

## Miscellaneous.

De Rheims (H.). Practical Lines in Geometrical Drawing, containing the Use of Mathematical Instruments and the Construction of Scales, the Elements of Practical and Descriptive Geometry, Orthographic and Horizontal Projections, Isometrical Drawing and Perspective. Illustrated with 300 Diagrams, and giving (by analogy) the solution of every Question proposed at the Competitive Examinations for the Army. 8vo, cloth.        9s.

Fyfe (W. T.) First Lessons in Rhetoric. With Exercises. By W. T. Fyfe, M.A., Senior English Master, High School for Girls, Aberdeen. 12mo, sewed.        1s.

Fuerst's Hebrew Lexicon, by Davidson. A Hebrew and Chaldee Lexicon to the Old Testament, by Dr. Julius Fuerst. 5th Edition, improved and enlarged, containing a Grammatical and Analytical Appendix. Translated by Rev. Dr. Samuel Davidson. 1600 pp., royal 8vo, cloth. 21s.

Strack (W.) Hebrew Grammar. With Exercises, Paradigms, Chrestomathy and Glossary. By Professor H. Strack, D.D., of Berlin. Crown 8vo, cloth.        4s. 6d.

Hebrew Texts. Large type. 16mo, cloth.
Genesis. 1s. 6d. Psalms. 1s. Job. 1s. Isaiah. 1s.

Turpie (Rev. Dr.) Manual of the Chaldee Language: containing Grammar of the Biblical Chaldee and of the Targums, and a Chrestomathy, consisting of Selections from the Targums, with a Vocabulary adapted to the Chrestomathy. 1879. Square 8vo, cloth.        7s.

Socin (A.) Arabic Grammar. Paradigms, Literature, Chrestomathy and Glossary. By Dr. A. Socin, Professor, Tübingen. Crown 8vo, cloth.        7s. 6d.

Bopp's Comparative Grammar of the Sanscrit, Zend, Greek, Latin, Lithuanian, Gothic, German and Slavonic Languages. Translated by E. B. Eastwick. 4th Edition. 3 vols. 8vo, cloth.        31s. 6d.

Nestle (E.) Syriac Grammar. Literature, Chrestomathy and Glossary. By Professor E. Nestle, Professor, Tübingen. Translated into English. Crown 8vo, cloth.        9s.

Delitzsch (F.) Assyrian Grammar, with Paradigms, Exercises, Glossary and Bibliography. By Dr. F. Delitzsch. Translated into English by Prof. A. R. S. Kennedy, B.D. Crown 8vo, cloth.        15s.

Lightning Source UK Ltd.
Milton Keynes UK
UKHW052356300123
416172UK00023B/419